THE TEMPERED STEEL OF
ANTIQUITY GREY

THE TEMPERED STEEL OF
ANTIQUITY GREY

SHAWN SPEAKMAN

GRIM OAK PRESS
SEATTLE, WA

Jacket artwork by Todd Lockwood.
Angelus crest illustration by Nate Taylor.
Map on page vii and circuit chapter headers by Shawn Speakman.
Interior artwork by Allen Morris.
Interior design and composition by REview Design.

Trade Hardcover Edition ISBN: 978-1-944145-69-9
E-Book ISBN: 978-1-944145-74-3
Also available from AUDIBLE

Grim Oak Press First Edition, September 2021
2   4   6   8   9   7   5   3   1

Grim Oak Press
Battle Ground, WA 98604
www.grimoakpress.com

For Kristin Speakman,

Whose love is in every word of this book.

THE TEMPERED STEEL OF
ANTIQUITY GREY

The fingers and thumb stuck out of the desert, unmoving, waiting.

Antiquity Grey bit her lower lip—a habit her grandmother scolded her for daily. It was a dangerous situation. The mech hand was more than just some slag the wind had brought to the surface. It had likely been buried since the Splinter War, when mechs battled over the planet's ore reserves during her grandmother's childhood. Chekker said shattered metal fell from the sky like meteors during the most violent of battles, burning hellfire that pockmarked the desert into glass. The wastes had once been a graveyard of broken mechs and plating, but no longer; those who pirated the past had scavenged it over the decades for profit, leaving almost nothing behind. Metal arms, metal legs, metal weapons. To be melted down and reconstituted on-world as well as off-world.

But no one had discovered this. *This* was hers. The people of Solomon Fyre would sing her name long into the night when she returned with it, a treasure worth years of rummaging the sands.

And who knew what else was attached to the hand, buried beneath the desert of this part of her world.

An arm.

A shoulder.

A torso.

Dare she hope possibly an entire body?

Excitement moved Antiquity toward her airbike. She would ride down to the mech hand, blast away the sand, and see for herself.

"Wait! You are not going down there, Grey-child."

Antiquity stopped, glaring at CHKR-11. The spherical bot spun in the air but was still safe behind the giant rock outcropping that hid them from metal scavengers who might be surveying the sands for an easy kill.

"You don't know what I am going to do, Chekker."

"Grey-child, I know you." Chekker whirred, slowly spinning and stopping as it considered her. Its soccer sport-paint was once proud but now faded with decades of time. "The moment you came upon this mech I knew your actionable intentions."

"There is no one around, Chekker!" She pointed in all directions, to the mountains at her back and across the entirety of the desert, to its north, east, and south. "Look to the wastes! I see no dust movement. None!"

"That is true. None. For now." The bot flew nearer her face in emphasis, his voice the static of his kind. "But I have been privileged to teach the children of your family for more than a century. None of them have possessed your proclivity for attracting danger."

Anger rose up inside Antiquity. She was no longer a child in need of a nursemaid. "Do you see what's down there, Chekker? Are your sensors shot? Look!"

The bot was unimpressed. "I do. I see trouble."

"Trouble finds me all by itself, you old bot!"

The ancient floating ball did not reply. It just spun in front of her.

"What do *you* think we should do then?" she asked, waiting for the fight.

Chekker wasted no time. "We return to Solomon Fyre. And inform the Elders."

"No!" Antiquity argued, wanting to hit the bot. She had done it before and it had been like hitting a rock face. "No. No. And no. Why should they take what I have found? Why should *they* get to own what *I* find?"

"Because of your family's past. And they are the Elders."

"They are thieves!"

"Maybe," Chekker said. "But your family is no longer in the position they once were, Grey-child. Grey has become your surname. And Grey is your legacy now. We will return to Solomon Fyre. If not the Elders, we will certainly tell your matriarch."

"No, we will not," Antiquity declared.

Before Chekker could respond, she gained the airbike's seat, released the grav-stabilizers that kept it from floating away, and punched the throttle. No electric tase from Chekker stopped her as she thought it might; he obviously did not think leaving her immobile would be safer than letting her reach the mech. Instead, the old bot followed as he was programmed, meant to teach but also protect. She did not know how he arrived at his decisions, but she was glad he did not prevent her.

Taking a final scan of the wastes and finding no evidence of scavengers, Antiquity rocketed down the mountain to the sands and pulled her airbike up next to the mech hand, its fingers resting on the ground longer than she was tall. Up close, she could see there might be more of it beneath the desert surface, lumpy hills of sand that could be other parts of the giant robot. Using her airbike's thrusters, she began blasting away the desert, revealing a forearm, an elbow, a shoulder. The sun beat down on her, blisteringly hot, but she kept at it, her excitement fueling her adrenaline even while sweat became the glue that adhered grit to her tanned skin. The shifting of the sands over time had reduced the mech from a painted dark blue to a greyish one, but the metal retained its make, unmolested by wear.

As her work continued through the afternoon and with enough desert removed, Antiquity could see the mech had landed on its stomach—and the white-tinted faceplate of its massive head stared right at her.

"Help me, Chekker." Antiquity could not see beyond the glass. "Run a diagnostic on the mech."

The bot flew to where she stood beside the head.

"I cannot, Grey-child."

"The mech is dead then."

"Quite the contrary," Chekker answered. "Its fuel cells are depleted from decades in the sand but they are not extinguished. It lives. But it is blocking my attempts."

The mech still had power. Antiquity stood stunned. It was a mystery what had brought down the giant warrior. But it hadn't been a lack of power.

"Can you access its last moments?" she asked. "See why it crashed?"

"I can try, Grey-child. Security will have been one of its primary functions. It is technology not unlike my own though, built at the time of my own creation. There is a chance, no matter how poor the odds."

CHKR-11 began spinning this way and that, each change in direction accompanied by a click as if unlocking a multi-number lock. Antiquity waited. She ran her hand over the smooth glass of the faceplate, wondering how the ancient treasure had been brought so low so long ago. After more than an hour and Antiquity's patience with the bot spent, a series of clacks reverberated through the glass. Shocked, she jumped back from the mech, trying to figure out what was happening.

Then an explosion sent her flying through the air.

She landed hard. Fighting the darkness swimming before her eyes, Antiquity gazed up at the massive head. The faceplate had shot open, knocking her aside.

Revealing the mech's cockpit—and a corpse.

"Are you safe, Grey-child?" Chekker asked, now hovering over her.

Chekker had somehow instructed the mech to open its pilot box. The heat of surprise still coursing through her, Antiquity waved the bot away and, regaining her feet, warily approached the giant robot again. Its driver remained strapped in his harness, twistedly slumped to the side, his long hair pulled back into a single platinum braid similar to the one Antiquity wore herself. She had seen dead bodies before, but not like this; the skin of the driver had sunk inward, paper pulled tight over his skull. Mummified, she thought, like one of the horrors told to scare children before bedtime.

To get a better look, Antiquity half stepped inside the large cockpit.

That's when she saw the crest on the driver's dark blue uniform.

"I had to copy and insert my system to gain access to the mech," Chekker said, hovering behind her. She barely heard him.

"What?" she asked absently, mind aswirl.

"Why are you not listening to me, Grey-child?" the bot said, annoyed. "I had to copy my system. Great skill built this mech. I believe it belonged to a person of high import. Its systems mirrored that. The security features did not allow access to the mech. Therefore, it required replicating my system. Two against one are better odds." Chekker went silent, a shadow at her shoulder. "If the deceased has left you unsettled, you may vacate the vehicle. Although it is my opinion you should have been prepared. These machines did not operate autonomously. All had drivers. You know this."

"It's not that, Chekker," Antiquity said, pointing at the crest—an insignia featuring flame between unfurled angel wings.

"As I said, Grey-child, danger finds you all too easily."

Antiquity thought Chekker meant their find—and maybe he did—but he had already disappeared from her side, flying toward the edge of the wasteland where her mountain home met vast desert distances. She scrambled over the sands, fearing to see what she already knew was there.

"Dust rising," she growled, barely able to breathe.

"It is."

"Scavengers?"

The robot gained altitude, just enough to get a better view without compromising their whereabouts. "Too far away. But the dust pattern suggests it."

"Close that cockpit, Chekker," Antiquity ordered, already moving to bury the giant mech again with her airbike. "Remember this location. And let's get out of here. Now."

"I could not agree more, Grey-child."

Antiquity went to work.

Eyes watched Antiquity as she returned to Solomon Fyre.

She knew whom they belonged to. This was not the first time. The Dreadth boys, who thought they were already men. Those who thought she was lesser than sand for being a Grey, despite that surname not belonging to her ancestors, her true family name once bearing the highest regard on her world. She cursed inwardly, as they darted from alley shadow to second-story broken window to burned-out machinery.

The road bristled with the Dreadths, more than a dozen. It was not the beating that they might try to give if they caught her that worried Antiquity. How long had they been watching since she realized they had been following her? Did they know where she had gone? If so, her find and its relevance for her family were not safe. If not, they knew the direction she had returned from and were just curious enough to track her grav-trail into the wastes below Solomon Fyre.

To possibly discover and steal the mech from her anyway.

She slowed her airbike to a stop, touching the ground to observe a desert flower that had broken through the shattered streets of the once bustling desert city—trying to act as if she didn't know of their presence.

If she surprised them, there was a chance at escape.

She needed that surprise.

"The Dreadths are watching," Chekker shared at her shoulder.

"Shut it. I know," she growled, viewing the tiny purple petals, remembering a time when she had done this with her mother so long ago, using her side vision while trying to come up with a plan.

As if the Dreadths could sense her thoughts, four airbikes larger and more powerful than hers glided out at the same time, two in front of her and two behind.

She looked up then—the ruse done—and brought out her best two weapons.

Her fists.

It would not be the first time she brawled to blood with the Dreadths.

The two airbikes in front of her then parted to let a third through, this last one finer than the others. Manson Dreadth sat its seat easily, his large blue eyes piercing her like a hunting desert hawk. Antiquity stared back; she would show no fear. Manson was the oldest of the group, tall and rangy. Soon he would join his father, Jackson Dreadth, as a council member, to one day take his father's place as lead Elder of Solomon Fyre.

Today that did not matter to him though. The sinking sun high-lighted Manson's smug smile. She was trapped.

And he knew there was nothing she could do about it.

"Where you been, Antiquity *Grey*?" the eighteen-year-old questioned, his last word a drawn-out sneer.

"That is none of your concern," she said, anger rising.

"With you Greys, it is always my concern." Manson looked around at his kin, who slowly melted from the city to surround her. He got off his airbike then, a coward made strong by numbers, and strolled toward her with his maddening smile. "You must be watched. You cannot be trusted. It was your great-grandmother who failed to protect Solomon Fyre when it needed it most. It is the reason even *speaking* your family's old name is punishable by *death*. Or have you forgotten history?" He smiled without a hint of humor. "Tell me, half-breed. What have you been up to? Mellex over there saw you leave this morning. And you've been gone all day, outside the safety of the city. So where? Where did you go, little *Grey* girl?"

"Dreadth-child, quit your advancement toward this position," Chekker ordered, still at Antiquity's shoulder. "It would be wise."

"I am no child, bot," Manson spat. "But you are right to worry."

When Manson would not stop his approach, the robot—originally built to coach sport but also protect those it tutored—flew to confront the boy. Manson did not slow. Just when Chekker was about to tase him, rocks thrown by the other Dreadth boys slammed into the bot. He went spinning through the air.

Giving Manson the space he needed to lunge at Antiquity.

She was ready. She threw the contents of her right fist—gritty sand she had gathered while looking at the flower. The boy fell back and raised his arms, but it was too late. Manson roared in surprise and then pain, momentarily blinded. His Dreadth family members froze, not knowing what to do.

This was her chance.

Antiquity hit the throttle on her airbike to escape.

Manson was faster. Before the airbike powered up, he grabbed her by the wrist and flung her from it like a rag doll. "You Grey bitch!" Manson yelled, standing over her, his eyes red from the sand. The other Dreadth boys cheered. "You have no power over me. Not anymore. Your family is dust. Just like you are going to be if you don't tell me what I want to know."

"I will *never* say," Antiquity hissed from the stone of the street.

"We will see about that."

Manson grabbed her again, his grip like steel. She fought and kicked and spit, but it did her no good. She could only watch as his fist punched into her midsection, sending her back to the ground and gulping air.

"Desist, Manson Dreadth!" a voice boomed, powerful and as unmistakable as a desert lightning strike. "Now!"

Manson stood over Antiquity, fists clenched in rage. But now he looked for the source of the command. Antiquity knew it all too well.

It was her grandmother.

Matriarch Vestige Grey walked slowly toward Antiquity and Manson as if she had all the time in the world, passing the two Dreadth boys and their airbikes at the top of the street like their threat didn't exist. Eyes, blinded during childhood, surveyed the scene with the intent of a thundercloud, her bitter lips' deepening wrinkles already aged craggy. Three tiny balls of blue light hovered around her: navigation bots, touching her lightly when obstacles entered her path. The leader of the Grey family did not deviate from her course—each step prepared, methodical, and precise.

To those who did not know her, she would seem serene as she glided down the ruins of lower Solomon Fyre.

To Antiquity, her grandmother had never been so angry.

"Manson Dreadth, you and your family will leave with the faculties that brought you to this moment," Vestige said coldly. "If not, you will find it difficult to do so. And once your father hears of this, I doubt he will be pleased with you."

Manson did not move despite Antiquity crawling back toward her airbike. "You have no power over me, you old crone." He laughed. "My fathe—"

"*Your father* knows I see beyond my lost sight," Vestige said. "If I stand before the Elders—especially at a time so close to your ascendance into their ranks—and reveal the video record of your assault upon my granddaughter, you will lose favor among many of them. Worse, you will weaken your father's standing as leader of the council. Are you willing to risk that and your future over so pert a girl?"

Manson looked at Chekker, who floated nearby. The bot possessed the ability to record events. The Dreadth boy gauged the blind woman. Were her words true? Antiquity did not know. It did not take long for Manson though. He grinned a nervous smile.

"I will be watching you, Antiquity," he said, pointing at her. "And watching for your secret out in the desert."

With that, he whistled at the Dreadth boys.

In moments, they were gone.

"I am fine," Antiquity said, dusting herself off while her grandmother stopped before her. The punch to the gut lingered.

Matriarch Vestige Grey gave her a disapproving scowl. "You are a Grey. You have to be."

"How'd you know they'd attack me? Know where I was?"

"Know? The blind always know." Vestige took a deep breath. "And I worry about you constantly, Antiquity. You are the last of us, our family buried beneath the power of history's Dreadths." The old woman paused, hands behind her back. "I worry because I know of your forays outside Solomon Fyre. I know you yearn."

"Yearn?"

"For something more. Like I did in my own youth."

Frowning, Antiquity turned away, preferring the ruins to her grandmother's always discerning gaze. The wasted city, after all, could not judge her. A century earlier, Solomon Fyre had been a bustling community, its roots deep and expansive mech eyries rising high above. The lower level of the city had long been abandoned though, much of it destroyed and left to decay when the Splinter War had come to their planet. Most of the inhabitants now lived in the upper city away from the numerous dangers prowling the desert. The ruins she now stood within were a graveyard, its ghosts silencing all.

Vestige Grey waited, leaving Antiquity further unsettled. Her grandmother always knew how to make her talk.

"Do you think they would have killed me?" Antiquity asked.

The old woman squinted. "Maybe. The Dreadth family has always delighted in violence against others. And that Manson . . . he likes it more than most his age."

"Why though?"

"Men teach boys, who eventually become men fathering more boys," Vestige said. "It is a vicious cycle. And it is the way of the world now. Perhaps it always has been."

"It wasn't always so," Antiquity pressed. "We once ruled."

"True. It wasn't always so. And yes, our family did once rule, my mother the last. Before the Dreadths took over. Before we became

Grey-shamed." The old woman frowned, looking at a fading sun she could not see. "The past. It is ever present in the now. Yet neither the past nor the present should be sacrificed for the future. You are that future. You have to be *smarter*, Antiquity. We will not be Grey forever. The time will come when we regain our true name. But giving those in power reason to kill us is not the way to that end. We will bide our time." Vestige gripped Antiquity's shoulder then. "Do not give Manson Dreadth a reason to *ever* attack you. Ever."

"He's older than me. Almost on the council, if street rumors are true," Antiquity said, shaking her head. "No one becoming an Elder should be so cruel."

"Rebelling is what youth does when faced with adulthood." Vestige gave her a look, and Antiquity couldn't tell if her grandmother meant the Dreadth or her. "Do not forget, Antiquity. Manson is his father's son, protected by him. You do not have that luxury," Vestige said. She paused, cocking her head. "Do you have a secret I should know about, my granddaughter? Manson mentioned such a thing."

Antiquity cursed inwardly, unsure of what to even say. She hadn't had time to figure out what she was going to do with her find.

"Antiquity unearthed a mech, just east of Solomon Fyre, Matriarch Grey," Chekker answered for her, the bot hovering over the airbike.

"Chekker!"

"A mech?" Vestige Grey asked, brow furrowing. "That can't be possible."

"It is quite possible," the bot replied. "We found it this morning."

Her grandmother's grip on her shoulder lost its tenderness. "Is this true?"

She couldn't hide her discovery now.

"It is."

Vestige had gone as still as a statue. Antiquity couldn't read her.

"The mech is complete, unmolested," Chekker added, hovering now before the matriarch. "Treachery brought it down, its systems compromised by a source from the outside, before it could even join the Splinter War. That's why it is intact. It never made it to the battle."

"I told you to stay away from these wastes, Antiquity, this very morning," Vestige said, voice low. She shook her head, thinking to say something more and deciding against it. Instead, she looked toward the desert. "How did you find this mech?"

"The wind storm yesterday. Must have tore enough sand away from one of its hands. And we came upon it," she said, shooting Chekker a dark look, but the sharing of her secret gave rise to excitement. "I uncovered enough of it and Chekker opened its cockpit. I covered it back over with sand, to keep it safe."

"Antiquity Grey speaks the truth, Matriarch," the bot said before Vestige could comment. "I opened the faceplate. The driver is one of your house and, based on uniform and biologic presence, it is my belief that it is your mother, Laurellyn Grey."

Chekker had not told Antiquity that. She had assumed the driver had been a man. Fresh excitement replaced any pain Manson had given her. Had she actually found her great-grandmother?

The blind woman did not respond at first. She had let go of her granddaughter's shoulder and folded her hands before her. Those hands were shaking a bit.

"Her surname was *not* Grey, Chekker," Vestige murmured finally.

"It is the surname I am charg—"

"What proof do you offer?" Vestige asked, cutting the bot off.

"None. The proof remains buried in the sands," the bot admitted. "I did not have time to copy the mech's system and data."

"Chekker broke into the mech. I can verify what he saw with the uniform, at least. It was of our family." Antiquity took a deep breath but tears sprang into her eyes anyway. "They killed her, didn't they? The Dreadths. It's the treachery Chekker mentioned. That's why she never joined the battle. She didn't run away as the Dreadths charged."

"Our two families have hated one another for a long time," Vestige said, fully composed once more. "And the one family that most benefited from her disappearance was the Dreadths. My mother was a strong woman. A stronger leader. I was young then, younger than you are now, and even I knew how dangerous she could be—and how precarious her position. We thought her mech obliterated, no evidence left. The Dreadths have ruled ever since that day, under the yoke of the Imperium. And they have worked hard to destroy our family name, erase it from history, and ensure it never rises again."

"If that's true, and the data inside the mech can be gathered, this could change all of that, Grandmother!" Antiquity said, her excitement returning again.

"How?"

"If the people of Solomon Fyre know the tru—"

"They will what, child? Revolt?" Vestige shook her head. "This is a hard life with harder lessons. They would find a way to kill us before such information could be used." The grandmother moved before the granddaughter and, taking the younger's hands in her own, gave Antiquity a solemn look as if her eyes could see all too clearly. "Once women held high offices on Erth. Women flew through its clouds. Women were every bit as strong as men. Especially in our family. Once," she said. "No more. Remember those days, Chekker? The strife. The blood. The death. The women of Solomon Fyre have been ground beneath the bootheel of Dreadth men for decades now. And there is nothing we as Grey women can do about it that won't lead to our destruction.

"I am ordering you, as your matriarch, to leave that mech buried. For now."

Antiquity pulled free of the other's leathery grip. It was all she could do to keep from screaming.

"No. That is the very thing we should *not* do."

Vestige darkened. "You are naive and foolish, Antiquity. I have seen what happens to those who challenge the Dreadths," the old woman hissed, growing angry. "The men, gone. Buried in the mines. Women too. I have lives to keep safe beyond your own. If you do this, I will have to denounce you as a heretic, in public before the Elders. You often do the opposite of what I tell you. It will be the only way to keep the few of us left alive. There will come a time when your discovery will matter. For all of us. That time is not now. Not yet."

"History has proven Matriarch Grey's words as correct," Chekker agreed, the bot now hovering before Antiquity. "I too have witnessed it."

"I will break that history then," Antiquity said defiantly.

Vestige stood tall and straight, like a blade about to slice.

Long moments passed.

Then with her three guiding balls of light swirling about her, she turned and walked back the way she had come.

) ◗ ● ◖ (

The next morning, Antiquity sat with elbows on table and chin on hands, bored.

The vid-view taking up the entire wall splashed vivid images of Erth's past, the lesson her grandmother gave Antiquity in a hidden room of their eyrie home. Vestige stood in the room's corner, talking about the Old Era's climate crisis and how it began, her three balls of light swirling about her head and notifying her of what scenes came across the vid-view. Antiquity sighed, fidgeting in her chair. All she wanted to do was sneak away and revisit the area where the mech remained buried. If it took sitting through a lesson to placate her grandmother so Antiquity could avoid suspicion of her true intentions upon waking, she would do it. But she didn't have to be happy about it.

"Antiquity, please pay attention," Vestige said, pulling her granddaughter back into the present lesson.

Antiquity stopped fidgeting and sighed again. "You should be telling me more about the mech," she said before she could take it back.

Rather than getting angry at her, Vestige took a deep breath. "Why do you think we are talking about all of this?"

"I meant how the mech works and the Splinte—"

"I know what you meant," Vestige cut her off, pausing the vid-view featuring the oceans of Erth rising as the polar ice caps melted.

The two said nothing more, at an impasse for how to proceed.

"You aren't mad at me?" Antiquity asked finally. "About finding the mech?"

Vestige gave her granddaughter a reproachful look. "Do try to focus, Antiquity. This is an important lesson, and it's one I have not taught you in many years. It is always wise to return to a lesson if it is important to do so."

"I don't understand why we are going over this again. What could be important about this one?" she huffed. She looked at the vid-view, with its grainy Old Erth footage. "It's not like it matters. It's ancient history."

"All history matters, dear heart," Vestige said. "Especially now. What is past may yet become prologue."

Antiquity looked down and picked dirt from beneath her fingernails.

"Whatever *that* means."

Vestige moved from the vid-view's corner and sat next to Antiquity. "It means pay attention. It will matter one day," she said, gesturing to the wall she could not see. "Now, let us look at the Old Era." The vid-view resumed, featuring an Erth that was quite different from the one they knew. The land masses were much larger while both poles featured massive glaciers. As the ice shelves retreated from a warming Erth, the melted water entered the oceans and land masses shrunk. "How did the Imperium come to be?" Vestige asked.

Antiquity gave into the lesson, knowing she had to complete it before her grandmother would let her go. "The Imperium is not an alien race as so many think. They were once us. They were an exploration colony sent into space to discover a new planet if our own could no longer support life."

"That's right," Vestige said. The vid-view changed to footage of an enormous colony spaceship traveling into the void of space. "Worried about planetary extinction, the Erth's people united to search space. There were life-sustaining planets discovered to be visited. These brave explorers traveled far into an unknown. But those left behind did not succumb to Erth's climate changes. They survived." She paused. "Meanwhile, space became a crucible for those who left, and after millennia, they evolved into the Imperium, ruled by an iron fist to survive among the stars, warped by fascist principles."

"And the generations in space without Erth's gravity and our sun changed their appearance," Antiquity shared.

"Yes, they are our kin but altered," Vestige said. The vid-view shimmered again, this time showing Solomon Fyre during the time it was Erth's capital city. "Before the Imperium decided to return to this planet, much changed during the millennia of their absence. Humanity survived on Erth too, adapting. Solomon Fyre became the capital city, although it maintained the sovereignty of other cultures like the *arabi*, the *persai*, the *cathari*, the rarely seen *atlanti*, and others. By the time your great-grandmother came into power, Erth had already harnessed the great power of mech technology, but Laurellyn continued to lead that effort. Until merchants from the Imperium reestablished contact with Erth. We now know the merchants were merely spies, used to learn how Erth fared before the Imperium's massive army retook the planet. Thankfully, your great-grandmother did not wholly trust those merchants, making her readier for the assault that would follow. It was all for naught though, obviously."

"Is that why the Imperium attacked Solomon Fyre first?" Antiquity asked, trying to understand why her great-grandmother was such a threat. "Because she was the leader capable of rallying Erth's other groups?"

"No one really knows," Vestige said, clearly pleased that Antiquity had decided to take part in the lesson. "We know they wanted the planet's natural resources, to maintain their empire and grip on us all. Most of the planet's mech might existed here, in Solomon Fyre. It makes sense they would eliminate the most difficult threat first. It's what I would have done, no doubt. Especially with the other ruling families here."

Antiquity nodded. "So why did the Dreadths sabotage my great-grandmother? Surely they are just as blameworthy as the Imperium. All the more reason to reveal their treachery to the world."

"I said to not provoke the Dreadths," Vestige said, darkening. She took a deep breath, holding her anger at bay. "Remember who the true enemy is, Antiquity. It is not the Dreadths. They merely took advantage of a situation. The Imperium took control of Erth and destroyed our way of life. Remain focused on the present and the future it may lead to in time."

Antiquity stared hard at her grandmother, not that the other could tell. "And what is that future, Grandmother, if we do not first take back what is ours from the Dreadths?"

"The Dreadths are only a part of the problem. The Imperium rules from Euroda, Erth's new capital. There, Star Sentinel resides. It is the only mech allowed by law on the planet and it is controlled by the Imperium Royals who live there. If Royal Ricariol Wit discovers what you found in the sands, Star Sentinel will likely raze Solomon Fyre to the ground," Vestige said. "Trust me. I am old and have seen much. I have a plan to deal with the Dreadths. Always."

"What plan?"

"In time, you will come to know it and see as I do," Vestige said. "In time."

Antiquity nodded. But she hated feeling like a beaten dog. She wanted to fight back, tired of being Grey-shamed and all it meant.

"Maybe you should go play with the twins," Vestige added, switching off the vid-view. She stood, hands folded in front of her. "I can tell that you care little for this day's lesson. Be safe. And stay away from the Dreadths. We will resume this line of study tomorrow. It is important to do so."

Antiquity leapt out of her chair, excited to be free. But she wouldn't be going to see her friends Kaihli and Elsana as her grandmother suggested.

She had plans of her own.

) ◗ ● ◖ (

As the heat of the day began to take hold, Antiquity Grey had already uncovered the helmeted head of the mech.

She had departed Solomon Fyre after her lesson, heading for the desert and its secret. It had not taken Antiquity long to remove Laurellyn Grey from her harness and gently place her within a mort-shroud. She had done so with special care. The mummified remains of her ancestor were light, nothing but skin, hair, and bone. She would be given honorable rest—fired to ash and loosed upon the winds of her former eyrie. Given the freedom she had earned.

Now, with the sun beating down on them, Chekker continued to copy what the mech knew. The gathered information would help Antiquity disprove the history that had resulted in the shaming of her family.

"The mech is named Saph Fyre."

"What?" Antiquity asked, pulled from her thoughts.

"The mech," the bot said from within the cockpit. "Its name is Saph Fyre. Quite clever, really, given its home and original appearance."

"Yes, that is the name of my great-grandmother's mech," Antiquity said, remembering Vestige's history lessons. "Hard to believe this is the last mech of Solomon Fyre. A lost treasure."

"When I was created, so long ago now, the eyries were occupied by more than a hundred mechs," Chekker shared, spinning while he continued his work. "Each one served a different secondary purpose, with distinct capabilities. But every driver was charged with the defense of the city. You have seen video of them taking to the skies." Antiquity nodded. "Even for one such as I, a machine, it was a marvel."

"Maybe the skies above Solomon Fyre will see it happen again," she said, imagining it.

"There is functionality here."

It took Antiquity a few moments to realize the bot had changed subjects. "What do you mean?" she asked.

Chekker left the cockpit and flew toward the mech's arm. There he began to spin, the hexagons of his round body becoming a blur, until light emanated from him.

On the steel plating, images appeared.

The interior of the cockpit. The view as the mech flew from a younger, brighter, and more civilized Solomon Fyre.

And its driver, Laurellyn Grey.

"The last moments catalogued by the mech," Chekker explained.

Antiquity watched as a woman, with younger but all too similar features to those of her grandmother, flew through the skies above her eyrie, to confront an invading force intent on pillaging Erth's ore resources. Before her, battalions of mechs flew, while she remained behind, orchestrating their efforts. When the Splinter War's first engagement arrived above Solomon Fyre, explosions tearing apart the skies as the two forces met, Laurellyn Grey was ready. She yelled orders and her commanders reacted, pushing the enemy back. As the battle continued beyond its initial clash, it was clear to Antiquity that the leadership of Laurellyn Grey would see them through the worst of it.

But then the interior of Saph Fyre went mostly dark. There had been no attack, nothing to warrant the cause. Laurellyn Grey panicked as the gear and goggles that allowed her to control the mech detached from her without permission. Saph Fyre immediately began to plummet. Tears filled Antiquity's eyes. She watched her great-grandmother scream into her com-link for aid. Dead air. No response.

As mechs exploded in the sky above, the rain of burning metal a storm falling to the desert, Saph Fyre plowed into the sands, her visuals of the battle going black, a void of misinformation.

The images Chekker had pulled from the mech died.

Antiquity felt ill, the kind of sickness that would never wholly go away.

"That is the end, Grey-child."

"Did you find out why that happened to her?" Antiquity asked.

The bot stopped spinning. "A hidden molecu-virus, activated when she gained a certain elevation."

"Sabotage then. The Dreadths?"

"The Dreadths are the probable culprits, given the time period. But no certainty can be gained from the evidence."

Antiquity wanted to punch something. She had wanted real proof that the Dreadths had been behind her family's fall. The video and the existence of the molecu-virus corroborated that Laurellyn Grey had been murdered. The effect of her death could not be ignored; leaderless, the mech corps lost the battle for Erth's capital city. The planet fell quickly then and resulted in her family's removal from power. Antiquity could clear their name and be Grey no more, but the Dreadths would still lead the Elders.

She suddenly realized how difficult all of this would be.

As she thought about what to do, Chekker gained elevation in a sudden burst, the bot sensing something.

"Danger approaches, Grey-child. Enter the mech cockpit. Now."

Antiquity struggled out of the mech's hole instead, first looking toward the desert. She saw nothing there. When she turned back toward home, her heart leapt up into her throat, pounding so hard she could feel it. Sand dust. Lots of it. It swirled up into the sky, higher than any one airbike could kick it.

"We have to get out of here, Chekker!" Antiquity yelled.

She reached her airbike. The sand dust that had come from the direction of Solomon Fyre whipped about her even as several airbikes flew past, circling the location of the mech in a blur. There were at least a dozen, maybe more. She looked over at Chekker, who hovered by her shoulder. The bot did not move, waiting. She did the same. Her grandmother always said keeping calm was the most important effort in life; she knew panicking now would avail her nothing.

There was no doubt though. She was in more danger than the previous day.

"Look, boys. A mech!"

Above her, on the sands overlooking Saph Fyre, Manson Dreadth sat upon his airbike, pulling back his goggles and looking at the mech. When his eyes finally met Antiquity's, he grinned all the more. She saw avarice there. And conquest.

"And look at this!" he said, laughing. Other Dreadth boys joined him, all of them snickering with evil intent. "Antiquity *Grey* and her broken-down soccer ball bot. Out here in the wastes where *anything* can happen." Manson gestured. The other boys spread out, taking up positions about the hole in the desert that contained the mech. "I wonder. Where is your *bitch* of a grandmother now, hmm? She certainly wouldn't leave the city, as crippled as she is." He paused, grinning all the more. "That means you are alone. That means you are *mine.*"

"Manson, you now know my secret," Antiquity said, turning to look at Saph Fyre and thinking quickly as she backed into the hole again. "You can have all of this. Impress your father with it. And the Elders. If—"

"If I let you go," the boy finished.

"This is a major find," she continued, taking a risk. She hoped Chekker had finished copying the mech's files. "Think about it. You would be the hero of Solomon Fyre! Remembered forever!"

"I will be anyway," Manson said, getting off of his airbike. "Especially if my father can use it against the Imperium. But none of that matters because you are Grey-shamed. And that deserves a permanent mark." Antiquity saw he would do more than beat her. "You are a Grey," he continued, pulling a knife. "There is nothing you can do to stop the shame I will carve into your cheek for all to see."

Violence in his eyes, Manson approached her.

"Grey-child, prepar—"

"No!" a small boy screamed. "Look!"

Manson spun around, pulling a lance-shot from his side belt. All

23

Dreadth eyes turned toward the vast wastes of the desert. Antiquity could not see what had caught their attention. But she knew terror when she heard it.

"They are upon us, Manson!"

"I will *not* leave this to *scavengers!*" Manson snarled.

Danger outweighing their leader's wishes, the Dreadths scattered. Most gained their airbikes and were already jetting toward Solomon Fyre's safety. Three others were not so fortunate—either cut off from their airbikes by the approaching threat or following the direction that Manson chose to take, they jumped into the giant hole with the mech.

With Antiquity.

"Do you have any weapons?!" Manson thundered in her face.

"Just Chekker," she stammered.

"Then we both die today, Antiquity Grey. Make it count," Manson growled, the large boy already leading them to confront what approached.

"What are we going to do?" Antiquity whispered to Chekker.

"You will fight. And so will I. Kick me into the midst of the scavengers when they appear," the bot ordered. "I will do what is necessary."

"You will be destroyed!"

"Trust in me, Grey-child. And after, enter Saph Fyre's driver seat."

Confused and frightened, Antiquity did as the bot asked. Grabbing Chekker from the air, she ran up the dune to view the desert. She almost dropped him. Scavengers were converging on them, undoubtedly drawn by the dust storm the Dreadths had kicked into the sky. Seven large airtrikes were approaching fast. She could see the desert-hardened men, women, and even children, their skin tanned to leather by the sun, their matted, greasy hair wild, and their tattooed bodies enhanced by off-world cybernetics. They reaped the sands for metal, killing all they crossed. The scavengers would be upon them in moments.

Down on his belly, Manson fired his lance-shot, over and over. Where he struck the airtrikes, armor sizzled and rent apart. But it did nothing to slow them down. They just kept coming, over twenty scavengers strong. All willing to kill for the metal they desperately needed to survive.

When the scavengers were almost upon them, so close she could see the implants in their eyes, Antiquity took one more look at Chekker.

And kicked him.

The metal ball flew through the air as he had been originally created to do, faster than his own flight could ever take him. All eyes watched as he arced and fell back to the desert. When he struck the sand in the scavengers' midst, he exploded, the detonation deafening and tearing apart the air, sands, and scavengers. Three of the airtrikes were blown off their grav-stabilizers, passengers screaming, dying, and flying in all directions. Antiquity and Manson both hid behind the dune as survivors shot back, their laz-cannons turning swaths of sand to glass and smaller handheld flash-fires discharging in Antiquity's direction.

She did not wait. Antiquity followed Chekker's final order. With tears stinging her eyes—tears of sadness for her friend's loss, tears of frustration for being unable to save herself—she tore back toward the mech, hoping she could figure out how to close the faceplate and have protection.

When she entered, the faceplate closed by itself.

"Strap in, Grey-child. It will enhance your safety."

"Chekker!" she yelled, wiping her eyes. "Is that you?"

"It is."

Sorrow changed to hope. "But you just blew up!"

"You saw a copy of me end, the one I made to unlock Saph Fyre today. I am very much here, in this new form. As is my duty, I will protect you at all costs. The mech does possess power, though limited. Strap in. And make it count."

She did just that. As Laurellyn Grey had once done a hundred years earlier, Antiquity strapped herself into the harness. It felt right, taking her great-grandmother's seat. The moment the last buckle clicked into place, the wall behind the chair opened and various pieces of gear settled onto her—the apparatus that would give her control over the mech. The mech adjusted for her smaller stature, the controls tightening about her, making her one with it. When the final piece of gear, a set of goggles, clicked into place over her eyes, a hum vibrated through Saph Fyre, its engines and machinery coming to life even as it kept her from death.

She was no longer Antiquity Grey. She sensed that. She was not the girl who had been raised to ignore hope. She was not the girl who had been subservient to all Solomon Fyre families, recompense for her great-grandmother's false failure. She was not the girl who hid from the Dreadths at every turn.

As she merged with the mech, feeling its energy joined with her own, Antiquity realized she had become so much more.

And never again would she turn back.

"Chekker, did you remove the molecu-virus?" Antiquity asked.

"I removed it when I discovered it."

"Good. I am free then."

Moving her limbs inside the cockpit, Antiquity drove Saph Fyre to rise from the desert that had been her grave for so long, the mech returning to the world even as sand slid off her to fall like rain. Antiquity could feel resistance in the mech's joints, but Saph Fyre's systems were already expunging the decades of grit that had accumulated, giving her more freedom with every moment. Through her goggles,

Antiquity saw what Saph Fyre viewed, the scavengers frightened and already firing whatever weapons they had at her. She also saw Manson and the other Dreadth boys still hiding, the looks of awe and hope on their upturned, sandy faces gratifying to her.

Still learning how to operate her, Antiquity got Saph Fyre to her hands and knees just as the scavengers attacked, their airtrikes spreading out and launching a barrage of cram-missiles and spike-rips.

"Incoming fire, Grey-child."

Antiquity braced herself. The blasts slammed into the side of Saph Fyre, knocking her sideways. To her surprise, they did little damage. Apparently the weapons were a negligible threat to her superior design.

Making a fist, she hammered the closest airtrike. It and its occupants vanished deep into the wastes.

"The Dreadths are about to be attacked."

Antiquity turned to look. Chekker was right. Two airtrikes had circumvented her counterattack, driving behind her to where the boys hid. Before she could do anything, one launched spike-rips at her knee and the other fired cram-missiles at the boys.

She didn't hesitate.

While the spike-rips hooked into her knee plating, rending parts of the joint, Saph Fyre batted the cram-missiles away, to explode harmlessly on her palm, far from where the boys hunkered.

They would remain in danger until the scavengers left or were destroyed.

"Do you trust me, Manson Dreadth?" Antiquity questioned, voice booming from Saph Fyre.

The Dreadth boy made no move, even as the others gripped him in panic.

"Who am I?" Saph Fyre thundered. Manson looked back toward the desert, where the scavengers were regrouping.

"Antiquity Grey!"

"No!" she said. "What is my *real* name?"

The scavengers were drawing closer, their numbers more than Antiquity could completely stop at one time. In a few moments, Manson and his kin would be killed. Darkness and understanding furrowing his brow, he stood, fists at his side. Angered by his only choice.

"You are Antiquity Angelus!"

Hearing her true surname exhilarated her as never before. It was all she could do to focus on the present. Saph Fyre used both of her massive hands to gently scoop the boys from their perilous situation. They were scared—more from her action than what transpired below—but Antiquity didn't care. It was the only way to keep them safe. And safe they had to be kept for this to succeed. She stood, the mech towering over the desert wastes. Kicking an airtrike that attempted to rope Saph Fyre's feet while the others circled about her, she took one step and crushed it, killing the murderous thieves within.

In her self-defense, she did not feel sorry for them. At least right now. Unlike her family, they had chosen their crime.

The remaining scavengers, understanding they were outmatched, sped away, leaving their dead behind, to vanish deep into the wastes again.

Antiquity took a deep breath. "Was all of that recorded, Chekker?"

"Every moment."

She lowered the Dreadths back to the sand. The three smaller boys did not wait to thank her. They jumped on their airbikes and were already speeding back to Solomon Fyre, without even a look backward.

All except Manson. He stood staring up at Saph Fyre's faceplate. He said nothing. There was nothing to say. She had saved his life and the lives of his brothers and cousins. And she knew he was trying to figure out why.

He would know all too soon. When his father and the Elders watched video of the sabotage that had murdered Laurellyn Angelus. When his father and the Elders watched video of him illegally screaming her true family name.

As well as saving his life.

Shaking his head, Manson left, riding his airbike back the way he had come, the small, singular trail of dust a reminder of the path she must take as well.

"I did it, Chekker." She smiled. "*We* did it. For our family."

"For our family."

If Antiquity could have hugged her friend, she would have. "Do you think Grandmother will be pleased by this?" she asked.

"She will be angry. And immensely proud."

"Do I have enough power to make it back?"

"Saph Fyre does. As long as you do not return by flight."

Delicately picking up the mort-shroud containing Laurellyn Angelus, Antiquity walked home, moving her legs in her cockpit, the mech matching her step for step. She had no idea how to use the other systems of the mech—its firepower, its flight—but she would one day. All of that would take time, time she had won for her entire family.

The days to come held promise.

And Antiquity Angelus would forge her own destiny.

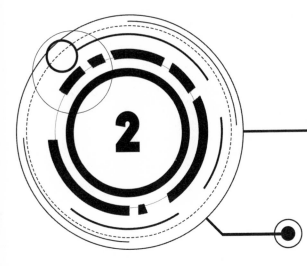

That promise dwindled over the next week.

Antiquity fidgeted while her grandmother glared darkly at her. The two were with CHKR-11 in an antechamber just outside the Hall of Elders, where the leaders of the city met. Few words had been spoken since they arrived that morning. Given new form after his destruction in the desert, Chekker hovered to her right, also quiet, his sentience now held within a new chrome sphere without blemish or markings. Vestige Grey and her robot companion crowded either side of Antiquity, as if to prevent her fleeing. It only left her feeling more annoyed.

They had been summoned by the Council of Elders. Antiquity guessed the reason easily enough. Saph Fyre. She had driven the mech through Solomon Fyre, excited to share her discovery with the city. It had not gone as she imagined. No cheers. No fanfare. Only fear from those fleeing before her. Whether the city remembered the mech or thought it part of the Imperium, it didn't matter. By the time she returned Saph Fyre to its former eyrie bay, only a few suspicious onlookers watched from the shadows.

Vestige had remained quiet since Saph Fyre returned home, choosing to focus on the moment rather than the events leading to it. She had touched the mech's faceplate for only a moment before sequestering herself with other Grey leaders who lived in the eyrie with them. Antiquity knew why. Having marched Saph Fyre through the city, the Imperium would undoubtedly learn of it, putting them all in danger.

Thinking it through again, Antiquity bit at the already shorn fingernails on her right hand.

"Stop that," Vestige snapped.

Antiquity did but glared at her blind grandmother anyway.

"And don't stare at me so, child," the old woman said, smoothing imaginary wrinkles from Antiquity's dress for what had to have been the hundredth time. "Or I will slap those eyes back front again."

Chekker lightly tapped her shoulder with his round body.

Even a robot could empathize.

Antiquity stared ahead once more, cutting off any number of angry retorts that sprang immediately to mind. One thing was for sure. The dress she wore did nothing to improve her mood.

"Why are you making me do this, Grandmother?" Antiquity asked again. She had not heard a good answer yet. "Why are we here? Why the dress? The Dreadths *cannot* be trusted. They will destroy our fami—"

"Every action has a consequence, Antiquity," Vestige answered. "And your actions in the desert have more consequences than most. Especially now."

"But I did nothing wrong!"

"No?" Vestige smiled tightly. "Yet here we are *anyway*. Although I foresaw this moment and have set plans into motion to remedy it."

Silence fell over the room, as thick as a sandstorm. Antiquity hated the feeling, hated the waiting. She had no idea what her grandmother meant. She also never would have thought that the discovery of her great-grandmother's powerful mech would result in such turmoil. The debating. The fear. And paranoia. The Elders, with Jackson Dreadth at their head, had moved to acquire the giant battle machine first. For the betterment of the city, they had all decided. When Antiquity—with her grandmother and family standing by her side—had not given in, Jackson Dreadth tried to take it by cunning. Several spies attempted to steal the mech from its berth. For naught. Members of their Grey community fought off every clandestine assault, leaving Saph Fyre safe. For now.

All while the Elders remained neutral, waiting to see how events played out. Politics. She hated the word now. Politics were the practice of influencing others for personal gain. Before discovering the mech, Antiquity had known nothing of politics. Over the last week she had learned all too quickly.

She wanted to roar her frustration like the dragons who used to roost within the mountains of Solomon Fyre.

Instead, Antiquity did not do so. Like her grandmother had advised, she waited to see what new ploy Jackson Dreadth now attempted to gain Saph Fyre for his own. "Let us leave, Grandmother," Antiquity pressed again, no longer caring what the Dreadth was up to after waiting several hours. "We've been summoned but no one is seeing us."

Just as Vestige Grey seemed uncertain for the first time that day, the heavy mechanisms of the great steel door unlocked and it finally opened. High Chamberlain Braun Pierce emerged, his long robes officious, his steely eyes as sharp as his role's reputation. She hated his pomp immediately.

"Family Grey," the man said with gravity, his hands steepled before him—an odd display of respect for a family so long shamed. He only acknowledged Vestige. "The council awaits your presence within the Hall of Elders."

Antiquity and her grandmother shared a brief look. Vestige patted her then on the lower back, more of a push forward than encouragement. They walked through the door and entered the large hexagonal chamber beyond, its walls burnished steel and adorned with vid-views of the city's past, its ceiling lost to the darkness. Antiquity suddenly itched with how small she felt. All seats at the semicircle taken but one, the Elders of Solomon Fyre turned their gazes on her from their high seats, adding to the feeling.

And one gaze was harsher than all the rest. Jackson Dreadth. He sat in the high-throne center seat while the Elders to his left and right remained one step below. A large metal fist rose behind him, once a part of a mech, a showing of strength. Antiquity did not shy from the Dreadth's gaze; she would not show weakness in front of him. It was the only power she had. The leader of Solomon Fyre stared thoughtfully at her, handsome in the way that a *heij* rattler could be, arrogance in his very manner. Manson Dreadth, who looked a great deal like his father, sat in the last Elder seat on her left, his inclusion in the proceeding unexpected since she had not heard of his ascendance to the council. Unlike the last time she had seen him—when Antiquity saved his life—Manson looked everywhere but at her. That suited Antiquity just fine.

The Elders sat in power, men who had ruled Solomon Fyre for years if not decades. No women were allowed on the council in that time. Not since her great-grandmother's era when Laurellyn Angelus ruled and supposedly failed the defense of the entire city.

"This day is one worthy of recording in the High Histories of Solomon Fyre," Jackson Dreadth began, his even voice filling the chamber. He looked to Vestige and inclined his head in recognition. "It is with great joy that I welcome a Grey family no more, but one proudly reinstated to Angelus."

The Elders lightly tapped their gem rings on the table, a sign of agreement and respect. Antiquity could not believe it. Her family had been like lepers for a hundred years, relegated to the lowest status in the city. To have the honor of the Angelus name reinstated was a dream not only held by her but all her relatives and forebearers as well. Maybe there was hope for her family after all.

Yet it all rang hollow. It made no sense why Jackson Dreadth would allow his family's sworn enemy to regain respectful standing in society.

Antiquity held her breath.

"It is time to let the past remain there, for the betterment of all," Jackson Dreadth continued. He gestured to the high chamberlain. The vid-views in the room came alive, each one showing various conflicts around the universe. "In some ways, the Imperium is at war with itself. As well as with those between the dark of the stars. These are difficult times. We have felt the effects of the chaos off-world. The planets of the government are fractured, and those larger conflicts draw the Imperium's gaze. We have an opportunity. For Erth to return to a role of prominence, this time within the Imperium. To be more than a speck in history." He paused. "The Grey-shame that has tainted one of the great ruling families of Solomon Fyre does not strengthen us, it weakens us."

Braun Pierce, whose role it was to record such meetings, was doing no such thing, his eyes piercing like a desert hawk's as he watched Antiquity. Some of the other Elders looked her way too from time to time.

"Vestige Angelus, I welcome your family returned to the Elders of Solomon Fyre. The vacant chair to my left shall now not be so. You bring wisdom to our city, with your years and your insight. Take it when you are ready, with all of our blessings. For it is not without giving up a piece of your own heart that you gain it." Jackson Dreadth gestured to the seat and then turned his gaze upon Antiquity. "Antiquity Angelus, in time, my dear child, you will be welcomed as the newest daughter named Dreadth."

Confusion at what had just been said crystalized into clarity when she looked at Manson Dreadth and saw his obvious misery.

He had known what she now knew.

New anger flooded through Antiquity. Vestige Angelus had used her sixteen-year-old granddaughter's life to barter. For societal standing. *Used her.*

One word echoed inside her.

Betrayed.

"The families of Dreadth and Angelus shall be wedded through the union of my son Manson and Antiquity," Jackson Dreadth said. "And in so doing, begin the revival of Solomon Fyre, to take its place once again among the powerful cities of Erth."

"No!" Antiquity yelled, finally finding her voice. Vestige gripped her arm in sudden iron, but Antiquity pulled angrily away. "This can't be!"

"It is already done," Jackson Dreadth said.

"This is how you repay me for saving your awful son?" she raged. Shock worn off, the words would not stop. "By enslaving me to him?"

"Hush, child," Vestige hissed in her ear.

"You did nothing of the sort, young one," the Elder leader said.

"I kept him safe!" Antiquity blurted, ignoring her grandmother's warning. The grip on her arm tightened, bony fingers filled with urgency. Antiquity did not care. "The scavengers from the wastes would have killed Manson and other members of your family if it were not for me and Chekker! We saved them all even though I didn't have to. You should be *thanking* me, not *ruining* my life!"

"If you had not left the safety of our city, to cavort in the desert wastes for your own amusement, he would not have followed you to keep you safe."

"To keep me safe?"

"That's right." Jackson Dreadth leaned forward. The smile remained but it had lost all of its humor. "He found the mech once known as Saph Fyre just as you did. It is a shared event. And in that event, we will share our families."

Antiquity now understood. The marriage allowed the Dreadths to claim Saph Fyre as their own. In return, the Angelus name would be restored and Vestige would gain a seat on the city council. Antiquity looked upon the Elders now, looking for help. She did not find it there. Even Prather Anil—the oldest and thinnest among them who had always been kind to the Grey-shamed family—looked away. The men before her knew enough of the truth by now and would not go against Jackson Dreadth. Worse, the leader of the Elders had likely promised each of them whatever they desired in return for their silence.

None of her discovery mattered, it turned out. The mech had been found and, with it, an uncovered lie about her family decades old. All for naught.

The lie and evidence would be buried now in a different way.

With politics and marriage.

"A great philosopher once said, 'Life can only be understood backward, but it must be lived forward,'" Jackson Dreadth continued. "We must *live*. This is a union that will invigorate Solomon Fyre's future. The past is the past and we have learned from it. Discovery of the mech is a fortuitous turn of events. *You* have the mech. *We* still possess the technology to replicate it, once proper stores of titanium are discovered. I have begun that undertaking. Putting aside this petty feud is the first step though. The mech belongs to the people of our city. To us, and our future."

"There is no *us*," Antiquity argued, hating the words and their selfishness the moment she said them. "It is mine. I found it!"

"You aren't capable of driving it. Of doing what is necessary," Chat Higgum chimed in, a portly Elder whose family also hated the Greyshamed. "You are just a girl."

"This *girl* was capable enough to kill those scavengers," she shot back.

"The Elders have watched the vid-cam footage of what happened, Antiquity. CHKR-11 had more to do with thwarting the scavengers than you did," Vestige said, finally weighing in.

She spun on her matriarch then. "You *sold me*, Grandmother. Betrayed me!"

"Vestige Angelus did no such thing, child. She is a practical woman," Jackson Dreadth said. Her grandmother did not turn toward her but instead kept her blind eyes facing forward. The fact that she ignored Antiquity hurt all the more. "Do not let yourself be foolhardy, Antiquity Angelus. It is a weakness I do not condone in my own family, and family Angelus cannot afford it either. Not during this time.

"You will marry my son Manson. And in turn, we will keep both families and an entire city safe."

) ◗ ● ◖ (

Once the assembly dissolved, Antiquity felt the burn of tears.

She fought them, unwilling to show weakness in front of these men. It didn't matter. The Elders departed their hall, nodding farewells only to Vestige, none of them giving Antiquity another glance. A means to an end, she meant nothing to them now. Only Manson gave her the briefest of looks, the younger Dreadth probably feeling as angry and cornered as she did. Antiquity ignored him. Instead she remained, rage and desperation mingling in ways she had never experienced. Jackson Dreadth had decided the Elders and the two Angeluses would reconvene in three days to work out the official details of the forthcoming union. No time would be wasted. She would be forced into marrying Manson as if she were living in the early days of Erth's Old Era.

The mech would be taken from her then, transferred to the Dreadth eyrie. The treasure of her past and the potential for her future lost.

All while her future became tied to a Dreadth she hated.

She rarely cried. Being Grey-shamed tended to harden hearts. But as her world collapsed about her, one thing kept her from shedding tears.

Anger toward her grandmother.

"That was unpleasant," Vestige sighed, finally breaking the quiet once the last Elder had left.

Antiquity said nothing. Silence was her only weapon.

"You need to *think* before you speak, Antiquity," Vestige chastised. But her voice carried no reprimand. "If you are to be any use to family Angelus at all."

She bit her tongue.

"Do you not see what I am trying to do for *our family*, child?"

Before she could stop it, her anger rolled out of her. "Apparently, I'm no longer part of that family," she said sharply.

And she ran for the door.

"Antiquity!" Vestige called after her.

She didn't stop. Vision shimmering, she fled the Hall of Elders, running through hushed hallways and finally out through the building's arched entry point into the hot afternoon. Dozens of people regarded her hurried appearance, but she paid them no heed, taking three steps at a time down into the primary square of Solomon Fyre, not knowing where she was going but getting there fast. She wanted to disappear. The upper city allowed for that, its populace bustling with cultures from all over Erth. Her own people were the majority, having settled Solomon Fyre's bedrock. The dark-skinned *persai* and their kindred *arabi*—the former in colorful silks, the latter draped in holy black—walked throughout the crowds too, most of them visitors from far beyond the desert. Even a few Celestials mingled, their tall, lithe figures and milky, transparent skin covered by off-world metallic materials to ward off the burning sun. All about their own business.

She got lost among them. None of them would ever know how important a discovery she had made. Whatever hope she had discovered with the mech had been stolen from her. By the Dreadths. By her grandmother.

Antiquity had never felt so hurt.

Or alone.

Sweat making her even more uncomfortable in the dress, she slowed to a stop in front of the cooling spray of a circular fountain. In the center of it, a dragon statue with wings spread to the sky sat perched upon a concrete mech hand, an homage to the beasts that had once roosted in these mountains. But it was also a memorial to the destruction of Erth's mech capabilities. What she wouldn't give to fly like dragons, to leap into the air and leave the worries of the ground behind.

Then she remembered she possibly could fly. One day. If Saph Fyre was hers.

What would she do now? What *could* she do?

The familiar soft whir of a bot glided up next to her.

"I suppose you are going to tell me to talk to Grandmother, eh, Chekker?"

"If you run again, he might."

Antiquity turned. Vestige Angelus stood there, hands folded and blind eyes watching Antiquity with the maddening solemnity that she always possessed, her three light orbs swirling over her head. Chekker floated beside her.

"I might have to," Antiquity said.

Vestige frowned. "I have never taught you to run from a fight."

"Hard to fight when you are sold to the very enemy you are to battle," Antiquity said, feeling the acid on her tongue.

Vestige stepped up to the rim of the fountain, beside her grand-daughter. "I want you to listen to me, Antiquity, and listen well," she said, her face as grave as Antiquity had ever seen it. "There is more at stake here than pride. Or family honor. There is more at stake than your heart or a single mech—even a mech as nostalgic and important as Saph Fyre. You discovered a remarkable secret, not only the mech but how your great-grandmother died at the hands of the Dreadth family." She kept her voice a whisper that the crowds nearly drowned out. "But you do not know *why* Laurellyn Angelus died. The true reasons. Or the secrets she kept." She paused. "Secrets she passed on to me.

"It is fortuitous for our family," Vestige continued. "If we are careful, we will no longer be Grey-shamed. You noticed the high chamberlain did not record our meeting with the Elders?" Antiquity nodded. "This whole thing can be plausibly denied by those men, and we must still tread carefully. The secret you discovered will right many wrongs. But we still do not have leverage quite yet, regardless of finding my mother's mech." When Antiquity didn't respond, Vestige squeezed her grand-daughter's arm, a longtime act of affection for the old woman. "You are petulant. And reckless. And how you've lived this long is quite beyond me. Likely more testament to Chekker than anything else. You have a lot to learn, child, and it is now time to grow into adulthood. And quickly. The events put into motion when you found Saph Fyre are a desert storm threatening to scour our lives away. It is not only those in power here that we must be wary of."

"Who else? And what secrets are you talking about?" Antiquity questioned, hating her sudden curiosity and the forgiveness it offered. "Off-worlders?"

"You do not understand. There are secrets long buried here in Solomon Fyre. And in the deserts. And in the great cities beyond the deserts, within the mountains and forests of Erth's mid-line," her grandmother said. "Secrets desired by the Imperium. Secrets that my mother kept safe." She paused. "Secrets I will not speak of while in public. We must discuss this with the other Grey families who we have welcomed into our eyrie home. They have just as much to lose as we do. It should be discussed behind closed doors."

Antiquity heard the worry in her grandmother's voice. Their home had become a refuge for several families, all shamed in Grey like lepers. Antiquity hadn't given thought to them or her twin friends, Kaihli and Elsana.

Lives were at stake, lives her grandmother protected too.

"I understand," was all Antiquity said. "And the marriage?"

"In this, we must be strong. *You* must be strong." There was something Vestige wasn't saying. "We will stand with the Dreadth family. For how long they've been enemies, there are enemies around Erth that make the Dreadth family close allies. Friends, even." Her blind eyes peered up into the sky. She looked almost sad. "And pieces upon a game board that must be moved no other way."

Antiquity didn't like the grim woman who now stood by her side. There were times in the past when her grandmother had appeared in such a way—wistful, tired, and melancholic. Men who had been fighting the fervently religious *arabi* a world away had the same look, one of taking part in a long war that would never end and having seen and done things of which they were ashamed. Such men broke over time in a way that could never be mended, wearing their inner pain on the outside. Vestige Angelus had the same appearance now. It unsettled Antiquity more than the meeting with the Elders.

"What do you want from me?" Antiquity asked, softening her manner.

"I want you to study. Pay attention. To my words now and after. Memorize. Watch. Challenge authority when you must. Walk the path only you can walk. I do not want to relinquish Saph Fyre any more than you do. That mech is our only hope. All will become clearer in the days ahead." She paused. "It is up to you, as my granddaughter and the great-granddaughter of Laurellyn Angelus, to see our family bloom once more in these desert sands. Do you understand that, Antiquity? Do you understand the power you will soon wield?"

"But I will not yield my heart," she whispered. "How can I wield power when I will be married to Manson Dreadth of all people? I will be caged for his benefit."

"Listen to me, please, my dear. It is important. One day all too soon, you will stand before High Chamberlain Braun Pierce with Manson. This marriage is the key to the future. Not only for you, but for Erth." Vestige took Antiquity's hand in her own—and slid a titanium ring upon her granddaughter's finger that she had produced from nowhere. "The young always believe they can see the future. You do not know what lies ahead." She adjusted the ring with tender care. "Chekker will aid your education, of course. Listen to him always. He is a conscience when you have none."

Antiquity looked upon the gift. Four tiny chips of sapphire—the gem of family Angelus—lay embedded equidistant from one another. They glowed in the sunshine and matched the ring that sat upon her matriarch's own finger. "What is this for?"

"A promise. My strength now becomes your own."

"Sounds like you are preparing me for the end of the world."

Vestige Angelus smiled and looked down on her with white-filmed eyes. There Antiquity saw the tough love that had bound them her entire life. Her grandmother kissed Antiquity's cheek with dry, thin lips.

"Be the change of the moment," the old woman said. "My love for you would be remiss if I did not prepare you for the world such as it is, not the world we wish it would be. And that world is coming for us even as we speak."

) ◗ ● ◖ (

"Awake, Antiquity," Chekker beeped. "And come quickly."

Antiquity woke from troubled sleep and rolled out of the bed placed in the makeshift living quarters within Angelus eyrie's workshop. The bot swirled in the air, waiting. As she dressed, rubbing her eyes, she looked from her sleeping friends on the floor to the giant standing mech just outside the large wall window, the head of Saph Fyre level with her floor, its body taking up the rest of the berth below. For nine days the mech had been housed in the ancient manse of her family, in the same position her great-grandmother had stationed it. While she could have slept in her own bed—her room was only three corridors away—Antiquity decided to guard the mech in person. She would die before letting someone thieve or destroy the mech in some way.

It also allowed her to closely oversee restoration. All of the tools, diagnostic systems, and repair bots that had lain unused since the destruction of Erth's mech corps in the Splinter War remained in the eyrie. Even Master Mechanic Brox Uphell still existed, as an artificial intelligence construct but one working to bring Saph Fyre fully back online.

She knew it was all for nothing though. Finding the mech had started a chain reaction of events in her life, each one worse than the last.

What new event did she have to deal with now?

"Why are you up, Antiquity?" a sleepy voice asked.

Kaihli sat up, blearily looking at her data-watch for the time. Her twin, Elsana, also stirred. They had helped Antiquity guard Saph Fyre, the longtime friends as excited as Antiquity by her find. The twins were Greys like her. In their case, their scientist great-grandfather had rebelled against the destruction of the city's university and de-education of the entire planet under the new authoritarian rule. It had cost his family their standing. Kaihli and Elsana knew Antiquity better than anyone; they also knew how dangerous life had become for the Angelus family and those who lived with them.

"Where are you going?" Kaihli asked.

"Yeah, what's going on?" Elsana rolled out of her bed, dark eyes already searching for her clothes and shoes. The twins were identical but whereas both of Kaihli's arms were muscled from working with machinery, her sister possessed one underdeveloped arm given her at birth.

Antiquity shrugged. "I don't know. Chekker?"

The bot flew to the door, obviously wanting them to move faster. "A spacecraft has entered the skies over Solomon Fyre."

"So what? It happens all of the time," Kaihli yawned.

Chekker shot back to the twin, clearly agitated. Antiquity had never seen him like this before. "Not a craft like this. It is not a materials transport from the capital or off-world. It is a Celestial delegation warship."

Antiquity could hardly believe it. "*That* doesn't happen all of the time."

"No, it does not," Chekker agreed. "Please hurry."

Worry at the bot's adamancy growing sharper, Antiquity followed him with added haste. She was not alone. The twins were already dressed in the colorful silks of the *persai* and pulling their black hair back. "Then we are going too. Maybe a once-in-a-lifetime thing," Elsana explained. "Besides. Someone has to watch over you."

Antiquity grinned at their new joke. The group left the room in a hurry, their pace quickened by the time they arrived at the ele-lift and called it to their floor. Antiquity couldn't believe it. A delegation warship. She had never seen one—none of them had—since the Imperium no longer needed that kind of might or presence after the Splinter War had destroyed all Erth mechs and the means to make them. The humor left behind by Elsana's joke vanished. For a Celestial delegate to arrive in an off-world warship could not be a good thing. It made Antiquity realize that she hadn't spoken to her grandmother since the council meeting two days earlier. Vestige had hinted at family secrets and then vanished into Grey meetings of her own.

Antiquity regretted not forcing her way into those meetings. She had spent her time in the eyrie working with Brox and Kaihli to return Saph Fyre to operational order. Now she worried this delegation had something to do with the mech.

With Chekker leading them, they made their way through the Angelus eyrie. Solomon Fyre butted up against a giant plateau, multiple eyries built into its sheer rock walls, once giving mechs easy access to the sky. Antiquity and her friends moved through corridors featuring doors to family units, eventually coming to another ele-lift. They rode it upward to a secured exit and, after Antiquity unlocked it with a genetic touch, made their way into the cool night.

Darkness still lay over the city, its sable shroud pinpricked with starlight. Ascending a thin path, they gained the rocky heights over the Angelus eyrie, giving them a sweeping view of the city below and to the east. There, one of the planet's two moons had risen, white and pregnant. Dawn would waken Solomon Fyre soon.

Movement in the sky caught her eye then. Chekker was right. In the distance moved a shape darker than the rest, sleek and silent. A massive thing pricked with laz-cannons and starbursts, it glided over the city in a grid-like pattern. It did not stop and neither did it repeat its path.

"Why is it not landing?" Antiquity asked. "Not descending to one of the ports?"

"I don't know," Elsana said.

Kaihli shook her head. "It's almost like—"

"Like it is looking for something." A sinking feeling fell over Antiquity.

The three girls continued to watch. Antiquity's uneasiness became a slow-gnawing fear. The events of the last few days had occurred because of the mech. And here was an Imperium delegation warship, a rare sighting, apparently scanning for something. She might not have understood the ramifications of her actions before, but the Celestial visit could not be coincidence. The delegate was here for Saph Fyre.

She suddenly felt really small. Long-standing conflicts with Solomon Fyre families she understood. She had grown up with that reality. The warship though? If it was here for the mech? Terrifying, due to the unknown.

After almost an hour, and with dawn brightening the east, the warship finished its search and began to move toward their location.

"Where is it going now?" Elsana hissed.

No one answered. Antiquity held her breath. The warship drifted over them, emitting a soft hum as it moved, its fold-engines shut down and mag-propulsion engaged. The girls hunkered down behind several boulders. For one moment Antiquity thought it had stopped above them. Then she realized it had slowed further, drifting on the air, to finally stop at the neighboring eyrie directly to the north.

The pinnacle of family Dreadth's eyrie.

"We are too far away," Kaihli said. "We can't see who will disembark from that warship. And maybe who is meeting it."

"We need a better view," Antiquity agreed. "Come on."

They left their hiding place above the Angelus eyrie and sprinted back to the ele-lift, shot down several hundred feet and, taking a different hallway cutting through the mountain's heart, arrived at the remotest ele-lift still within Angelus control. After a quick ride upward, Antiquity and the others were outside again, upon an outcropping overlooking the landing platform of the Dreadth family. Even though they were too far away to hear, they would at least be able to see who exited the delegation warship—and who had possibly come for the mech. It didn't take long. As soon as the ship landed and anchored itself magnetically to the port, a large door at the ship's stern opened and a Celestial emerged, the man's skin so white it almost glowed in the night.

"A high-ranking Celestial," Kaihli whispered. "From the heart of the Imperium. Or maybe Erth's capital. This visit is an important one."

"How do you know that? All Celestials look the same, to me anyway," Antiquity said, frowning.

"Look at his guard retinue."

Antiquity did. While the Celestial elegantly glided onto the Dreadth landing platform—calm and serene, the folds of his white robes billowing—his guards spread out to protect their master, each one carrying a high-tech laz-rifle at the ready and wearing a white starburst insignia upon their helmet.

The warship had not come from the stars. The insignia, only used by Erth's Celestials, denoted a retinue from the planetary capital city of Euroda.

"He is part of the ruling family of Erth," Antiquity guessed.

"That's not all," Elsana said. "Look."

It took Antiquity a moment before she realized what her friend meant. Moving to meet the Celestial from the eyrie's port doors came a middle-aged man and a familiar old woman—the latter possessed of three glowing orbs spinning about her head.

Vestige walked beside Jackson Dreadth.

"What is my grandmother doing down there?" Antiquity hissed.

Elsana shook her head. "None of this makes any sense, Antiquity. What have you gotten yourself into?"

Kaihli gripped rock. "Too far away to hear."

"You will. I have been given access to audio from Vestige Angelus's walking spheres," said Chekker. Antiquity continued to watch as the two heads of enemy families stopped before the Celestial, the delegate overlord to both.

After a few clicks, sound emanated from Chekker.

". . . honored to meet you, Royal Declarion Wit," Jackson Dreadth said, bowing.

"I am not interested in the pleasantries of Solomon Fyre. Or your forced respect." The man had a high, tinny voice that unnerved Antiquity right away. "I am here for one reason. Residents within this city have reported the presence of a mech, one that walked through the city recently and then vanished." He looked around, frowning his disgust of the place. He clearly did not like coming to Solomon Fyre. "This is a violation of the Splinter War's compact with those of Erth. I am here to retrieve the mech and all information gathered by its discovery. And to deliver sentences of treason if need be."

"I am unsure of what you mean," Jackson Dreadth said. He stood defiant, shoulders squared, but his hands showed supplication.

"This is your only facility, yes?"

"It is my home."

"I would have ignored one report. Royal Ricariol Wit, my older brother and great lord general of the Imperium's Erth, would have as well," Royal Declarion Wit said, his tone cold. "But there were numerous reports. And my patience wears thin, even now."

"I have not seen this mech you speak of," Jackson Dreadth said. He hadn't, Antiquity thought, so not a lie. "I am the head of Solomon Fyre's Council of Elders. If there was such a mech, I would have seen it by now. These halls and mech ports once contained the mech might of an entire planet but not for decades. Not since—"

"Not since the Imperium quelled your savage ways."

"We are not our rebellious grandsires," Jackson Dreadth pointed out.

"No," Royal Declarion Wit said. He had gone as still as a statue. "But perhaps more devious in bondage."

"'Freedom from the soil kills the tree,'" Vestige quoted, an ancient adage from the *arabi*, looking as solemn as Antiquity had ever seen her. "But in our case, even if there was a mech discovered—and even if the people of Solomon Fyre possessed the ability to mechanize once more—Erth now lacks the precious ores of its former soil to produce the titanium needed. The Imperium is under no threat."

The Celestial turned his icy blue gaze upon Vestige. Even from the great distance, Antiquity saw the look Royal Declarion Wit gave her grandmother.

It was the look of a *heij* rattler before it struck.

"Who is this old woman, Dreadth?"

"She is Vestige Angelus, matriarch of her family."

Royal Declarion Wit's eyes narrowed. "A Grey. Is it not also Erth law to never mention the name of a family that has been Grey-shamed?" he said, eyes lazily ignoring Vestige.

"It still does not change the truth I have spoken," Vestige said. "Grey-shamed or not, Royal Declarion Wit."

"Why do you speak as if you have some say here," the Celestial said.

"You waste my time and that of Royal Ricariol Wit. He has ordered me here. To remove the mech. To restore the balance that this planet has enjoyed for generations. Speak again, Vestige Grey, and I will silence that voice."

The threat slithered into the large space between Antiquity and her grandmother. Knowing her grandmother so well, Antiquity dreaded what she knew would come next.

"If speaking means dying, let my death roar into these mountains," Vestige said, pointing with an open palm, her blindness looking upward. She seemed to gaze directly in Antiquity's direction, as if she knew her granddaughter watched there. "And may it echo through our world."

"Dreadth, this crone must be here—in your home—at your behest," Declarion said, his voice carrying no change of inflection with the accusation. He nodded to one of his guards. "We will be discussing more than just the mech, it seems."

A lone blast punctured the air.

Milky eyes filled with surprise, Vestige crumpled like a rag doll, smoke rising from the hole in her chest created by a laz-rifle.

Her grandmother's orbs fell dead with her.

"No!" Antiquity screamed at the realization of what had just happened, voice filling the mountainside.

All eyes below turned toward her. The Celestial was saying something to Jackson Dreadth, but the Elder ignored him, staring hard at Antiquity. Even as the guards split—some running into the warship while others swarmed into the Dreadth eyrie—Antiquity could not remove her gaze from her dead grandmother.

"You must flee, Grey-child," Chekker said, hitting her shoulder. "Now. The guards of the Celestial will attempt to enter these environs."

"Come on, Antiquity!" Elsana screamed, yanking her hard.

Tears blurring her vision, the death of her grandmother emblazoned into her mind, Antiquity let herself be dragged back the way they had come.

Into the new emptiness of the Angelus eyrie.

) ◗ ● ◖ (

"Run, Antiquity!" Chekker buzzed in her ear.

Some part of the bot's urgency brought her back to the world and she quickened her pace. But images played over and over in her head. Her grandmother. Murdered. Falling to the ground. A smoking hole in her chest. The orbs that had aided her to walk shattering upon the rock of the mountain. The images played over and over even as her friends to either side guided her along, gripping her arms and stumbling toward the first ele-lift. Once within, a jolt rocketing downward. And hallways. Suddenly at the entrance needing her genetic input to open for all of them, the quickest way back into the safety of her mountain home of rock and steel. But she knew that safety was an illusion. Nothing would be safe again.

The sightless face of her dead grandmother stared after her.

"She's gone," Antiquity choked.

"If you do not run, the Celestial and his retinue will kill you. And your friends. The mech is your only chance." Chekker pushed her in the shoulder.

She barely understood what the bot suggested. The mech? Vestige had been a guiding light her entire life and now that light had been extinguished. She was lost. Cast adrift. On her own. Tears began to swim again, the weight of it crushing.

She steeled herself from it though. Took a steadying breath. And anchored herself to her friends, who still pushed her along. She would not fail them.

No one else would die because of her.

"The mech then," she said, now hurrying.

Back in their makeshift bedroom, Antiquity gathered the clothes and supplies they needed. The twins did the same. In a matter of minutes, they were moving into the eyrie berth, crossing the steel walkway to Saph Fyre's head and cockpit. Antiquity was about to yell for Chekker and Brox to get the mech and eyrie ready for parting when she pulled up, her eyes falling on a shadowy figure standing within the opened faceplate.

She knew him at once—and prepared for a fight.

"Let us pass, Manson Dreadth," Elsana growled.

The oldest son of Jackson Dreadth did not move. Instead he looked at them, defiant, gauging them and Chekker. He held no weapons. But there was something in his manner that worried Antiquity, as if a coiled spring lay just beneath his surface, ready for release and violence.

"How did you get in here?" Antiquity growled, ready for anything.

"The same way you did, I'd imagine," he said, his humorless smile maddening to Antiquity. "Through the closest outside door."

She couldn't believe it. "The door just opened?"

"It did. And I rode the ele-lift up here."

"You lie."

"*Why* are you here, is a better question?" Kaihli asked, having pulled one of her heavy electro-wrenches from her pack, their only weapon at hand.

"To wait, of course. For you." Manson snorted, meanness in his eyes. It was then Antiquity saw that the older boy had a large pack upon his back, of a type the residents of Solomon Fyre used when leaving the city for weeks on desert forays. Before she could ask about it, an explosion rocked the mountain, the sound reverberating through the eyrie.

"The Celestial and his guards," Elsana said. "Trying to get in here."

"What's going on? A Celestial did *that*?" Manson asked, pointing back the way they had come. Real fear crossed his face—the first time Antiquity had ever seen it.

"No time for this, Dreadth," Antiquity said, striding toward him. He stepped aside at the last second; the twins followed their friend. "You need to get out of here. Now. Hide in the eyrie. Or go back the way you came in."

"If you leave him here, he will die," Chekker said, hovering at her shoulder. "He must come with us."

Suspicion took root in Antiquity then. She sensed a plan, one that had been put into motion long before the events of this night. She looked from her friends to Manson and back again.

"Fine. We will be talking about this later, Chekker."

Elsana grabbed Antiquity's arm. "Are you sure about this?"

"I will explain later," she said, already putting on the mech's control gear. "For now, get below. We have to get out of here."

"I am not going anywhere," Manson said stubbornly. "I am here for the mech."

"Did you question why your father gave you that pack, Dreadth?" Antiquity guessed, seeing immediately in his eyes that Jackson Dreadth had a scheme beyond his son getting the mech. She stepped into the cockpit's chair and the harness began to click itself around her. "Don't you wonder how you got genetic access to this eyrie, the enemy house of family Dreadth?" The back wall of the cockpit slid open and live pieces of gear snaked over her limbs, hands, and feet. "We have been lied to, Manson. You now have a choice to make, one that is your own. To live. Or die."

Another explosion shook the mountain—louder and stronger. Giving her worried looks, the twins vanished, scurrying down a side ladder into the crew hold of the giant robot. They knew where to go; they knew where to strap in.

"You don't have much time," she said.

Shaking his head, Manson made his choice. He moved deeper into the cockpit and, giving Antiquity a hard look, disappeared below as well.

She couldn't believe this was happening.

"Chekker! Where did you get to?" Antiquity yelled as goggles slid over her eyes, the hum of machinery and power coming to life, pulsing through her senses.

"I am here, Grey-child," the bot responded in her ear, having joined with the mech's systems.

"Is Brox aboard?"

"He is here with me. Although he is not happy about it."

Antiquity nodded to no one. She would deal with Chekker and Brox later. She powered up the mech, her mind entering its metal skin, making her one with the giant. She was more than a girl; she was more than a machine. As she joined with Saph Fyre, some part of the machine soothed the grief burning in her heart, an echo of some part of her great-grandmother Laurellyn Angelus. Once she had sat in this same place. The continuity of the family line was comforting. Those women were a part of Antiquity. It kept her focused on wielding the awesome might of Saph Fyre to escape.

And even though she had no idea what to do about the Celestial, his warship, and whatever machinations she had been caught up in, Antiquity would at the very least keep her friends safe.

She lifted her hands before her and flexed the fingers to fists.

"Open the outer eyrie doors, Chekker," she said, readying herself.

The massive steel doors slowly split apart. Light from the new day's dawn dazzled her.

Laz-fire struck her titanium skin immediately.

Antiquity could not back away from it, Saph Fyre still pinned within her berth. While she didn't feel pain from the mech's superficial damage, it registered in her mind, insects stinging a thousand times over. She pushed off and leapt out of the eyrie and into the morning, landing beyond the door in a crouch and gripping rock to gain a better look at her assailant. She already knew what it was. The Imperium warship hovered in the skies just above her, its laz-cannons unleashed. They could not penetrate her hardened titanium with single shots, but Antiquity knew the warship had more capable arms aboard and she could not let them be brought to bear.

Having learned more about Saph Fyre's abilities in the days since the scavenger attack, she fired her own weapons, rocket ports popping out along her arms and ordnance released. The decades-old rockets were still live, slamming into the warship. The craft twisted to the side but continued its assault on the mech, barely daunted.

Saph Fyre had more weapons but Antiquity didn't know how to use them. She realized there would be only one way to end the fight. Antiquity put her mind into flight, willing the thrusters in her feet and hands to fire and launch her into the sky.

Saph Fyre did not respond.

"Why aren't the flight thrusters working?" Antiquity roared into her headset.

"Brox has informed me that they are working. I will double-check," Chekker replied in her ear, even as the warship shot a trans-harpoon at the mech. Antiquity ducked it, the tearing weapon imbedding into the side of the mountain.

"All is operational," the bot assured a few seconds later.

Antiquity cursed, trying to make the thrusters work again, sending her mind racing into the mech.

Nothing happened.

She sensed it then. Some sort of barrier. Within herself.

Confusion became white-hot anger and frustration. She couldn't do it. She'd have to find another way to reach the warship. She pulled herself up the side of the mountain, leaping between gaps, gaining elevation. She'd have one chance at this. Finding what she wanted, Antiquity tore apart a rock outcropping, the boulder larger than the mech's head.

The warship rose in the air to continue its assault, blowing apart the rock at the mech's feet, now trying to unseat her. Antiquity didn't wait. She threw the massive rock toward the top of the warship.

It had the desired effect. The ship dropped in elevation to evade being struck.

Allowing Saph Fyre to jump.

Antiquity leapt from the mountain, driving the mech's powerful legs toward her foes. Those piloting the warship saw their mistake, but it was too late. Saph Fyre landed on the ship, and Antiquity plunged the fingers of the mech's left hand into the hull, anchoring to its metal. Gripping with her knees, she pummeled the ship with her right hand—over and over and over—the hull of the ship buckling with every strike. She screamed at the top of her lungs, rage and the sorrow of losing her grandmother mingling together and infusing her every movement. She and Saph Fyre were one, and she would not let those of the Imperium escape.

The warship careened to the side, flying crazily away from the city and its buildings, trying to unseat her. But Antiquity held on. In a matter of only minutes, the warship began losing elevation and control over the desert. Then an explosion ripped open the entire rear of the craft, where its engines were located. Antiquity held on to its shattered front hull even as its remains fell toward the desert they now flew over. With a crash that would awaken anyone in Solomon Fyre who had not been awake already, the warship slammed into the sands, a smoking and fiery ruin.

Unsure how much heat the mech could take, Antiquity pushed Saph Fyre off the disintegrating hull and took them to a safe distance.

"You did it!" Elsana screamed from below. Antiquity didn't know what to say. Manson and her friends had undoubtedly been watching footage of the battle on vid-views in the crew quarters.

Chekker buzzed in her ear, barely a whisper.

"It is but the beginning, Grey-child."

Antiquity took a deep breath, gazing into the fire of the burning warship. She knew men and women died within it, but she didn't care. They had helped kill her grandmother. She hoped that Royal Declarion Wit had been aboard, but there was no way to know.

"We must leave," Chekker said. She could hear the anxiety in the bot's voice. "The Royal will have informed his brother."

"I know. Grandmother had a plan."

"She did."

Just mentioning her grandmother brought tears to her eyes, battle adrenaline unable to quell her sadness. There were answers to be had though. Chekker had a lot of explaining to do. But first, she had to keep her friends safe.

And Manson. What role was the Dreadth playing in this?

Antiquity turned away from the dying warship. The Imperium would find it, no doubt. They would hunt her. Fortunately, the sands of her homeland would hide the massive mech's passing.

She turned, and Saph Fyre ran into the heart of the desert.

Rage helped her continue through the day and long into the night.

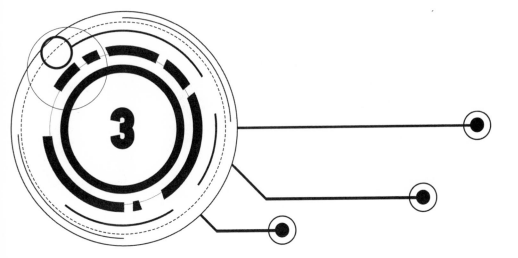

Wearied and feeling dry to the bone, Antiquity could not sleep.
She sat upon a boulder away from Saph Fyre and her
friends, arms wrapped around drawn-up knees as she viewed the
mech. It lay sprawled at the bottom of a narrow desert canyon where
she had left it, a perfect place to hide. The canyon walls were high and
littered with crystal veins that wove through the orange-and-red rock,
creating the appearance of cascading water. She had stopped here in the
night, exhausted beyond physical and emotional limits, not because
of the beautiful setting but because the desert's end had revealed the
ravine, giving Saph Fyre a natural shield from aerial searches—those
in the air as well as from space. Sleep had not come though. And as
the stars moved overhead, her tears had fallen until their well dried
up and she was left alone with the sounds of a world bereft of Vestige
Angelus. The memory of her grandmother's last moments haunted
her through the night.

She shook her head to no one. She had once felt exhilarated at finding Saph Fyre. Now she looked upon the mech and saw only a curse on the Angelus family.

Nothing would ever be the same again.

She twisted the titanium ring on her finger. It was the last gift her grandmother had given her, identical to her own. It connected them, even now.

She would never take it off.

At least they hadn't been found. Overnight, Saph Fyre's sensors had picked up a dragon flying from the direction of Solomon Fyre. But the beast had flown farther north and east, leaving them alone. Thankfully, no one had discovered them.

Yet.

"Antiquity?"

She turned. Elsana stood in the dawn's weak light, silks covering her dark skin, thick black hair pulled back. Having already met the day as her faith required, the twin carried her *seccade* prayer rug rolled up under her arm. The uncertainty in her voice stabbed Antiquity all the more. Of the twins, she was the more sensitive, wearing her heart on her sleeve, her shrunken hand giving her emotional perspective.

"I am okay. Where is Kai?" Antiquity asked, rubbing her eyes.

"With Brox. Working on Saph Fyre. There is a great deal more work to be done, I guess. And minor damage from the fight needing repair. Kai is better at machines and tools than I am. Always has been." She held up her hand in apology. "And Brox is happy to have the help."

Antiquity looked back toward the mech. She was glad Brox had come along. The artificial construct had resided within the eyrie's memory banks for several decades, his mind copied from an old dwarf of a man with a woolly beard and penetrating, serious eyes.

She had no idea how Saph Fyre worked beyond a rudimentary way, and the mechanic for family Angelus knew its science like no other.

"Are you okay, El?" Antiquity didn't like the weariness in her words.

Elsana nodded, meek as usual. "I should be asking you the same thing but I know nothing is okay. Instead, I'll simply say thank you for saving us."

"Did I? Save us?" Antiquity snorted. She took a deep breath. "Or did I just put you in worse danger, out here, in the middle of a situation we know nothing about."

Elsana sat next to her friend. "You did what you had to do. Kai and I both are grateful. That Celestial would have killed us outright. Or worse. The Imperium has never been kind to my people."

Antiquity nodded, understanding of her dark-skinned friend. In many ways, they were similar despite their different heritages. Outcasts. The *persai* followed an ancient and peaceful faith that had existed on Erth for millennia. But they were always likened to and feared like their extremist, black-clothed cousins, the *arabi*. The former believed in peace with others; the latter once subjugated people to their faith by the sword. Antiquity had never been religious—the Grey-shamed were not allowed such community endeavors—but she had always been fascinated by the duality that Elsana must live with.

Kaihli, on the other hand, decried the faith her sister embraced. It was a difference that defined them to their cores.

"Matriarch Vestige would be quite proud of you," Elsana said.

Antiquity hated hearing her grandmother's name. Her eyes welled up again. She looked away. Would the tears ever stop? "I got my grandmother killed," Antiquity said, the words tumbling out of her. She squeezed her eyes closed against the tears but all she saw was her grandmother falling to the ground. "Why did she push that Celestial? Why?"

Elsana put her arm around Antiquity. Of the twins, she always knew what to say and do. "Only she knows that. But I doubt Vestige Grey ever did anything in her life that was not by choice."

Antiquity sniffed, blinking the tears away as she looked at the sky. "You are right. She would have done it for a reason. Even during our last lesson, she said she always had a plan to thwart those who hated her."

"Maybe she sacrificed herself to—"

"Set me on a path of her making," Antiquity finished, daunted by the realization. "But to what end?"

The two sat in silence. Antiquity mulled over the words. She couldn't believe her grandmother would sacrifice herself for any reason. Yet, what her friend said about Vestige ran true. The enormity of it all could not be ignored.

"You should know. Manson is talking about leaving," Elsana broke in, looking back toward the little camp.

Antiquity frowned. "Where would he go?"

"I don't know." Elsana shrugged, looking down at the beautifully made *seccade* she held. She used it to pray to her god every morning. "He doesn't like Kai and me very much either." She paused, considering her next words. "What made you bring him anyway? And how did he even get into the Angelus eyrie?"

Antiquity didn't respond right away. She had an answer for the former question and a guess for the latter. She still had to talk to Chekker. And Manson. Looking back on the night, the bot had been instrumental in ensuring that Antiquity woke, moved into position to observe the meeting with the Celestial, Jackson Dreadth, and her grandmother, and transmitted the audio from the meeting.

The bot would have also been able to give Manson Dreadth entrance to the eyrie. "Where is Chekker?" she asked.

"With Brox and Kai, in the mech." As Antiquity pushed herself off the rock, she realized how tight her muscles were from driving the mech.

"And Manson?"

"He *was* on the other side of Saph Fyre, sitting."

Antiquity nodded. "I will go talk to him. Alone."

She walked away from her friend before Elsana could say anything. This wouldn't be easy. For as long as Antiquity had known him, the Dreadth had always been a bully, thick-headed and absolute in his belief that he was superior to the other children. That his family's standing gave him amnesty from his actions. He was stubborn and arrogant, and convincing him of anything would be a challenge. She needed to know what he knew.

After that, she would have to convince him of the truth.

Antiquity walked by Saph Fyre, the giant mech towering over her, finding Manson on the other side where Elsana had said he would be.

When he saw her, Manson's already glowering demeanor darkened further.

"We must speak. Now," she said simply.

"I don't take orders from a Grey," Manson declared.

When surrounded by his family members, he had seemed invincible. It had led Antiquity to flee from him more times than not. But here, in the wilds of Erth where neither held sway, she found she didn't fear him—and certainly not after the events of the last two days.

"I am going to be blunt about this, to get it through that thick skull of yours, Manson," Antiquity replied, the irritation in his eyes driving her vindication. "Right now, the Imperium is in control of your life. They will have already gone into my home and discovered the eyrie, with its recent use and updated files. They know about Saph Fyre and the battle we waged. And since my grandmother and your father met with Royal Declarion Wit in the Dreadth eyrie, I am betting he is either dead or imprisoned. That means your family name isn't worth the Elder council seat you just ascended to. The Imperium will be hunting you as it is likely hunting me."

"And what of your grandmother?" he spat. "She planned all of this."

"If so, it was a terrible plan. She is dead, Manson, killed by the Celestial. I watched it happen," she said, unwilling to let the words make her cry in front of him.

Manson hid his surprise at the news. He hadn't known of her death. "Why would my father be a part of it? Or even care about that old blind woman? This all sounds like a lie, an Angelus lie. Meant to topple my family from power."

"Let me ask you this," she said, crossing her arms. "How did you end up in my home with a travel pack on your back? Who told you to do that?"

"My father told me to head to your eyrie. That I could possibly take the mech. Said he had arranged that the door would just open." He looked over her shoulder, disgust twisting his mouth. "I didn't know you'd have *persai* filth with you as protection."

Reminded of words once spoken by her grandmother, Antiquity kept her anger in check. It would avail her nothing if she got in a fight.

"You are right about one thing. My grandmother did have a plan," she said instead. "But I am betting your father helped with that plan."

"That is ridiculous. Dreadth and Angelus have hated one another for decades."

"Maybe. But what if that hatred was to be directed at an enemy of both?"

"Laurellyn Angelus made that mistake," Manson said, eyes dark. "United the families against a common foe and couldn't protect the city. Destroyed Solomon Fyre. Never again, as my father says."

"The Dreadths planted a molecu-virus that shut down this mech!"

Antiquity said angrily, pointing up at Saph Fyre. "Your family betrayed the coalition."

"Not *my* ancestors," Manson argued.

"And perhaps you believe that," Antiquity said. It was like speaking to a child. "But I have proof!"

They stared at one another. Unrelenting.

After a long minute, Manson shook his head. "Why should I trust you?" he asked with a sneer. "And your *persai* friends?"

"Because we are all you have," Antiquity said. "The Imperium commands loyalty through many parts of Erth. They hunt Saph Fyre. They hunt us. By now, they will be wanting anyone with the Dreadth name or genetic signature. That means you." She decided to take another angle. "And, by the way, you are now an accomplice to family Angelus. I doubt they will take too kindly to that."

Manson looked away. He either didn't believe her, or he did and was having a hard time coming to terms with it. Either way, it didn't matter to Antiquity. She couldn't let him leave. If he left, he could be caught and forced to give up where Saph Fyre and her ragtag crew were hiding.

"Can you prove any of this?" Manson asked finally, squinting at her.

"We are about to find out. Come with me," Antiquity said, turning. Not waiting to see if Manson joined her, she strode back to Saph Fyre.

The canyon had lightened and Antiquity became acutely aware of the new day with all of its sounds and smells. The mech had brought them far, through the deadly desert of her entire childhood into a new part of Erth she had only seen in vid-views. The odor of water tinged the air, not far away. The dryness of the nearby desert mingled with the sound of a slow wind as it caught the giant redwoods that lined the lip of their ravine. Birds had been singing but she just now noticed them, flitting through those massive trees above and occasionally below.

She climbed into the body of Saph Fyre through a small hatch in its torso. She found Kaihli and the artificial construct hologram of Brox working on the massive joint of the mech's shoulder, one of the areas the Celestial warship had partially damaged. Elsana was right about her sister; Kaihli possessed a keen mechanical intellect that surpassed them all. The twin had become covered in lubricant, her dark skin glistening with sweat, as she and Brox—his old bearded face critical of her every move—worked side by side, the ghost of the mechanic instructing Kaihli in what needed to be done. Even in such a short time, the two were working as if they had done so their entire lives.

Elsana sat nearby, her *seccade* rolled up and placed back in a bag at her feet. Chekker spun above them all, watching. Antiquity rapped the titanium hull with her knuckles, drawing the attention of the hologram, the bot, and the twins.

"We still do not know where we go or what we do," Antiquity began, dreading what her friends might say. She turned to Kaihli and Elsana. "Manson and I are caught up in this. There is no going back for us. That isn't true of you. You have a choice."

"A choice?" Kaihli sniffed. She wiped sweat away from her brow. "There are vid-cams all over the city. The Imperium knows who your friends are."

"And that Celestial and his guards saw us," Elsana added.

Antiquity breathed in silent relief. The twins were very different. But sometimes they acted as one.

"Then we are decided," Antiquity said. Some of her fire had returned, stealing away her weariness, for a time at least. "We are together in purpose."

"And what is that purpose, Antiquity?" Manson growled, having followed.

She gave the Dreadth a brief nod. She would do what her grandmother would want, no matter where it took her. She would be strong. For her grandmother and the memory of strength that she had left behind. For the rest of the Angelus family. She owed the old woman that.

And let the stars fall from their heavens and break upon the rock of my world.

"Chekker, it is time we talked," Antiquity said.

The bot floated through the air toward her. "Time transcends our hopes and dreams, Antiquity. Vestige knew this to be true. She knew this moment would come."

Antiquity swallowed the pain that rose in her chest. To think her grandmother had foresight to know of this moment left her humbled in a way she had never experienced.

"It is best we speak privately, Grey-child," the bot continued.

"I am going to tell my friends anyway, Chekker. Might as well do so now."

"Very well," Chekker said. "That is your choice. Be mindful though. The knowledge you will come to possess is of the most dangerous kind, the sort that leads the powerful to end those who come by it." When everyone in the mech's compartment looked at one another, Antiquity sensed a pact forming. The bot seemed to understand it as well. "Place your titanium ring within me. This is the command I have been given by Vestige Grey, matriarch of family Angelus."

Antiquity looked down at her hand. Earlier she had decided she would never take it off. Now she was being asked to do just that. The sapphires within the ring shone with a lustrous blue light not unlike the illumination of her grandmother's orbs, as if they understood they were being called on for some higher purpose of guidance. Her grandmother had put the ring on her hand, and even now, she could feel those bony fingers sliding the cold metal onto her finger.

She only hesitated for a moment. She understood there would be no going back. Doing as instructed, Antiquity spun the warm ring free of her hand—even as a pocket within Chekker's chrome exterior opened.

Antiquity placed the ring there. The bot accepted it. The hole closed.

Almost immediately, a new hologram began to form in the mech's hold, light molding into human features. An image formed of a woman she knew, the resolution becoming clearer and clearer, the face similar to her own in many ways. Hair pulled back. Eyes round and bright. Cheekbones proud and a strong chin beneath.

The woman who stared at her was not her grandmother, as Antiquity had assumed it would be.

"I can't believe it," Antiquity whispered.

With a brief nod and a wry smile, Laurellyn Angelus greeted her great-granddaughter.

"I am here, Antiquity Angelus, my great-granddaughter. My great hope."

Antiquity could barely breathe, unable to find the words. She stared at a woman who had been dead for decades, a leader who had failed at protecting everything she held dear and been blamed for it by history, a person she thought she had lost to the erasure of time and law. She wondered what else lay hidden from her. Artificial constructs were not available to everyone, only to those with great family worth and wealth. Brox, for instance, possessed knowledge of mechs that few could hope to know or emulate. He had been given the honor of having his memories downloaded at some point before his death, ensuring his knowledge would not be lost. Laurellyn Angelus died so young that it had never occurred to Antiquity that her great-grandmother could possibly be accessible to her in some form.

Yet here she was, staring at a woman out of legend and myth, her memories bound to the ring that Antiquity now possessed.

"I am here, Great-Grandmother. I have questions for you."

"I have answers," the hologram said.

Antiquity took a deep breath. If getting answers from Manson had been difficult, this would be triply so. Constructs were often limited in what they could answer, particularly from those who had been dead a long time. "First, how do you know my name? You lived long before I was born."

"I have access to information through CHKR-11 as well as the Angelus eyrie data banks," Laurellyn said. "I know what has transpired and the hardship you are about to undertake as my great-granddaughter."

Antiquity nodded and, taking a deep breath, tried to organize her thoughts. "Why did my grandmother have to die?" Antiquity asked, not the most important question to ask the long-dead but one that came unbidden from her very depths.

"She died with purpose. With the honor of House Angelus," Laurellyn said, her eyes sad and matching Antiquity's own. "She sacrificed much—for you and for her family—to keep safe the treasures of Erth. My daughter is no more, but her purpose remains in you. In that death you will find meaning."

The gravity of her words left Antiquity feeling the weight of discovering the truth in all of this. It also echoed what she and Elsana had surmised, that Vestige had a plan.

"And what is that purpose?"

The artificial construct shimmered in her hologram. "To keep safe secrets that have remained hidden from the Imperium since before even the Splinter War. Secrets that led to the Splinter War. Secrets that started the Splinter War. And secrets that were not discovered by the Imperium after the Splinter War. I am dead. The secrets of an entire planet are not. It is now time to wield those secrets to their end."

"Grandmother spoke of secrets. She even wanted me to marry a Dreadth to keep those secrets safe between two families," Antiquity said, very aware of Manson standing near her. "I guess she did that in case all else failed. But now I'm not so sure. Now I'm thinking she put plans in motion that have led me here."

"You are perceptive, my great-granddaughter," Laurellyn said. "That will serve you well in the coming days."

"So I'm not to marry Manson Dreadth?"

"That is entirely up to you."

Antiquity shuddered at the idea but was glad she now had a choice. She also realized she wasn't asking the right question.

"Why was it important for Manson and me to believe we were to be married?"

"The Council of Elders has members who would not agree with the actions my daughter and Jackson Dreadth have decided to put into motion. These are men who are self-interested. Who would report betrayal to the Imperium for personal profit. The marriage allowed for the heads of families Angelus and Dreadth to meet without arousing suspicion. More, it kept blameless those Elders who would continue to lead Solomon Fyre in case those plans do not succeed."

"And it gave Manson access to my home, to be saved," Antiquity finished. She saw a glimmer of truth then. "We are rebelling from the Imperium. Why now?"

"Erth has long been rich with ores," Laurellyn Angelus said. "The Imperium knew this before returning. A new source for them to plunder. When I was young, I came into power of Solomon Fyre and the entirety of Erth. It was not an easy time. I worked hard to unite the planet's mech forces. Because of that, Solomon Fyre became the first target of the Imperium, to remove Erth's leaders. Before the war began, the Imperium claimed Erth as its own, and in that claim I saw our destruction. I knew even as the Council of Elders did that the Imperium would strip us of our natural resources beneath a bootheel of subjugation—particularly the ores that go into the Celestials' fleets, machinery, and mechs. We fought back before it could happen. It led to the Splinter War.

"I helped hide those ores. The Imperium has been hunting for the largest stockpile of titanium ever mined. It is the reason the Imperium continues to hold dominion over Erth. They may harvest redwoods and farm exotic fish and animals for consumption, but they desire the titanium."

"Hide?" Antiquity asked. "How does one hide such a large part of Erth?"

"That is for you to discover," the hologram said. "There are other parties who must be vetted, parties who once knew about the existence of our plan. A great amount of time has passed, however, and loyalties have a tendency to change over time."

"That's what you want me to do?" Antiquity asked, thinking. "Meet with . . . someone? They have to be long dead by now."

Laurellyn Angelus gave the same wry smile as earlier. "Some are. The knowledge has passed from the dying to the living. Some still live, if they have lived wisely."

"Why was my father a part of this?" Manson added from the side, large arms crossed over his chest. "He never told me anything."

The hologram shimmered toward him. "Manson Dreadth, your father is a noble man from a dishonored house. The Dreadth of my time aspired to greater heights and he gained them by sabotaging my

73

mech and, with it, our counterattack and the fate of our world. I made sure if an event like it ever happened, the truth of hidden ores would not be easily discovered. The secrets have remained so buried ever since. Information acquired by Antiquity from Saph Fyre made its way to Jackson Dreadth via my daughter, an interesting choice given our family histories. I always described Vestige as being sage, even when she was little." She paused for only a moment. "Jackson Dreadth understood it was time to set matters right—not just with our families but with the Imperium."

"And he likely didn't tell you about it because he knew you'd fight him about this, especially since the Angelus family was involved," Kaihli spoke up, answering for the construct.

"You do choose to fight a lot, Manson," Elsana added.

Before he could argue, Antiquity intervened. "What happens next?" she asked.

"The *arabi* have an ancient saying: 'Know the path before the path knows you.' You must embrace the secrets I saved. Only in them will you survive. The past serves the future. It was not meant to be so but it has become so. It is you who exists in that present rather than another, and in the present you shall remain, to be that which is needed as long as you accept it," the construct said. "CHKR-11 has guided you to the edge of our home's deserts. That is the briefest of beginnings. You must make your way over the Dragonell Mountains and through Woodlock Forest to Luna Gold, to meet with the Celestial merchant Vodard Ryce, a friend to Angelus and one whose family has no love for their kin. The way was once perilous to Luna Gold. I have no doubt that is still so."

"We must be careful," Kaihli said. "While we are relatively safe here in the Dragonell Mountains, home of the *persai*, Luna Gold sits within the western Muthlaj Mountains. That is where the same *arabi* you just spoke of live. If the scavengers don't get us first, the *arabi* will."

"You appear to be of the same faith, Kaihli El-Amin. Splintered apart but similar enough to understand. You are Grey no longer. You are needed, and in that need you are absolved of the shame on your family."

"My sister only understands machinery," Elsana deflected.

The Dragonell Mountains. Woodlock Forest. Luna Gold. Ancient Celestial friends. The *arabi*. Antiquity suddenly felt overwhelmed, anxiety tightening her chest. "I still don't know what to do. The Imperium is after ore, great," she said, exasperated. "What other secrets are there?"

"I never thought you this stupid, Antiquity," Manson said, annoyed. "The titanium could rebuild the entire mech fleet of Erth. We could fight back again!"

Antiquity was as surprised by the idea as the twins were.

"To free Erth," Manson said quietly.

"Saph Fyre was once my mech," Laurellyn Angelus said, eyes shining in memory. "She has secrets of her own. She is yours now, a part of your bloodline, an inheritance of grave import. Use her to find Vodard Ryce, find the stockpile. On this, all depends. For your family. And the world."

"I will, Great-Grandmother."

"Wear my ring, my dearest descendant. Remember me," the hologram said, beginning to dim as the ring ejected from Chekker. "Courage comes from within, and you will have to be courageous beyond measure."

Before she could ask more questions, the light that had been Laurellyn Angelus vanished. Antiquity suspected her great-grandmother had given what she could. She was now on her own with even more questions.

The first question being: What if Vodard Ryce and his family were no more?

That wasn't the only thing Antiquity had wanted to talk to her ancestor about. Luna Gold had been a thriving city during Laurellyn

Angelus's time. But even Antiquity—who did not know much about the rest of Erth—knew the history of the city they were supposed to travel to.

For decades, Luna Gold had lain in deserted ruin.

) ◗ ● ◖ (

Stunned silence replaced the void left by Laurellyn Angelus's departure.

"Well, that complicates our lives," Kaihli said, wiping her sweaty brow.

"I can't believe we just saw her," Elsana said. The twin looked as if she had just seen a miracle. "Only her ghost, but she felt real, as real as any of us."

"Did you know everything she talked about, Chekker? Brox?" Antiquity asked.

"I knew enough to keep you safe, Grey-child," Chekker said. "To get you free of the eyrie after discovering the mech."

"She was powerful in life," Brox said with a deep baritone voice. Made entirely of light, the dwarf tugged at his thick beard, a mannerism that translated to his artificial construct. "I have no memories of her being deceitful or dishonorable. She was a woman of many secrets—as leaders must be in the worst of times."

"We have a lot to talk about now because we know some of those secrets," Antiquity said, looking from face to face. "I took you all with me from Solomon Fyre because I wanted to keep you safe from the Imperium. But what my great-grandmother asks is something different. Entirely different. Last night, we were running. To hide. If we do what my great-grandmother requests, we won't only be running but—from the sounds of it—trying to free Erth. By now, the Imperium knows I have Saph Fyre and my connection to it." She paused, looking to the twins. "Manson probably can't go home. And I certainly cannot.

I shudder to think what has happened to the other Grey members in the eyrie. But you two could go back, find your parents, and hide elsewhere. You two have a choice. I'm not so certain you should come with me in this."

"We aren't leaving you, Antiquity," Elsana said, giving her friend a look that said no argument would be worthwhile. "Besides, Kai has always wanted to see the world."

Kaihli hugged her sister, while nodding to Antiquity. "And if you ask us again, I'll beat you with this electro-wrench."

Antiquity grinned to hide the burn of tears that threatened anew. She loved her friends.

"And you, Manson?" she asked, turning to the young man. She didn't know why her grandmother had made sure he was a part of this, but she also knew her well enough to not second-guess it. Manson had been a bully with little guidance. But now Antiquity realized he could possibly be a strong ally if given direction.

"The only thing I know for sure is I've been thrown into a situation I don't really understand," he said. He looked a little defeated, something that pleased Antiquity more than it should have. "I know I'm stuck with all of you."

"We aren't too thrilled either, Dreadth," Kaihli said under her breath.

"I don't think we can be enemies and get through this," Antiquity said to all of them. She glanced at Manson. "Friends now?"

He gazed hard into her eyes. "I saw you as the threat before. As the family that hated mine so badly you'd do anything to regain power." He paused, clearly choosing his words carefully. "Now the threat—the true threat—is out there, it seems."

"Coming for us," she said.

He nodded.

"What comes next then?" Elsana asked.

"Luna Gold is far away. If we go by land to keep hidden from the Imperium, it will take days to drive Saph Fyre through these mountains and the dense redwoods of Woodlock Forest," Manson said, using his data-watch to pull up a hologram map of the area and then looking at her pointedly. Antiquity was happy the Dreadth did not mention flying as a possible course to take, given her inability to do so. "And unless I'm mistaken, we have virtually no supplies. Barely any food. Little water. No weapons besides the metal around us. And even knowing how to use this mech as a weapon is suspect. Then there is the problem of Luna Gold itself. Everything I've read and heard say it is a ghost city, broken and empty. I am betting whatever Antiquity's great-grandmother wants to happen ended when that city and everyone in it died or moved on. Not to mention this Vodard Ryce is probably already dead."

"We don't know that for sure. Celestials are long-lived," Elsana said. "He very well could still be alive."

"Not in the ruins," Manson argued. "How would he survive? Besides, if he isn't dead from old age, the *arabi* would surely have killed him as a heretic by now."

"We survive in a desert, with *arabi* living in Solomon Fyre," Kaihli countered. "And even if he did leave, perhaps we could find him. In one of the surrounding cities or villages."

"Right," Manson said sarcastically. "And *I'm* a *persai.*"

"Chekker, do you know anything else that could help?" Antiquity asked, mostly to defuse the mounting fight.

"I do not, Grey-child."

She sighed. "Well, Manson is right. We do need supplies. I could eat an entire bloxen right now," she said. The others nodded their agreement. "Saph Fyre is large. Hard to keep hidden. But thankfully, we are on the edge of the Dragonell Mountains and they are covered by the Woodlock Forest. The redwoods are tall—taller than the mech—so as long as we stay within the forest, we should remain undetected by the Imperium as we travel."

Manson looked to his map again. "Holstead is the closest village of any size. We should go there. It will have the things we need."

"Being discovered would be the end of us," Antiquity said.

The Dreadth nodded. "More than cautious. Once we get close enough to Holstead, we will have to leave the mech. And be fast. Can't leave Saph Fyre too long in fear of it being found by others. But we can sell one of the mech's four airbikes in that town to get the money we need. Just have to be careful."

The twins nodded. Antiquity couldn't disagree. It pleased her that Manson was being helpful. Wanting to be a part of the solution. In the past, he had been a detriment in every way to her life. She wondered if, when he had no pride at stake, he was not the bully she had grown up with every year of her life.

Time would tell.

"What do you think, Chekker?" she asked, already thinking about what all of this would mean. "You are the one always telling me to stay out of trouble."

"I have also always said that danger finds you, no matter the situation," the bot said. "It is sound reasoning, acquiring food and water by selling an airbike. But the wilds are dangerous and it comes in many forms. The mech is your best defense but if you leave it, there are many who will test your resolve. The *arabi* are formidable in numbers, even for Saph Fyre, but the *arabi* city of Bayt al-Hikma is a long distance away and we shouldn't run into them. Scavengers do venture into the Dragonell Mountains from the desert. And the peoples of Holstead will not likely take kindly to strangers. It is my place to keep you safe but my job has become much more difficult since Matriarch Vestige appointed me with your well-being in this quest. I will not always be by your side. The teachings of your family will have to take my place at times."

"Then we will go to Holstead first. Get the things we need," Antiquity said. "And from there, try to discover the secrets my great-grandmother hid from the Imperium."

"And if we do, Antiquity?" Elsana asked.

"I don't know," she admitted. "But if the ores for titanium still exist and they are in a quantity that makes a difference to Erth, we will do something about the Imperium."

"Only if you are doing this for more than revenge," Manson said pointedly. "Are you? Doing this for more than avenging your grandmother?"

She paused, at a lack for words. She hadn't considered how her own pain could affect what was to come. She *did* want revenge, she realized, shocked by the sudden desire for it. But what if Royal Declarion Wit had not been aboard the warship? The anger that had fueled her ability to drive Saph Fyre across the entire desert without sleep rose up within once more. She knew what the Dreadth was getting at, but it was not his place to offer such a worry.

"If the Imperium killed your father, you will feel as I do," she said quietly.

Manson Dreadth did the unexpected. He approached her, took her hands in his own, folded their fingers together in the Council of Elders manner of respect between two people. She was so surprised that she didn't pull away.

"Let's hope my father is still alive. Because we will need allies in Solomon Fyre when all of this is done," he said. "And I am sorry for the loss of your grandmother."

With that, he turned, climbed a ladder, and vanished into the mech. The twins just stood there, mouths agape. Then a sly smile crossed Kaihli's lips.

"He doesn't hate you as much as you think."

Antiquity dropped her hands, at a loss for words.

"Your grandmother had an ability to read people," Chekker quipped. "*All* sorts of people, Antiquity."

Antiquity repressed the impulse to smash the bot out of the air.

) ◗ ● ◖ (

Antiquity climbed into Saph Fyre's head, leaving grogginess behind.

The twins had forced her to take a nap, one that lasted longer than she wished but which she had definitely needed. Antiquity looked out the faceplate, taking a deep breath in the stillness. The afternoon waned and soon the colors of the desert would emerge. Sleep had given her a reprieve from thinking about her grandmother, and eating what few supplies they carried prolonged the peace a bit longer. But now that she was alone and had time to sit and reflect on the new knowledge she possessed—and when Manson had mentioned revenge—a fire blossomed inside again. She would see her grandmother's killers dead. She would see her great-grandmother's charge completed. Or she would put up the most hellish fight anyone on Erth had seen. And she could do that with Saph Fyre.

It helped that Elsana, Kaihli, and even Manson agreed to go with her, even though she would have done it on her own.

It would take knowing Saph Fyre completely to have the best chance.

Manson had brought up a good point. She needed more answers.

"Brox?" Antiquity said into the silence.

The hologram of the long-dead mechanic appeared before her. "Yes, Antiquity Angelus? How may I assist?"

"I tried to fly Saph Fyre when the Imperium warship attacked our eyrie," she said, letting the controls snake their way over her, onto her. "But I couldn't do it even though I willed it. Chekker said that all flight capabilities were functional. What happened?"

Brox nodded. "I have seen it before. Not an easy thing to fix."

"What do you mean?" Antiquity asked. "You can fix anything on this mech."

"It isn't an easy thing to fix because the problem is not with the mech," Brox said, folding his hands before him. "The problem is within you."

"How so?"

"In the time of Laurellyn Angelus and my own life, to be a mech pilot was a mark of experience and ability. Mechs were a precious commodity—so much technology, energy, and time going into them—and only the most skilled were given that honor. Rigorous testing was given to all thirteen-year-olds. Only a few went on to train. Fewer still received a mech." He paused, almost as if his artificial brain was deciding what to say next or how to say it. "You have not had that training—training that was intended to remove those who did not possess all attributes required to become part of the most powerful legion on Erth. Emotional attributes as well as the physical—to control a mech in its entirety. Including its flight capabilities."

Antiquity frowned. "So. What you are saying is this," she said. "I might not be able to fly Saph Fyre."

"It is possible you may not, Antiquity Angelus."

Antiquity sat there, stunned. The thrill of destroying most of the scavengers who had tried to steal Saph Fyre infused her memory. The robot. Hers to command. And now? She might not be able to fly. The thing she had looked forward to most.

The function that would best keep her friends safe.

"Is there a way to train my mind to accept the flight protocols?" she asked.

"There is one test that I possess," Brox said. "But it would require a full day, and you would not be awake but in a dream state, leaving the mech susceptible to attack. It also may not work, this setting not conducive to testing."

Giving up an entire day. When those around her needed her most. Cursing the reality of what she had just learned, Antiquity nodded, thinking.

"Thank you, Brox."

The hologram vanished.

She'd have to come to terms with that later. Antiquity kept focused on the task at hand. She might not be able to control Saph Fyre in all ways, but she knew what she could control now. She let the last few controls and headgear cover her body. Saph Fyre grew in her mind even as she entered the mech. The melding got easier each time. It was time to travel over the Dragonell Mountains, through the vastness of Woodlock Forest, and eventually make their way to the ruins of Luna Gold. Feeling power thrum through her and knowing the others were secured below, she climbed out of the ravine, her hands made colossal, her legs strong, and her will powering the awesome might of the mech.

Once at the top, she gazed about. She had been so tired when she piloted into the ravine that she missed the world about them. The desert gave way to the beginnings of a lush forest. Redwood trees, sporadic at first but thickening into the hilly distance, grew toward the sky. With every massive step she took, the ground changed—first dry grasses clung to shattered rock and sandy soil, changing as the hours passed into verdant green fields of ferns, small flowers, bubbling creeks, and dark soil. She hadn't thought that leaving her desert home would affect her, but she found the overwhelming color a shock to her senses. And her excitement rose at another new sight in the distance—the Dragonell Mountains, their heights craggy and snow-covered. Each step by Saph Fyre brought them closer to Holstead, a necessary first step to Luna Gold.

She returned to the moment and looked for Chekker. She saw him after a few minutes, the bot scouting ahead for anyone who might encounter the mech. It was good having him there. Saph Fyre's sensors were a part of Antiquity's senses now, but using the mech was a new experience and having her longtime friend out in the wilds gave her comfort.

They would have to stay one step ahead of everyone else if her great-grandmother's vision had any hope of coming to pass. There were a great many to stay ahead of besides scavengers and the Imperium. There were dangers everywhere on Erth and especially beyond the Dragonell Mountains, according to the bot. The *arabi* were zealots, known for adhering to even the most conservative tenets of their faith. There were also dragons in the mountains, some living among the *persai* but most wild. And probably others Antiquity didn't even know about, the unknown possibly even more dangerous.

Thankfully, as midnight approached, they had crossed none of them. The blip of Holstead pulsed on the map within her mind, driving her. The village was still two hours away, shorter by airbike since the smaller machine would navigate the giant redwoods more easily.

Antiquity decided it was time to stop, tired from the journey. She found the largest redwood she could, its trunk as thick as one of Saph Fyre's legs, and sat the great mech against it.

When she depowered Saph Fyre and its wires and headgear disappeared, she went down the ladder to see the others.

"We are far enough away from Holstead to not come under

suspicion. I hope, anyway," Antiquity said, looking from face to face. "But close enough to ride into the village and do our business."

"Then this is a great place to stop," Elsana said.

"Brox, the airbikes are operational, right?" she asked.

"They are, Antiquity Angelus."

"They were one of the first things we fixed," Kaihli said, clearly proud of the achievement as she unbuckled from her crew harness. "Early instruction from Brox before working on . . . more difficult things."

"Good, because we are going to need them," Antiquity said. "We will sleep here tonight. First thing in the morning, all of us will go into the village. Strength in numbers. It shouldn't take too long. We sell an airbike, get what we need, and get out. We are not doing anything else. I have no doubt the Imperium has sent our pictures, names, and possibly our genetic codes out to every city, town, and village of Erth. We must be careful. We can't risk drawing attention."

"What if someone comes poking around while we're here?" Manson asked. "When we are asleep. Or gone to Holstead."

"Chekker will keep watch for intruders, circling the area in rings of surveillance, while we sleep and when we are away from the mech," Antiquity said. She sighed. "What else can we do? Let's sleep now. I want to finish our business in the village and get Saph Fyre as far away from Holstead—and anyone who might discover the mech—as soon as possible."

The others nodded, even Manson, who did not argue. She could tell they hadn't slept well either since fleeing Solomon Fyre, unrolling their sleeping mats without a word. She gave no worry to the others. They could create their own beds. When her head hit the pillow, days of exhaustion caught up with Antiquity. Sleep took her and she didn't put up a fight.

It felt like only minutes when a hand shook her out of the void.

"Antiquity, wake up," Elsana said, worry in her voice.

Antiquity glanced at her data-watch, its glow adding to the dim light within the mech. Hours had passed. According to the time, the sun would be lightening the east already, the new day and the trip into Holstead upon them.

"What's wrong?" she asked as Kaihli awoke nearby.

"We have a problem." The twin pointed over to a vacant mat.

Antiquity didn't have to ask. She knew what had happened and Elsana would have already checked the mech for the answer. A dozen different curses came to mind, none strong enough for the rage that now overtook her.

Manson Dreadth was gone.

He had deserted them in the night.

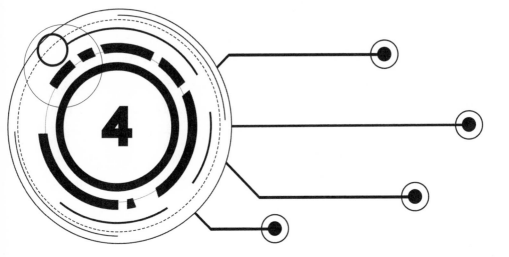

4

"He lied," Antiquity said, so angry she wanted to punch a redwood.

"What did you expect?" Kaihli said, shaking her head. "He's a Dreadth."

Kaihli's comment just made Antiquity fume more. After they discovered the Dreadth had vanished, Antiquity and the others investigated the mech. Manson had taken one of the airbikes, some of their limited food and water, and somehow been able to avoid detection by Chekker, who had spent the night on perimeter watch. They had no way of knowing when he left. She doubted he would have wanted to arrive in Holstead while the village still slept, which gave her hope he had left right before they had woken. It wasn't much to go on. But she had survived on less in the past.

Now Antiquity and Kaihli rode across the wooded landscape, each with their own airbike in case they had to split up. Antiquity looked at her data-watch, its hologram arrow pointing them toward Holstead.

They had been riding for an hour, having left Saph Fyre beneath a thick copse of redwoods, the trunks so large and the foliage so thick that someone could be standing nearby and still not see the mech. Elsana stayed behind—her sister the stronger fighter—while Chekker and Brox guarded the mech. Neither the bot nor the hologram could operate it, but Antiquity knew Chekker could enact some of its defensive capabilities if he had to.

"He lied. Said the things we wanted to hear. So he could take an airbike and leave. Unchallenged," Antiquity spat, the very idea like acid in her heart. "Why would my grandmother believe in Dreadth honor?"

"Is he heading back to another city in this part of the world?"

"I don't know."

"Do you think he could be going to contact the Imperium? Get his family back in good standing with those who want our deaths?" the twin asked.

The questions only fueled Antiquity's fire. "He can't be that stupid."

"He wouldn't have ridden the airbike all the way back to Solom—"

"I. Don't. Know," Antiquity cut her off. "Doubt it though. Too far."

Kaihli didn't ask another question. She had gotten the cue. Instead she followed closely after Antiquity as their airbikes wove through the forest toward Holstead. Antiquity was happy Kaihli had come along though. Nothing about her appearance suggested a weapon but Antiquity knew she had several hidden large tools that the twin knew how to wield, at least in the mechanic sense.

"Well, is he trying to turn us in at Holstead?" Kaihli asked after they crested a large wooded hill and slowed down, the trees dwarfing them.

Antiquity stopped, looking for any clues. They had already found a few signs of someone's passing—redwood needles on the ground disturbed, broken branches or fern fronds, footprints when he had to relieve himself.

"I certainly hope not," she said. "But if yes, we need to be vigilant."

Kaihli growled low. "I hope we catch him, show him what he deserves."

"I hope we catch him before he gets to Holstead," Antiquity said, knowing that they wouldn't but hopeful all the same. "If we don't, we could be walking into a bigger mess than if we had let him go."

"No time to waste then."

Antiquity agreed. She throttled her airbike, and Kaihli raced after her. With the rising sun warming the air and the smells of a vibrant and lush forest perking up her senses, Antiquity moved the airbike over steep, rocky inclines, shallow creeks, and downed redwoods, pursuing the boy who had lied to her. Anger bolstered her resolve but that wasn't the only thing that did so.

Manson Dreadth, for all his past sins, was innocent in the discovery of the mech and the Imperium's wrath. He had no idea what was right and what was wrong. If she could, Antiquity would fight to save him from himself.

She didn't want more blood on her hands.

They came to a large road after what seemed an eternity, one paved in stone so thick even the roots of the massive redwoods on either side could not buckle it.

"We will ride into Holstead, like any other travelers," Antiquity said.

Pulling up next to her, Kaihli nodded. "What are we looking for?"

"Manson, of course," she said. "Or a business that looks like a merchant where he'd sell the airbike."

"Or the local Imperium enforcement. Where he'd sell us out."

Antiquity nodded, hating the idea of being without proper weapons or Saph Fyre. But they wore large hooded coats to help conceal their identities.

It was the best they could do.

They continued along the twisting road, one that climbed into higher hills, the two friends quiet, Antiquity trying to quell the uncertainty of what was to come. The first glimpse of people other than the few stragglers they met on the road took Antiquity by surprise—they were in the tree canopy hundreds of feet above on ropes and pulleys, collecting cones, cones the Imperium craved for their resin. Eyes followed them as they passed. It reminded Antiquity that they were strangers in a new land. Buildings appeared next, small at first, mostly farms that helped support the community. She knew somewhere in the looming mountains whole swaths of acreage were being logged as well; the Imperium used the beautiful wood to accent their homes and public buildings.

Finally, after the forest thinned considerably, they entered a valley with steep mountains to either side and a silver stream running through its heart. Following it, they reached a larger river, which they crossed on a wide stone bridge. At last the two friends spied the outer fringes of Holstead proper.

Chekker had called it a village. That wasn't entirely accurate. It was no Solomon Fyre, the city of her birth massive by comparison, but Holstead seemed newer if smaller, made of better materials than she thought possible this deep into the wilderness. More people joined them on the road as they entered town. The travelers gave them curious looks—most likely due to their city clothing—but they never went beyond general interest.

After riding up and down different thoroughfares in their search, they finally came to the local mercantile of Holstead. And it was massive. It was clear to Antiquity that it was the merchant for the entire area, one who had a hand in most if not all of the economic transactions that took place. Food. Water. Goods both large and small, imported and exported. There were several merchant princes in Solomon Fyre, all vying for the last coin, willing to swindle to win the best deal. Money tended to corrupt in that way, at least in Antiquity's experience. She'd have to be careful here. From the ornate building to the guards posted around it, the owner of this establishment had the power of the purse at his disposal. But that's not what initially drew her eye.

The airbike Manson had stolen sat parked outside, along with several other conveyances and even three horses.

That wasn't all. Men and a few women watched them from the street. They appeared to lead hard lives, clothes dirty and eyes hard. A man with scars crisscrossing his face gave her a cursory look before taking steps two at a time into the mercantile. Even one *arabi* scrutinized them from the shadows across the street, face covered as was their way and body robed in black.

"Being clean must draw attention around here." Kaihli snorted.

"Looks that way."

"If Manson's turning us in, he's doing a poor job of it," the twin said. "These people might finish the job."

Antiquity tried not to stare too long at any of the onlookers. They both parked their airbikes next to their twin, nodding to one of the guards who had also taken an interest in them as they walked up the stairs to the main entrance. "Let's see if we can find him."

Once through the large double-gated door, the inside seemed larger than the outside could hold, the ceiling high and running into the distance. All manner of merchandise littered the selling floor, and even Antiquity—who enjoyed going to such merchants in Solomon Fyre—was impressed. Advanced technological creations sat alongside the most rudimentary needs of country living. Data-pads next to farrier tools. Digital appliances next to hand pumps for drawing water from the ground. Even a large vert-flyer upon a podium, a vehicle only really needed in large city living. It was an amalgamation of cultures and time periods, meant to appease even the pickiest customer.

Dozens of people were taking advantage. Most appeared to be citizens of Holstead, their clothing a mix of the greys, greens, and browns of a people who lived in the forest. A few wore the colorful silks of the *persai*. And even the lone *arabi*, who had followed them into the store, gazed at wares, the tall figure's black robes and headdress concealing everything but dark eyes that looked once more in Antiquity's direction.

She felt exposed but she soon spied Manson, his pack fuller than she remembered, as he walked in through a doorway at the side of the large room, followed by the man with the facial scars they had seen outside and a new roguish man with good looks and grey at his temples.

When Manson saw them, he did not look happy.

"What are you doing here?" he sputtered, walking up to Antiquity.

"I could ask you the same thing," she hissed angrily. It was all she could do to not throttle him senseless.

"I am selling the airbike," he mouthed, keeping his voice as low as possible. He held in his hands a pouch of what Antiquity assumed to be gold dirham, the currency of this part of the world. "Sold the airbike, actually. Time to get the things we need."

"Why did you leave without telling us?" she growled low.

"It is best we do not talk here," Manson said, looking over his shoulder. The two other men spoke quietly with one another, eyes on Antiquity. "I got a bad feeling about the owner of this place."

"Oh, it is a great day! A great day, I say," the rogue said to no one in particular, walking up to Antiquity and Kaihli while clasping his hands before him. "Today has brought us not one rare ride but three. *Three*, I say. Mech airbikes. Beauties too. New looking. From my new friends." Other customers looked up, curious at what was happening. Antiquity frowned at Kaihli. This was already not going the way she had hoped.

"My airbike and my friend's ride are not for sale," she said flatly, confronting him and giving the owner a dark look. Manson gave her a quick warning head shake. She ignored him. "The other one is already yours, I believe. That's it and that's all."

"My name is Beven el Ordett. I own this store. And whether you like it or not, everything is for sale in Holstead, young lady. Everything." He walked closer, using his size and proximity to intimidate as he looked her over, avarice glinting in his eyes. Another bully. "I am either the buyer or the seller and I decide which at any given moment. Do not think about taking my new ride." The merchant leered at her before striding to the entrance. "Let us look at it instead and maybe you will change your mind about the other two."

Antiquity hit Manson hard in the lower back and, along with Kaihli, hurried after the rogue.

Sunshine blinded her as she exited, her eyes having adjusted to the dark interior of the store. It took her a moment to see clearly again.

That's when Antiquity noticed the eyes watching from the alley shadows.

"Three airbikes," Beven el Ordett said, gesturing at the trio. "Prizes, to be sure."

"They have been in my family for generations, scavenged from the sands outside Tungstone," Antiquity lied. "We've kept them up."

"Tsk, tsk, I am not so sure," he said, shaking his head. "I have never seen airbikes look quite so new as these." He paused. "No, I think they were found with a much *larger* prize."

Antiquity knew exactly what the owner meant. They were in real danger now. "I don't know what you mean."

"Do not lie to me, young lady. I—" Beven el Ordett stopped, looking beyond her. Anger replaced his playful banter. "You've been followed here," the merchant growled low, even as Antiquity caught the first coordinated movements of men and women approaching from the alley—all wearing gear and ragged clothing very different from those of Holstead. "Very foolish or smart to deceive me this way. It makes no difference."

"I don't know *you*. I don't know *them*," she shot back. "We just want to leave."

The merchant frowned, his men raising their weapons as they all backed toward the building's entrance. "Everyone leaves this world one day, young lady. It looks like your day is today." With that, the owner fled behind the protection his walls provided and slammed the doors.

"Surrounded." Manson broke the sudden silence, already puffed up as if he could take on all dozen or so that closed in a semicircle about them. "You have really got a knack for danger, Angelus."

"Me?" Antiquity erupted, drawing her knife while both she and Kaihli moved closer to the larger boy. "You are the one that deserted us!"

"Deserted? I did no such thi—"

"Focus, you two!" Kaihli pulled a heavy wrench from the pack on her back. "We'll need two airbikes at least and fast."

Antiquity knew the attackers, had known them the moment she saw them. Scavengers. Maybe even the survivors from the day she exhumed Saph Fyre from the sands outside of Solomon Fyre—the day she killed their friends and family. They glared with bionic eyes at Antiquity and her friends while arms and legs featuring crudely welded bits of cybernetic steel twitched in anticipation. No one from Holstead would come to their aid; they were strangers in this city. And no one stuck their neck out against scavengers for strangers.

"You be the bitch that killed Old Rizzo. And Smelly Nelly. And kin I did not even like but they were kin," a scavenger growled, his teeth mostly gone. A bionic eye implanted in his forehead whirled, his agitation clear.

"Crock Bob was right. It is you," a skinny woman from the side said, tongue licking cracked lips as if about to taste something sweet. "We caught your face on vid. He knew you the moment we saw you, he did."

"How did you find us?" Antiquity asked.

"The desert is our home, city-born," another spat. "You should have flown your precious mech. Left a trail even a toddler could follow through the sands, you did." He paused, eyeing the airbikes. "And now we want your rides. And that mech. You will give it. Or die."

"I don't think so," Manson said, trying to shield the two girls.

The one known as Crock Bob grinned wider.

"Was hopin' you'd say that."

The dozen desert people swarmed them, all brandishing various blunt and sharp weapons. Before she knew it, Antiquity was grappling with unwashed bodies for her life. She lashed out with her knife, her two companions doing the same with their own weapons. A fire rose inside until Antiquity burned with it. She would not die this way. Not against these derelicts. Not in this foreign town. Four of the scavengers went for Manson—his size making him the obvious threat—as several others went after her and Kaihli. Manson beat them off and helped the girls, roaring while his fists broke both bionics and yellowed teeth. The scavengers did not weigh much, but they were wiry strong and even Manson couldn't keep them all at bay. In a few seconds, they had him pushed away and to the stairs, taking punches and bludgeoning until he could only shield himself.

Kaihli was having none of it. She swung her huge wrench with muscle corded from years of machinery work, breaking free of her attackers to help Manson. She smashed a scavenger in the head; he crumpled, falling away down the stairs.

She went after the others, howling, surprising the scavengers with her fury and allowing Antiquity to pull the Dreadth to his feet.

When she turned to find the next attack, Antiquity saw their danger. Too late. A net shot from an air-cannon flew toward them, the three easier to catch in one spot. The thick cords spread out and settled over them, heavy and rough—even as scavengers pulled and others swarmed. Antiquity cut at it with her knife, panic fueling her need. A skinny man with pocked skin drove her to the ground with his weight, his wretched breath hot in her face. She stabbed him, repeatedly, each thrust burned into her memory, until he rolled off, screaming and dripping crimson. The net did not give even though Manson and Kaihli fought to be free as well. More weight pushed them down and her face got jammed into the sharp edges of the stone stairs.

She was dead. The realization fell on her like a hammer to anvil. These were her last moments. She had failed. Her grandmother. Her friends. Their cause.

It was only a matter of time.

Then suddenly, without knowing why or how, that deadly weight disappeared—even as the mewling scavengers fell silent. Through the holes in the net, Antiquity spied one thing that gave her a small inkling of hope.

Fear in the eyes of the scavengers.

Her attackers backed away uncertainly, all of them gawking at one another for direction. Behind her, Manson and Kaihli lifted the net away, sweating freely and breathing hard. Like the scavengers, they were not looking at Antiquity either.

She turned.

A tall black-robed man descended the stairs toward the fight.

The *arabi*.

All eyes now on him, he glided downward like a hawk on the wind's hunt, smooth and pure and without stopping, danger in every graceful movement he made. The day grew even more silent.

"The sun shines and, beneath it, the coldness of a hatred grown in the sands," the figure said, the voice clear and oddly musical despite the black cloth that covered his mouth. "Warmth is the calling of the All-Father, He who tests the will of such men as these."

"Religious zealot," Crock Bob spat venom, his forehead's bionic eye raging red. "Riddle Will Master. This is not your fight. These are ours."

With a clean, sure motion, the *arabi* drew a sword from his robe's folds, its blade black and slightly curved. Antiquity could not look away from it. The weapon shimmered then, as if it swallowed the day's light and winked it back at her.

"She is worth a fortune," another scavenger whined.

"Yes," the *arabi* said. "She is. But not for you."

Crock Bob spit upon the stairs—and charged. He had made his choice in the matter. Surprised, the other scavengers did the same, yowling and brandishing their weapons, ready to fight the one figure who stood in the way of their bounty.

In a fluid motion, the robes of the *arabi* flew upward, cloth and wind creating chaos and movement that seemed to envelop the entire set of stairs. Even Antiquity couldn't register it all. The scavengers reacted as she did, confused by the display—an uncertainty that turned to screams of pain. Before Antiquity could say a word , the *arabi* was by her and cutting through the scavengers like a hot knife through butter, a blur of movement without sound, the black of his blade a scythe to all before it. Bodies fell, the dead making no sound, only mute surprise on their faces as the sword cleaved into the afternoon.

Those scavengers who were not stunned by the display pulled into a group, trying to find some protection from their killer. One even blasted her flash-fire, burning one of the scavengers instead before try-ing to hit the *arabi*. It did not matter. In such close quarters, the *arabi* was the deadlier, sword carving the group in a flurry that seemed to defy physics.

Antiquity had never seen anything like it. It made her sick with hope.

When only two scavengers were left standing—both stunned and on their knees pleading for their lives—the *arabi* stopped suddenly. His sword returned to the folds of his robe and he stood, impervious and unmoving, not even breathing hard.

The *arabi* turned to Antiquity then. Their eyes met. She felt drawn into them. There was no hate there or evil. But they were liquid pools of darkness. Empty. Devoid of emotion.

And strange in a way Antiquity couldn't define.

"It is best we leave," the *arabi* said, moving toward Kaihli.

Antiquity thought the man meant to hurt her friend. She moved to intervene but then noticed the problem—and her heart sank. Kaihli still stood but she breathed shallowly, crimson staining the silks on her left side, making them sticky. Manson had already placed a hand on the wound even as the twin had gone deathly white.

"Kaihli!" Antiquity said, wrapping one arm around her friend as Kaihli slowly sank to the stairs. The *arabi* knelt and pulled Manson's hand aside. Blood seeped when the foreigner probed and prodded the area.

"I will be fine, Antiquity," her friend breathed, gritting her teeth. "Rusty knife did it. Damn scavenger scum."

"Is it bad?" Antiquity asked, dreading the answer.

"She will die if we are not quick about it," the *arabi* said. He looked around. A few of the people in the streets were dispersing, clearly afraid of the robed figure, while others still stood in the square below, masking that fear with a violence that only needed a spark to ignite. "And we are no longer welcome here." He looked to Manson. "You. Idiot. Carry her to one of the airbikes."

To Antiquity's shock, Manson did not argue. He moved immediately, getting his strong arms under Kaihli and cradling her gently.

Movement caught Antiquity's eye. The *arabi* turned as well. Beven el Ordett stood in the opened doorway of his store, his demeanor dark like a storm cloud.

"They are coming with me," the *arabi* declared.

"I know, Will Master. You will forever be welcome here," the merchant said with deferential respect he probably rarely showed. He nodded to the airbikes. "And I understand. Take all three. For the years of your patronage."

The *arabi* gave a curt nod, already moving toward Antiquity's airbike. "Blessings upon you, Beven el Ordett."

"You cannot take it," Antiquity said, regretting the words even as they tumbled forth.

"I am no thief," the *arabi* said, mounting its seat.

"Neither am I," Antiquity said. "Leave one. For the merchant, for what's happened on his store's steps." Looking around and realizing the danger they were all still in, she nodded to Manson even as she threw her leg over the side of the bike. The Dreadth did the same, placing Kaihli in the front position, his long arms able to operate the airbike even with the wounded girl in front of him.

"Why did you let those two scavengers go?" Antiquity asked, the two airbikes shooting back into the street and out of town, aware of the arms like steel around her waist.

"If one of them dies of their injuries, the tale may still be told, of course."

Wondering what the *arabi* meant, Antiquity became aware of an awesome truth, one she hadn't recognized in the heat of the battle and its aftermath until now, although the lilt in his voice should have been proof enough. It was a truth that was contrary to everything she knew about the fanatical faith of the *arabi*; it was a truth that resulted in the stoning of those who wielded a sword outside of their faith's tenets, no matter the reason.

The person who had saved them so artfully was not a man at all.

The *arabi* was a woman.

) ◗ ● ◖ (

"Where are you taking us?" Manson asked as his airbike pulled alongside.

Antiquity sat upon her own bike, thinking, unsure if he was talking to her or the woman behind. It didn't matter. They had been riding over an hour, heading back in the general direction they had come but not exactly, making few stops and only when Manson needed a break from cradling Kaihli in his lap. The twin's wound was now taking its toll; in the last hour, she had sunk against Manson, wilted like a desert flower. Antiquity feared for her friend's life, and it was that fear that drove her to listen to the *arabi* and do exactly as she was told. The grief of losing her grandmother still burned in her; losing Kaihli would be too much to bear.

She looked at Manson—his eyes stabbing her with reproof—and looked around. The redwoods had thinned somewhat as they gained elevation, the air growing cooler with every twist and turn. While the *arabi* had assured them that they were going to a place where Kaihli could be helped, Antiquity had begun to question their path. Her heart screamed indecision. Saph Fyre did not have medical care beyond the rudimentary. Antiquity was forced to trust the *arabi*—and trusting others had never come easily for her.

"Where are you taking us, Antiquity?" Manson asked again, clearly agitated but focusing his ire on her. "This is not the way back to—"

"I know, Dreadth," Antiquity growled, silencing him about the mech.

Before he could respond, the *arabi* looked at him, her eyes hard. "You do not deserve a say," she said. "You put these lives in danger."

"You know nothing of us," he spat, still cradling Kaihli.

"I know what I see with my own eyes," the *arabi* said. "It is clear your friends were upset to find you in Beven el Ordett's mercantile. I saw it in your eyes; I saw it in their eyes. The heathen wayward of the desert found you, you who brought the danger. The will within the world has an eye that never closes."

Manson almost went cross-eyed. "What is *that* supposed to mean?"

"Your youth makes you volatile."

"I only wanted to keep you all safe!" Manson roared, echoing into the trees. "No one is looking for me. At least as far as we know!"

"Did it ever occur to you that we don't need protecting," Kaihli said through clenched teeth, trying to sit up.

"Says the one bleeding out in my arms," he snapped. He didn't let her go.

Antiquity appreciated the way he had helped her friend, but years of being bullied by the Dreadth fueled her anger. "It seems to me that girls ended up saving you, Manson. Not the other way around. Perhaps you should consider that."

He sat there, at a loss for words, like a landed pond fish gasping for air that would never come. He had nothing to say because there was nothing *to* say.

"What's the matter, Dreadth?" Kaihli coughed, a pained grin on her face. "A girl put one over on you again?"

"Can we all agree on one thing?" Antiquity cut in, taking hold of the conversation. "Do you agree if one of us plans on leaving, you tell the others? That seems simple enough. Even for one so stubborn as you.

This cannot happen again." Manson looked at the *arabi* as if gauging her and then looked off into the trees, keeping quiet, the rising color in his cheeks an indicator of his anger.

Antiquity didn't care if he stomped off into the forest and died there. Instead she took in the woman behind her. "You said you were taking us to a place where my friend can receive aid. Where? You can tell us that much."

"Somewhere your friend can get the care she needs. That is all I can say," the *arabi* said, eyes suddenly soft as she looked at Antiquity. "Beyond that, I am sworn to the secrecy of the mountains."

For the first time, Antiquity understood what the scavenger had meant about the woman's riddles. They were maddening. "I give you my thanks," she said instead, not wanting to start another fight. "What is your name?"

The *arabi* hesitated. "Sadiya."

"I am Antiquity. Point us in the right direction."

The black-clothed woman nodded slightly and pointed up the hillside, a track that led them toward the mountains that towered beyond. And farther away from Saph Fyre.

Antiquity sighed.

There was nothing she could do. Kaihli needed care. The *arabi* offered it.

What that care looked like remained to be seen.

Antiquity throttled the airbike forward. The other followed it. They continued to climb even as the sun banked behind the western forested hills, the light now at their back as the *arabi* turned them north, deeper into the Dragonell Mountains. Antiquity knew nothing about the territory they now entered. Every dip, bend, or rise in their path brought new and beautiful country that grew increasingly more dangerous—taller cliffs, rockier terrain, and redwoods growing at strange angles above them and roots gnarled along the path. She sensed the *arabi* did not wish them harm; if she had wanted it, Sadiya could have easily killed Antiquity and her companions. There was more to her and why she had saved them than Antiquity knew. When they stopped, Antiquity would make sure Kaihli got the help she needed. After that, a lot of questions asked.

The path took a sharp bend upward where large boulders littered the mountainside, the airbikes running slowly around rocks that had fallen into the path. Kaihli slept, her skin taking on a waxy pale appearance. The help she required would have to come quickly.

Just when Antiquity was about to pull over and question Sadiya again, a turn of their path brought them to a glen cut into the side of the mountain, one featuring a small waterfall that fell from heights above.

And in the glen below, a house.

"We stop," Sadiya said, fluidly dismounting from the slowing bike.

Antiquity rode the airbike up to the structure, Manson pulling up beside her. "What is this place?" she asked.

"What passes as my home these days. I have learned the hard way though that days change and with them where our heart resides. The same is true of home," the *arabi* said. She gestured to Manson. "Put your friend inside."

The Dreadth did not argue. He carried the limp twin into the house. Antiquity followed.

The home was just as small inside as it appeared without, a two-room hut really—nothing on the rock-and-mortared walls, simple furniture, and few possessions. An open-faced fireplace with hood leading smoke outside had been built into one corner. Supplies of various nature were stockpiled on one wall. Antiquity followed Manson into the small adjoining room where two sleeping mats with heavy and colorful blankets lay folded neatly for sleep. Antiquity wondered who used the second spot; the thought vanished just as quickly as it came.

"Give me the gold from Holstead," Sadiya said after Manson had gently put Kaihli into one of the beds.

He looked to Antiquity and back again. "What will you do with it?"

"Always what I must," she said, hand out.

Antiquity nodded to Manson. What had they gotten into now? He finally handed the bag over. The *arabi* hefted its weight, gauging its worth. With Antiquity and Manson following her, she walked out of the home and hung the pouch on a branch at ground level out near the path, the gold dangling, before she walked back into the house and returned to the room with Kaihli.

"What are you doing?" Manson asked, and Antiquity wondered the same thing.

"The gold is worthless to you."

"How can gold be worthless?" the Dreadth argued, the very thought ridiculous to him. He was on the verge of losing his temper. Yet again.

"Gold is a simple rock of the world without someone who deems it more than that," Sadiya snorted, gathering her robes about her. She looked down on Kaihli. "It is worthless to you here. I certainly do not value it, can you not see? But your friend needs it. And I have friends who can help."

"What friends?" Antiquity asked.

"You will see. If it is meant," the *arabi* stated, kneeling down to the twin with a basin of water and wet rag. "In the meantime, leave this house. I will do what I can about your friend's fever. Hide the air-bikes around the back of the home, from the sky and the path. Eyes are everywhere."

Kaihli moaned in her sleep as the cold rag met her forehead. Manson left and Antiquity reluctantly followed suit. The two of them did as they were told, hiding the airbikes beneath redwood boughs that draped from the mountainside above.

"Why do you think she wanted the airbikes hidden from the sky?" Manson asked, crossing his arms.

"When we were crossing the desert, I saw a dragon, one that flew this direction. Perhaps she is worried of that." Antiquity shrugged. "I'd rather know who her friends are. Kaihli is not doing well."

"Did coming into these mountains kill your friend?" the Dreadth asked. "Surely there were other places to receive aid."

The thought had crossed her mind multiple times on the ride upward. It still took all of Antiquity's will to not hit him, scream at him, or both. Before she could do any of it, a shadow passed overhead, catching the last golden rays of the day. "What is that?" Antiquity asked, already knowing the answer.

"Dragon, from the looks of it. Maybe the dragon you saw," Manson said, shielding his eyes from the sun. "We are in their mountain domain. And of those who more than likely ride them."

Antiquity looked again to the sky, watching the winged creature vanish from view. She had never seen a dragon up close, only on vidviews and the statues in the main square of Solomon Fyre. She knew they were fiercely territorial, highly intelligent, and that even some *persai* communities had bonded with them as companions, the former able to ward off their more warlike extremist *arabi* brethren with the might of their winged friends. Antiquity wondered if the dragon flying in the sky was part of such a community or if it was a wild creature. And what it must be like to fly in such a way.

She grimaced for a second at the thought. It made Antiquity think about her own inability to fly Saph Fyre. Some part of her mind lay blocked from the mech's flight capabilities. She had reflected on the reason since her conversation with Brox. But she had come to no conclusion and it grated on her the more she used Saph Fyre. Vestige had always been in control, in every aspect of her life. Why couldn't Antiquity be the same?

"You are sad beyond your friend's condition," Sadiya said. She had joined them silently, wiping her hands on a cloth.

"It's nothing. Are we in any danger?" She pointed at the dragon circling back into view on wind updrafts.

"No. Not here. And certainly not from the dragons," Sadiya said. "They live in the cliffs above, much higher elevation where they can better control the temperature of their nests and see their futures in the distance." The woman said it with such belief Antiquity had to wonder if the dragons could indeed view the future. "Let us go indoors. It will be dark soon and there are creatures in these woods far deadlier than what you've just witnessed. Man and beast. I will begin dinner. It is a rarity to have such visitors."

"No, we must get Kaihli help," Antiquity argued.

"Aid is already on the way." Sadiya motioned to the gold. The pouch had vanished from the branch without them even noticing.

"Where did it go? Who took it?" Manson asked.

"You will see. If the winds blow that way. Inside. Both of you."

Antiquity gave Manson a look before they did as they were told. Within the home, the *arabi* had already set up additional beds in the front room where now a fire blazed from its small hearth. Where the bedding had come from, Antiquity did not know. The first odors of something cooking over the fire assailed Antiquity and she realized how hungry she had been for a great long while. After only a few minutes, their host rose to fill earthenware bowls with a green-brown paste and thin pieces of bread to scoop it with. She handed the food to Antiquity and Manson, both carefully tasting the contents of the bowls before quickly devouring the spicy meal.

When Antiquity had finished her bowl and turned to look in on Kaihli, a dark-cloaked figure lay hunched over her.

"No!" Antiquity screamed. The *arabi* gripped her arm with iron.

"Let the healer be, Antiquity Grey."

Antiquity did not fight the woman. "What is she doing?"

"What healers do."

Antiquity had a hard time letting it happen but relaxed, and Sadiya let her go. She watched as the figure did things to the twin that she couldn't see. Antiquity felt even more helpless than before. No sounds came from the room besides Kaihli's broken breathing. How the person had escaped notice and snuck into the home, Antiquity did not know, but she watched as long minutes passed. Manson watched as well but did not seem concerned about the healer's administrations.

After what seemed an eternity, the dark-robed figure rose with a large satchel and, with a brief nod to the *arabi*, departed into the night. Sadiya said nothing.

Antiquity went into her friend's room. Sadiya did not stop her. Kaihli now breathed easier and her color had improved, even in the short minutes the cloaked figure had been in the room. The twin's torso lay exposed but bandaged. Antiquity could feel no fever emanating from her friend, a good sign.

"Why?" Antiquity whispered to the *arabi*, not wanting to wake Kaihli. "Why do you find it necessary to help us? To stick your neck out against the scavengers and again helping my friend get well. We don't know one another. You have no cause to help."

"Because I follow my path," she said, eyes boring into Antiquity's own. "And that path is before me, with you on it."

"You might have saved my friend. But I do not trust you."

"When you begin to trust, the friendship the world has spun for us will be put in motion. And what a wheel it will be," Sadiya said.

Antiquity could tell she was smiling underneath her scarf. "Until then, we will learn to trust. And be more than what we are."

Unsure of what the woman meant but intrigued all the same, Antiquity nodded, finding she liked the *arabi* quite a bit. The woman was of a stubborn sort, no different than Antiquity's grandmother. A pang of that fresh loss hit Antiquity but she tamped it back down. "You still didn't answer my question. Why do you find it necessary to help us? Following your path is not reason enough."

The *arabi* nodded, eyes gone solemn. She reached for her sheathed sword, which had up until that point been propped against the wall behind her. She fingered the handle of the sword in her lap, tender care for such a deadly weapon.

"The mech you told Beven el Ordett doesn't exist," Sadiya said, looking back at Antiquity, all friendliness gone.

"Yes?"

"I have seen it."

) ◗ ● ◖ (

"You are an Angelus. All of Erth will know it soon, I think."

Antiquity felt exposed, her secret known, and she was unable to do anything about it. The *arabi* had called her a Grey at Kaihli's bedside, but somehow she had known more. Antiquity should have picked up on that immediately and felt sheepish she hadn't. After the startling revelation about the mech, Sadiya had left to keep watch outside, telling them the morning would bring discussion. Anxious for most of the night, Antiquity lay awake, listening to Kaihli softly breathe next to her as she had done many times before—even as Manson snored unaware in the next room—going over the events of the previous day. The real danger had been in the knowledge Sadiya somehow possessed. So many questions Antiquity needed answers for. Thankfully Kaihli woke in the morning with renewed health—the visitor's care had restored her friend. Now the twin sat next to Antiquity as if her bodyguard.

The *arabi* seemed unconcerned about it all. She moved before them, having cooked a simple breakfast of eggs and stripped meat for the group, still wearing her faith's robes, face covered in the black veil. As far as Antiquity could tell, the *arabi* never took them off.

"How do you know about the Angelus family? And the mech?" Kaihli pressed, still moving gingerly from the stitched wound but well enough to have an edge to her voice.

"History is bound to the world, and the world to it," Sadiya said.

"The scavengers called you a riddle master. They weren't lying," Manson scoffed.

"We are living in history, us four."

Antiquity frowned. "What do you mean by all of that, Sadiya?"

The *arabi* smiled but her eyes held no humor. "Angelus and Dreadth were hunted for several days. The Imperium after them. That news reached even Holstead. It even came to me, who lives a quaint existence outside society. I did not seek you, at least not in the way you think. Though when I saw you, I knew you. I am betting Beven el Ordett did as well. He was happy to see the Dreadth and airbike arrive at his establishment; he was *not* pleased to see the scavengers, I could read that on him like the wind in the trees. But he is wise enough to not alert the Imperium and suffer my displeasure."

"What drives you then?" Antiquity asked. She wanted to trust the *arabi* but knew she couldn't. Too much was at stake. "You know about us, about the Imperium. Do you not have interests similar to that of Beven el Ordett?"

Sadiya had become like a statue, solid and immovable. "All my life,

I have sought meaning. Purpose. Honor. I have searched for it throughout the land. It is the course of one's life to search for these things. I found it in you when I saw you."

Before Antiquity could respond, Manson grunted. "We owe you our thanks for saving us and especially Kaihli," he said. "But you are a barbarian. And a woman without honor even in her own culture, if that sword means anything."

"The news spread by the Imperium did not mention how doltish you are, boy. It's a wonder you have not already been captured." Power resonated in the words, a warning. "And you know nothing of my people, Dreadth, not even the smallest kind. You do not know me, where I've been, how I've traveled. You do not know my past and how it informs my future. Antiquity's future. Your future. And you certainly do not know what honor is, not if your honor runs akin to that of your family."

"Just like you do not know *my* past," Manson argued. "Why I am the way *I* am."

"Sadiya, you have seen what happened at Solomon Fyre? Vid-cam footage. Of what made us flee with the mech?" Antiquity was trying to allay any fight between the *arabi* and Manson.

Although now she did wonder why the Dreadth acted the way he did, and the possible truth of his words. He had only ever been a bully. But she had to consider there might be more to Manson beneath the surface.

"I have seen it. Or a semblance of it. I tend to not believe vid-cams. But word spread fast over the sands and I know it to be true."

"Then that is how you know of my great-grandmother's mech," Antiquity said.

"No." Sadiya sat up a bit straighter. "I saw it long before you were born, if truth be told. I was once afforded an education, one unlike most receive on Erth. And certainly, one truer than the histories the

Imperium allow people. I know of the mech named Saph Fyre. The exploits of one Laurellyn Angelus, a cunning leader and formidable foe. And I know of her place in the Splinter War and how the day of her death changed the course of all histories, even those beyond Erth. When I saw the vid-cam from Solomon Fyre—even though the mech I saw featured paint blasted by sands and time—I knew its origin and who had found it. Only family members can power a mech. It had to be an Angelus."

"But you are not turning us in?" Antiquity asked, unable to fully believe it.

"If the Imperium wants you, you are friends walking along my path."

Antiquity nodded. "And where does that path take you?"

"To freedom," Sadiya said finally.

Antiquity couldn't help but think the *arabi* knew more than she was telling them. It was in her eyes and the way she looked at her; it was the words she didn't say between the ones she did. First her great-grandmother had asked Antiquity to confront the Imperium; now the *arabi* echoed those same sentiments. One unalterable truth could not escape Antiquity though.

She had friends. But what she needed were warriors.

"We travel to Luna Gold," Antiquity shared. "You are right. We are being hunted. And I know you saved us. But I also know that you will be in danger because of me."

"Only prey know danger," Sadiya said. "Danger is where you go. The ruins of Luna Gold will bring only pain to you. As they have for so many in the past. It is a ghost world, one buried with broken promises. You should not go there."

"We are going to Luna Gold," Antiquity said firmly.

"A simple question then," Sadiya said. "Why?"

"In time, perhaps," Antiquity said. "Trust first. Or you can stay here."

The *arabi* stared at her with eyes so dark brown they looked to be onyx. They bore into Antiquity and again she felt she was being scrutinized all the way down to her core. After a few seconds of silence, Sadiya looked away, that gaze gone, and began to move about her small home, gathering items and placing them into a pack.

"Then learn to trust we shall. I will go with you," she said. "It is clear you do not know this part of the world. Do not know its dangers or hardships. Do not know who to trust." She said this last bit with mockery as she looked at Manson. "I would see you arrive safely to Luna Gold, to see fulfilled whatever quest you think is needed. What you seek is not there though."

"How do you know this?"

"A Will Master knows what is hidden from the world," Sadiya said. "A Will Master knows when the hidden should remain so."

Antiquity weighed the issue. She did not know what a Will Master was, although she remembered Crock Bob cursing that title at the *arabi* in Holstead. It left her uneasy to not know the black-robed woman better. But she needed allies.

"Do not do this, Antiquity," Manson pressed.

Antiquity and Kaihli looked at each other. The friends nodded to one another. "You may join us—until I say otherwise," Antiquity said.

The *arabi* inclined her head. Manson rolled his eyes.

"Let us go then," Sadiya said. "And see your great-grandmother's first and last joy."

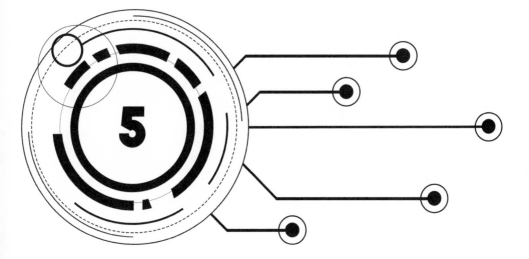

5

The two airbikes traveled familiar territory, returning the way they had come.

Antiquity still rode with Sadiya, Kaihli with Manson. The *arabi* had said nothing more, her demeanor as stoic as when they met. Like Antiquity's grandmother, Sadiya possessed secrets and she kept them locked away. There was much Antiquity didn't know about the *arabi*, but she knew she was willing to find out. Not only that, she was willing to allow Sadiya into her life in a way that few had entered. The twins were her closest friends in the world, Chekker even closer. Even though she had known Manson longer, Antiquity did not trust him in any meaningful way. Not yet—certainly not after his stunt at Holstead—and likely never. Whether she trusted the *arabi* one day would depend on how she reacted to seeing Saph Fyre. Antiquity had come to realize all too clearly that every person had selfish wishes they wanted fulfilled. What Sadiya wanted was still unknown.

The day grew warm, the smells of the forest all around them as they traveled. Suddenly Sadiya gripped her shoulder, head cocked to the side.

Antiquity slowed her airbike. Manson did the same behind her, he and Kaihli looking confused. It didn't take Antiquity long to hear what the *arabi* already had. A hum born of fast-moving machinery permeated the forest, growing louder. She had heard it before but it had always been accompanied with a desert dust trail.

"Do you hear that?" Antiquity asked Manson.

He gave her a dark look. The sound grew to a roar that seemed to engulf the entire forest.

Scavengers. A lot of them.

"It is what I had hoped," Sadiya said. "One of our escaped friends from Holstead has done his job." She sounded almost pleased. "Do we have far yet to go before we reach the safety of your mech?"

"We must push the bikes for all they're worth," Kaihli said. "Now."

"She is right," Antiquity said. "It's still a ride."

"But the *arabi* tore them apart back there!" Manson said, gesturing at Sadiya. "She can do it again, if we are smart about it."

"Not the entire set of families that are likely out there. I am no match for that many," Sadiya said, eyes flashing. She pointed at Antiquity. "But she is."

"If we can get to the mech, yes," Antiquity said. "That's a big *if*."

"Then I suggest getting to the mech with all haste."

Antiquity throttled the airbike. It sped forward like a shot arrow. She tore down the path, the trees becoming a green-brown blur, adrenaline sharpening her skills and control of the bike. She couldn't see if Manson kept up but she knew he would. He could focus every bit as well as she could.

The descent seemed shorter than the ascent. Before Antiquity could believe it they were upon level ground once more, the redwoods thicker but scavenger vehicles growing louder and drowning out the sounds of the forest. She didn't know which direction they were coming from—had they somehow gained the heights above Sadiya's home and followed after them or were they ahead? Could they be boxed in? Antiquity gritted her teeth, wanting to curse. Every day had been dangerous since they had been driven from Solomon Fyre. She wondered if it would ever stop.

When the first cram-missiles lit up the forest in front of her and disintegrated trees became flying shrapnel, she got her answer. She veered away from the conflagration, pushing the airbike to its limits, feeling heat even as she flew by the fire. The scavengers came into view then, tearing through the redwoods on their airtrikes from the east, trying to cut them off. They were too late. Both airbikes got ahead of those who pursued them, the scavengers left behind, raving and continuing to fire cram-missiles and the smaller laz-rifles. One glance gave Antiquity a look at the madness and fury that gripped their attackers; they would die before allowing their prey to escape. They would not flee like they had before in the desert. They would keep coming.

And the scavengers were gaining. The airbikes were fast but they did not take turns well. The scavenger airtrikes were larger but they possessed grav-stabilizers that corrected their turns if they were about to tip.

A series of spike-rips hit the back of the airbike then, tearing into the protective metal there. The attack almost unseated her and Sadiya, but both held on.

"Antiquity!" Manson roared from his airbike.

She understood without even asking. In another few moments, the scavengers would have them—would be close enough to kill them.

"It will be fine, Antiquity!" Sadiya screamed from behind, squeezing Antiquity's shoulder in support.

Antiquity had no idea how that could be.

Then, as she was looking back to gauge the next spike-rip shot, a giant shadow leapt from the trees onto the lead scavenger airtrike.

Antiquity could not believe her eyes. The behemoth creature ripped at the airtrike and its driver, grabbing him with its teeth and flinging him free of the machine, his body hitting a redwood trunk with a wet thump. The monstrosity leapt clear, back into the redwoods. Without its operator, the airtrike caught its front air-grav and flipped, the vehicles behind sliding to a halt or slamming into one another. The airbikes left the scavengers behind.

What was that thing?

Antiquity felt some hope return. The path began to change. The redwoods thickened and she knew they were close to where they had left Saph Fyre.

"How close are we?" Sadiya yelled over the roar of the wind in her ears.

"Close!"

The path veered around redwoods as thick as Saph Fyre's legs, heading directly to the area where Antiquity had hidden the mech. The airbike rocketed over ferns and fallen limbs, and before she could believe it, there was Saph Fyre—exactly how she had left it but surrounded by more scavengers. Before she had a chance to slow, Chekker was there, flying into the midst of the desert thieves to get their attention. It worked. The scavengers opened fire on the bot as he wove this way and that, her friend able to avoid being hit even as he gave the airbike riders cover from the threat.

Antiquity wove her airbike through it all, hunched down against metal, heading to one spot, Saph Fyre's left foot, even as Manson went into the right. The sounds of the pursuing scavengers rumbled in the air as they tore through the forest, already firing at the mech. Antiquity did not look to see if her companions were safe; she jumped off and scampered up through Saph Fyre, working her way up to the neck where she climbed the final ladder to the cockpit. Hoping the others would take care of themselves, she strapped herself into the harness as it came alive at her touch, scavenger fire already shaking the mech from the outside.

Chekker was suddenly there, yelling at her. She ignored him. Instead, she powered up the only thing that would protect them, the mech's senses becoming her own.

Antiquity and the mech were one again.

Saph Fyre stood and struck out immediately, kicking at those scavenger vehicles that had formed a circle too close even as she pushed the giant mech to stand. The battle did not last as long as the first one. Attuned to the mech in a way she hadn't been when she discovered it, Antiquity lashed out in multiple ways—firepower, fists, and feet.

The forest shook with her anger, fear now the adrenaline driving the great machine. Scavengers died by the dozens.

Smoke lay thick on the air. Saph Fyre could smell it, hot and acrid.

When the last airtrike and its occupants were crushed beneath her foot, Antiquity took a deep breath, steadying the power that had thrummed through her. She looked at the vid-view for footage from her interior. Thankfully, everyone was safely aboard.

Chekker remained, spinning in the air.

"Where have you *been*?" the bot hissed.

"Hello to you too, Chekker," Antiquity said, still one with Saph Fyre.

"Those scavengers have been attacking the mech for an entire day. It was all I could do to keep them at bay, Grey-child. I could not control Saph Fyre; I could only activate the mech's defense systems."

"You don't seem too worried about me and what I've gone through," Antiquity said, annoyed. "I am happy you kept the mech safe though."

"Tell me what happened then, Grey-child, and let me ridicule."

Antiquity did just that as she left the fiery remains of destruction behind and began heading toward their next destination—Luna Gold. In her mech mind, she saw the flashing dot location of the ruined city on an electronic Erth map. It would have only taken a day to reach in the air, but traveling by foot, it would take longer and be more difficult. With the billowing smoke from broken scavenger vehicles revealing their whereabouts—and some of the Holstead citizenry surely interested in the Imperium's bounty on Saph Fyre—it was best that she move away from the area as soon as possible.

When Antiquity finished telling Chekker what had transpired in Holstead and after, the bot did not speak for some time, clearly thinking it all through.

"What of this *arabi*, Antiquity?" he asked finally. "Do you trust her?"

"I do, in a way. She saved Kaihli."

Chekker spun, jerkily. "That is hardly reason."

"You sound like Grandmother."

"I did know her a long time," the bot admitted. "I carry a bit of her inside."

Antiquity nodded. So did she. "I think Sadiya has a much longer story to tell. She has secrets. But who doesn't? Grandmother did. Great-Grandmother did. Even you did. Probably still do. How many of them are Angelus secrets remains to be seen."

"*Arabi* are a powerful faction, one of the most extreme elements among Erth's religions. *Persai* like Kaihli and Elsana are the more moderate and understanding of that same religion. The *arabi* and *persai* are two peoples broken by time and ancient anger buried in the sands. This Sadiya could be quite dangerous without saying a word or finishing an action. Where she goes, animosity and hatred follow, no matter her intentions."

"No different than Manson's nature then," Antiquity pointed out.

"I am not sure he should be here either," Chekker said, humming. "Although your grandmother believed in him. And so did his father. Perhaps she would think the same of this spirited, sword-wielding *arabi*."

"Sadiya is also a Will Master."

"She has said that?"

Antiquity thought back on their conversations and shook her head. "No. She hasn't. She did mention what a Will Master's place in the world is, not that she's one of them. But Beven el Ordett, that merchant in Holstead, titled her that. And I saw her as she fought. It was unlike anything I've ever seen. What is a Will Master, Chekker?"

Chekker whistled then. "She is a rare creature, that's what she is. I have limited information about Will Masters, but there are few of them and they are held with great esteem in the *arabi* culture. They have abilities that some deem unnatural. Others believe they merely possess a focus—a sheer will—that goes beyond what the human condition is normally capable of. Sadiya will have secrets. She is beholden to her All-Father. And she may have motives of her own and a plan for the world. With control over both."

"An ally until she's no longer one, is that it?" Antiquity surmised. "I just know we have to reach Luna Gold quickly. With whatever help is given. I need answers."

"If they still exist."

Antiquity hoped her bot friend was correct. "Can you check on the others, please?" she asked. "Make sure they are all fine. I jostled them around quite a bit during that fight, more than likely. Especially Kai. She still has a long way before she's healed. And I can't do it. All of that black smoke billowing into the air . . . it could draw the wrong kind of attention."

The bot spun once in agreement and vanished down into Saph Fyre's hold.

Already in the harness and seeing no reason to get out of it soon, Antiquity drove the mech onward, into the giant redwood forest, toward that dot that flashed in her brain. They had been lucky so far; the Imperium had not discovered them. She hoped the destination Laurellyn Angelus had pointed them toward would be easier than the road thus far. She prayed the answers she sought were still there despite the decades that had passed. And she hoped no one else would get hurt on her account.

Given the last few days, she knew those were likely unattainable wishes.

) ◗ ● ◖ (

Once night fell, Antiquity powered down Saph Fyre and joined the others.

The terrain had changed considerably during the day, the redwoods still thick and tall but the Dragonell Mountains losing their grip on the world and giving way to flatter land, forcing Antiquity to weave the mech through them. Her ability to understand and use Saph Fyre's finer capabilities improved, but doing so left her sore, using muscles she didn't know she had. She crossed numerous streams and strange foliage but the land to the east of the Dragonell Mountains lay pockmarked with large craters. Two-headed deer and other mutated animals coexisted here, watching their passage with unconcern. Several times they came to a wide-open space populated with baby redwoods growing out of buildings fallen to disuse, remnants of towns now reclaimed by nature. People had once lived and died out here in this wilderness but no longer. The land had been mined extensively for its titanium—and then been left to die, polluted and desecrated.

Saph Fyre registered the poisons but they were now at safe levels. Decades helped heal, no matter its leprous look and strange life-forms.

It gave Antiquity hope. Life always found a way.

But it didn't answer where all of the titanium had been hidden.

"Another night of water and whatever we can forage," Manson grumbled, huddled around a fire like the others.

"Maybe if you hadn't botched getting us supplies in Holstead, Manson," Kaihli growled. "If you had just told us you were going, we would not be hungry right now, ya know?"

Before Manson could argue, Sadiya stood. "The Dreadth there is not exactly accurate about this evening," she said. "Look."

From the darkness, a shadow materialized, a massive hulk padding on silent feet. The others gasped, frozen in place. The cat stood taller than even Manson, thick at its shoulders and haunches, the muscle beneath its sleek velvety grey fur rippling with power. Large paws hid claws that would be as long as Antiquity's hand. She recognized the cat the moment she saw it. It was the beast that leapt upon the pursuing scavenger airtrike, crippling their pursuit and giving Antiquity time to regain Saph Fyre.

Now faced with giant lantern eyes that smoldered like a falling piece of ash still burning at its edges, Antiquity knew what desert hunters felt when confronted with predator desert lions.

It was a fear that struck at the heart.

"There is no need for alarm here," Sadiya said, standing. She strolled toward the cat with a familiarity that defied logic.

"We have two visitors, it seems," Elsana whispered.

Antiquity stood slowly, worried that any quick movement might be her end. It was then she saw the cat's companion, a rider upon its back, dwarfed by the size of the mount. Despite the distance to the ground, the lithe figure dismounted smoothly. He was just a boy, not older than twelve summers, his boyish youth slowly giving way to the man he would one day become. His shaggy hair glowed golden and his eyes were a dazzling blue even in the weak firelight, but his garb was similar to that of *arabi*—black robe and a thick belt keeping the cloth close to his body for unhindered movement.

"If you move, she will kill you, you know," the boy said to Antiquity, his smile more roguish than his years should have allowed.

"I do not question that," Antiquity said simply.

"My kitty loves to play first. Bat a toy around a bit. Have some fun. Toys don't usually survive that, of course." He grinned broader. The boy wasn't a true *arabi*, not in the way that Sadiya was. "Can get a little bloody sometimes."

The cat stepped just inside the edge of the firelight, large eyes assessing those who sat about the fire.

"Soren, call Cinder off of us," Sadiya said, the *arabi* not even troubling the hilt of her sword. "We have had a long day. And the day is as long as my patience is short."

"Come on, can't I have a little fun?" the boy pouted.

"No."

Manson stood then. Antiquity noted he kept the fire between him and the cat. "You know this kid, *arabi*?"

Soren frowned. "My cat does not take kindly to improper address, city-man," Soren said. He had become deadly serious. Cinder growled low in her throat. It was clear she did not like it one bit. "Nor do I."

"Yes, Dreadth, I know him," Sadiya said. "You should be thankful for that. He brings exactly what you wish."

"And what's that?" Elsana asked.

Soren turned back to his cat and from large leather bags slung over the feline's back the boy pulled pouches of various sizes and shapes and began tossing them all at Manson. "Food," he said. "Enough for several weeks if you are careful."

Antiquity couldn't believe it. "How is this possible?"

Sadiya shrugged. "The gold was used for more than saving your friend."

Antiquity understood then. She was now even more grateful for the initial trust she had shown Sadiya. The boy and his cat had saved Kaihli. Soren had taken the gold, brought the healer from who knows where, and then tracked them down as they fled the scavengers and traveled to Luna Gold to deliver the food they needed to survive.

"Then we are thankful," Antiquity said.

"Why did he do that? Risk himself and his cat there," Manson asked from the side, gesturing to Cinder. "Is he your slave, Sadiya? All *arabi* have slaves, from what I hear."

"We do not have slaves, boy. Not since the Imperium abolished that unholy act," the *arabi* growled. Her voice had become dangerous. "Regardless of what you may have heard in your safe city confines and privileged upbringing. He is my friend. They both are. You would do well to remember that before speaking again and creating a situation you cannot possibly desire."

"Yet women in your culture are treated exactly like slaves," Manson argued, as if he hadn't heard the threat. "Except for you. Alone. In the wilderness. Carrying a sword that breaks the covenants of your vaunted religion. You are not what you say you are. Maybe you should tell us what you are doing here?"

"Manson, maybe you shoul—"

"No, Antiquity, I will not be quiet," Manson said, voice raising. "What is she doing here? Because she saved us from scavengers? A situation she probably set up to gain your trust?"

"I do what I must," Sadiya said, cutting Antiquity off before she could speak. "As the All-Father commands all of His children." She stood then, danger in her movement. "You are one of them. But you rage from a deep place within. A dark place. Created by a past you hate. The words you speak are a reflection of you, not me. Why do you not trust me? And where does that anger come from?" She paused. "A father most likely killed by the Imperium and a son whose ire is as misplaced as his bigotry. A boy who parades as a man but saved by a young woman more capable than he gives her credit. With a mech of ancient design risen from the sands of time."

At mention of his father's possible death, Manson was already moving to confront Sadiya. Chekker flew into their midst, hovering above the campfire. "Dreadth, you will stand down now or find yourself without a home in this wilderness." The bot swirled to Sadiya. "He is not wrong though. You have a story to tell, *arabi*. I would know it. The Grey-child would know it. We all would know it. It is my role to protect Antiquity from threat. My Grey-child will be protected, from the unknown as well as the known. I would hear how you came to be by her side."

Antiquity noticed then that the bot had moved closer to the *arabi*, his chrome form prepared for violence. She saw that anger simmered in the group and she had to do something about it. It dawned on her that her companions did not know all that had transpired. They each possessed bits and pieces. To bring understanding to them all, she began at the beginning—with the discovery of the mech, saving Manson and the plans for their marriage, the ring bequeathed to her by her grandmother, and how that had brought them to this moment, on their way to Luna Gold. She choked down the emotion that threatened when she spoke of her grandmother. Antiquity powered through it, finishing with her trip into Holstead and meeting Sadiya.

When she finished, she felt drained in a way she never had before. But calm filled the campsite, each person focused on her.

Soren whistled. "It will take Beven el Ordett a long time to forgive what occurred on his doorstep."

"He will. All too soon. Greed will change his mind."

Soren snorted. "Or fear of you."

"The merchant is the one that said you are a Will Master," Antiquity said, using the boy's comment as a way to broach the topic. "Is this true? Do you control some kind of magical abilities that we should all know about?"

"It's not magic. And no one controls the Will, Antiquity Angelus," Sadiya said, clearly amused. "No more than you control the wind around Saph Fyre when you are one with the mech."

Elsana leaned forward, eyes bright. "You use the Will." The twin said it with such certainty that Antiquity wondered if her friend knew something that she had missed.

"The Will answers my call when the All-Father deems it time," Sadiya said.

"You see! She's a witch!" Manson sniped, hot again.

"There is nothing heretic about the Will, Dreadth," the *arabi* said, looking up at the stars above as if they held impossible patience.

"Shut up, Manson," Elsana said, the usually meek girl surprising Antiquity.

Chekker had not moved. "It is time for your tale, *arabi*," he said.

All eyes turned to Sadiya. "'The leaves give of their essence to the tree that carries them,'" she quoted, a proverb Antiquity had heard Elsana say from time to time. "You have shared your story, I will share mine. Home is where the great epics of the past begin. I will begin there as well. The home of my birth is distant, yet home travels with me. If I have what you define as a home, it would be what Antiquity, Kaihli,

127

and the Dreadth there saw—a hut in the mountains removed from all Erth societies. Isolation is by choice as well as necessity. Still, the *persai* who live in the mountains above are gracious neighbors. After all, we are not that different. Not in the ways that matter. Honor. Acceptance of our long-splintered traditions. And love of home. I have lived among them for more than ten years. In that time, as a lone soul in the wilderness, I have known the peace that all of our faith seek daily.

"I was not always alone, of course. Not before I traveled here. My father was a man of some import and I had a life of luxury, family, and friends," Sadiya continued. "He felt strongly that his scions be able to protect their interests, especially their persons. Alongside my two brothers, I trained. It is with a humility the Dreadth there lacks that I can say I was a prized pupil. My brothers bled at my feet more times than I lay bleeding at theirs. My father enjoyed it. But anger at my training and the breaking of thousand-year-old doctrine festered. My older brother did not take the same pride in his sister as my father did in his daughter. The animosity ran deep." She paused, her eyes looking far away at the past. "I did not have a choice. It is impossible to deny that which our parents make us while having to take responsibility for what that is."

"You were better than them because the Will had already touched you," Elsana interrupted, captivated by the woman's story. From her *persai* roots, she clearly knew more about the *arabi* culture than Antiquity did.

"Perhaps. The Will is not to be used in such ways. But I was young and eager to prove my worth," Sadiya said. "Staying became hard after the realization that my brother would never embrace my path. Great evil would have blossomed if I had remained. I fled my home. To protect it as well as to defend it. In so doing, I shamed my father, my family. I will never be welcome there again. Home is where my sword resides and right now that home is here, among you."

"It seems you are the only one here who *is* home then," Kaihli said a bit stiffly. "You mentioned the Will. Did we see it when you saved us in Holstead?" she asked.

"An aspect of it, yes. The Will has many facets within the All-Father, and protecting others who are innocent is a main tenet."

"Did you know who I was in Holstead when you killed those scavengers?" Antiquity asked.

Sadiya hesitated a moment before answering. "I did."

"Then you lied to me."

Sadiya shook her head. "I did not. I omitted. They are not the same thing."

"And you just *happened* to be there, at that mercantile store," Manson mocked, his disdain clear.

"The All-Father places paths, and paths are meant to be taken."

Manson shook his head, stood, and strode off into the darkness. "Riddles, riddles, riddles. An *arabi* woman wielding a sword is enough for me. What a crock."

The others watched him go. No one tried to stop him.

"That life story is a sad one, Sadiya, no matter what he says," Antiquity said after Manson had vanished into the woods. "I can see why Chekker is worried though. You know more about my family and our escape than is comfortable. You also seemed quite adamant that we should not go to Luna Gold. Why?"

"Ghosts live in these lands," Sadiya said, shrugging. "And ghosts tell no worthwhile tales. What you seek is not in these mountains."

"What makes you say that?"

"I am no fool. These lands have long been void of their precious metal. It has been their only worth and that worth was in their past. Laurellyn Angelus and her mech vanished long before that occurred, before the Imperium mined the titanium empty. You are here at the behest of your great-grandmother. But Luna Gold is much changed since she lived, and the city is not what it once was—now ruined by blight."

"The Will offers possibility. The obvious is not what has been hidden," Elsana said. "You speak the obvious."

Antiquity had never heard her friend talk like that—or ever about the Will. The *arabi* gave the twin a look as if seeing her for the first time. Elsana did not flinch from it. Something crossed between them, unspoken, but Antiquity could not be sure what it was.

"You feel you are here for a different reason entirely, don't you, mirror-child? Beyond what you have been told. You *feel* it deep within," Sadiya said.

"I do," the twin said.

"My sister has always been a bit strange," Kaihli assured teasingly. "A screw loose somewhere."

"The Will works in strange ways," the *arabi* said. Whether she spoke about Elsana or their conversation, Antiquity couldn't tell. "I may be wrong. I do not ask why you are here, I only know where it will lead. That direction is certain to anger the Imperium, for it is against the Imperium in every way. You see, I know what *I* feel."

"Where does that feeling take you, *arabi*?" Chekker asked.

"Imagine an army of mechs with Saph Fyre at their head once again."

Antiquity did not try to hide her thoughts. Sadiya had been able to discover them entirely on her own. Instead she thought back to the vid-cam footage from the Splinter War. Such an army would be formidable, particularly since the Imperium thought Erth quelled and devoid of military might. It scared Antiquity to think about it. For Erth to see such an army again, it would take Antiquity not only fulfilling the quest set before her but going beyond anything she likely could even fathom. It would take steel within.

She realized with more clarity than in the days before what her great-grandmother might be wishing of her. It left her feeling outmatched.

Antiquity found Sadiya looking at her again, that stare penetrating deep.

"Manson should not have left," Antiquity said, turning away from that look, viewing where he had gone.

"He will be fine," Sadiya said. "As I said, ghosts haunt here. Ghosts can only harm the living if the living allow it. He knows ghosts. We all do. But he is capable—if foolhardy—a great amount of the time."

The fact that the *arabi* said positive comments about the Dreadth made Antiquity realize how much more she liked Sadiya, even in such a short time. Mulling on that, Antiquity left with Chekker to talk to Brox about Saph Fyre and her fuel cells. When she returned to the fire, she accepted food Kaihli had prepared and greedily consumed it, hard bread and soft salted jerky. Manson still had not returned. Soren lay against Cinder nearby, both asleep. Elsana and Sadiya talked quietly, huddled close to one another in conversation. It bothered Antiquity for some reason that she couldn't define. Elsana had always been a bit different. Perhaps she had found some sort of kindred spirit, allowing her to open up a shyness that before had been almost debilitating.

Antiquity caught a hint of movement. Manson appeared from the edge of the woods, eyes glittering as he stared at Sadiya's back. He saw Antiquity watching him.

Then he disappeared back into his darkness.

She knew he wouldn't leave. Not so far away from home. He would stay close to the mech and its safety. But he was also the type who needed to blow off steam in his own way. To rage even if that anger was pointed at nothing.

She did wonder about one thing above all others though, a thought that she was ashamed of the moment she had it.

Antiquity wondered if she had made a mistake saving him.

) ◗ ● ◖ (

Antiquity stepped out of Saph Fyre, yawning into the following morning.

"Where are Elsana and Sadiya?" she asked Soren, looking around.

Soren scratched behind Cinder's ears as the cat sat upright before the dead fire, eyes closed. Antiquity could feel the feline's contentment vibrating in her chest. "Over there. At the edge of the clearing," Soren said with barely a gesture. "A forsaken Will Master of the *arabi* and a deformed twin of the *persai*. We are a strange troupe of souls."

Antiquity nodded, looking. Elsana and Sadiya were in deep discussion. As the *arabi* gestured to the twisted trees, the twin did the same but with her shrunken hand, evidence she already deeply trusted Sadiya. Nearby Manson stared up at the enormity of Saph Fyre with hands on hips, Chekker floating at his side, the bot projecting a hologram of Brox pointing to this joint or that plate or that weapon—giving a lesson to the Dreadth. Antiquity was pleased to see he took part. She had slept late but the others had let her sleep, probably at Chekker's request, and they had found other things to do.

At least they weren't fighting, she thought. They couldn't when they headed into the danger that would be Luna Gold, to find the Celestial merchant Vodard Ryce.

Or his kin, anyway.

"We have not heard your story," she said finally, looking over at Soren, who seemed bored by all of it. "Or what you know about Sadiya. It seems you two are quite close. What do you know about her? How did you two meet?"

"I know little about her past," the boy admitted, now examining the pads of Cinder's paws. "I only know what the dragon *persai* whisper and what those in Holstead gossip. Some say she was cast out from her people because she broke her faith's rule of women not picking up arms against humanity. Others say it has to do with the sword she carries, one she stole from the royal family of Bayt al-Hikma, the *arabi* capital to the east. Still others say she killed a family member there and has been hunted ever since." He paused, thinking. "I know her as well as anyone probably. She raised me, found me after my own mum died. She is like a mother. A very strict mother, but one nevertheless. I don't think it is any of those stories but could be all of them. She is a complicated person to know, even after knowing her for so long."

"And you adopted the *arabi* religion?" she asked.

"I wear the robes, don't I?"

Antiquity frowned. "But you are blond. Blue-eyed. Very unlike the other *arabi* I have seen or met."

Soren shook his head, a condescending grin playing across his lips. "'Appearance is the first gateway to misunderstanding.'"

"I'm sorry," she said. "You're right. Judging you on how you look is wrong."

Cinder sniffed, as if agreeing that Soren was quite right.

"You mentioned Sadiya's sword," Antiquity said, changing the subject. "Stolen?"

"I do not know how she came by it. It is precious to her though. It never leaves her side. Even I have only seen it a few times and never at any length," Soren said. "It is rarely drawn, only with serious need as dictated by the All-Father. If someone sees its blade, it is usually the last few moments of their life on Erth."

Antiquity thought back. The scavengers had cornered them in Holstead. Sadiya had appeared from the merchant store, robes flowing and sword drawn. The weapon had been a blur then, almost as if the woman hadn't wanted people to see it. It had carved through all materials—flesh, bone, leather, and even metal. Antiquity had heard of swords like it, blades forged in the heat of the deep desert and cooled in the cold waters of the highest mountains. How the *arabi* had come by the blade was one more mystery.

Kaihli appeared then from the mech, wiping grease from her hands with a rag. She looked over at her sister and grunted. "El has always been closer to the *arabi* than the *persai*," she said. "Spiritually, at least."

Antiquity nodded. She didn't disagree. "Are you worried about this?"

Kaihli shook her head. "It pleases her, I have no doubt. That she and I can be that different out in the open now."

"You've always been quite different. Must be tough being the uglier one."

Kaihli punched her in the shoulder. It hurt. "You deserved that."

Antiquity grinned. "How are you feeling?"

"Whatever that healer did, it worked. I'm sore but alive," the twin said. Kaihli waved at her sister to join them. Aware that they were suddenly being watched, Sadiya and Elsana returned from the edge of the woods, heads lowered, still in conversation. The *arabi* went to Soren's side. Cinder nuzzled her briefly in greeting.

"It is time for you and Cinder to return home," she said to the boy.

Soren could not hide the hurt that he felt. "But I want to stay here, with you. And them. I want to go onward, explore where I haven't—"

"You know why you cannot," Sadiya said, cutting him off. "You are the only one who can do that which is required. There are many paths that lead to the future, but only one will reach it successfully. I must help them make that future."

"No," he said, crossing his arms. "Then I will go with them. And you can stay. It is dangerous for you to go anyway. The mountains beyond hold your past."

Sadiya clucked as a mother hen would to a chick. "That path you must follow is separate from mine," the *arabi* said, gripping the boy by the shoulders. "We will meet again if it is the Will's way."

Soren did not budge.

"Do as I say, Soren."

The final words from Sadiya left no room for argument. Antiquity could hear the power in them. Sadiya outstretched her hands, palms up, in supplication. Despite clearly not wanting to do it, Soren gripped the hands of the *arabi* firmly, each one looking into the other's eyes. Then Soren let go and mounted Cinder.

"I hope you find what you are searching for," Soren said to Antiquity.

And just like that, the boy and his cat were gone.

"Soren is like smoke in a breeze but can be as stubborn as a mule." Sadiya breathed deep. She returned her gaze to Antiquity. "Luna Gold is still distant. It is time we move on. Only ghosts may live in this forest but that does not mean the living can't visit them any time."

The *arabi* did not mean the scavengers—but the Imperium. It would not give up so easily. Antiquity knew that. And now, even though her great-grandmother had assured her it was the correct way, they went to meet a Celestial who could easily betray them with a single communication. What if her great-grandmother erred? What if Vodard Ryce was dead, his secrets gone with him? Or worse, the death of his titanium trade had removed the ties he had once enjoyed with

Laurellyn Angelus. The more Antiquity thought about it, the more she worried Sadiya was right—this was a pointless pursuit.

Yet they had no choice. They needed direction, needed answers.

And Luna Gold was the only course they knew.

After gathering their things, Antiquity drove Saph Fyre throughout the morning, heading toward the Luna Gold that blipped on her mind-map. The land continued to show signs of heavy mining the farther they traveled, although nature had tried its best to counteract the damage done to it. Animals showed more signs of mutation—extra arms, feet, heads, or eyes. Even the redwoods had grown thicker and taller than usual, their trunks broad and boughs high. Chekker scouted ahead as he had done before, the bot aware of Luna Gold's location too. She wondered what her bot friend thought. Could he even understand how insane all of this was? She watched behind her, worried in case of pursuit. None came.

The land climbed and so did Saph Fyre. By late morning on the fourth day after Holstead, the Muthlaj Mountains came into view, Luna Gold nestled somewhere in its western slopes even as the home of the *arabi* capital Bayt al-Hikma existed in the east. The distant snowy peaks glimmered coldly in the sunlight, mirroring their current surroundings. The temperature had cooled, the valleys become deep-cut ravines with sentinel ice spires above. At times, Antiquity gripped the side of a granite outcropping to continue on the path, its way too narrow for the mech to walk upon. Mechs had no need for such roads back when the city was a living thing; they simply flew into the mech ports. It was a reminder of her inability to fly.

Just after noon, as Saph Fyre was almost upon the mind-map's dot representing Luna Gold, Chekker returned, flying before her faceplate. "You must be cautious, Grey-child," he said over their shared com. "This will not be easy."

"What did you find?"

"Luna Gold," he said. "Or what is left of it."

Antiquity knew the great city had been left to ruin, but she could hear Chekker's worry. "How bad is it? Must be pretty bad for you to mention it."

"You will see."

Saph Fyre rounded another bend and Antiquity peered down into the valley below.

Luna Gold lay shattered before her, far larger than Solomon Fyre but reduced to rubble and overcome by nature. The massive city had once been a sprawling metropolis of luxury and sport, the money from the surrounding titanium ventures flowing into its restaurants, businesses, banks, and populace. The excess created large skyscrapers of titanium, steel, and glass, once as tall as the mountains around them but now brought low and broken, the titanium looted and other precious metals stolen. Only concrete and glass remained. Antiquity took it all in as she navigated Saph Fyre downward to the city's mech port, its surface flat but covered in grasses, shattered boulders fallen from the mountain slopes, and broken ships.

From the port a large road fed into the city's heart. And around Luna Gold's lower climes, smaller residences could be seen, built into the very stone of the mountains.

"You are right, Chekker. Finding Vodard Ryce will be nearly impossible in all of this. What would you have me do?" Antiquity asked Sadiya, who watched within the pilot box of Saph Fyre.

"It depends why you are here."

"My great-grandmother led me here," Antiquity reminded the *arabi*, moving Saph Fyre behind a large fallen building for cover now that she had at least surveyed what she had gotten them all into. She powered down the mech, its controls snaking away. "Or at least a hologram of her did. We need answers that she says lie buried here."

"You did not answer me," Sadiya said. "What are we here to find?"

Antiquity thought about telling her of the hidden ores. She decided against it. "That is a family secret that I do not feel comfortable sharing. Yet." The *arabi* nodded but without much enthusiasm. Antiquity looked outside the faceplate at the flying bot. "Do we have any record about where this Vodard Ryce used to live, Chekker?" Antiquity asked, bolstered by the city now that she was here. "We can't possibly find him in all of this. He's a grain of sand in a dune."

"He had numerous residences here, according to my records," the bot said. "There is also no guarantee that he chose one of them to remain."

"Or if he is even still alive," Sadiya said.

"Chekker, can you scan the city?" Antiquity said.

The bot flew away.

"Now we wait," she said to the *arabi*.

"Waiting is the truth tree's strong roots."

Antiquity had no idea what that meant but she suspected the Will Master meant power existed in patience. They waited for Chekker, not speaking. The *arabi* shared from the folds of her robes food that Soren had brought them. Antiquity accepted it eagerly. At one point, Manson climbed into the cockpit to discuss what plan they should adopt, and when he learned they already had the beginnings of one in place, he disappeared back below, grumbling about not being included. The women took great amusement at that. When she became bored with the waiting, Antiquity called Brox, asking for a report on the mech's functions. The ghost mechanic informed her that Kaihli had restored all functionality to Saph Fyre that the desert sands had stolen.

After more than an hour, Chekker returned. "I discovered signs of life."

"Sounds like more life than one person," Antiquity said.

"There are several groups of people living in different quadrants of Luna Gold. I did not fly close to learn more as I did not want to alert them to our presence. One such area is the former entertainment house of Vodard Ryce, a large residence built into the bones of the mountain cliffs overlooking the city due east. It seems the most promising."

"I say we check there first," Antiquity said to Sadiya.

"Within the safety of Saph Fyre, if you please." Antiquity thought back to the danger the scavengers had posed without the steel skin of Saph Fyre around her. A similar group could be living in these ruins. She couldn't argue the idea. On one side, Saph Fyre offered protection from possible attackers lurking in Luna Gold; on the other was the danger of one of those people contacting the Imperium. Both choices had risks.

She just hoped no one could still communicate with the outside world.

"We travel within Saph Fyre," Antiquity decided.

"I think that wise, Grey-child."

"Sadiya, can you call everyone up here."

The *arabi* went below, and after a few minutes, Antiquity informed the group of her decision. No one disagreed—not even Manson. All in agreement with her choice, she let the gear snake over her body again and Saph Fyre strode through the remnants of one of Erth's mightiest cities, toward a possible residence of Vodard Ryce. Antiquity hoped that all of this was not in vain. She didn't know what she would do if the Celestial or his family were no longer alive.

"This seems so very familiar. Must be the vid-cam footage I saw taken when it was a vacation destination," Manson said. He had a strange look on his face as if remembering a dream from days earlier. "It is incredible how low this great city has been brought."

"Ironic, isn't it," Elsana said, sitting nearest to the *arabi*. "Vodard Ryce had a hand in the destruction of this land and now, if he's alive, he survives in its destruction. Can't say he doesn't deserve it."

"The metal of the mech you sit safely within was probably mined somewhere nearby," Kaihli reminded her sister.

"And then the Celestials stole it all," Manson chimed in.

Antiquity kept her focus on driving. "We know little about Vodard Ryce. He was a friend of Angelus. Once, at least. Maybe he regrets his role in all of this and remains here out of duty."

The others went quiet then. Antiquity was fine with that. It helped her concentrate on the desecration of Luna Gold and keeping clear of possible threats from the other areas where Chekker discovered life. Saph Fyre moved through destroyed city blocks, over rubble, and around parks grown wild. Nothing moved, not even birds in these environs. Tarnished silver corroded away and tubes once holding ionic gases lay shattered, business signs no longer readable. Various conveyances—some once powered by solar energy, others meant to be pulled by mutant six-legged giant horses—lay scattered on the roads, their owners long gone. It was exactly what Sadiya had called these lands several days earlier—a ghost world.

After Saph Fyre had crossed half the city toward the far cliffs, Chekker paused in flight, waiting for Antiquity to catch up.

"We are being watched," Chekker said over his com.

It took Antiquity a moment to understand what the bot meant but she did once she gained her friend's side. In front of them, some distance away but discernible, was a flying bot no larger than a robin but shaped like a dragonfly, its wings a rainbow blur on the air and its shiny body a bright sliver of silver in the sunlight. It was as if the bot and Chekker were facing off, unsure whether to meet. Antiquity could make out a small laz-gun mounted to the bottom of its body. She had never seen its like before and had no idea what such a small bot could do with such a minuscule weapon. She likely didn't want to find out.

Just like that, the dragonfly flew off—directly toward the residences carved out of mountain rock.

"It wants us to follow," Chekker notified her.

Saph Fyre did just that. The building rubble increased the closer she got to what had once been a residence of Vodard Ryce, and Antiquity realized that it had been brought from the rest of the city and deposited here to form a large half-circle maze that butted up against the cliff. The mech stepped over the maze, able to ignore its route. Whoever lived in the residence must have set it up, but for what purpose, Antiquity could not figure out. After half a mile of organized rubble, they came to a large area clear of debris that the maze fed into. There, in the cliff, a giant black hole gaped at them, a mine tunnel cut into the cliff face. The dragonfly stopped there, watching. It was joined by another. Then another. Until there were several dozen dragonfly bots, shimmering in the air, preventing them from continuing farther.

Movement from the mountain residence above caught Antiquity's eye.

Upon a balcony on the highest level of the home stood a man.

He was old, old and broken like the ruins around them, back twisted and bony shoulders stooped. Leaning heavily on a long steel staff, the Celestial had once been tall; now he was thin, like an ancient knife. But whereas his brethren were usually well-kept and stately, the old man's hair grew in wild tufts on his head and face, and his blue eyes burned with the conviction of emotion his kind typically lacked.

Several dragonflies flew beside him as if in protection.

"Welcome, Saph Fyre!"

The voice boomed through dragonfly bot speakers.

Antiquity didn't know how to respond. "Hello, Luna Gold."

"Oh, I am far from Luna Gold, although I am certainly a part of her. And perhaps some part of her is in me," the old man said, growling a low cackle. He became more serious. "You know who I am or you would not be here. The only question is, Antiquity Angelus, will you join me long enough to share your secrets and how it is you have finally arrived here in Luna Gold?"

Antiquity paused. She looked to the others around her and all were oddly quiet, even Sadiya, who had become still like stone. No help came from Chekker either; the bot remained in the air between Saph Fyre and the dragonflies.

"Brox," she said to the air.

The mechanic's hologram appeared before her. "I am here."

"Can you keep Saph Fyre safe if I leave? Like you did against the scavengers?"

The artificial construct nodded. "I can to a point. The mech has defensive capabilities that are a match for any of those who still reside here."

"Great," she said. Antiquity moved the mech into the mine shaft. As she did so, the dragonflies separated and let her pass. The shadows would have to conceal Saph Fyre from aerial surveillance. Then she sent her mind into Saph Fyre and the mech let her go, the harness lightly putting her down and unwinding from her extremities. "Let's see what this Celestial has to say about it."

"All of us?" Manson asked, frowning.

"I think I need all of you," Antiquity said, giving the Dreadth a shrug. "Unless you don't feel up to the task."

Manson bristled, exactly what Antiquity wanted. "I will go, yes."

The others said nothing but nodded her way. Antiquity nodded back. She had a sudden moment of love for them, even the ones she now grudgingly had to admit had become friends. They followed her lead as she made her way down the ladder and into the innards of Saph Fyre. The emotions were almost overwhelming. The possibilities of what she might discover ran through her mind as fast as light speed, how it might shape the next few days, weeks, or even years. She knew one thing for certain though. The last week had led her here, to this moment; she would not shrink from it. She would face it with her chin up like her grandmother would demand and expect of her. And she would make her grandmother proud.

When she stepped from Saph Fyre's foot into the mine shaft, the odor of stale decay laced with a hint of metal met her. It did not take her long to find out where to go. Deeper in the tunnel, a large doorway opened, its thick steel door pulled partially back but providing enough room for Antiquity to see the darkness that lay beyond.

A dragonfly shimmered there.

"Vodard Ryce," she breathed to herself. "I hope my great-grandmother chose wisely."

She passed through the door, the others following behind. The moment she entered, the darkness fell away and lights in the floor illuminated, leading deeper into the mountain and away from Saph Fyre. She hesitated only a moment before striding ahead. The rock had been laser cut and was smooth and precise, a perfect square large enough that it could have also admitted Saph Fyre farther into the mountain. After a few twists and turns—and several other large passageways that seemed to lead deeper into the rock—the tunnel came to a massive ele-lift capable of holding hundreds of people. It only needed to move five and Chekker. Antiquity's heart raced as the ele-lift traveled upward.

When the ele-lift stopped and the doors opened, the ruins that had been in evidence everywhere in Luna Gold disappeared. Opulence greeted them, the room before the ele-lift one of stately grandeur. All rubble and destruction gone in a moment. The most beautiful art and finest materials met them—steel baubles upon granite tables, and life-size statues of men and women against the walls, and high ceilings painted in a fresco long since out of style. The amount of wealth to create such a home staggered her. It made Antiquity feel small until she realized that was exactly its purpose. She could see what Luna Gold had once been—a beautiful city vibrant with life and culture. This home was a museum of sorts for a long-dead city.

"Welcome to the last of my homes, Antiquity Angelus, and welcome to your friends, of course," Vodard Ryce said, his frail form visible through an arched doorway the next room over. "Please, come in. There is much to discuss."

Chekker took up a defensive position between the Celestial and the group. "Tread carefully here, Grey-child."

"Yes, yes, your bot companion is not wrong," Vodard Ryce agreed. "But do not fear me. Only that which hunts you, the stars in the sky and the winds above."

Antiquity strode forward, unafraid. She kept telling herself that her great-grandmother wanted her here, in this place at this time. "I will decide that, Celestial. Chekker, can you scan by record and ensure this man's identity?"

"Ah, stubborn like your grandames," the other said. He grinned, which brought a light into his cold blue eyes and wrinkled features. "I have aged but remain the same. Do your scan, bot, and be done with it."

Chekker did so, a swath of light scanning over the old Celestial's features.

"He is Vodard Ryce."

"Of course I am," he snapped. "And do not forget it."

"My great-grandmother told me to find you," Antiquity began, taking a seat upon a large plushy divan that the Celestial had offered, heart beginning to slow as her mind focused on the moment. The new room they were in was a large rectangle that featured a long bank of floor-to-ceiling windows and the balcony where Vodard Ryce had been standing earlier, the ruins of Luna Gold spreading into the distance. "A construct of her, at any rate."

"That is not all, is it, young Angelus," the Celestial said. "I have watched the vid-cam footage of your work in Solomon Fyre. The Imperium is quite keen on finding you, your faces and names spread like wildfire throughout Erth. But first, decorum. May I offer refreshment? Surely you have need."

Before she could say anything, Vodard Ryce cocked his head to the side and several dragonflies raced from the room. It was clear now who had brought them to his door. It hadn't been a lone dragonfly bot's choice.

"You control them?" Kaihli asked, clearly interested.

"I do," Vodard Ryce said, tapping the side of his head with a long finger. A small node beneath his skin there denoted an implant of some kind. "They once mined these mountains, their size able to infiltrate even the smallest titanium deposits and their numbers able to do it quickly and efficiently." He paused, looking out the windows. "Now, they are my bodyguards and servants. If I had wanted it, they would have torn Saph Fyre apart one laz-cut at a time."

Antiquity knew the mech had defensive capabilities to prevent that. She thought Vodard Ryce likely knew that too.

"Are you alone here?" she asked.

Vodard Ryce nodded even as the bots returned carrying trays bearing cups and simple fruits and thin crackers of some sort. "All have left me. I have my books. I have constructs of my own similar to your great-grandmother's kind. It is a peaceful existence."

"Seems boring to me," Manson said, looking around at the opulence.

"To the young and reckless, I would imagine so," the Celestial said.

"One day, if you are so lucky, Manson Dreadth, you will also find my kind of peace."

"You know who we all are?" Elsana guessed.

Vodard Ryce nodded to a blank wall. One of his dragonflies flew up to the ceiling and began projecting light into images and shapes and colors. Antiquity watched Imperium footage taken days previously as Saph Fyre erupted out of the Angelus eyrie and fought Royal Declarion Wit and his Celestial warship. It was strange seeing it from outside of the mech. Accompanying the video along its bottom were pictures of those who had perpetrated the craven crime, wanted by the Imperium. Antiquity stared at photos of her friends, even Chekker. Only Sadiya had seemingly escaped the interest of the Imperium.

"You have been quite the celebrities as of late," Vodard Ryce said, grinning even as he sipped tea from a steaming cup one of his bots had supplied.

"You know us then," Antiquity said. "Tell us about you. Why would we be sent here?"

"First," the Celestial said, eyeing Sadiya. "Tell me about the *arabi.*"

"You can ask me that yourself," Sadiya said.

"There are many things I would ask of you," he said, clearly amused. "Let me look upon you though, standing at the ready to defend your friends. Yes, I see you. As those here do not yet. Your posture, your stance, even how your robe falls about a weapon those of your gender are not allowed to carry. You are a riddle, in more ways than the one, I bet. It intrigues me when little does anymore." He paused, sitting forward a bit. "Do not be shy. Before I help the lot of you against the empire of my forebearers, I would like to see the sword that is kept shadowed from the world but will one day see its light of day for all to witness."

Antiquity looked to Sadiya. A heavy silence filled the room. The *arabi*'s brown eyes were fixed on her blue. Antiquity could tell she didn't want to but had to.

"Do take care, Child of the Rose," Vodard Ryce purred. "No need for blood this day."

In a flurry of decision and movement, Sadiya swept aside her robes and before a breath could pass among them drew forth the sword, holding it parallel to the floor by its filigreed hilt. Antiquity looked closer now, noting the beautiful roses and thorns engraved into its titanium cross guard. But its black curved blade had not changed, absorbing the light as if drinking it.

"I suspected elegant beauty," the Celestial said, leaning forward to get a better look, eyes further alight. "I was not wrong."

"What's so important about her sword?" Manson asked. "There are many like it."

"Not so, young Manson Dreadth," Vodard Ryce said, his eye traveling over the weapon held out for all to see. "'A sword is the relevance its hand decides,'" he quoted the ancient *arabi* proverb. "Do not be so quick to dismiss a venerated Will Master. Such a sword is not given lightly. The last such weapon I saw belonged to the most extraordinary of men, a king by more measure than simply birthright, a man whose youth, strength, and honor saved his people during the Splinter War. He is sadly gone these many years, a decade almost, dead at a time that needs one such as he." He paused. "Seeing this sword gives me fond memories of him just as Antiquity brings back memories of her great-grandmother. Today is a day of hope. What is your name, *arabi*?"

"Sadiya." No hesitation.

"A beautiful name," the Celestial said. "And what name does the sword bear?"

The *arabi* frowned, eyes going darker than usual. Antiquity had never seen her bothered by anything. It was a bit disconcerting.

"No name was given at its gifting," she said.

"The person who gave it likely wished you to discover its name. History is replete with such moments. One day, you will." Vodard Ryce looked back to Antiquity. "Be sure to care for this Child of the Rose. She is a great ally, like those already in your company."

"I am fortunate in my friends," Antiquity said, looking over the gathered group. "You mentioned my great-grandmother. How did you know her?"

"You look a bit like her, especially the fire behind your eyes. It is an honor, even after all of these decades, to still owe her such a great debt, one that transcends time and our secrets," Vodard Ryce said, staring off at the ruins of Luna Gold. "Yes, I knew her. As well as anyone could. I was one of the first merchants to return to Erth, a decade before the Imperium would enslave the planet. I helped her build consensus here in Luna Gold, to bring the titanium out from rock to fight the stars if those stars attacked. They did, the Imperium's plans unbeknownst to me or my wife." He darkened a bit at that. "I even had a hand in your mech. The titanium for Saph Fyre came from these mountains. And more besides."

"It is hard to believe that you would betray your people," Manson said, eyes narrowing. It was clear he did not trust the Celestial.

Vodard Ryce looked at him, not with anger or annoyance but pity. "Yet here you are, a Dreadth, blood rival to Angelus, aiding the enemy. War makes enemies but also odd friends. You will learn that is all too true before this business is done." He sipped at his tea again. "But to address your ill-conceived point, discretion has ever been a part of my trade and my life. I kept my brethren close for many years even as I became close with those here." He nodded to the wall again. "Until an event changed my entire life."

The dragonfly projection took on new video, of a tall Celestial woman, beautiful and fine, her bearing strikingly similar to Vodard Ryce's. She strolled what could only be a Luna Gold garden, laughing, another shorter woman at her side, also smiling brightly at some hidden joke. Laurellyn Angelus looked young, far from the severe leader Antiquity would later know her to be. The two walked together, lost in amusement, until they vanished around a large hedge blooming with yellow flowers. More images took over then, the two women sitting upon a giant mech hand, surveying the horizon.

"My great-grandmother and your wife, I assume? They were friends?" Antiquity asked. She had never thought what her family was like before the Splinter War. It surprised her, seeing Laurellyn Angelus outside of Solomon Fyre.

"Like sisters," Vodard Ryce said, smiling fondly at the images as they played out. "Two very different people from two different cultures finding commonality in the most important of life's endeavors—living life itself. Also fierce. Loyal. And worried about their families and their peoples. Titanium brought Madylia and Laurellyn to one another but it was the future of Erth that made them friends." The image changed on the wall again, to one of Madylia asleep in bed. She looked haggard, sick, thinner than even a Celestial should look. And Laurellyn sat beside her as she read a book to her friend. "My wife became ill. Terribly so. A wasting disease caused by Erth's heavier gravity compared to our home in the stars. The medical technology to heal her did not exist here on this planet. And when we tried to receive it or travel to the stars . . ."

"Your own people did not help," Kaihli surmised. "But why?"

Vodard Ryce gave the twin a sad look. "Politics. Economics. Revenge. The minds of monsters are hard to know. Off-Erth technology could have saved her. But even one as rich as I could not circumvent the power of the Imperium. I built Luna Gold with my wife's help—a more ruthless business woman Erth has never known. The Imperium leveraged my heart's hardship against me. Used her illness against the woman who had bartered so strongly for decades." He took a deep breath, eyes seeking the floor. "There was nothing I could do. And Laurellyn was by her side, holding her hand, when her spark vanished from the universe."

"My great-grandmother showed you more compassion than your own people," Antiquity saw, eyes tearing up.

"She did. It was long before your birth, but I can still see the two of them together."

"I am sorry for your loss," Antiquity said, fresh grief born of her grandmother's death rising inside her.

"The past has become an unburied present," Vodard Ryce said, taking a steadying breath even as the images on the wall went cold. He sat up straighter, eyes turned hard once more. "It is with the future that we of the past have placed all bets."

Antiquity felt again the weight of decades. "You have been waiting for me. A long time."

His eyes narrowed. "That's arrogance speaking. Or misunderstanding. Either way, the traits of youth will not serve you in the immediate future," the Celestial said, partly amused again. "I have been waiting for the *right* one. We did not cast the future and place all hopes on one woman or man. Are you that person?" He tapped his finger on his lips, eyeing her like Sadiya did from time to time. "Perhaps, perhaps. I'm reminded of an old saying: 'Know the path before the path knows you.' If you do that, Erth stands a chance to be sovereign once more."

Antiquity nodded, understanding. Her great-grandmother had used the same *arabi* saying in her hologram discussion days earlier.

"My great-grandmother said this is about titanium," Antiquity said. "How do you hide titanium in quantities that would matter to the Imperium? It'd be too much."

"Very carefully. With planning."

"How do you know?"

"Because I'm the one who hid it."

"At those quantities, not possible," Manson said, shaking his head. He went to the windows and looked out instead.

"Manson has a point," Antiquity said.

Vodard Ryce raised his hands in supplication. "I have done what I can. Even Laurellyn Angelus did not see all, and in the time since her passing, other events have altered our original vision. The titanium that once flowed from these mountains remains safe, for the moment at least. But other leaders have risen and fallen since the Splinter War took your great-grandmother, and those leaders improved upon the original intent of Laurellyn Angelus, for better or worse. It will have to be enough."

"Who were those leaders? Are they still in power?" Antiquity asked. "And what has changed?"

"That, my dear, is a secret even I cannot share with you. 'The unseen thorn most bleeds the flesh,'" Vodard Ryce said, using another *arabi* proverb. He looked to Sadiya as if she'd agree. She remained silent instead. Antiquity couldn't tell if it was distrust or something else. "Most of you are hunted by the Imperium even as we speak. Royal Declarion Wit has unleashed his Lion upon you. And if the Lion finds you, it is best the knowledge remains a secret. Until another can fulfill our hopes." When Antiquity was about to ask more questions, Vodard Ryce raised his hand in denial. "I know, I know. You wish to know more. But this is not a game lost by loose tongues. The duty I feel is to your great-grandmother and the defeat of the Imperium. Remember that."

"You can at least tell us where that titanium went?" Antiquity pressed.

"It has vanished in the most unexpected of ways, in ways even

Laurellyn could not have suspected. Sundered and spread. It is safe. For now, at least."

"Riddles," Manson snorted. "You are just as bad as the *arabi* over there."

"I will take that as a compliment, young Dreadth," the Celestial said.

"Will you point us in the right direction, at least?" Antiquity asked. "Help us fight the Imperium?"

Vodard Ryce placed his teacup upon a side table, stood, and walked to the window. He stood near Manson; Antiquity could tell it unnerved the Dreadth. Or maybe it was something more. In the day's sunshine, Antiquity saw how powerful Vodard Ryce had once been; he carried it in every graceful step and movement. "That depends. Will *you* fight the Imperium?"

Antiquity was being interviewed. She hadn't even considered what this meeting would be like beyond trying to stay alive and find the titanium. "I'm nobody," she said, thinking back on what had already been said. "But I will fight for what is right."

"You are hardly a nobody, my dear, but if you are, you are one surrounded by somebodies." Vodard Ryce gazed at the others. "I see strength in all who stand before me—and most of all in you. I believe your words. More importantly, I believe you can do this. Despite the danger I'm helping send you into, a Will Master is a powerful ally. Journey to Bayt al-Hikma. It is not far, over these very mountains to the east. Your black-robed companion will know," the Celestial said. He looked at Sadiya. "Once there, visit the House of Wisdom. An *arabi* will meet you, along with a bot whose designation number will be all-important. Embrace the wisdom you discover there. It may just prove to be the Imperium's undoing."

"How will this *arabi* know we are even there? Or who we are?" Antiquity asked, perplexed by the very idea.

"The House of Wisdom has many visitors," Vodard Ryce answered. "And I can send a coded message ahead of you to ensure the meeting takes place."

Antiquity still worried how that could be. "You won't join us?"

Vodard Ryce breathed deep, smiling a sad smile. "This is my home. Always has been. It always will be. With no regrets. I have found that a world can seep into someone and make them feel whole, change them," he said. "These ruins of Luna Gold are a part of Vodard Ryce, and Vodard Ryce is a part of what remains of Luna Gold." He caught the gaze of each of them before settling on Antiquity one more time. "The puzzle pieces you need are all about you. Trust in their placement. They will be the shoulders you need, to remove the yoke of absolutism from the Imperium and set right the wrongs of the past."

"Wheels within wheels turn, cranking against one another, until one breaks and it takes the rest with it," the *arabi* said.

"Just so, Sadiya," the Celestial said. "To break the shado—"

A flash of light hit them then through the windows, brighter than the day's sun.

"CITY OF LUNA GOLD!"

The voice thundered outside, infiltrating his home and cutting off Vodard Ryce. All turned to the windows. Fear gripped Antiquity. She knew exactly who the voice belonged to—and what it meant.

"ANTIQUITY ANGELUS," Royal Declarion Wit's angry words boomed.

An image coalesced in the air over the city, projected there by the massive ship that now hovered above the ruins. Several small ships separated from the larger, surrounding the once great city, their armaments pointed with deadly intent. Antiquity could not take her eyes off the hologram though. The face staring outward was a grotesque sight, especially for a Celestial. Royal Declarion Wit bore severe, ragged burns along the right side of his long face. He had survived the battle in Solomon Fyre but not unscathed. Revenge burned in his eyes, the Celestial's earlier cold demeanor gone.

"ANTIQUITY ANGELUS AND MANSON DREADTH," the hologram roared above again. "The footprints of a mech are not that hard to track. You are surrounded. It is over. Leave the old traitor and hand over the mech."

Antiquity froze, unsure what to do. The Imperium had found them, undoubtedly from the smoking destruction of the scavengers outside Holstead. Saph Fyre hid within the entrance to the mines, unseen from the sky. But it was only a matter of time before Royal Declarion Wit discovered it, leaving Antiquity no choice but to hurry back, take over piloting Saph Fyre, and give her and her friends a fighting chance.

"You must go, fly high and away from these bastards," Vodard Ryce hissed.

Antiquity didn't have the heart to tell him that she hadn't been able to fly Saph Fyre. "Is there another way? Out of the city besides flying?" she asked.

Vodard Ryce frowned before nodding. "Under the mountains, yes. Through the mines."

"There is no way Saph Fyre can go through the mountains," Manson said.

"The mines beneath these lands are numerous and large," Vodard Ryce said. "My dragonflies cut deep. They will take you far, but most of the other mine shafts have been blocked from the world. You will need to muscle your way out on the other end."

"Dreadth! I know you are there!" Royal Declarion Wit said. "Look south."

Manson and the others did so. Where Saph Fyre had entered Luna Gold, a massive mech lion as formidable as Saph Fyre sat upon a hillside, its titanium painted a matte black and silver eyes turned toward the last bastion of Vodard Ryce. Then a second hologram appeared in the sky, this one projected from the four-legged mech and those within it, featuring a Celestial as old as Vodard Ryce but with wild, shaggy hair like a lion's mane.

The Celestial gripped another man by the neck. In the hologram his eyes glared defiant, but his face showed the deep purples and swollen lesions of one who had taken a beating. The Celestial brought a raz-knife to the other's neck, its keen edge glowing red. Antiquity knew the man the moment she laid eyes on him.

Jackson Dreadth.

"No," Manson breathed.

"The Lion has found you, tracked you," Vodard Ryce said. "You have to leave. Now. I will do what I can to cover your escape."

Antiquity understood then. The two were in different ships. The hunter had found their trail and called Royal Declarion Wit to the ruined city.

Antiquity was cornered.

"We have to go after that Lion," Manson hissed to Antiquity.

"Come out, come out, wherever you are," the Lion teased as if he had heard Manson's words, malevolence in his grin.

"I'm going out there," Manson growled, moving toward the room's exit.

Vodard Ryce stood and with speed that belied his age held the Dreadth back, his bony arms strong. "You will only be caught. The Imperium does not take prisoners unless they lead to further prey. Once Declarion Wit has you, he will execute your father and eventually you. Without mercy."

"I will make an example of you, Angelus," the Celestial continued, glee in his eyes. "I will destroy all you love—destroy your loved ones and the Grey-shamed in your beloved city—if you do not surrender. I will make them watch. Better, I will make the entire planet watch. It will be a history lesson unlike any Solomon Fyre has witnessed before." Royal Declarion Wit paused, obviously relishing the moment. "If you do not come out," he said, smirking, "I will have my Lion slash the Elder Dreadth's throat. And his death will be on your hands, not mine."

Silence fell upon them all, a heaviness that choked the room. "Antiquity," Manson breathed, shaking his head. She almost thought that he would push past Vodard Ryce, but he didn't. Instead he stood there, paralyzed, the love he bore his father clear but so too the allegiance to their cause. "There is another way. We can get him back. *You* can attack that mech lion. Those ships. Saph Fyre is battle ready. And tested."

Antiquity felt her heart drop. "I can't fly."

"You can," he said. "You must!"

Torn, Antiquity looked from Manson to his father's hologram.

"Royal Declarion Wit will not tolerate an insurrection under his planet command," Vodard Ryce said firmly, hand making a crushing fist. "You have to go. I can give you cover, enough to get away. Go to Bayt al-Hikma, through the mountains. But be careful. There are those in *arabi* circles who have agendas of their own, who will try to control or even destroy you as the Imperium would."

"Manson. My son. If you are out there, look at me," Jackson Dreadth said from his hologram.

The Lion still held him. But there was a peace in the man's eyes. Antiquity knew what he had decided.

"Remember what I told you about your mother," Jackson Dreadth said.

"No, Dad," Manson breathed.

"Remember the face of your mother, and remember it well."

"No!" Manson roared even though his father couldn't hear him.

Tears streamed down his face. The others watched as Jackson Dreadth did the unimaginable. With the back of his head, he butted the hunter as hard as he could. Blood exploded from the older man's nose as his front teeth vanished. The raz-knife sunk deep into the Dreadth's neck and through it like a flame through wax, and the head separated cleanly as the hologram became washed in red.

"No!" Manson screamed again.

"We must go!" Sadiya said as she pulled the Dreadth along. The young man did not fight it. "Nothing is keeping those ships from attacking now!"

"Go then, Angelus!" Vodard Ryce said with steely confidence as he gripped Antiquity's shoulders in farewell. The little flying machines now buzzed throughout his home even as thousands more flooded the air outside of the windows like desert locusts every eighteen years. Antiquity tried to pull him onward but he fought back. "You must find your way in this. My own way has been known a long time. Beware of my son if you meet him. He is not to be fooled or trifled with. And beware the entire city of Bayt al-Hikma. The secret you seek is there and buried deep."

Antiquity tried a final time. "Come with us!"

"I cannot." He tapped the implant on the side of his head. "Someone must maintain your cover. If I leave, I lose all command over my little friends."

"What will happen to you?"

"What should have happened long ago! Go!"

Antiquity sprinted then, after her friends, all taking the elevator down to the city level. She looked up into the sky. The dragonflies had already begun their attack on Royal Declarion Wit and his ships. The Imperium vessels fired into their midst, but they were too many and spread out too much to be killed quickly. The ships blazed away at the tiny bots, but even though large swaths of them died in the hail of gunfire, many more surged out of the mountain. The Celestial ships were darkened by their swarm even as their mounted lasers lit up their titanium hulls.

Antiquity tore up through Saph Fyre into her pilot box, the mech coming to life as the controls snaked around her. Soon, the power of her family's heritage thrummed through her. She felt big. She felt strong. She felt like she could take on the world.

From the giant mine entrance, she gazed with her mech eyes at the Lion and the warship. Anger at what had been done to her and Manson gave her a moment's pause to fight back. She tried to engage flight, her mind pushing against whatever prohibited it. She found the problem fast this time, the blockage in her head that kept her from flight, unsure why it existed. She pushed against it but it wouldn't budge.

Frustrated she returned to the moment and Saph Fyre turned to thunder into the old mine, shaking the rock with every giant step as she followed several dragonflies into the deep recesses of the mountains. But with one final look back, she saw the Imperium fire that would eventually incinerate and consume the dragonflies that had given them a chance at escape.

Her eyes burned with the reality.

She would never see Vodard Ryce again.

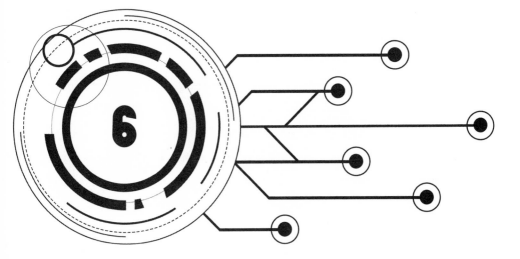

6

Bayt al-Hikma loomed before them, a sprawling thing, alive with life. Antiquity and Sadiya sat upon a large outcropping of rock that jutted above the cave entrance they had just exited. Saph Fyre remained within those dark confines, sheltered from the sky and any eyes that may have been watching. Antiquity had to admit, it was nice being outside once more. The mountain mine trip from Luna Gold had taken longer than she expected—three days by their data-watches—and been more dangerous, the old mines not cared for since their ore deposits ran dry. All sorts of sharp-clawed creatures inhabited the mines, eyes glowing with malevolence at the mech's passage, but only one had proven a real fight. Several dangerous tunnel collapses also required clearing, slow going. They had given Antiquity an idea though. She collapsed long stretches of tunnel behind them as they fled. The new rubble would mark their passage but the Lion would spend time digging it out, giving them time to flee.

The others weathered the trip well, all except Manson, who alternated between raging at his father's murder, seething with the need for vengeance, and weeping for the loss.

Now Antiquity sat with Sadiya.

Bayt al-Hikma, the fabled great city of the *arabi* faith, glimmered in the distance.

"No city on Erth rivals Bayt al-Hikma," Sadiya said with a fondness that Antiquity did not miss. "No equal in the Occident, no equal in the Imperium. It is the most wondrous city in the region, in importance, in prosperity. No one is better educated than the scholars here. And no one is as dangerous as the educated."

"You speak of it as if you've been here," Antiquity pressed, trying to learn more.

"This was my home," Sadiya admitted. She gestured to the bulk of the city. "It is a crossroads between the west of your home and the east of the Imperial seat. I have no doubt it has changed since my leaving."

Antiquity breathed in the cool night air. "It is a marvelous sight."

"Bayt al-Hikma began as a single stone tower in the deserts you crossed, so many centuries ago its original location is long forgotten. The irony of that is not lost on those who live here. For knowledge has ever been the power of my people. The tower existed as a simple place for translation, housing a small library of texts to bridge the cultures that grew in various directions about it." She looked around and pointed. "You see that area void of buildings in the north of the city?" Antiquity nodded. "The tower is there, moved stone by stone, a holy place, a garden now cradling that past. It became a place to protect knowledge soon after, a library for subjects such as philosophy, astronomy, science, mathematics, and the literature of the wise *el-hajida*."

"And your people moved it here," Antiquity surmised.

"At a time of great conquest, yes. My people pushed into other areas of the world. Bayt al-Hikma grew, a jewel of information."

"And the tower grew with it."

"More than that," Sadiya said. "Knowledge within it grew. It was a flower of our Golden Age that merged those peoples with others and therefore expanded intellectual traditions for all. Much has been lost since that time, I think. But also gained."

Antiquity realized then how educated Sadiya truly was. She knew the history of this city and her people. But it was more than that. It was how she spoke, how she moved. Antiquity bet she had come from a wealthy family, where education was a given.

"The Imperium even tried to remove the tower. We fought," Sadiya said. "They failed, discovering the price of trying to eradicate a people's culture."

Antiquity was surprised. She had not known that. The Imperium had always been so entrenched in her life, so powerful, it was hard believing that there was something they could not do. It made sense though. Her grandmother had always said knowledge was an enemy to those in control. Despite their Grey-shame making it illegal, Vestige had tutored Antiquity in secret. Antiquity always hated it, keeping her from her friends. Now she saw new value in it, a new light.

"Speaking of knowledge, you knew we didn't need to go to Luna Gold," Antiquity said. "You tried telling me but I didn't listen."

"You are as stubborn as other women in your lineage, it seems," Sadiya stated, nodding. "A boon but not without consequence. I knew the best place to venture would be the House of Wisdom. Ultimately, we seek knowledge. What better place to go?"

"And, with Luna Gold, now more are dead," Antiquity said sadly.

"One more is dead, a man whose family had a great deal to atone for. Vodard Ryce and his family were a part of a large wheel and they were a cog that spun and spun, to the detriment of Erth. His noble sacrifice atones for those earlier transgressions against the people the Imperium has enslaved."

"Two are dead," Antiquity corrected. "Manson's father died also."

"He made a choice," Sadiya said. "It was an honorable one. I do not weep for him as his sacrifice likely saved us all. He knew even as I did that Manson would want to fight and save him—putting at risk everything he, your grandmother, and Vodard Ryce worked hard to attain. The young Dreadth has become a powerful tool, one his father sharpened to an edge with his death."

Jackson Dreadth had done just that. Antiquity knew it to be true. But who would control that tool? Was it even right to think of Manson that way? She had hated Jackson Dreadth for so long, a man who ruled Solomon Fyre with an iron fist and who made the lives of her Grey family a poverty-stricken hardship. She realized now that larger issues had been involved, secrets that tied their families together, Jackson Dreadth and Vestige Angelus working together in case it ever became mutually important. It wasn't just his death, though, that made Antiquity sick. Others sacrificed too. She hated the violence, hated the killing. She had been on the run for over a week, the days blending together, and they had begun to wear on her. She could feel her own role in all of this, flashes of memory. The dead. The dying. The death.

And now, she had driven her family's mech, her friends, a Dreadth, and a mysterious *arabi* woman to a city of unknowns, all while being pursued by the Imperium. She realized more than ever this was a game of life and death, for Erth itself.

Life and death, without the fun of a game, she thought wryly.

"We will go into Bayt al-Hikma in late morning, when visiting travelers are plentiful," Sadiya said, gazing at the pink of the rising sun. "We will mix in with them."

"Saph Fyre will be safe here?" Antiquity asked, unnerved by the thought of leaving that kind of powerful protection behind.

"You certainly cannot take her into Bayt al-Hikma."

"I know," Antiquity said, annoyed by the obvious. "Do you know anything about what Vodard Ryce said? About meeting an *arabi* in the House of Wisdom?"

"I know enough to trust the All-Father. You should too."

"Growing up Grey-shamed, I had to trust myself."

Sadiya nodded. "That is a wisdom of a different sort. One I embrace alongside my faith." She paused. "I know that whoever you meet will not be a friend of the Imperium, if that's what you mean."

"Do we have anything to worry about? With the Imperium, I mean?"

"Not likely," Sadiya said, eyes twinkling. "If there is one last free bastion on Erth, it is Bayt al-Hikma. The king who ruled during the Splinter War kept his might close to his empire, the might of economic trade, the might of the unknown buried within those walls. The Imperium has tried to bring Bayt al-Hikma under their control, but the *arabi* here are quite self-sufficient. Even Royal Declarion Wit and his brother know not to poke a sleeping mountain cat. For it, there is an uneasy stalemate between the two."

"The danger to Saph Fyre is out here then."

"Oh no, there is danger in the city as well. A different kind. One I hope to navigate as a ship upon storm-tossed seas," Sadiya said. "Let us hope we do not cross it."

Antiquity frowned. "How will we avoid it?"

"By wrapping thorns about the rose, of course."

Antiquity had no idea what the *arabi* meant, but she was glad the other seemed to have a plan.

) ◗ ● ◖ (

Within the next hour, Sadiya vanished.

Antiquity had returned to Saph Fyre, to break her fast and see how her friends fared. Elsana sat in the crew quarters, reading a supple leather-bound *arabi* book that Sadiya had shared with her. Manson lay on his bunk in self-imposed exile, dark circles under his eyes and his back turned to the room. Antiquity left them both alone. After finishing her meal, she went in search of Kaihli, who had gone out into the large cave to look over Saph Fyre with the aid of Brox and Chekker, the mech having sustained minor damage while they traveled through the cave network.

"Is she all right?" Antiquity yelled up at Kaihli, who worked on the mech.

"She weathered the trip and battle fine," the twin shouted back, using an electro-wrench between two titanium plates at Saph Fyre's elbow. "She only needs some minor adjustments. At this elbow. Her wrists. And some fingers are partially out of alignment."

"I am so happy you are my friend, Kai," Antiquity said, hands on hips as she watched from far below. "All of this is beyond *my* ability, I know that."

"What can I say?" Kaihli said, grunting with her efforts. Sweat poured off her but she clearly loved the work. "I'm a hot commodity now. Where's my payment?"

Antiquity laughed. After a few moments, she became serious. "I'll be leaving soon," she said. Kaihli and Brox looked worried even as Chekker zoomed down to her. "I know, I know. Don't say it, Chekker. It's not what you wanted to hear probably. Sadiya and I are going into the city alone though. It will be easier for us if we are few."

"When will you leave?" Kaihli asked.

"I'm waiting on Sadiya. She left to gain needed items, I guess."

"I suppose if you are to go, the *arabi* is best to keep you safe," Chekker said. "Do try to make wise choices, Grey-child. It would not do to lose you now."

Antiquity left them as the others continued work on Saph Fyre. As early morning made its way to late and the waiting had begun to grate on her nerves, Sadiya appeared on the hillside below, hiking up the steep grade to the mountainside.

"Where did you go?" Antiquity asked, perturbed by the other's secret exit.

"To the outskirts of the city," the *arabi* said, unslinging a new satchel from her back and opening it. From it, she pulled a black robe. "You will need this."

Antiquity caught it. The cloth of the robe was soft and thick, but it also stretched in her hands without losing its solidity.

"What's this for?" Antiquity asked.

"A disguise, of sorts," Sadiya said. "There are those within Bayt al-Hikma who hold no love for the Imperium, but there are also those who would profit from your discovery. Even with the many cultures visiting and living in the city, your golden hair and blue eyes will draw the interest of those we pass. It is best to be cautious. But it is more than that. You must walk in the steps of the *arabi* if you are to visit our most holy place." She took the robe from Antiquity. "Let me help you put it on."

Antiquity let Sadiya do just that. She removed her great-grandmother's flight suit from over her normal clothing, allowing the robe to fall over her shoulders. Sadiya wrapped it about her, folding there, tucking here. It was a strange feeling, being dressed by another.

In minutes though, the robe settled, the black scarf hiding her face last of all.

"You look uncomfortable," Elsana said.

"How on Erth can you tell?" Antiquity said, laughing.

The twin grinned. Only Kaihli saw no humor in it, casting a dark look at her sister. "Looks like I'm losing my best friend and my sister at the same time."

"You believe in nothing, Kai," Elsana said.

"Not true. I believe in what I can see and touch. What I can fix."

Elsana rolled her eyes. "Steel. And that's about it."

Kaihli shrugged. "When we get home, I think Mother will have quite a bit to say to you. Switching from the colorful silks of the *persai* to those black will most certainly result in a talk."

Sadiya stepped between the sisters and placed a hand on Kaihli's shoulder. "The division of the *arabi* and *persai* was foretold by the All-Father long ago and our eventual reunion is also foretold. Time is an immutable river, one we all must cast our lot upon, and all flows into the one body of water known as the soul."

"Why do you wear the robes?" Antiquity asked, curious but also trying to change the course of the conversation. "Beyond the obvious, of course. The robes are a part of your faith and your culture. But from the moment I met you, you've never struck me as someone who adheres to norms of the culture. The exile. The sword."

Sadiya looked away. "What you say is true, to a point. But like the currents beneath the surface of that river, there is much you do not know about me."

"'A well is deep, but its waters derive deeper,'" Elsana quoted.

Sadiya nodded, her eyes soft. "You have read far already. This pleases me."

Just as Antiquity was about to ask about the book and its importance, the data-watch on her wrist blared an alarm, vibrating too.

She knew exactly what it meant. Someone was trying to steal Saph Fyre.

Before the others could even ask, Antiquity tore back into Saph Fyre, surprised the robe did not hinder her movement in the least. She climbed fast, already knowing who was within the mech's pilot box, anger fueling her. When she gained the cockpit though, she was not prepared for the sight before her.

Manson struggled, suspended in air, the controls of the mech having snaked around him and gripped him tight. He fought against the wires, but it was no use. His brawn was held fast.

"Get me out of this thing!" he roared.

"What do you think you are doing?" Antiquity yelled back, furious, already knowing the answer.

"I said. Get. Me. Out of this thing!"

Antiquity crossed her arms, even as Sadiya and the others gained the pilot box. "You cannot control Saph Fyre any more than the others here can. She is compatible with my genetic lineage and only it. You know better than this. I ask you again, what were you thinking about doing while we were outside the mech?"

Manson strained harder against his bonds.

"Let me go!"

"No, not until you tell me what you were thinking."

The Dreadth stopped fighting but he glared hotter at Antiquity than she had ever seen him do. Their two wills collided. Antiquity could tell this was going to be a fight unlike any the two had ever had before.

"Manson!" Antiquity said.

"I want them to pay," he snarled, muscles in his neck and face corded. "I want them to die. Horribly. As my father died."

"And you thought using Saph Fyre would see that done?"

Manson flexed his fists. "Your mech is a weapon. It should be used as such. All you have done since the murder of your grandmother is run. Run. Run. Run. The mech has been great at it because you are great at it. A girl using a great gift in fear. You are weak. Pitiful." He spit this last word out with venom. "I would do what you can't bring yourself to do. Fight."

Antiquity was taken aback. She knew the pain the young man felt but had not spent much time considering their situation from other points of view, only doing what had been required to survive. It hadn't occurred to her that she had been running when she could have fought back, especially in Luna Gold. She saw it from his point of view now, and even though his father's death made him emotionally unbalanced, Manson was not wrong. Antiquity took a deep breath, thinking how best to approach this. She knew exactly how he felt; she carried the same thirst for revenge after her grandmother's death. She realized he had become a mirror, one she had to look into and know. Her grandmother always said that hatred could destroy even if it felt right. She did not want to become the creature who was held before her.

"We want the same thing, Manson," Antiquity said, trying to remain focused on the importance of what her great-grandmother and grandmother had set into motion.

"Then you kill Declarion Wit! And his Lion!"

"Killing them will not satiate the vengeance of your heart. There are other paths to take," Sadiya interjected. "A truth that will see your will done, if in a very different manner."

"And you," he sneered at the *arabi*. "Filling her head with these words. Words. Words. And more words." He turned back to Antiquity. "Are you turning your back on your own people now? Your own *friends?"* Manson growled, eyes fevered. "Joining that *arabi* bitch? I see her already twisting the mind of Elsana. Who's next?"

"No one controls me, Manson." Stepping closer to him for emphasis, Antiquity narrowed her gaze. "Sadiya saved our lives. You will not speak of her that way again."

"Let me out of this mess," Manson said.

Antiquity nodded to Chekker. The bot contacted Saph Fyre in his electronic way and the wires that held the Dreadth let loose.

Manson dropped to the floor.

He regained his feet immediately—and grabbed her by the robe, the wildness of grief and anger in his eyes.

"You need to do this. Kill them, Antiquity," he said, fists shaking.

She stood against his strength. Agitated, Chekker spun in the air near them. Antiquity knew the bot would let no harm befall her, especially from Manson. But she no longer feared the Dreadth as she once had. She could take care of herself and would do so here. "The Imperium is more than the Royals and their Lion. I know how you feel. I feel the same way. They will be dealt with at a time of our choosing."

"Choosing? You and that *arabi* let my father *die!*"

"I certainly did not want him dead. I do honor his sacrifice," Sadiya said, brown eyes solemn. "You are a scion of a brave man. The blood of family within your veins will see you through this day and many more like it."

"Will you promise to kill them?" Manson asked Antiquity, anger abated by the *arabi*'s words, but his features hard with the request. "Will you kill the Royals and their Lion? Fight instead of run next time."

"I promise to fight, Manson," Antiquity said. "We will see them ended."

The Dreadth nodded. Antiquity reached out as he pushed by her, already taking the ladder down into the mech. She looked at Sadiya and the others. All were silent. Letting her hand fall to her side, Antiquity realized that she had tried to comfort the bully, a boy who had terrorized her for so long. For the first time, she truly felt a connection with Manson Dreadth. They shared the same emotions of having loved ones killed.

Antiquity realized one more thing.

The conviction of her promise had taken root in her heart.

) ◗ ● ◖ (

"You should not have promised the Dreadth revenge."

Antiquity and Sadiya had descended from the mountains to a long, winding road that they spied from the cave entrance. The words were the first either of them had said since traveling toward the sprawling towers and walls of Bayt al-Hikma. That had suited Antiquity just fine. No distractions meant keeping an eye out for danger in a land she knew very little about. So far, nothing presented itself. They blended with others upon the road, most of the women wearing similar robes to that of Antiquity and Sadiya, the cloth hiding all features besides the eyes. Now that they traveled beneath the morning shadows of the enormous city, Antiquity felt more at home than she had since leaving Solomon Fyre. True, there were different smells. Different sounds. And a different culture about her.

She didn't know how long it would take to reach the House of Wisdom. Or to meet Vodard Ryce's mysterious *arabi*. She just knew she had to return to Saph Fyre by nightfall. Mostly at Chekker's behest.

"I want what Manson wants," Antiquity admitted finally. "I just have larger designs that he can't possibly understand, feeling the way he does."

"Revenge is a self-administered deadly poison if not handled with

170

absolute care—like any baby viper," Sadiya said. "The All-Father calls it the death of the soul if not practiced with honor."

"Is that in the book that you gave El?"

Sadiya kept up the pace, striding ahead. "It is, a small piece of its wisdom."

"Will wisdom bring back my grandmother? Manson's father?" Antiquity said, still feeling the fight with Manson and not liking the biting tone in her own voice.

"No," the *arabi* said. "But it may keep you safe. Emotions left untended burn hotter than the desert sands at noon."

"Why are you trying to teach El your religion?" Antiquity asked.

"She requested its education."

Antiquity frowned. "And you gave it over freely? Seems like an important text to you. One you wouldn't give to a stranger, which my friend is to you."

"She does not know it yet, but she has great potential," Sadiya shared, stopping before a large cart filled with deep red apples for sale. She tossed a coin at the vendor, who caught it deftly even as she selected her fruit. "She feels the world as it is, not as she wishes it to be."

Antiquity thought of her friend, with a hand born crooked and misshapen. "I've tried to get Elsana to come out of her shell. I've hoped she would see the strength I knew she was born with. But how do *you* know? You just met her."

"It is uncommon, true. I noticed her strength before I saw her hindrance though," the *arabi* said. "Elsana has lived a very different kind of life from others. The handicap she was born with has resulted in a larger awareness. In time, you will see your friend become stronger than even her healthy twin."

"Does that mean you are training her or something?"

Sadiya laughed, the first time the *arabi* had done so. "No, I will not train her. That is not my role. Will Masters are chosen by the All-Father, but they respond only when the time is right. Elsana has the gift. But it is up to her to embrace that calling."

Sadiya lifted the apple under her veil, took a bite, and turned to make her way through the crowded streets of Bayt al-Hikma. Antiquity followed, trying to make sense of the *arabi's* words while being vigilant and taking in the wonders of the ancient city. Bayt al-Hikma was a massive construct centuries in the making, every new generation and ruling family adding to it. She knew the *arabi* and *persai* had been one desert people, fractured by philosophical differences and separated now by region and belief, the *arabi* settled in the high eastern mountains of the Muthlaj Mountains whereas the *persai* and their dragons had chosen the Dragonell slopes. Now that Antiquity was surrounded by the world of the *arabi*, she could tell the differences between the culture and that of Kai and El's life. Few colors existed. Black, white, and grey created an austere feeling to the world about her. The walls were high and thick, the buildings square and severe. It was a vibrant, living city but made cold by the extremism of design choice.

"Want an apple of your own?"

The voice turned Antiquity. A teen boy stood before her, dark-skinned, about her height but rail thin, and with big brown eyes appraising her. In his left hand, he offered a red apple similar to the one Sadiya had bought several streets back.

"And to what do I owe this generosity?" she asked.

"You have beautiful eyes. Exotic. Your blood has Fyre in it."

"I am different, yes," Antiquity said, acknowledging her Solomon Fyre lineage. She had been worried her blue eyes would attract attention. Looked like her fear was well founded. "Does that bother you?"

The boy waved off the question. "No. Not at all. You are just different."

Sadiya returned to Antiquity's side. She took the apple instead. "The All-Father does not appreciate thieves of any mettle."

The teen frowned. "'Take of this world as little as a rider's provisions, beware of associating with the rich, and do not deem a garment worn out until you have patched it.'" The boy gestured at his ragged, street-urchin clothing. "As you can see, I abide by the Word."

"At least you have read His word," Sadiya replied. "Even if you do not follow it fully."

"My name is Azik. Where do you travel?" the boy asked, excitement shining in his eyes. "I can take you there faster. I promise."

"For a price, I am sure," Sadiya said.

"A small price, for such a powerful Will Master such as yourself."

Sadiya turned, already walking away. "Leave us be, street child. The path we take is dangerous and not one for the young or faint of heart."

Antiquity smiled at Azik before catching up to Sadiya. She looked behind her. No hint of Azik was in evidence. But if he was like any of the street children of Solomon Fyre, he could hide and follow with the best.

"How did that boy know you are a Will Master?" Antiquity asked.

"He did not know. He was attempting to inflate my ego for money."

Antiquity shrugged and followed. This world was strange and new to her. Sadiya walked them deeper into the sprawl, away from the merchant quarters existing in the outer rings of the city. Larger buildings rose overhead, towers stretching for the sky, not built in the shining metal of Solomon Fyre but in the stone and woodwork of older times. Bridges connected them high above the ground, a latticework of pathways that residents could take without having to travel upward and downward. Men and children walked the streets, wearing black, grey, and white clothing, all dark-skinned and dark-eyed like Azik. But the women were all robed and fully covered in the same black Sadiya and Antiquity wore, the culture of the *arabi* clear about the presentation of the female form. Antiquity couldn't fathom why a woman would let longtime cultural identity make choices for her. Then she was reminded of the male Council of Elders in Solomon Fyre and how much power they possessed.

Sadiya continued on. She knew exactly where she was going. It was clear to Antiquity that the *arabi* knew Bayt al-Hikma quite well from her time living in the great city. It left Antiquity wondering about that time in her friend's life.

Sadiya left the main throng of people to take a different path, one less used. At one point, the buildings parted and the most ancient part of Bayt al-Hikma appeared, a large tower of square construction that rose above all others.

"The seat of the ruling family—Airtafae al-Hisn."

"What does that mean in *arabi*?" Antiquity asked.

"It translates to the Rose Stronghold."

"We are going there?"

"In a way," Sadiya said. "Just not one that is known."

The *arabi* kept going, taking main streets, side streets, alleys—and even entered several small buildings, taking stairs to the sky bridges above and traveling from building to building as the late morning transitioned to afternoon. By the time she returned to the ground, Antiquity felt dizzy, turned around, and fully unable to find her way back again. It occurred to her Sadiya was zigging and zagging through the city with purpose, likely to prevent Azik or anyone else from following.

After cutting through a small park filled with a green lawn and ringed by beautiful flowering hedges, Sadiya stepped beneath an oddly shaped bridge that formed a wide tunnel of sorts that angled softly to their right. Once in the middle, one could not see the back entrance or the one ahead. Sadiya looked about for watching eyes.

"Turn away, please," the *arabi* requested.

"What are you doing?"

"Please turn."

Antiquity did so, the other's lack of answer grating on her. Before she knew it though, Sadiya hissed at her. When she turned, Antiquity saw a small open doorway cut into the stone of the bridge's tunnel wall.

"I didn't hear a thing," Antiquity said, stunned by the door's appearance.

"Let us go quickly."

Sadiya slid into the darkness. Momentary fear met Antiquity as she entered pitch black, a fear born out of the unknown. As she stepped through, the stone door closed silently behind her, leaving her breath ragged in her ears.

Then light blossomed, cupped in Sadiya's hands.

Before she could tell the origin of its source, the light expanded, brighter and brighter, until the gloom of the tunnel they stood within pushed back. The door brought them to the interior of the bridge, the smell of dry stone and stale air surrounding her. The tunnel traveled through the meat of the bridge above and—from what she remembered—toward a high, thick, surrounding wall fronting the Rose Stronghold.

"This is how we will get into the House of Wisdom?" she questioned.

Sadiya lifted what appeared to be an orb, shedding even more light deeper into the passageway. "It is."

"How did you learn of these tunnels? Does everyone know them?"

"No, they do not. If they do, they lack the ability to open them," Sadiya said. "When I was young, I adventured, as children do when left to their own devices. Parents can only keep a bird caged for so long before the bird discovers more about its home. And this home is ancient, filled with secrets and ghosts."

Antiquity did not respond. Instead, she watched her companion. Sadiya moved down the narrow corridor, her black robe an inky blotch in the strong white light. They traversed several crooked tunnels and multiple staircases that led up, leaving her thighs burning. The *arabi* never slowed. After a time that left Antiquity wondering how far they had gone, the tunnel stopped before a wall where no other way branched. Sadiya hummed a steady note that Antiquity could easily hear in the silence. One hand held the orb while the other pressed against the rock, fingertips extended as if they meant to meld with the rock. Sadiya bowed her head, concentrating. The *arabi's* low hum penetrated Antiquity's chest but it was more than that—there was some element to it as images filled her mind, a call to the world and beyond, a way summoned to step through stone. The rock began to glow with a soft light that matched the orb before all illumination snuffed out and a vertical crack let afternoon light into the darkness.

It was said magic had once been used on Erth, fairy tales of wizards and witches who employed the mystical arts long before the technologies of man replaced them. Antiquity had no idea if the Will Master possessed that kind of magic or if it was something else. Either way, Antiquity continued to be amazed by the *arabi*.

"How did you do that?" Antiquity asked.

"Calm mind, sound heart, soft words," Sadiya said. "I asked the world for help and it saw fit to answer my song of supplication."

"And one day Elsana will be able to do that?"

"Perhaps. If the All-Father grants it and she chooses that path."

"Where does that kind of power come from?"

Sadiya pushed on the door, clearly not worried who might see on the other side. "As I just said, it is granted. It is a gift that few can feel, fewer can know, and fewer yet can master."

Pocketing the orb in her robe's folds, the *arabi* walked through the open wall. Antiquity followed—and, having returned to the fresh afternoon air, stood stunned.

An immaculate courtyard spread beauty about her in a vast walled circle, a building at its center drawing her eye, built of stone she had seen in the desert outside of her home city. But it was the garden about the building that fixated her. Sunshine brought all of its colors to vibrancy, as Antiquity stood in the shade of a giant flowering tulip tree where their tunnel door had deposited them. Similar trees grew about the outer circle and rows upon rows of roses circled the center structure— some so ancient their vines were as thick as Antiquity's waist, so tall she could walk beneath them. Antiquity had never seen so many roses in one place, so much color, the air fragrant with their heavy white, red, yellow, and other color blooms besides. It was a lot to take in.

Sadiya gave a soft look of understanding, knowing the garden's effect, before walking along the closest path toward the lordly building. Antiquity observed the House of Wisdom more closely. It was less a house than a short tower, wide and squat at its bottom with four diagonal tiers stacked up and growing smaller with each added level. The garden grew right up next to the tower, as much a part of the beauty as the flowers.

Antiquity followed Sadiya, the path weaving back and forth like a snake. The *arabi* did not slow, her robes a black stain on the beautiful day, until she came to a rosebush that was much younger, smaller and less gnarled than the others. Sadiya went to her knees, bowed her head, and began to pray, the words a whisper on the air.

Antiquity did not interrupt. She waited, feeling the solemnity of the moment, the sun warming her through her own black robe.

"He was a good man," Sadiya said then, regaining her feet.

"Is this a grave?"

The *arabi* nodded, taking a deep breath. Her eyes shimmered, tears on the brink.

"Who is buried here?" Antiquity asked, looking around. "Is every rosebush marking a grave?"

"They are. This is a place of earned peace," Sadiya said. "Those who rest here have protected the House of Wisdom for centuries. The man buried before us is the last interred here. Almost ten years ago."

Antiquity thought back a few days. Vodard Ryce had mentioned to Sadiya that he knew a man with a sword similar to the one she carried—a man who had been a king beyond mere blood, a man who had died about ten years earlier.

"It's you," Antiquity said, mind spinning. "You are the *arabi* I am to meet."

"Your insight pleases me. I sought you out, to keep you safe, but I am happy you are strong in intellect as well as spirit," Sadiya said, fondly touching one of the dark red blooms of the grave before her. She turned then, her brown eyes hard with strength once more. "One may say fate brought us together for future tidings. I like to believe the All-Father has found a purpose for the both of us."

"Who are you? If you knew the man Vodard Ryce knew, then you are more than a homeless *arabi* living out her days with dragons and their riders," Antiquity said, more curious than angry with the secrets the other had kept.

"I am a Will Master. Nothing more, nothing less," Sadiya answered. "I will always be who I am, who the All-Father has made me." She pulled her sword free, the sun captured by its black blade, the roses and thorns glowing in its titanium cross guard. "Like the Celestial in Luna Gold, I am the guard of a great secret. Even I know it not. It is time to see it revealed. The past has entered the present to benefit the future for all."

"At least we are getting somewhere," Antiquity said, ready for the answers her grandmother had kept from her. "Are there no guards here? For such an important place, I would think it deserves protecting."

"Guards are not allowed upon these hallowed grounds," the *arabi* said, gesturing at the colorful roses. "The House of Wisdom is a long-held holy place. And like most religious places, only those who have a right may visit here. I have been given that right, although there are some in Bayt al-Hikma who would disagree. We must be cautious."

"That returns to me to my previous question. Who are you really?" Antiquity asked, shaking her head. "Surely you are no commoner, if what Vodard Ryce said is true."

"No, I am not. I have family buried here."

"Which person represents the rose you were just praying at?"

Sadiya sighed. "In time. His name shall not be spoken here, among the others who cannot speak for themselves. He would ask that I maintain decorum." She paused, already walking ahead. "Follow me. There is a room I wish you to see, within this great library of my forebearers. I have never seen it. It will be a first for both of us. Come."

Antiquity followed as Sadiya took the winding path toward the House of Wisdom. From afar, the building looked small underneath the much larger tower of the Rose Stronghold looming in the sky behind it. Now much closer, Antiquity could feel the weighted importance of the House of Wisdom. It possessed a solidity and exuded an aura of ancient power that she could not ignore. The path wound around the side of the building where wide stairs led to a set of double doors closed to the afternoon. Antiquity noted the doors were made of a black ironwood, riveted and banded with thick iron and featuring large representations of golden jackal heads biting large rings.

Sadiya walked silently up the stairs and pulled on one of the rings. The door opened and both women slid inside.

The interior was a well-lit masterpiece of architecture and artwork. Antiquity had never seen anything like it. Solomon Fyre existed in sterility in its technological growth. The inside of the House of Wisdom warmed her in an unexpected way. It was more a university than a mere library, filled with globes of various sizes and colors all featuring Erth, gold statues of ancient and dignified personages keeping watchful eyes from corner placements, and glass cases holding leather-bound tomes of significance. Well-maintained tapestries depicting desert battles, the splitting of *arabi* from their *persai* brethren, and important moments from past eras hung upon walls. And above, painted in a swirling fresco that spanned the ceiling's entirety, glowed the creation of Erth and all forms upon it. The opulence and craft of art starkly contrasted with that of the black-and-white city outside.

That wasn't all. Shelves rose to the ceiling—on every wall where tapestries did not interrupt. Books sat upon those shelves, books of all shapes, sizes, and colors just waiting for readers. The wealth of knowledge in the House of Wisdom could never be fully catalogued.

Antiquity peered about. Only the library greeted them.

No one else was around.

"The upper levels of the House of Wisdom are filled with books as well—and much more," Sadiya said, looking up as if she could see through the painted ceiling to the other levels. "All knowledge saved before the Great Cataclysm exists here. When other nations were reduced to poverty and ignorance, the *arabi* faith took upon itself the need to preserve what had come before. Science. Mathematics. Physics. Chemistry. Even the arts like literature and paintings are represented here, all aspects of humanity that existed on Erth so long ago." Sadiya's voice carried an awe and wonder. She moved ahead toward the vast open interior of the structure, her footfalls so silent that no echo chased. "If we had but more time, I would show you many of the secrets here. You would never want to leave."

Antiquity nodded, already feeling that way. Being a Grey-child from a fallen family, she had never been given a proper education. Her grandmother taught Antiquity history, math, physics, and other disciplines in private, but Antiquity had despised it. Now she was surrounded by volumes of knowledge and all she wanted to do was move about it, through it, and discover it for herself.

Instead, she walked past it all, following Sadiya into another room with a series of deep-recessed alcoves featuring treasures of the past.

One of those treasures instantly brought her to a halt.

Antiquity looked about, heart thumping wildly in her chest as if an attack was imminent. The mech hand stood upon its wrist—fingers and thumb partially open, four times her height and drawing her attention like iron to a lodestone. It was of a different model than Saph Fyre, each finger featuring tiny *arabi* runes. Antiquity was suddenly reminded of the mech hand in the Council of Elders back home. It was quite different from the mechs she had seen in Splinter War footage. The *arabi* of Bayt al-Hikma clearly had their own cultural style; that style could be seen here.

"This is incredible," Antiquity breathed. "Where did it come from?"

"I do not know its history, only that it sits here, a reminder of the past and a hope for the future," Sadiya said. She still held her sword but cradled, as if it were a newborn. "It remains hidden here, far from seeking eyes. If the Imperium knew this portion of a mech existed, they would raze Bayt al-Hikma, even if it took the Sky Legions of the Emperor, even if it took their entire might and a million lives to lay waste to our city. They would hunt and hunt and hunt until they discovered this hand's origin, to ensure the technology for building mechs could never be duplicated. For it is their doom that they would see. Their fear would be well founded."

"The hand has remained secret for a very long time then," Antiquity surmised. "Otherwise, the House of Wisdom would be no more. Perhaps the entire city."

"Just so," Sadiya said. "This is the most hidden room in all of Bayt al-Hikma. The hand did not come here by luck."

"Someone placed it here. Who?"

"That is a much longer tale," the *arabi* said. She looked down at the sword, eyes shining. The reverence she gave the weapon made Antiquity wonder after the bond she shared with the sword's previous owner. Before she could ask more, Sadiya turned the weapon until its blade pointed downward, and walked into the midst of the mech's hand.

When the sword entered the space within the mech's fingers, a hum not from Sadiya filled the House of Wisdom, a whirring of machinery coming to life from all around the two companions. Antiquity tried to find its source but couldn't pinpoint it. Sadiya did not stop. She touched the sword's pommel to the palm of the giant titanium hand, her head bowed as if appealing to a higher power.

The effect was instantaneous.

Electricity sparked along the hand, snapping and traveling over the metal and arcing between the fingers. They moved, curling as if to grip the sword that had been placed at their center, alive again.

Sadiya withdrew her sword and stepped back—as the floor at her feet slid open to reveal stairs. The electricity died. The hum stopped.

The doorway down remained.

Understanding dawned on Antiquity. "Vodard Ryce did say secrets are buried deep," she said. "Looks like he meant it literally. You have done this before?"

"No, I have not. It was my first time," Sadiya said. "The sword was entrusted to me by one who not only loved me but who loved this city and world. I saw him do it only once, the day he wanted to reveal the secret of this sword. I did not venture into these depths. He would not allow it and said my time would one day come. That day is today."

"Did he tell you anything more?"

"He said sometimes a sword is a weapon of death, sometimes it holds the key to life. Through knowledge, power," she said. "He also said I was not then prepared. I hope I have honored him with the many days since of preparation."

"That was ten years ago?"

"A long time to wonder, yes."

Antiquity nodded, stepping up to the doorway. Stairs vanished downward, each step made of metal grating. Where they went appeared to be much newer than the ancient stones of the House of Wisdom. "Shall I go first?" Antiquity wondered out loud.

"I think it is your right."

Antiquity hesitated before taking the first step. Sadiya had protected her several times since they met—the *arabi* certainly would not send her into a dangerous situation now. The light from the House of Wisdom above only infiltrated so deep before the orb Sadiya carried came to life behind Antiquity, brightening more of the stairs but not much else. When the door slid quietly closed behind them, she tried to not let it bother her. Ever since her meeting with Vodard Ryce, Antiquity had expected to eventually see mountains of titanium, the ore kept safe, the building block that would allow for a new army of mechs to rise from the bowels of the world to confront the Imperium. Vodard Ryce had hinted at such. If the Celestial helped store large quantities of his mined titanium here, it opened up possibilities— futures of a free Erth.

Thinking about all of those futures and how to fulfill her family's charge, Antiquity did not recognize the giant when it stood before her.

She froze, heart racing with surprise. Sadiya stopped behind her, raising the orb higher. Gathering her wits, Antiquity gazed at the mech. It was every bit as tall as her Saph Fyre but all other comparisons ended there. The design was not that of Solomon Fyre's culture but that of Bayt al-Hikma, the artisans and engineers who had created the mech clearly from this part of the world. The mech had a full titanium-plated beard in place of its faceplate, its eyes a thin line visor. Antiquity could just make out a gigantic sword collapsed and latched into place along its right forearm; a laz-cannon was affixed in a similar placement to its left arm, an arm that ended in a stump.

The missing hand from above.

The stairs continued downward to a barely glimpsed floor, the mech standing guard over the entrance into what had to be a massive room.

"I cannot believe what I'm seeing," Antiquity breathed, trying to penetrate the gloom to see what else the room offered.

"I have always wondered about the hand above," the *arabi* said, just as stunned as Antiquity. "And where the rest of it might be. I always thought it had been destroyed in the Splinter War, its wreckage buried or sold off by scavengers."

"Why would it not be attached to this mech?" Antiquity wondered.

"It very well could be a warning," Sadiya said. "And a promise. But it is more than that. The hand, in the *arabi* culture, represents the immediate action for the Will. It contains all forms of strength—it can be gentle, it can kill. A hand enacts judgment even as it can deliver love. It can war and it can find peace. In a way, showcasing the hand above is telling us to be wise with acquired power and forthcoming decisions."

"I haven't had much time to contemplate wisdom. I've been

running for my life," Antiquity said, watching a pinprick of light in the distance form. It flew toward them, growing larger as it approached. "What is that?"

Sadiya pulled her sword free. "I do not know."

They watched the light advance and develop into a solid form.

A small spherical bot.

"Welcome to the Great Hall of Rostam. I am CyTak-5. How may I be of assistance?"

Antiquity and Sadiya looked at one another. More surprises. "Who or what is Rostam?" Antiquity asked.

"An ancient hero of my people," Sadiya said. "A holy paladin. He journeyed on seven quests, defeating all sorts of demons and beasts. He protected his people but fell prey to men's treachery." Seeing no real threat, Sadiya hid her sword anew. "Not unlike your great-grandmother Laurellyn Angelus. An interesting parallel there, I think."

"Hello, CyTak-5," Antiquity said, unsure what to expect. The bot was smaller than Chekker but had obviously been placed in the cavern with a purpose. "Do you have the ability to light this entire space?"

The bot flew a bit closer. It emitted a beam of light then, scanning her. She stood still, waiting for the bot to finish. The scan ended, the bot bobbing up and down.

"I can, Mistress of House Angelus."

Antiquity shared a look with Sadiya as the bot fulfilled the request, his chromium form emitting a different type of light that expanded into nothingness. Other lights along the walls, ceiling, and floor flickered to life, illumination flooding the underground room. Antiquity caught her breath. In the distance, mechs materialized from their imprisoning darkness, rows of them, an army of titanium standing at the ready. Antiquity did a quick count. There were sixty mechs in all, with different designs in evidence but none painted in the colors of their houses, as had been done in the time before the Splinter War. She forced herself to breathe, knowing what she now looked at. Power. Absolute strength of arms. This was sovereignty from dominion, the secret now found.

"Sadiya, did you know about this?"

"I did not, Antiquity," she said, the companions now hastening down the stairs. "This is a secret best kept safe by the ignorance of all."

"Vodard Ryce did this," Antiquity said.

"The titanium is from his mined mountains," Sadiya agreed. "He did not build these though. That would be beyond him. He was a powerful Celestial but he would not have the ability or the machinery to produce these. CyTak-5, who built this place, stored these mechs, and assigned you as its warden? And why has no one found it?"

The bot spun in the air, considering. "The Rose King of Bayt al-Hikma programmed me. He was a most astute master." The bot paused. "As to your last question, I cannot fully answer as it would be conjecture. I can share that my programming kept a magnetic seal about the entire room, one that could only be deactivated by a certain key. Since you are here, I believe one of you possessed said key."

"Your sword," Antiquity said. Sadiya nodded. "Then the Rose King knew your weapon's previous owner. Wheels within wheels, indeed."

Sadiya said nothing, gazing upward at the towering mechs.

"Well, we need to get them out of here!" Antiquity said, excited, already thinking how their might would help her cause. "There has to be a way. CyTak-5, can you conduct a system check on these mechs?"

The bot left them, flying to the first mech. Then a second. A third. As it went, the bot scanned their innards. When it returned, Antiquity was not prepared for the results.

"They are nonfunctioning."

"Dead?" Antiquity said, shocked. They couldn't be. "They have no power?"

"They have cells and those cells do contain power, although based on fuel levels I believe they would not function for long without another fuel source being introduced," the bot said. "They do possess enough power for pilots to fly them from this room that has housed them for so long."

"Then what is the problem? How are they dead?"

"They have no memory," CyTak-5 said. "They are nonfunctioning because they lack the operating system needed to connect to a pilot."

Antiquity stood there, stunned. She needed these mechs. Needed them in the worst way. The excitement of discovering this room with its treasure died inside of her, leaving her cold, angry, and even more confused. There were new problems to navigate. The operating system was one of them, sure, but she lacked the pilots to fly them from Bayt al-Hikma. From the old videos shot before the Splinter War, she knew pilots were recruited at an early age—and that had not happened in Solomon Fyre for decades. Not that she would have been one of them with her inability to fly. She ignored that thought, thinking on the moment. Attaining the right operating system to bring them to life had to happen first, and there was only one entity that could help her with that, a bot who had already helped achieve this.

"CyTak-5, when we leave and close the door, will the room protections be reinstalled?"

"They will, per my programming."

"We need Chekker," Antiquity said, already taking the stairs two at a time, adrenaline pushing her toward the surface and a return to Saph Fyre. "We need his help in figuring out how to make this work. He will know best."

Sadiya kept up. "We must be wary. This is a dangerous secret to know. If it falls into the wrong hands, it could be disastrous for Erth."

Almost forgetting the final words of Vodard Ryce in her excitement, Antiquity stopped and turned back to the bot. CyTak-5 spun in the air, waiting on them. "CyTak-5, what is so special about the designation number of your name?"

The bot clicked as if processing the question and choosing what to say. "I am five."

"But what is so special about your number?" Antiquity pressed. "Does the five mean anything?"

"It is a number given me when created."

"Did you know a man named Vodard Ryce?" Antiquity asked, hoping to unlock the secret of the bot's number.

"I did not."

Antiquity mulled it over, thinking, but then turned, focused on her return to the sunlight. The cryptic words of the bot bothered her but she had other worries to consider. When they regained the staircase's top, the door slid open once more and they returned to the first floor of the House of Wisdom. Sadiya touched the tip of her sword to the mech's enormous thumb. The door closed again, hiding its secret once more.

They left the House of Wisdom then, the late afternoon dimming to orange and sunset's eventual purples and pinks. Antiquity was already trying to figure out how to best leverage the power she had found and make it her own, to free the people of Erth from Royal Declarion Wit, his Lion, and the Imperium. The discovered secret threatened to overwhelm her. She would have been running if she had not needed Sadiya to open the tunnel. They rushed down the stairs of the House of Wisdom, around the graveyard with its roses and thorns, toward the wall with its hidden tunnel—and Antiquity slid to stop on the gravel of the path.

A black-cloaked figure stood under the tulip tree.

Broad-shouldered and unmoving, hands folded within the robe and head bowed as if asleep or in prayer, the man glanced up at them, black eyes as cold as winter's night. He wore his beard close-cropped to his chiseled features, face weathered by time and life. Antiquity had been around many different kinds of men but this one exuded danger the others lacked.

He lowered his cowl then, tilting his head with respect.

"Welcome home, Will Master," his deep voice intoned, little warmth behind it. "The years have been far too many, my *namur.*"

Antiquity waited for Sadiya to draw her sword, to fight the man, to bring him low so they could escape and return to Saph Fyre.

Instead, the *arabi* bowed her head in return.

And offered her wrists for binding.

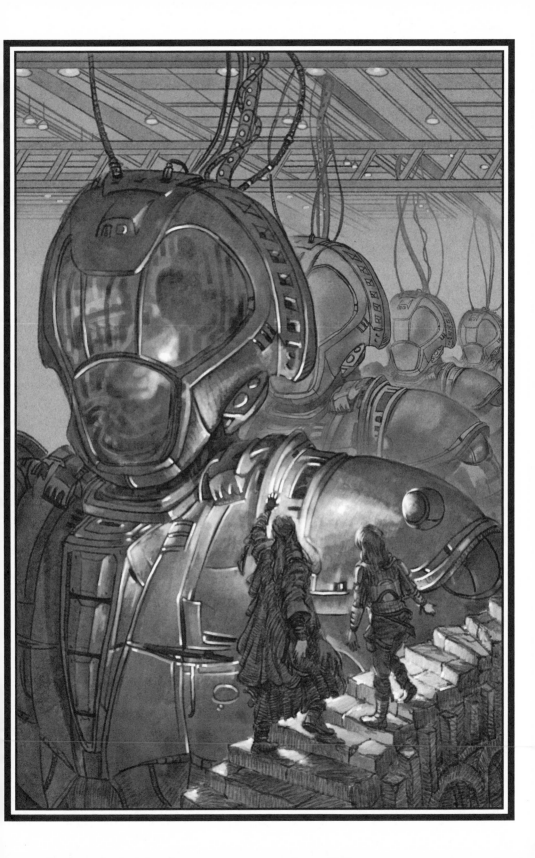

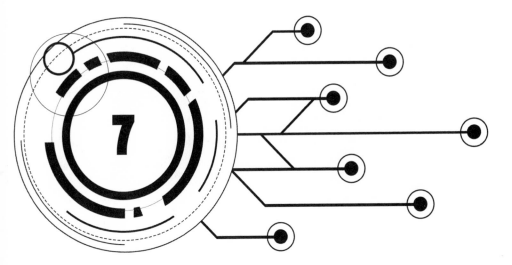

7

A ntiquity paced like a caged desert lion, seething.

Sadiya exhibited the opposite, sitting in repose in their shared cell, unmoving and eyes closed as she prayed. If Antiquity could have shaken her to gain answers, she would have. Venting her anger at someone—anyone—would have helped. She knew it was useless though. Sadiya had said very little since their capture, refusing to answer all questions put to her. The guards had merely deposited them behind bars. Since then, the silence had unnerved Antiquity even more than Sadiya's lack of response.

Antiquity thought back to the capture. The robed older man had not shown a weapon. He had not even threatened them. When Sadiya offered her wrists, the man merely laughed, a deep-throated and pleasing sound, quite odd given his gruff appearance. He walked from beneath the tulip tree and down the pathway—right by them without a word—without so much as a glance backward. He vanished around the

House of Wisdom. Sadiya had followed, nodding for Antiquity to do the same. Once they left the rose garden through a rounded gate in the thick wall, two dozen bearded men with weapons drawn surrounded them, an escort.

Their captors took them to the Rose Stronghold, the giant tower lording over all of Bayt al-Hikma. *Arabi* watched them pass but their curiosity faded with the robed man's stern looks. They entered the tower proper and, blindfolded, were led up several series of stairs and placed in a cell.

The cell could only be called that due to the locked door.

The room reminded her of Vodard Ryce's home, beautiful and comfortable. Art hung on the walls. Rugs covered the floor. A table and chair were against one wall; two beds, pillows, and blankets on the other. Fruit, dried meats, and small goblets of wine awaited on two silver trays.

She couldn't tell if all prisoners were treated with such care. Or if it was because of Sadiya. Ultimately, it didn't matter, she realized.

Either way, she couldn't escape.

"We should discuss nothing. This is a tower of many ears." Sadiya glanced around to illustrate the problem. "Sleep. No one will come for us this day. Argument will keep them busy until morning," she said as the afternoon outside the barred window purpled to twilight, when Antiquity should have returned to Saph Fyre.

Antiquity asked a flurry of questions then, not mentioning their meeting and quest. Sadiya answered none of them. Instead, she went into a trance, eyes closed, breathing slowed, movement still. Starving, Antiquity went to eat the food and sip at the wine. Wondering about what would happen was pointless. Instead, she thought of her friends. She wondered what they were doing. Were they worrying about her being gone? Would they risk looking for her? Chekker would be the voice of reason while the twins would want to find her. She doubted Manson had come to his senses, still angry at their last exchange. The worst part of being in the cell was that without her, Saph Fyre would be vulnerable. She was the only person who could operate it. She hoped her friends would prevent it from falling into the wrong hands.

Antiquity was sure of one thing though. The mechs she discovered below the House of Wisdom had to remain secret.

She wondered anew about the robed man and who he was.

Antiquity fell asleep with those thoughts.

She awoke just after dawn pinked the sky. Sadiya stared at her, sword in her lap.

"They did not take your sword," Antiquity pointed out.

"Nor would they," Sadiya said, taking a deep breath. She exhaled it with slow calm. "Even my former mentor would have tasted its blade, although the outcome would certainly have been in question from the moment our weapons met."

Antiquity shook her head. "You are speaking now, eh?"

"Today is for words, yes."

"That robed man was your mentor? But he arrested us anyway?"

"He is named Mir Muhktar. He is a complicated man, a Will Master in service to the Rose Crown, making him a religious figure as well as a political one," Sadiya said, fingering the rose- and thorn-scrawled cross guard of her weapon. "Before I left Bayt al-Hikma, he taught at the Airtafae Madrasa, the most prestigious university for mastering the Will. I, his student. He was a powerful figure in those influential circles. He has been placed in a most unusual set of circumstances since I left, one that will test his loyalty and his faith."

"You are speaking in riddles again," Antiquity growled. Manson wasn't the only one who found it annoying. "Please, what have we gotten ourselves into?"

"We will go before Rose King Sayf al-Din this morning," the *arabi* said.

"And?"

"He is a young king. Rash and impulsive. I will not speculate how it will go, Antiquity," Sadiya said. "The former king, whose grave I knelt at, would hear all arguments and uncover wisdom. I do not think his son practices life that way."

"If you knew the old king, did you know this son?" Antiquity asked.

"I did. A long time ago."

The *arabi's* wistful tone made it clear she didn't want to talk about it. A void of silence returned, but anxiety rushed in to fill it. Secrets extended to the royal family of Bayt al-Hikma, it seemed. She didn't say anything—the listening ears of the tower, as Sadiya had put it—but Antiquity wondered how close the Rose King was with the Imperium and if they were in danger of being transferred into enemy hands. Bayt al-Hikma had long been a free stronghold. But they had no love for one another and it was only their beneficial trade agreement and the *arabi* technological and martial might that had kept the Imperium at bay for a century.

After minutes of Antiquity pacing again, a knock came at the door. She stopped. The door's locking mechanism tumbled and turned within the stone before the door opened and a robed and veiled young woman entered.

"It is my great honor to escort you," she said, eyes demurely down.

Sadiya stood from her cushions, sword vanishing again. "Thank you for your service. We are honored by your presence."

The woman left the doorway. Sadiya followed. Antiquity did the same, straightening her own robe and veil. The newcomer paid no attention to Antiquity, already walking to a set of stairs that would take them down through Airtafae al-Hisn. Guards met them on the first floor, weapons drawn and taking up positions in front as well as behind. None of this seemed to bother Sadiya; she acted as though they didn't exist and strode through the hallways as if she owned them.

The throne chamber of Airtafae al-Hisn was as grandiose as its surrounding rooms, halls, and city. Antiquity expected it but was still awed by it. She had never been amid such grandeur. Massive statues lined both sides of the thoroughfare that led to the throne at the room's far end, each reverent stone figure bearing the load of the ceiling and each different from the one next to it—kings, paladins, scholars, and even several robed Will Masters. The high vaulted ceiling between the carved columns exhibited exquisite art tiles, a mosaic created with delicate care. None of the statues were women, Antiquity noted, recalling the criticisms Manson had made about Sadiya carrying a sword. In this part of the world, Antiquity and her *arabi* companion were heretics for very different reasons, both soon to stand before the most powerful man in Bayt al-Hikma.

The guards led them past the carved personages—those stone eyes following them, it seemed—as well as dozens of attending *arabi* who watched them with mixed animosity and curiosity. Antiquity ignored them, keeping her eyes ahead.

To the Rose King.

Light falling on him from sky-glass set in the wall behind him, Sayf al-Din sat rigid upon a marble throne raised above the hall's polished floor. He was younger than she expected—quite unlike the men who ruled in Solomon Fyre—his close-cropped black beard showing no signs of grey and his face free of wrinkles. He wore a loose-fitting shirt tucked into a wide black belt, the latter buckled with an open-petaled gold rose above black baggy pants tucked into shining black boots. He glared at the two women as they approached, rage in his dark eyes.

To his left, a tall, thin black-skinned and grey-bearded paladin stood, bearing a round shield upon his back and two hands upon the pommel of a curved sword whose blade touched the dais. On his right, Will Master Mir Muhktar watched, stoic as stone.

Antiquity realized she was sweating beneath her robe. She had no idea what to expect. But the fact that the Rose King had requested their audience with so many people watching meant he wanted this meeting to be public—for whatever purpose, she couldn't guess.

The *arabi* woman and the guards who brought them departed, leaving Antiquity and Sadiya at the base of the stairs leading up to the throne.

Antiquity had no idea what to do.

"Take those robes off," Sayf al-Din ordered Antiquity, eyes burning into her and his voice carrying to all who watched. "You are an affront to our culture, unbeliever."

The room had gone deathly silent. She looked to Sadiya, who nodded. Antiquity disrobed, the black silks coming off easily and dropping to the floor, unveiling her Solomon Fyre clothing, her origins now known to all.

It had an unexpected result. It empowered her. Fear of the unknown dropped away. Once again she was the girl who stood up to her grandmother and the Dreadths alike. With no more need for the disguise, she felt able to stand before Sayf al-Din and his burning gaze.

"And *you*," the Rose King hissed at Sadiya. "Return what you stole. Now."

"I will not," the *arabi* woman said, the steel in her voice carrying to all corners of the room. "Theft did not bring it to my side, rather it was a gift from a dying man who knew his end came on swift wings, a man whose most burdening secret had to be protected from those who would subvert it to their own ends." In one smooth motion, she withdrew her sheathed sword for all to see. "No hand not of my own shall touch it."

"Insolence!" the paladin said, hands upon his sword trembling with anger. "How dare you lie to your king!"

"The only lie here is that which slithers over your tongue and out between your teeth, Rukh al-Za," Sadiya said, her voice carrying as strongly as the king's. "I will not hear your voice again or respond in kind."

"How dare yo—"

"Quiet, Rukh," the Rose King said, eyeing Sadiya with disdain. "Why have you returned?"

"The All-Father compelled it. The Will required it."

"You and your precious Will," Sayf al-Din spat. "I remember it all too well. A riddle without answer. You have never known your place. You will tell me what I want to know, or I will pry it from you until your tongue is yanked from your corpse."

"We come looking for allies. But I see your past prevents you from seeing the importance of my visit. Threatening is a child's ploy. A higher power guides. Erth is at a tipping point. I am here on its behalf," Sadiya said, looking first at Mir Mukhtar and then around the room at those in attendance. "The young woman at my side has seen her grandmother killed by the Imperium, her family name destroyed, and has spent days fleeing those who find her a danger. To their power, to their star-strewn hegemony. She has knowledge that can free peoples and planets."

"We know who she is," the Rose King said, pointing at Antiquity. "She is an enemy of Bayt al-Hikma, an Angelus of Solomon Fyre and wanted for questioning by the Imperium."

"She is that, and much more," Sadiya said.

"Yes, she is much more," Rukh intervened. "She is a murderer, from a cursed family. She tried to kill Royal Declarion Wit and is responsible for dozens of Celestial deaths. Sire, kill her now and be done with it."

"'When the mongoose invades the den of the fire-cobra,'" Sadiya quoted, "'do not be surprised when fangs sink deep.'"

"Do not quote *that book* to me," Sayf al-Din growled. "I know it."

"Then you also know the Imperium is the mongoose."

"I know one thing," the Rose King said, sitting higher in his throne. He gestured to the side, where guards awaited orders. "I doubt the Royal or his Royal governor brother would like to be called that."

A door opened in the wall. Tall, thin men moved into the hall, all carrying combat gear and laz-rifles slung over shoulders. They wore the bright and shiny technology and weapons of the stars—Celestial soldiers of the Imperium.

And the Lion led at their forefront. Royal Declarion Wit's bounty hunter stopped beneath one of the pillars, eyes sparkling with the knowledge that he had caught up with his prey. The memory of the assassin slashing Jackson Dreadth and his lifeblood spilling free still haunted Antiquity. The Lion grinned with shattered teeth. She went cold. He called a halt to his guard retinue. He held no weapons; he didn't need to. They would not attack her. Not while within the Rose King's hall, the Celestials unwilling to accidentally start a war, instead waiting on permission to carry out their orders.

A range of emotions gripped Antiquity, confusion the worst of them. The Lion had been invited to the hall at the behest of Sayf al-Din. That much seemed clear. Had the Lion found Saph Fyre? Were her friends killed? Would the Rose King hand her over to the Royals? Would Sadiya finally fight? Questions paralyzed her with no answers.

"I see the fear in your eyes, Angelus," Sayf al-Din said, nodding as if it had been expected. "Maybe you can answer. Why are you and the traitor here? No riddles from you, I bet. Perhaps I will spare you from the Celestials if you please me."

"I will never tell you," Antiquity said, voice smaller than she wanted.

"You do not have a choice in the matter. Not once we are done here," the Rose King said, grinning without humor. He leaned forward. "Where is your mech? Yes, yes, I know of your mech. It has been all over the vid-views. An impressive machine. I understand why the Imperium wishes it destroyed. Can't have a new army rising from the sandy ashes of the old. But with certain . . . friends, perhaps we can help one another."

"No."

"Very well, two traitors then," the Rose King said, sitting back.

"Sire, you do not want to do this," Will Master Mir Muhktar finally spoke. He had said nothing or even moved since Antiquity and Sadiya entered the throne room, but he obviously felt the need to do so now. "Let me speak with my former student. Alone."

"She may be your former student, but she is no longer under your protection," Sayf al-Din said. The Rose King sat up straighter, waving aside the other's words. "She has forsaken her family, her people, and you. She has no rights."

"My Rose King," the Will Master said, leaning forward ever so slightly as if he were talking to a child. He whispered further discussion. The hall was not privy to the words being spoken. It was clear Rukh al-Za could hear what was being said; the paladin flushed with anger as the conversation continued.

"No, Mir! She will not be given those considerations!"

"Once the All-Father has ordained a Will Master, the religious and kingdom laws are quite clear," Mir Muhktar said, this time loud enough for all.

"I want justice!"

"For a Will Master, justice comes by the hand of the *Allamah*."

"How convenient—the protégé protected by her once master," Sayf al-Din scoffed. He pointed at the Will Master. "You will arrest her immediately and let the law lead you to the conclusion I have already come to. She has stolen from my family, and for years she has borne a weapon against the tenets of the All-Father and those who follow Him," the Rose King said, growing angrier with every uttered word.

"She can be held accountable for that," the Will Master said, keeping his voice strong yet calm. "After the process of the law has been fulfilled."

"Then disarm her. Now. Return the blade to me," Sayf al-Din ordered. "And fulfill your role as leader of the *Allamah*."

Before Mir Muhktar responded, Sadiya moved to stand upon the bottom step leading to the throne, drawing all eyes. There she turned to face the hall and those who watched, eyes hard above the veil.

"The Rose King has asked me to relinquish a weapon, a gift of love. It is one I have carried since it was bequeathed to me, an honor I accepted and one I have carried righteously. As a woman who follows the All-Father, I am forbidden by law from carrying any weapon that can be used to cause harm to others." The *arabi's* voice carried to the far reaches of the throne room. She lifted her sword high for all to see. "A weapon is nothing without its wielder though. We are one. I will not accept theft of the gift by any hands, especially those of my brother—as our father gave his sword to me of free will with kindness.

"I am Sadiya al-Din, daughter of Rose King Baz al-Din, sister to Sayf al-Din and Mohab al-Din, princess of Bayt al-Hikma, and rightful wielder of my father's legacy. I will not be intimidated for executing his final wish."

Then Sadiya tore off her robe in a flourish that left the black silks floating on the air, to gently fall to the ground.

"Ancient laws upheld only by tradition are not laws at all. I will not be oppressed.

"I will not be silenced. I will be who I was born to be.

"And the All-Father will guide me as He has always done."

Shock changed to angry growls and even shouting. Antiquity couldn't believe her ears. For the first time, she saw Sadiya without her culture's black silks—strong, regal cheekbones and full lips, close-fitting black clothing over whip-thin strong limbs, and braided black hair falling down her back. It was clear no one had recognized Sadiya for who she was beyond her brother and small court, one of thousands of women wearing the black robes of an *arabi* woman. Now she stood exposed before them all, sword in hand, defying her brother the Rose King. It was more than that though. She was defying an entire culture, her own. Antiquity now better understood why Sadiya had gone into exile.

If the Rose King had been angry before, he was livid now. "How dare you remove your black robes in public for all to see!" Sayf al-Din yelled, echoing many of the men in the hall. "Defiler! Heretic!"

"I am of royal blood and I have the right to speak," Sadiya argued.

"You are no one! Cursed to death as our forefathers swore! Rukh, kill her!"

Rukh moved from the raised dais even as his guards joined him, all advancing with weapons drawn. The room held its breath, even Will Master Mir Muhktar, who had clearly chosen not to interfere. Drawing the sword once belonging to her father, Sadiya waited. She did not move, eyes never leaving those who circled her. Antiquity held her breath. Even after what she witnessed in Holstead at Beven el

Ordett's mercantile store, Antiquity didn't know how Sadiya would be able to take on so many trained guards at once with only a sword. It didn't seem right.

On silent feet, Sadiya prowled like a tiger then, muscles taut and limbs corded, watching how the others reacted to her steps. The guards surrounded her with equal measure, hemming her into an airtight circle, one from which she couldn't possibly escape. The *arabi* held her sword ready.

And closed her eyes—lips moving.

A prayer? Part of her connecting to the Will? Antiquity didn't know.

Rukh al-Za walked around the outside of the guards. He wielded his own curved sword. On his left arm was the round shield, a bloomed rose etched into the center of the titanium. The paladin taunted Sadiya, hoping she would look his way—just long enough for his guards to take advantage.

Sadiya was not distracted. She moved this way and that from the closing guards, keeping them off balance, but her dark eyes took in the entire room and that included Rukh and his guards.

"Attack!" Rukh al-Za commanded, feeling the time was right.

Antiquity waited for the inevitable death to fall upon Sadiya. It never happened. One moment she was there within the circle; the next moment, gone like smoke on a breeze. The guards looked about, bewildered, and Antiquity did the same. Sadiya had vanished. In that briefest of seconds when chaos gripped Rukh and his sentries, one of them fell, sword dropping from nerveless fingers, blood bursting from a severed artery in his neck. The others looked to the dying man, some even falling back and breaking the circle. It was all the distraction Sadiya needed. The Will Master was even faster than before, a blur of motion, there one moment and striking before on to the next.

Her blade carved darkness from the light, a swath of ink too fast for the eye to see.

More guards fell, their blood slicking the floor. Unlike the first guard whom she had killed to confuse the others, Sadiya only wounded them. Howls and groans echoed even as hands and feet were cut from limbs. Sadiya had become a storm, sweeping through the men as if they were paper.

Before a minute ended, the circle of guards was no more. Sadiya disarmed the last one, pinning him to the floor by his neck. She crouched over her last fallen prey, crimson running the length of her black blade, eyes glimmering at Rukh al-Za.

She had saved the paladin for last. It was not lost on Rukh. The way Sadiya moved mimicked a deadly desert viper—slow tension ready to strike like lightning. The two stepped around and over broken bodies, paying them no mind. Rukh al-Za was an older man but he had years of experience. Sadiya lacked the experience but possessed youth and had been taught by a Will Master. Antiquity wondered what would happen if Sadiya won.

She worried more about a loss.

Then Sadiya and Rukh were at each other, swords shattering the stillness.

The room watched as the two battled. Antiquity had never seen anything like it. Both were precise in their movements but fighting at such a furious speed it was hard to witness any particulars. Rukh possessed height over Sadiya; she had a lower center of gravity. One would strike, the other parried, and both would spin away from the other. Again, it happened, a different type of attack; again, it left the room stunned when they parted. Antiquity realized they were testing one another, trying to find weakness. She couldn't fathom the amount of training that had brought both of them here.

The Rose King sat upon his throne, eyes on fire for his sister's death. Mir Muhktar watched, a silent apparition of darkness, his arms folded within his robes. The Will Master kept out of the confrontation, showing no emotion.

The battle continued.

With a feint to her right, Sadiya moved left, meeting his sword with her own as she came inside his defenses to slash his side. But he was ready. While she overextended, he elbowed her in the face, sending her backward. She blocked his following thrust—but he had planned for that too, his momentum carrying forward into a solid kick to her chest.

Sadiya slammed into one of the carved pillars, her breath exploding.

"Your mentor did a poor job of training you," Rukh growled. He pointed his sword at the older Will Master. "I know his style. You fight like him."

Sadiya wiped the blood from her nose.

"It's the last time you touch me," she said, bringing her sword up.

The two met again. A flurry of titanium followed. Neither seemed to have the upper hand. Antiquity could tell they would not back down, but the fight had taken a different turn, one where both were breathing hard from their exertions, their weapons meeting less frequently than before. It would come down to whoever made the most egregious mistake.

Then overconfident, tiring, or both, the paladin thrust as he had several times, to push Sadiya back, to give himself more room to maneuver.

She didn't react the way she had before.

Instead of giving him more distance she shortened it, slashing the sword aside even as she kicked low.

The strike to Rukh's knee bent it forcibly to the side.

He crumpled, crying out.

In a blink of an eye, the fight was over.

"It appears as though I have learned a few things since I left my old master," Sadiya said, slapping his sword aside. She stood over the defeated Rukh, the old man breathing hard and glaring up at her, placating hands out in front but his eyes baleful.

"The All-Father has judged. He is with me today, Brother," Sadiya said, never taking her eyes off of the dangerous paladin.

The Rose King clenched his teeth. "You will be stoned for that."

"I am a Will Master," Sadiya said, stepping back. She kicked Rukh's sword away. It clattered across the floor. "I will not die by your hand, Brother. The Will has forbidden it, this day anyway." She stopped and turned, her voice filling the great hall. "The Rose King has no authority over my life. The All-Father has chosen. The law protects a Will Master to carry out the wisdom He sees fit. I will see that Will done." She paused, lifting her sword for all to see. "When I received my father's gift, he said the day would come when it would unlock the very power of Erth, beyond the walls of Bayt al-Hikma. He said I would understand its forging, from the hottest sands of the desert, because I too would be forged in the heat of battle."

She lifted the sword for all to see. "The sword is no longer my father's weapon. I accept its honor and burden today, before you all. It is the Will that names the great swords of the past. It is my right to do so here in our present.

"I make it my own. And name it Syd Alyamin—Oathmaster."

"Sire, do not let this deadly woman leave," the Lion said, stepping forward. His Celestial guards were already moving toward Sadiya and Antiquity. "The Will Master is too dangerous to be left alive. Give me the Angelus as well as her friend. Royal Declarion Wit will deal with them as they deserve."

"You will hold your ground, Royal Lion," Mir Muhktar said,

paralyzing those who moved toward his former student. He had brought his Will to bear to make a point. "The Imperium shall not intercede in this. The law forbids it. If you did, there would only be more bloodshed this day and those after, and not of your making, I feel."

"You may regret this. In the not too distant future, *savage*," the Lion cursed the final word when he saw Sayf al-Din would not intercede. He gave a short bow to the Rose King before ordering his Celestials from the room.

He would not give up so easily, Antiquity knew.

"The last I checked, Sayf al-Din sits upon the throne of Bayt al-Hikma," the Rose King said, standing. The Lion gave him a final look. "If you wish to maintain our relationship, please notify Royal Declarion Wit that we will give Antiquity Angelus to the Imperium once we question her. And question her we will, thoroughly."

"If you harm her, another will sit on that throne," the Lion threatened.

"Threats are for the weak," Sayf al-Din said. "Action matters."

"Action is what you will get then."

The Lion swept from the room, face flushed with outrage. The Celestial retinue followed him. Before he left, the Lion gave Antiquity a dark look. She knew the other would not stop until he had captured her. What that meant for Bayt al-Hikma, she didn't know. She knew one thing though. Sayf al-Din had kept her from the Imperium.

What that reason could be beyond getting Saph Fyre, she could only guess at.

The Rose King viewed his sister anew.

"I may be hampered by doctrine but there are those in the streets of Bayt al-Hikma who bend the rule of law to their own use," he said. "Flee, if you want, Sister. Will Master or not, woman or not, you won't see another day on Erth."

"I will do what I must," Sadiya said.

"Then leave. Guards, seize Antiquity Angelus."

Sadiya moved to Antiquity's side as guards tentatively approached. They gave the *arabi* woman a wide berth. She ignored them, leaning in close. "I will come for you when I can. You must promise. On these things, all future events hinge—stay strong and do not die. My brother will not kill you. You are valuable while Saph Fyre remains hidden. You are the mech's pilot—its only viable pilot—and your strength must keep him at bay. He will not torture you, but he will try to gain information. Through any means necessary. He will try to find the others he has seen on the vid-views and use them against you. I will try to prevent that from happening."

"I am to be a prisoner here?" Antiquity asked, dreading the answer but already knowing it to be true.

"Not for long if I have my way," Sadiya said. "The All-Father has given me His Will."

"Will that be enough?"

Sadiya smiled sadly. "It will have to be."

"Keep my friends safe, even Manson," Antiquity said, head swirling with the enormity of what was happening. The sting of anxious anger threatened tears. "They do not deserve being killed or even tortured. I am the one who led them here."

"I will do what I can," Sadiya said, gripping Antiquity's hands.

Then the *arabi* turned, striding from the hallway. No one moved to stop her. Antiquity stared after her friend, hoping she would survive whatever city assassins the Rose King would undoubtedly hire. Mir Muhktar's words still resonated; he had made sure no one could stop Sadiya while within the Rose Stronghold, the laws of their religion sacrosanct. Sadiya held her head high as she went, as if no one on Erth had threatened her life in any way.

One person knelt as she passed, knees to the floor, head lowered. Then another. And another. Until the entire room's attendance knelt, heads bowed in respect for a daughter and sister all had thought lost.

The Rose King and Rukh al-Za whispered with one another, watching her go.

The paladin limped from the room.

Bowing to a king who ignored him, Will Master Mir Muhktar vanished through a side door—giving Antiquity a short nod before doing so.

With Sadiya gone out the hall's far doors, a fear Antiquity had not felt in a long time crept over her, made all the more poignant when guards bound her hands behind her back and pushed her from the room.

For the first time since fleeing Solomon Fyre, Antiquity was alone.

) ◗ ● ◖ (

The girl plays in the sand, letting the hot desert fall through her little fingers.

The day is a beautiful one but all days are gorgeous to her when she is outside with her parents. They left their eyrie that morning with a small picnic, heading to the edge of the desert where few go. It is one of her first memories, one that fills her heart with love and dread. Her father has a present for her. She is giddy with excitement. She rarely gets gifts of any kind. She understands her family fell out of favor with others who live in Solomon Fyre and that continues to this day. They have lost a great deal while other families seem to have more. She suspects that her real last name is not Grey but far different—but she doesn't have the courage to ask because it would only make her father angry and her mother sad.

She knows what not to say. Her grandmother taught her.

She is only seven years old.

"Antiquity, are you ready?" her father asks. He smiles like the rising sun.

"I am! I am!" she shouts, jumping around, clutching her hands before her. Her mother wipes away the sand that has been kicked up on their picnic blanket.

"Wait here," he says. With a skip and a jump that makes her giggle, her father disappears around a large boulder.

She can barely contain the anticipation.

When he reappears, he is holding a small airbike, a perfect size for only one of the three.

She cannot believe it.

"Where did you get it, Daddy?" she breathes.

"From an old junker, at the edge of the city. I suspect he didn't know me. Here you go, Sweet Rose," he says, grinning all the more. She loves it when he calls her that. "Want to try it? It will take some practice but I think you are old enough now."

She does want to try it. More than anything. She has had to watch other kids playing with one another and each other's toys. She is not allowed to play. Every time she tries, she is pushed away, told to play alone with her own toys. But she has very few, and the ones she has are ancient and broken. The airbike is her first real gift. One that can't be taken away from her.

He holds the airbike steady, the machine floating above the sand. He nods to her. She swings her leg over the seat. The airbike bounces a bit but stays aloft. She looks back at her mother, whose hazel eyes are shining with happiness.

It takes all her effort but she holds on to the bars to steer while getting used to the seat. Her father points to the throttle and braking systems. She tries to memorize it all but it's too much. She depresses the throttle as he lets go. She falls off. Determined, she gets back up, dusts herself off, and lifts the airbike up herself. She gets back on. She focuses on balance, on gripping the handles, to stay on the bike. She throttles it up again like her father showed her. The bike responds, edging forward slowly above the sands. She wobbles *a bit, fighting the gravity that threatens to unseat her. She focuses while giving it a bit more thrust. It moves faster. She holds on, excitement building, learning how to balance more effectively even as she controls where the airbike goes.*

She learns quickly. Soon she is flying over the sands. She circles their picnic location, the sands flying up every which way. She is giddy with happiness. She can't hold it in. She laughs and laughs at her new freedom—her new toy.

Grinning, her mother hugs her father from behind as both watch her.

It is a fun day.

"Grey!"

The voice shatters the moment. Scared, the girl tries to brake the airbike. She does it too quickly. It jerks her forward, and she teeters off the seat to the sands. Fighting tears, she stands up even as her mother rushes to her side.

Her father is not there though, as he usually is when she is hurt.

Instead, he faces the owner of the voice.

A group of men are walking down the arid hillside from the direction of the city. The girl has not seen them before. But they are like many in the main part of the city beneath the eyries where the girl and her family live. They are poor. Broken. And angry about it.

She realizes her father stands between the men and his family.

"You should not be here," the man growls. He points at her new airbike. "And she should not have that toy. You are Grey. You are nothing. You own nothing but your former home. You pay forever for what you did."

"Why must my family pay for the sins of the past?" her father asks. "For what my wife's ancestors did or did not do? I am not them. My wife and daughter are not them."

The man leading the group walks up to her father. He is larger and muscled. He has lost much of his hair while his red beard is bushy and unkempt. The girl has seen people look at her strangely—sometimes even with disgust—but never the hate glimmering in this man's eyes. He gets into her father's face, staring him down.

"You married that half-breed there, had a child with her. Worse, your family destroyed our city. You are shamed. To stop it from happening again."

The other men join the first. They surround her father. Like all children, she knows a fight is going to happen when she sees it.

"Please," her dad says, hands up. "Not here. We don't want any trouble."

"You shouldn't have left your precious eyrie then, Grey."

With that, the man strikes. A heavy fist crashes into her father's face. He goes down like a dropped doll. The girl screams. So does her mother. As the other men descend on her helpless father, they kick him even as he tries to defend himself. It is clear he will not walk away.

"Run, Marxa!" her father yells, already bloody.

Her mother doesn't hesitate. She picks the girl up with wiry strength. They are fleeing. Jostling. Chaotic. Her mother is crying. Fear unlike any the girl has known blooms inside and she begins to cry as well. She doesn't look back for her father because she's afraid of what she might see.

"Ox, get the woman!" she hears the leader scream.

"I won't kill her!"

"A little fun then before I do the deed."

The girl looks back as a scrawny man runs after them. Ox closes quickly and grabs her mother by the hair. He yanks her back so hard all three tumble to the hot sands. Her mother lets her daughter go as she fights back, punching as hard as she can. The man gets on top of her. She bites their attacker even as she tries to blind him with her fingernails. It only angers him further. He grabs a nearby rock and smashes her head.

Her mother goes limp.

Ox drags her back down the hill, behind the boulder that had hid the girl's gift.

But she is already running, back toward the city.

She cries until the world is a blur. She cries until she can't breathe. She cries until her legs burn with agony and she falls into the arms of a stranger on the first city street she comes to.

She cries for hours at what she has seen, in the arms of her grandmother. Until sleep takes her.

The horror of the memory blends away into a new one.

)◗●◖(

She sits before a giant vid-view, one placed in a hidden room of the eyrie.

Her grandmother is there, thin and hard-edged, eyes blind and the three orbs that help guide her steps swirling overhead. She is irritated; so is the girl. It is another boring lesson filled with tedious information. History, mostly. Current events, sometimes. All woven together to help the girl learn more about their world—its past and its present. The time before the Splinter War and the hardships since. The mechs and their power, and how Erth misses that power. The girl cares little for it all. She wants to be outside and exploring the city with her bot, Chekker. Every day that passes, she resents the lessons more and more. And more and more, her grandmother is increasingly annoyed by her pupil's lack of interest.

The girl is sixteen years old. She sometimes thinks her grandmother is one hundred years old and was born that age.

"You must focus, girl," Vestige Grey says again.

"I still don't understand why any of this is important!" she says. "We are Grey."

Her grandmother sits up straighter, knife-thin. Despite her blindness, her eyes still manage to convey daggers at her granddaughter. "If you say that again, I will slap it from your mouth and keep doing it until you stop. We are only Grey-shamed if we embrace it. I won't let you do that. Not to yourself, not to me, and not to our family."

"Grey-child, listen to your matriarch," Chekker says, the soccer-like

bot hovering in the corner of the room. "The information is important. She means well."

"If she meant well, I would not be in this room," she says. "I'd be outside."

"I know you, Antiquity," Vestige says. "You are wont to do the opposite of what I tell you. Every time you venture into the city and beyond, you place yourself in danger. Every. Time. It is the reason Chekker is your companion, as he was once my guardian so long ago and your mother's guardian as a girl too. You are getting to an age where you want to push beyond the boundaries of your known life for those of the unknown. The only way to truly protect you, my strong-willed granddaughter, is to give you the tools to do so on your own. I will not be here forever. Neither will Chekker. Knowing about your heritage and Erth's history will aid you. One day. Trust me."

"I'm not even supposed to study," she gripes. She knows the words will anger her grandmother, but she doesn't care. She says them anyway. "If people of the city found out about the vid-view, they would take it away. Or worse."

"Again, don't fall prey to being Grey-shamed. It's exactly what they want."

"They could kill us if they knew about the vid-view."

"Then they can't know, can they?" Vestige snaps back.

She remembers the first lessons her grandmother taught her. Of family. Of honor. Of doing the right thing no matter the consequences. And how all three of those things brought low her family name. She remembers hearing the name Saph Fyre and about the other mechs that had once flown alongside her great-grandmother. Saph Fyre had been a large part of her studies right from the beginning. Her grandmother shared secrets, ones that excited the little girl. She was told they must keep their lessons private. They are Grey-shamed and that means no one speaks of their past—but it is still a past that she must learn about. She was enthusiastic at first about the

secrets, about the stories of the great mechs that darkened the skies with
their flight.

Now, much older, the secrets are a boring reminder of what her future
can never be.

For when a family is Grey-shamed, the label exists forever.

"I can hear in your voice you are done for today," her grandmother says.
She stands and the orbs above react accordingly. "Get out of here, scamp.
Enjoy the day. Adventure as you will. Perhaps I will go for a walk as well
and join you later. Will serve these old bones, yes."

The girl frowns, surprised. Her grandmother has never suggested an
adventure.

She is the least adventurous person her granddaughter has ever met.

The thought is gone as quickly as what she learned that day. The girl
races from the room, excited to be done for the day.

She travels the labyrinthine levels of her family eyrie. It is a large com-
plex. Once, it housed hundreds of extended family members, workers, and
assistants.

Now, barely two dozen various Grey-shamed families call it home.

"Grey-child, where do you wish to go?" Chekker asks.

The girl ponders this. The city market, maybe. Or the dragon fountain
where the poorest among them perform plays of past greatness. Or maybe
out to the sands, where she looks across the hot desert and daydreams about
the exciting world that lies beyond. She wonders if she will ever venture
there—into the unknown.

"The sands?" the bot presses.

"Why would you recommend that, Chekker? You've never done so
before."

"Grey-child, perhaps it is because you do what someone tells you not
to do," the bot says, swirling in the air. "Obstinate like your grandmother
during her childhood."

"So you are secretly trying to stop me from venturing out of the city?"

"It is my job to keep you safe. The sands are dangerous."

The girl makes up her mind. She locates her airbike—one that her grandmother gifted when she turned thirteen years old—takes the ele-lift down toward the base of the bluff, and heads out of the eyrie into the late morning sun. Chekker follows. He is her constant companion and her clos-est friend—even closer to her than the twins. Once, the girl thought having the bot's protection was not needed. Until she asked about her parents and her grandmother shared all the details of their murder. It is a memory that hurts, more now that she knows more. Her grandmother had done it to drive home a point—that some Solomon Fyre residents want their family dead for what transpired in the past. The girl never questioned Chekker's role again. After all, she remembers what happened to her parents.

Throttling the airbike, she rides from the eyrie. Something makes her stop. She turns to look at the high, rocky bluff, her family home built along its face and into its depths. Once, her family led Solomon Fyre. Once, mechs used to fly the skies. She can imagine the mechs taking off to fight their last battle, one they never returned from, one that left them vulnerable to the Imperium.

She is about to throttle up the airbike again when she sees her grand-mother. The old matriarch has followed her. She has never done it before, her duties to the eyrie hindering her free time. The girl feels disquiet. Why is she watching now?

She shakes it off. Chekker is allowing her to explore the edge of the des-ert. It will be a fun day. She turns to look back again. Her grandmother is still there. The old woman nods to her. That's not all. She raises a hand also in farewell.

It is one of kindness. Affirmation. And something more.

Pride?

The girl waves to her grandmother and then she's off, blending into the city and its bustling populace. She knows every street, every shop, and every nook and cranny. She rides the airbike, exhilarated by it. It is the only time she feels unfettered from the Grey-shame upon her.

She leaves the city behind, riding down to the edge of the desert. She looks off into the distance, looking for signs of danger.

She notices none.

That's when she sees the giant metal hand sticking out of the sands.

The fingers move and it becomes another memory.

The weight of the mountain and the cavern's darkness press down on her.

She is a part of Saph Fyre now, infused by its technology even as her humanity guides its great power. The past she once hated learning about embraces her as pilot and she has left her home to fight for a future bequeathed by her great-grandmother. It has come at great cost. She has lost her home, her grandmother, and the innocence of her youth. Friends have lost much too. It is not an easy thing rebelling against the Imperium; it is even more difficult to uncover secrets of a world buried long before she was born. She has crossed desert sands, hidden in canyon trenches, and walked beneath redwoods. She has visited the fabled ruins of Luna Gold and watched a Celestial of the Imperium save her. Now she drives the mech carefully through ancient titanium mines bled dry, a young woman in command of rare titanium and tempered heart.

Saph Fyre progresses through the caverns with great care. The mech is powerful but in such close quarters, a cave-in would kill them. Worse, she knows the Lion seeks them. Her friends below require her to keep them safe. Too many lives have been lost—her grandmother, the Dreadth, the Celestial. She can't lose more. Losing more just might undo her. She used to feel strong, invincible.

That was before finding the mech.

Now she knows better. Life is tenuous at best. It can be taken from you in a second.

Saph Fyre looks back the way they have come. Nothing is there. The mines are a labyrinth in the deep. She follows a map supplied by one of the Celestial's dragonfly bots before it ceased working when its master died. She has never known darkness like the one they travel through, claustrophobic in nature. She fights the feelings. They will not serve her and she is responsible for her quest as well as her friends. To lose her way or her mind now would lead to oblivion.

When she spots the first clawed creatures clinging to the mine walls and ceiling, she does not panic. They are small compared to Saph Fyre, about as big as her mech's thumb—six limbs lean and gnarled with muscle, snouts lined with sharp teeth, gimlet eyes flashing. Whether they have gathered because of the mech or because Saph Fyre has entered their territory, the girl doesn't know. It matters not. Either way, she must deal with them if they become aggressive.

They stare at her passage, eyes following. She is careful not to crush those who skitter across the stone. She does not want to provoke the beasts by harming one. Any use of her weaponry could bring the mine crashing down on her. She navigates past them, entering a different corridor, one that is devoid of life.

A mewling sound makes her turn then. The creatures are following her. She continues onward. She hopes they will eventually fall back. They don't. When the first creature leaps from its place on the cavern wall, it lands on the mech's upper arm, raking its claws at the titanium. It does no damage. She shrugs it off. It falls to the stone. It cries out, wounded. She feels bad but is happy it didn't damage Saph Fyre.

But what if a hundred of them attacked?

The arabi *enters the cockpit from below. She is alone. "It looks like we have company, and dark company at that."*

"What are they?" the girl asks.

"Glocks," the arabi says. "Underground dwellers."

"Are they dangerous?"

"Quite, to miners," the other said. "To Saph Fyre? Maybe. As the ore was removed from these mountains and the tunnels created, miners would exterminate whole masses of glocks. They are natural to underground catacombs. Mining simply made more areas for them to live. Now that the mines have run dry of their titanium and all mining efforts have ceased, the creatures are flourishing with no miners killing them."

"What else do you know about these mines?" the girl asks. "Other creatures I should be made aware of?"

"There are bigger threats. In the deep. The bones of the world are ancient and the All-Father mentions the beasts that were here at Creation," the arabi says. "All are big, all would be a threat to Saph Fyre."

The girl is contemplating this when the tunnel ends suddenly—to a massive black void. She has entered a cavern so large she can't see its ceiling, walls, or other side. The floor is cut smooth. Dust swirls up from her every step, the world coated in it.

The glocks have stopped on their own. Instead, they pace back and forth at the tunnel's edge, mewling their low language, eyes glimmering in the dark. Pleased they are not following, the girl breathes a sigh of relief. Saph Fyre looks at the new environs instead. She floods more light into the space. She stands within a huge room, a former miner staging area, massive square pillars holding up the ceiling. Archaic machinery rusts in its corners; refuse litters the ground. It is a world that hasn't been seen in a long time.

"I wonder why the glocks aren't following?" the girl thinks out loud.

The arabi looks out the faceplate, taking it all in. "Perhaps they fear the lingering smell of humanity."

The girl doesn't think so. It's been too long. She drives Saph Fyre forward with caution. The mech's steps echo in the stillness and its blazing light casts strange shadows about the pillars, leaving her more disquieted. The words the arabi shared about the All-Father's beasts in the deep linger and she begins seeing them wherever she looks.

But nothing attacks. The darkness is their only companion. She is starting to feel better about getting out. The glocks have left them alone; the Lion hasn't caught them. The far wall and a new tunnel are now visible, another way to freedom.

That's when a white mass of scales falls heavily upon Saph Fyre. The girl reacts instinctively, yelling in fear, rolling forward and away. The arabi holds on for dear life as up becomes down, down becomes up. The girl brings the mech back level, hoping her friends below are strapped in, and realizes the white mass is a behemoth snake, coils thick and settling about the mech's shoulders and arms. A roar fills the cavern, louder than anything the girl has ever heard. Massive dragon jaws twist into view, rows of teeth razor sharp gleaming in the dark, and huge emerald orbs blink at her, glaring hate.

It is a creature born of speed and lethality, a dragon with a snake's body and tenacity, an animal of unbelievable size.

"Wyvern!" the arabi warns.

The coils of the beast squeeze about Saph Fyre, tiny wings on its back throwing up dust on the air. Pressure systems on the mech blare a warning. The wyvern is crushing the mech, the titanium stressed from the attack.

The wyvern's jaws close down then on the mech's right forearm.

Pain stabs the girl's mind. She yells out in agony. She is one with the mech and she feels what happens to Saph Fyre. She grabs the wyvern below its head, pulling it free from her arm. It twists from her, snapping, trying to get at her neck. She can feel the entire creature wrapping about her—even its tail has coiled about the mech's legs. Thoughts race through the girl. She knows the wyvern will not let go; she has to discover a way to make that happen, and fast.

"In the corner! Look!" the arabi points out.

The girl glances. Stone rubble from the mountain fills the corner, but it's organized in a wide-brimmed circle. White orbs as tall as a human glimmer in its midst.

"We have to get out of here! It's a wyvern's nest!" the arabi *yells.*

"Easier said than done," the girl growls back, trying to get them free. The wyvern has her so wrapped up that she can't direct any of her weapons at the beast.

There has to be something else.

She allows the wyvern to pull her down to the ground. The mech falls, shaking the stone beneath. It has the desired effect.

She is closer to the nest.

She blasts her flamethrower at the nest. The reaction is immediate. The wyvern howls in rage at the threat to her eggs. The dragonkin tightens its anger about the mech more, even as a part of it wants to let go and defend its young. The girl feels the change. The wyvern unwraps just enough to free Saph Fyre's arm. It is exactly what she needed. Using the newfound freedom, she grabs the wyvern by its loosening tail. It is weaker there. Saph Fyre unwinds it further. She throws flame at the nest again. The wyvern screeches—let's go more. The opening Saph Fyre needs is there. The girl smashes the wyvern alongside its thick head with a mech fist, sending the terrible beast limp to the ground.

"Get out. Now!" the arabi *yells.*

The girl doesn't have to be told twice. She flees into a new passageway similar to the one that entered the cavern. A thought occurs to her then. Before the wyvern can give chase, she shoots one of her various cram-missiles at the exit's roof.

The weapon explodes. Rock from above cascades down, blocking any pursuit.

It will stop the beast from giving chase.

It will also slow the Lion from catching his mech prey.

The memory blurs, darkness replacing it. It is a void of alien sentience. Something is not right. The girl is not alone inside Saph Fyre. Another presence fights for her will, to control it. When she battles back, it becomes painful. Blinding hot. She would scream but she can tell she is no longer a participant in her own body. It feels like she is splintering. It feels like hot sand is pouring into her brain and burning it from the inside out.

The pain is the only thing she knows is real. The pain grounds her. The memories vanish. The alien blackness recedes as well.

She is alone in her own mind.

For now.

) ▶ ● ◀ (

When Antiquity opened her eyes, an *arabi* man glared down at her.

"You are tough, Angelus. Tougher than you look."

Heartbeat slamming in her chest, Antiquity looked wildly about, trying to come to grips with reality again. The memories were still thick about her like flies, overwhelming her with emotion. She gritted her teeth. She clenched her fists, back arched against leather restraints keeping her pinned to a table. The room blinded with its whiteness until she noticed medical holograms floating in the air. That wasn't the worst part. She had not thought about the day her parents died in a long time. She fought pain as her heart still wailed. She fought for a recent memory—how she had come here. Then she recognized the man staring at her. Sayf al-Din. The Rose King. Other memories returned to her. Infiltrating the great *arabi* city. Taking stairs beneath the House of Wisdom. The lighting of secret mechs. Her capture. Sadiya's fight.

The Rose King had wasted no time. He ordered Antiquity from the throne room even as Sadiya strode from it.

Antiquity wanted to scream for help but it was too late. Machines hummed about her. Electrodes and wires hung from her. Yelling for help would be in vain. Sayf al-Din had already made up his mind about her fate.

For above her, a hologram of a brain slowly spun in the air, different parts lighting up and becoming more crystalized in resolution.

It took Antiquity a second to realize it was her mind.

"Beautiful, isn't it?" Sayf al-Din remarked. "Your brain, in one spot, and every neural pathway, nerve ending, and, in essence, memory. This is you, floating outside of your body."

"Why are you doing this?" Antiquity breathed.

The Rose King looked at her as if she were a strange insect. "I thought that obvious."

"The mech?"

Sayf al-Din nodded—but not to her. To someone she couldn't see.

A new intrusion began at once. It started as a tender touch, one that probed the edges of her mind, the same sentient void from her last memory. It was another intelligence worming into her mind. Rage came to her aid, pushing away the foreign invader—if not out of her mind, at least preventing it from entering further.

She needed every ounce of her willpower to do so.

"You are strong. Still. But I want you to realize something," the Rose King said, hovering over her so close she could smell the stink on his breath. "As soon as you give in, the pain will stop. I give you my word. But I will have what I wish, make no mistake. Look there," Sayf al-Din said, pointing. She viewed a middle-aged *arabi* man wearing a long white robe just within her vision. He paid her no attention, instead waving his hands this way and that over a digital interface hovering in the air. "He is Abdur Hazim, the Rose Stronghold's expert on all things artificial and intelligent. Even now, you are giving up secrets as we harvest your genetic code. A mech is useless without its pilot, the driver linked to it by body. But a suitable proxy can be built." He paused, his voice a whisper when it returned. "Tell me. Where is the mech? I am no fool. You escaped Solomon Fyre with your great-grandmother's machine. Then you show up here, hunted by the Imperium and accompanied by my sister. I had to let her go but you . . . you know what I wish to know."

"I will never tell you," Antiquity spat. "You will kill me before my memories are stolen from me."

"That could be true. Full memory retrieval is only successful with those people who accept the process." The Rose King leaned back. "This could be easier. Right now, Sadiya is making her way through and out of the city. I do not know where she intends to go. But she is being followed. Make no mistake. I also have others sweeping the countryside, seeking the mech. Without you at its controls, the mech is defenseless, easy for the taking. Either my sister will lead me to Saph Fyre or I will find it on my own."

Antiquity fought the return of the void. It pushed harder but she repelled it. She would never give up her great-grandmother's mech.

No matter what pain came her way.

"The Angelus fights, my Rose King," Abdur Hazim said from the side. "There is still much to retrieve. We have enough for a rudimentary copy. But I need more."

"A copy?" Antiquity gritted between her teeth. "Of what?"

"Of your mind, dear, of your mind," Sayf al-Din said. "For instance, that last memory you had is helping Abdur Hazim bio-wire the new golem so your mech cannot tell the difference between your nervous system and that of your replacement."

"You are making an artificial construct of my mind and body?" Antiquity said, horrified by the idea. By the intrusion. "Golems are illegal in the Imperium."

"I am not part of the Imperium, no matter what the Royals in Euroda think." The Rose King laughed with no humor. "I will do what

I wish. I am taking the necessary genetics from your body to build a golem, one that will be infused with the copy of your mind. Only your genetics and mind can unlock the mech," Sayf al-Din said. "If I am to gain any of its secrets, I must have you. Or some kind of you, at least."

"Then bring the pain, you bastard," Antiquity spat. The Greyshamed anger that had always served her well against bullies came to the fore. "I know pain better than someone as spineless as you will ever feel."

The Rose King frowned darkly. "Very well."

Adrenaline rushing again, Antiquity fought, even as Abdur Hazim pumped a new purple fluid into her veins. She felt it instantly, inducing a fraying at the edges of her will. The mind assault began anew, urgent. More memories swirled out of her subconscious, all threatening to pull her down into their depths where they could be recorded, stolen, and added to the golem's mind that shimmered above her. But she knew what was happening now and that knowledge bolstered her battle against the Rose King and his artificial intelligence expert. Time stopped even as it sped up, and Antiquity slowly felt the loss of herself.

Until the door to the room burst open and Rukh al-Za appeared.

"Sire, we are under attack!" he breathed hard.

"That can't be," Sayf al-Din said, already moving toward the door. "Who? Where?"

"The Imperium," Rukh al-Za said, sword drawn. "They are bombarding our outer walls from the air, while keeping all retaliatory craft grounded. They want the girl. And her mech."

"The Lion. And the Royals," the Rose King snarled. "They are not truly attacking, only making a show of force to get what they want. Tell them we still have the girl but not the mech! Do it, now! We need more time before we hand her over." He pointed at Abdur Hazim.

"I will return shortly. Continue with any means necessary. Even means that are excruciating."

The *arabi* doctor nodded as his king left the room. Abdur Hazim stood and moved to her side. On a screen hovering in the air above Antiquity, he selected various light buttons and intensities. The machine powered up again. Electricity thrummed and entered her body. She jerked from it. She bit down, unwilling to give in to the void—the void became a powerful tiger in her mind, clawing to free the knowledge she possessed.

It was only her mind that prevented its theft.

Long minutes passed. The holographic brain above her continued to fill in, pieces of her being copied and inserted into an artificial intelligence matrix. When Abdur Hazim finished, Sayf al-Din would turn her over to the Imperium.

Antiquity fought as if the world's safety depended on it.

The next time the room's door opened, Antiquity thought she was hallucinating—a blur of spherical chromium flying in, its electric tase slamming into Abdur Hazim and catapulting the doctor into the back wall where he lay broken.

Chekker!

Behind the bot, Kaihli, Elsana, and even Manson rushed in, the twins grinning at her and the Dreadth already moving to undo the restraints on Antiquity.

And behind them all, with sword drawn and wearing her black robes once more, Will Master Sadiya al-Din.

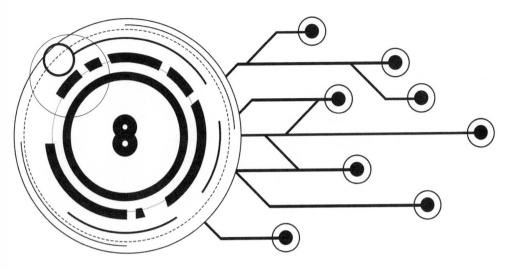

Restraints undone, Antiquity rolled weakly from the table, crying. Manson grabbed her before she could fall, his strength buoying against what the Rose King and his artificial intelligence designer had done. She couldn't find words of gratitude—they were beyond her—but her weak smile and tears told the truth of how she was feeling. Happy to see her friends. To be alive. Clear of the table and the memories. Away from the machinations of Sayf al-Din and what he had planned. The strongest emotion—to be *free*. She shook in the Dreadth's arms even as Sadiya ordered their next steps. Antiquity let her. The *arabi* knew the Rose Stronghold better. Antiquity didn't have to ask about getting out of the city. Sadiya had come for her as promised. Stumbling, Antiquity could barely get one foot in front of the other. Memory of what had been done chased after her, driving the young woman forward.

A torn mind, a broken soul. A part left behind.

"We have to get out of here as quickly as we can," Kaihli said, holding a laz-rifle she couldn't have gotten from Saph Fyre.

Sadiya nodded. "The All-Father willing, we are doing just that. And we may have some help yet."

The *arabi* took the lead then. The others followed. Manson held on to Antiquity until she grew strong enough to move on her own. It didn't take long. Anger mixed with understanding at what had been done to her rose to the surface, bolstering her strength. Manson also carried a laz-rifle—a massive weapon perfect for his size—and even Elsana held a laz-pistol in her left hand. Chekker brought up the rear as twists, turns, and staircases took them all over.

No alarms sounded, despite the little company passing numerous *arabi* denizens who gave them curious glances but did not try to stop them.

"Where did you get the weapons?" Antiquity asked Manson.

"Sadiya wouldn't say," he said.

The *arabi* brought them to a halt at a passage intersection. She glanced around before turning back, her eyes meeting Antiquity's. "My brother is not the brightest star in the sky, Angelus. He and that dog Rukh al-Za wanted me dead. Assassins followed me the moment I left the Rose Stronghold. They did not fare well." She paused. "But they were well-armed."

Even through the veil, Antiquity could tell Sadiya grinned.

They left, moving swiftly. Stairs took them upward, so many that Antiquity's legs burned and her energy flagged. But she continued on, unwilling to be captured. She would not end up on a table again. She had no idea where they were going, but the *arabi* had a plan and Antiquity trusted her.

A tremor shook the stone of Rose Stronghold. One of the explosions from the Imperium's attack on the city, Antiquity thought. It only quickened their pace.

When the alarm horns blew throughout the corridors, she knew it was for her.

After their long climb, the group came to a large door.

The *arabi* moved next to her.

"I hate to tell you this, but Saph Fyre is lost," Sadiya said, eyes grave. "My brother already had soldiers searching the areas around Bayt al-Hikma. They were closing in on the cave. It was only a matter of time, and I could not kill them all. Far too many, even for a Will Master. Best to get your friends free."

"But that mech is our only hope! We have to go back and fight!"

"While it may feel that way, it is *not* our only hope," Sadiya said, raising a finger to make a point. "My brother still does not know of the mechs beneath the House of Wisdom. They are our true hope, the one your great-grandmother created. And he no longer has you. The mech is useless without you. You were still on that table when we saved you, meaning the construct of artificial intelligence was not complete. We have time to plan, to fight back. But we have to get you free of here, free of my brother. We cannot risk you being captured again. We can do this. To fight another day."

"But surely your old Will Master mentor will question what we were doing at the House of Wisdom, and the Rose King will conduct an exhaustive search," Antiquity pressed. "Even if the mechs are protected by CyTak-5, they won't be safe for long. There are ways around any security system."

"My mentor will not."

"How can you be so sure? He didn't raise a hand to help you!"

Sadiya unbarred the door, pushed it open, and stepped into darkness on the other side. With weapons raised, her friends stepped out into the night, the air cooling them. The *arabi* did not seem worried, sword now sheathed.

"Loyalty falls first for those leaders losing power," Sadiya said.

Antiquity found herself beneath the stars, the illumination of Bayt al-Hikma drowning out most of the starlight but the sky a welcome sight. One of the moons rose over the horizon, a silver scythe lighting their way. Antiquity had no idea why they were on the roof of the Rose Stronghold. Another blast echoed throughout the city. Antiquity saw the fight on the far side of Bayt al-Hikma, warships and *arabi* weapons engaged against one another. She wondered how far the Imperium would go to capture her. Would they be willing to destroy the city of their trade partner? Only kill the Rose King? Or something in between?

She looked around, hoping Sadiya had acquired them some sort of transport. She saw nothing though. Only a flat roof with several smaller towers around them. Antiquity and the others would be safe until the fight shifted in their direction. It would eventually.

The hope that had kindled inside began to dim.

That's when a black shadow stepped free of the night. Manson brought his laz-rifle up but Sadiya deftly pushed it down again.

"These are the times that ruin power," Mir Muhktar said, hands folded within his black robes. The Will Master wore his cowl close, but his dark eyes glittered with interest.

"My teacher," Sadiya said, bowing.

"You are now mine," Mir Muhktar said, returning the bow. "You brought honor against your brother and to your fight with Rukh al-Za. A lesson learned."

Antiquity held her surprise in check. "Is he coming with us?"

"My place is here, Angelus. For better or naught," the older *arabi* said.

"How are we getting away?" Kaihli asked, unwilling to lower her weapon.

"With fire," Mir Muhktar said.

The Will Master withdrew a black sphere from the folds of his robe. He tossed it to the edge of the stone roof. It exploded there, soundless fire, the blue flames leaping twenty feet into the air and sustained. Antiquity looked around her. Another thunderous explosion tore through the city. All eyes turned there. Antiquity moved to the edge of the roof, seeking the cause. Large Imperium warships hovered over Bayt al-Hikma. They could have been firing their large cannons at will. Instead they seemed to only be sending warning fire below.

"The Imperium is attacking. There," Antiquity said, pointing. "Your brother left me so he could rally his defenses. That flame is going to draw one of them right to us!"

"I know all of this," Sadiya said, her eyes shining. "Who do you think made sure the Imperium knew you were still here?"

"Why would you do that?"

"We need the diversion," Mir Muhktar said, looking west. "And Sadiya has always been good at that."

"Who have you called with that fire then?" Antiquity asked.

"You will see."

Antiquity gazed where Sadiya already looked. Shapes darker than the distant mountains approached them through the night, far from the city but moving fast, five of them from what Antiquity saw and flying so low they could almost graze the land. Whoever approached, Sadiya and her mentor had called them. And drawing closer, they became silhouettes she recognized.

Dragons.

"You don't expect us to ride those things?" Manson asked, fear in his voice.

"If you wish to leave, yes," Sadiya said. "Or you can stay behind for my brother and his dog to kill you. Or the Imperium. Up to you, Dreadth."

Manson grunted. "No choice then."

The *arabi* nodded.

The dragons grew larger, drawn by the blue flame. They were massive beasts, wings spread wide, so large several people could ride each one. Her mind still struggling with the events of the last few minutes, Antiquity had a hard time understanding what was going on. Where were these creatures flying from? Why were they ready at short notice? And did someone guide them? Could dragons even be controlled?

As wind from the first dragon's landing hit her, she couldn't believe who she first saw. The young man grinned at her from upon the dragon, seated behind an elderly *persai* woman whose colorful silks floated everywhere in the dragon-made breeze.

"Told you we would see one another again," Soren said, grin bright.

In another life, Antiquity would have been elated by his appearance. Instead she nodded and said nothing, too numb to even be surprised but feeling a spark of hope reignite in her breast. Four more dragons landed upon the roof, all different in size and coloring, there to aid them.

"We must leave. Now," Sadiya said.

The *arabi* ushered Antiquity to the dark-green dragon that had landed second. Sadiya pointed at short steel rungs bolted into thick leather-harness straps that led up toward the rider and her long, curved seat. Chekker flew over the newcomers, appraising them for danger. She knew he wouldn't find any. She climbed the rungs as Sadiya let the others know who they'd be traveling with. Her malformed hand hampering her ascent, Elsana had a hard time of it but gained her seat behind a burly bearded man who helped strap her in. With the others aboard their dragons, Manson and Kaihli lowered their weapons and moved to the last two dragons.

"Move it! We have to get to the skies," Soren said, turning around in his seat.

As Kaihli and Manson climbed their own mounts and the two Will

Masters said their farewells, the door the companions had just passed through burst open.

Rukh al-Za and swarming guards stormed out.

Kaihli acted first. She dropped back to the roof, unslinging her laz-rifle. She fired into the midst of their foes, scattering them, felling several before they even knew they were dead. Mir Muhktar and Sadiya leapt aside and separated, swords drawn, robes flowing as they charged at the soldiers. Antiquity began undoing her harness buckle but the young woman dragon rider she sat behind prevented it, holding her hand fast. She watched as the two Will Masters worked together, confusing their attackers as they leapt into the midst of the soldiers, cutting them down and using the resulting wild fear to their advantage.

Mir Muhktar engaged Rukh al-Za, who had already pulled his weapon free. Their swords rang within the laz-fire.

Another guard contingent swarmed from the door, free of the *arabi* chaos. One of them fired toward those who attempted to flee upon the dragons.

And hit Kaihli in the chest.

"No!" Elsana yelled.

Antiquity felt her heart stop. Unable to help, she watched Kaihli collapse. The world moved in slow motion. Her mentor taking over and sword vanishing within robes, Sadiya rushed to the fallen twin's side.

Kaihli did not move. The hole in her unmoving chest smoked. Eyes stared vacant.

"Sadiya! Flame!" the old *persai* woman screamed.

"Back, Muhktar!" Sadiya roared.

The *arabi* heard the warning. He leapt aside just as Soren's lead dragon belched flame at the doorway, flooding the entire area with heat. Rukh al-Za saw his danger, vaulting back through the doorway to safety. His underlings were not so observant. Screams of agony punctured the night as the fire incinerated them.

Antiquity barely heard them. She couldn't take her gaze away from Kaihli as the rider in front of Elsana accepted her twin's limp body. He cradled her in his strong arms even as his dragon leapt into the night with broad, rushing wings.

"You must go!" Mir Muhktar roared. "Others will come. I will give you time."

Sadiya nodded to her former mentor.

Antiquity held on to her harness. The woman rider in front of her had strapped her down tight. Manson scrambled up and gained the seat behind her. The last to mount, Sadiya strapped herself with Soren and the *persai* woman.

With bunched muscles and a flourish of powerful wing strokes, the dragons entered the dark sky, the buildings falling away.

Swallowed by tears, Antiquity barely saw it.

Her friend. Gone. Killed protecting her.

Her fault.

Bayt al-Hikma grew small and soon faded away.

) ❱ ● ❰ (

"She helped save us. Save you," Manson said in her ear.

The flight's wind cooled cheeks made hot by tears, and dawn's first glimmers colored the sky behind. Antiquity took a steadying breath, finding it difficult to respond. She didn't want to break down again. The five dragons flew west over the Muthlaj Mountains, three carrying companions, two flanking as escorts. Chekker followed, the bot checking on Antiquity at intervals but mainly keeping an eye out for pursuit. As far as she could tell, no one pursued. They had gotten away. It was hard for Antiquity to take any joy in it. Several hours had passed on their journey, but the simple fact remained—Kaihli. Her friend. Dead. Protecting her and the others. Her grandmother had been old, Vodard Ryce little more than a stranger. But her friend had sacrificed herself, a young life not fully lived. It wasn't fair.

And there was still Elsana. Antiquity viewed the rust-colored dragon flying near. The bullish rider still held Kaihli in his strong arms, Elsana slumped against his back. Antiquity could just make out her friend. Eyes open but not looking at anything.

Her eyes matched the defeat and sorrow in Antiquity's own heart.

"Did you hear me, Antiquity?" Manson asked, pushed up against her.

She took a deep breath. "I did. Doesn't matter much."

She could feel Manson tense. "We have lost a lot since we fled Solomon Fyre."

Antiquity refrained from snorting. He had no true idea what she had lost.

"I know this is terrible solace and . . . I've never been good with words. You know that. But it could have been worse," he continued, as if it helped. "If the Rose King had kept you, Saph Fyre would have been his. And if he had gained Saph Fyre, the mech army buried back there would have been his too. Sadiya told us about it. He would have become the most powerful man on Erth. No doubt about it."

Antiquity nodded. "My friend is gone."

"She stopped you from falling into the Rose King's hands again."

"My friend is dead," Antiquity repeated, feeling the first stirrings of anger. Looking back at Manson, Antiquity had never felt so defeated in her life. "I can't do this," she breathed, feeling tears come to the fore again.

Manson stared deep into her eyes, his rugged face blurry from her tears. There was steel in him that Antiquity had not seen since his father's passing.

She wished she had some of it.

"Kaihli didn't die because of you. They killed her. Like your grandmother."

"I can't do it, Manson." The tears wouldn't stop.

Antiquity felt how close he was then, a solid presence in a life that had become all too fragile. He was close, closer than he had ever been. A part of her wanted to sink into that strength; a part of her wanted to blame him for everything that had happened.

"I am sorry, Antiquity," he said simply. "But you have to do it."

She rubbed the tears from her eyes. She had nothing to say.

What could she say?

"She was a powerhouse of a girl. Strong in ways many of my boy cousins aren't."

"Girls can be strong too, Dreadth."

"I know. I just meant—"

"I know what you meant. It's more than that," she growled, pushing back pieces of hair come free by the wind. "She was . . . my best friend. Have you ever had a friend that could finish your sentences, show you love, fight *with* you and the next second fight *for* you?"

"No. You are luckier in your friends than I have been," Manson said. He leaned into her, whether it was a sort of hug or by accident, Antiquity didn't know. "I will say this though. She would want you to keep fighting, Antiquity." When she was about to say he didn't know Kaihli, he continued. "That one night, before we arrived at Luna Gold, I got angry and stormed away from the fire. I didn't leave you all because I was angry about the *arabi* and her place among us." He paused. "Well, maybe a small bit was that. No, I left because I couldn't help but hear my father in her words—words about paths placed by some kind of higher power—and I was worried about him. He was doomed even then. I miss him. I know he is gone. And there's nothing

I can do about it. *Not one thing* that will change what happened.

"Let's get these bastards for what they've done," he said. "Let's end them. All."

"We don't even have Saph Fyre," she said, feeling the weight of their new problem. "And even if we did, they have hundreds of war machines in space ready to drop to Erth and level us."

Long seconds passed. Antiquity turned her mind to Saph Fyre. The Rose King possessed the mech. Or maybe the Imperium did now. Either way, it would require returning to Bayt al-Hikma on their own terms to retrieve the hidden mechs. But she didn't think that was even possible. Too many ifs and not enough assurances.

She'd have to leave everyone except maybe Sadiya behind.

Two would have a better chance than many.

"What did your father mean right before he died?" she asked finally. "Something about remembering the face of your mother."

As if seeking an answer, he looked off toward the Dragonell Mountains, their slopes highlighted by the coming day. The sun would be up soon. "My mother. She was . . . special. More than that. She loved me. In a far different way than my father does . . . did."

"What happened to her?"

"The black scarab virus, the one that tore through Solomon Fyre," he said, stonily. "It ravaged her, left her a husk of what she had been. When she finally left this world, my father pulled me aside and made me promise that I would never forget her face. Not the sick one but the beautiful one—the one that shone with her love for me. He said if I kept her in my heart and remembered her face, I'd know love still. I promised him and I have held on to those final moments ever since."

"Your father was saying he loved you, then," she said. "He was saying goodbye."

Manson nodded and looked away.

Antiquity sensed his sadness. She felt like she understood him in a way that she never thought possible.

"It doesn't matter," he sniffed suddenly. The hulking brute of a bully had returned, a young man angry and seeking revenge. "Somehow, you are the key to all of this. You are the answer to setting us all free again."

"I only wish I knew what I'm supposed to do," she said, feeling helpless. "I'm nothing without Saph Fyre."

"Then get her back."

"What?"

"You heard me," he said, a sudden grin on his face. "Let's get her back. And do it in the name of Kaihli. Your grandmother. Even my father."

"You going to help me?"

Manson shrugged. "What are friends for?"

"Is that what we are, Manson?" she asked. "Friends?"

"Let's say we are no longer enemies, if that makes you feel better."

Antiquity returned the smile. It did not last long. She thought of what would have to happen ahead. Simply planning Saph Fyre's retrieval would not return the mech. Getting it back would be a daunting task, especially if the Imperium had it. Antiquity fingered her great-grandmother's ring, remembering her words, considering their overall goal. She needed Saph Fyre. And that meant being bold at a time when she just wanted to lie in bed and cry for the loss of her friend and Elsana's pain.

The thrum of dragon wings kept her awake with her thoughts.

) ◗ ● ◖ (

A shoulder shake roused her from fitful dreams.

"Where are we, Manson?" she asked, rubbing bleary eyes, overcoming her initial confusion and resultant fear of being woken while in the air.

The Dreadth pointed in answer. Jagged peaks loomed ahead, spread as far as the eye could see and stabbing the sky, the upper reaches like razor-sharp teeth and coated in ice and snow. Below, a great forest grew, pushing up against the mountains in a green carpet, streams and rivers like silver veins flowing to the south. It all left her a bit dizzy. The group no longer flew low to avoid detection but instead high toward whatever destination they ventured. Antiquity then realized she had fallen asleep against Manson, his warmth keeping the chill from her. Feeling uncomfortable, she sat forward, trying to uncramp muscles and sort her wits.

Memories of the previous day surfaced. She had been violated. Mind torn apart, memories copied. What Sayf al-Din had done to her woke her fully.

Then she remembered what had happened to Kaihli.

Rather than cry, she filled the hole in her heart with anger.

Nothing would ever be the same again.

"I still don't know where we are," she pressed.

Manson shrugged. "That is likely a question for Sadiya and her boy prodigy. I'm all turned around after last night's flight."

Shielding her eyes from the midmorning sun, Antiquity looked about. The other dragons formed a line. All were there. A bright spot of chrome far back proved Chekker had kept up. Looking ahead, the dragons flew toward a giant gap between spires, a break in the mountain line. They passed through minutes later, coming out the other side, and Antiquity could see the deep desert in the far distance.

But that wasn't all. Dragons in multitudes watched them pass, some circling on drafts of air, others clinging to rock and sunbathing, while still more sat upon diagonal nests made of limbs and stone—dragons in all sizes, colors, and shapes. If finding a cavern full of mechs had awed her, seeing a mountainside of the great creatures did so even more.

There were so many dragons they would blot out the sky if they all took off at once.

And where the forest met the mountains, stone buildings grew upon a wide shelf of flat land featuring pathways leading below.

Even at a great distance, she could see people, all wearing colorful silks like the dragon riders.

Persai, she thought.

"What is this place?" she asked.

"Home," the woman rider said, the first words she had spoken during the flight.

Antiquity took a broader look at the world, piecing the past and the present puzzle together. She understood then where her saviors had traveled from.

"We're back," Antiquity said.

"What do you mean?" Manson questioned.

"The Dragonell Mountains," she said, pointing. "We crossed that desert. We met Soren and his big cat, Cinder, in the Woodlock Forest there, when the scavengers were after us. We took solace in Sadiya's hut somewhere down there too. And that dragon we saw so many days ago—"

"Lives here, part of a *persai* community," Manson finished.

Antiquity nodded. She remembered the argument between Sadiya and Soren. The boy had wanted to come with them to Luna Gold. The *arabi* had denied him, telling him to follow her wishes. Now Antiquity knew why. Sadiya had foreseen the possibility of events in Bayt al-Hikma not going as smoothly as they hoped. She had known Antiquity and her friends might need saving and ensured an escape route.

With the possibility of danger on their heels.

The Will Master had many secrets still.

The five dragons spiraled downward, one after another in a careful descent. When her own dragon touched down, it was as if they were a feather. The dragon moved with grace to a side arena of young tenders waiting to unharness them, to finally lay their great weight on the ground and rest.

The rider turned and freed the strap around Antiquity.

"Take it slow," she said.

"What is your name?" Antiquity asked, straightening her legs out in front of her as Manson swung his leg over and began taking the rungs down to the ground.

"Leesa."

"Thank you for your aid, Leesa," Antiquity said.

The dragon rider said nothing. She helped Antiquity down from the dragon, eyes dark and unforgiving.

When she had stretched legs and back, Antiquity looked for Sadiya.

The massive dragon the *arabi* rode now settled on the other side of the paddock. Antiquity realized the enormity of the creature when she compared it to those around it. Even tucking its legs beneath itself in rest, the dragon's head rose above all others. As Sadiya, Soren, and the old rider dismounted, the dragon looked right at her as if sensing her thoughts. Antiquity glanced aside, unsure what to do. When she looked back, she was pleased to see Sadiya waving her over.

Soon Antiquity stood staring up at the marvelous creature.

"You may touch her," the old *persai* woman said, having examined both wings for any damage before coming to stand next to Antiquity. She smiled wryly, wrinkles cutting deep into her weathered face. "You will not be bitten. Or worse, eaten whole."

Not sure what to do, Antiquity grinned nervously, stepping closer to the dragon. The *persai* nodded acquiescence. She reached out, touching its foreleg. The dragon held its head high, just how a knightly king of the Old Era had been depicted in decayed paintings. The skin was rough with tiny scales but also silky, a strange feeling beneath her fingertips. She felt heat radiating from deep within the creature, the furnace that had blasted Rukh al-Za and his guards there at all times.

The head swiveled down to her level then and deep eyes took Antiquity in. She saw herself reflected in large green orbs and marveled at the creature's design. Humanity during the Old Era had needed to eliminate climate-destroying machines and created in their place new beasts to travel long distances. Using genetics and selective breeding, dragons had become a dominant species, myths from the old world become real.

"He is magnificent," she said.

"*She* is that and much more," the *persai* said, pleased.

"Antiquity Angelus," Sadiya said, reverence in her words. "I have the pleasure of introducing Tamantha Wre, mistress of the Pelail Eyrie, leader of this *persai* sect, and a friend to me when no one else would be."

Antiquity began to bow—as seemed fitting—but the *persai* shook her head.

"Come, child, formalities matter not, not once dragon fire has been shared."

Antiquity straightened. "I know little of your ways."

"But you keep *persai* company," Tamantha Wre said, gesturing to the side where Elsana returned to the ground, followed by her dead sister in the arms of the burly dragon rider. They walked into the city, vanishing from sight. "If you call *persai* friends in Solomon Fyre, you will be called friend here in Pelail Eyrie."

"Where are they going?" Antiquity asked.

"To the House of Mourning Flowers," Tamantha Wre said. "Your friend Kaihli will be prepared there for her final journey."

"I should be there with Elsana."

"In time," Tamantha Wre said, eyes earnest. "You have been hurt to the deep."

"I have been. To my very heart. So much these last days."

The ancient *persai* took Antiquity's arm.

"Walk with an old woman, please."

Antiquity did that. While she knew the other was quite old, there was a wiry strength in her movements and a steely strength in her black eyes as she walked a different route into the city. Sadiya followed behind, her black *arabi* robes a stark contrast to those of the *persai* around them.

"You need refreshment. Rest. And counsel. In that order," Tamantha Wre said. "On our flight, Sadiya shared the events you witnessed on your journey to this very moment, and those events are troubling. Solomon Fyre. Luna Gold. Bayt al-Hikma. And the power of the mech that you discovered, one that is an affront to the Imperium and its governor in Euroda. Even here, in these wayward mountains, we have heard of Saph Fyre's return—and her new pilot. You need aid, although only you can know what that looks like."

"Aid," Antiquity tasted the word. It was bitter. "Most of the aid I've received has led to someone dying."

"Care to hear wisdom from my grandfather—an *arabi* warrior, Will Master, and diplomat living in the times after the Splinter War?"

Antiquity nodded.

"'To the All-Father is your return all together; then He will inform you of what you used to do,'" Tamantha Wre quoted. "While I do not follow the All-Father of my forebearers, I like that particular passage. Make sure what you do in this life matters. Those are words of wisdom for everyone." Tamantha Wre took Antiquity's hands in her own and drew her through a home's curtained doorway, leaving the day behind. "My home. I share it with you. Let us make sure the aid you have received and are about to receive do not go for naught. Dying for what is right is better than without cause." She let go and turned back to the doorway.

"Take your leisure here. Food is upon the table. Rest. Sadiya will visit when you have had time to recover. We have much to discuss."

Antiquity watched the old woman leave. When the colorful heavy curtains fell back into place and she was alone, she looked about. The home of Tamantha Wre featured charm that only those who have lived long years possessed. The multiroom dwelling had been built with mountain stone, rock cut so cleanly that Antiquity saw no mortar. Comfortable furniture, shelves of books, paintings of dragonkind upon the walls, and no discernible technology of any kind. Small mementos and personal prizes littered the place, each telling a story. Pieces of memories. The old *persai* lived in comfort but it was one of simple pleasures. Antiquity liked her all the more.

She went to the round table in the corner, with its plate of fruit, cheeses, nuts, meat satays, and a pitcher of water. She hadn't realized how hungry she had become. Chewing on cheese and several grapes, she went into the washroom. After splashing water on her face, she looked at the girl in the mirror. Unkempt, greasy hair. Dark circles under eyes. Hollow stare. She saw someone who once had grand plans, placed upon a path not of her choosing but one she had accepted all the same.

It was now a woman's face she barely recognized.

Who had she become?

She took a soft cloth next to the bowl and toweled the water from her face.

When she finished, Elsana stood in the doorway.

Before either could speak they were hugging one another and crying, their tears and shaking sobs binding them in shared grief.

They held one another a long time.

"She loved you, you know," Elsana said, stepping back and wiping her eyes.

"And you," Antiquity said. "Is she kept safe?"

"She is in the House of Mourning Flowers," the twin said. "A sort of mortuary but with great beauty, a solemn place. She is being prepared for whatever my end wishes are. Even though she was not the most devout *persai*, a part of our faith was in her heart. She will be cremated as my parents would wish it. I could only see her for so long before . . . before . . . I had a hard time even breathing."

Tears came to Antiquity again. Words she didn't even know she possessed tumbled out of her like a landslide. "I should have done more. I shouldn't have been captured. I never should have brought either of you on this journey. I never should have left Saph Fyre and you all and thought of a different way. She died becau—"

"You have nothing to feel guilty about," Elsana said, coming to stand by Antiquity again. The twin had strength in her eyes that Antiquity had known existed but had hoped to witness one day. "Kaihli was her own soul. She always wanted to work on giant machinery. That was her dream. You gave that to her. She would have been angry if you *hadn't* taken her along."

Antiquity laughed a little and sniffed. "She would have been furious. But she'd be alive."

The brief spark of strength Antiquity had seen was now gone. Elsana moved to a small chair in the corner of the washroom and, looking down, she cradled her malformed hand in the other, her *persai* silks as limp as she suddenly looked. "The book Sadiya gave me. I've read most of it. The *arabi* faith, their religion, and how they deal with life. All wise words." She paused, shrugging. "It talks about death too. 'Say: the Angel of Death who is given charge of you shall cause you to die, and then to your All-Father you shall be brought back.'"

"Angel of death, a hand of the All-Father," Antiquity said, frowning. "I wonder. What does the book say about revenge?" she asked.

Elsana stood then. "If one is patient, forgiveness is better than retaliating."

"Where are you going?"

"To see my sister again. Then sleep." Elsana's dark eyes were sad. "I spoke to Tamantha Wre. She stopped me before I entered here. She wishes to share something with us. But only when we are rested and ready."

"Do you think we are safe here?" Antiquity asked.

"For now. But not for long. I sensed that from the Tamantha Wre."

"Sensed? Part of your Will Master talents?"

"I don't know what it is," the twin admitted. "But how can a disabled young girl ever become the fighter that Will Master Sadiya is?"

Before she could respond, Elsana was out the door.

) ◗ ● ◖ (

A soft knock at the guest bedroom door woke her from deep sleep.

Antiquity sat up and rolled out of bed. It was still light outside, the colorful silks over the windows casting the room in various shades of blue, red, and yellow. Aches as deep as the hurt in her heart had sunk into her muscles, the flight upon the dragon taking root in her bones. She ignored the pain though, dressing in *persai* clothing that had been left for her. She thought of Kaihli and Elsana then, the twins having worn their silks every day she had known them. A part of her felt like she was betraying Kaihli—the twin had never particularly enjoyed that aspect of her life—but Antiquity didn't have much choice in fresh attire and she knew it would please Elsana as well as Tamantha Wre.

"You may enter," she said once she was dressed.

Sadiya entered the room, dressed in her usual black robes.

"You look more rested than before," the *arabi* noted.

"I could have slept for days. Is it time to meet with Tamantha Wre?"

Sadiya nodded. "Follow me."

The two left the home of Pelail Eyrie's leader. Few *persai* were upon the cobblestone paths connecting home after home. The sun had sunk far into the west, the gold of its descent casting the mountain in its color. Night would fall soon. Antiquity gazed into the sky and toward the spires above them, seeking out dragons. Even at such heights, she could make out hundreds of them settling down to roost among one another.

"Thank you, Sadiya, for coming back for me," Antiquity said. "And for saving my friends from your brother. I will forever be in your debt for that."

"I apologize I couldn't save Kaihli and Saph Fyre as well," the *arabi* said. "The All-Father puts us upon a path to fulfillment but sometimes that path is uphill and winding." She paused. "I did take the liberty of notifying the others what we discovered beneath the House of Wisdom. I thought it only right that they know."

"I know you did, Sadiya. Manson told me. And I am fine with that," Antiquity said. "Do you think we can get Saph Fyre back?"

"I do," Sadiya said. "But we need information. Has the mech been found? Who found it? And what are they doing with it?"

"The *persai* don't seem to have much in the way of technology."

"We will not discuss it here," the *arabi* said mysteriously.

Curiosity aroused, Antiquity kept quiet. She had no idea what Tamantha Wre wanted to share but it was obviously something for her ears alone. Once they navigated through Pelail Eyrie, Sadiya took a sharp turn into the massive redwoods that lorded over this part of Erth. Antiquity would never get used to being beneath trees so large, such a sharp contrast to her life in Solomon Fyre. Soon the path snaked upward into the craggier parts of the mountains where jagged boulders littered the ground as if torn from the cliffs by giant hands and tossed aside. The air had become colder again and soon small crevices filled with snow became common. Behind her, the sun dropped down behind the horizon; nightfall had come and with it the stars of the east.

After an indeterminable walk, Antiquity caught sight of a square stone building built into the side of the rocky slope, guarded by a familiar beast. Cinder looked up at them, lantern eyes bright.

Sadiya walked by the feline and opened a wooden door bound in dragon-shaped iron. Antiquity entered after her. She was surprised to see Tamantha Wre, Manson, Elsana, Chekker, and Soren were already in the warm room, one ablaze with light from dozens of large vid-views upon the walls.

When they turned to her, she saw friends who were pleased to see her.

All except Elsana, who looked like she hadn't slept, her face pinched with grief.

"Welcome, Antiquity Angelus," Tamantha Wre said, coming over to embrace Antiquity with a quick and gentle hug. "Did you rest well?"

"Yes, it was much needed."

"And the food was adequate?"

"Better than I've had in quite a while," Antiquity said, smiling.

"That is well," Tamatha Wre said. She folded her hands before her. "You probably noticed that my home contains no technology that connects with the outside world. We *persai* in Pelail Eyrie prefer it that way. But there are times when matters in the outside world deserve our attention, that we may be prepared for dangerous lives, dangerous minds. I did not always think so. But when Sadiya arrived and my people gave her sanctuary, I saw the wisdom of the Bayt al-Hikma *arabi* way." She gestured to the vid-views. "The Will Master uses this building for that purpose, discovering what occurs in the world through contacts in major cities. While she was gone with you, I took the duty upon myself."

"I thought you said you hated technology."

The old *persai* shrugged. "I am no fool. Just because we're divorced from technology does not mean those who rule around us are not in need of watching. There are times when the timber wolf must be watched to keep safe the rabbit hole."

Antiquity liked Tamantha Wre. She reminded her of Vestige. As she mulled that over, she looked to the vid-views, trying to understand what she saw. Each one showed different videos from around Erth.

"These feeds transpire now?" Antiquity asked.

"Some do, yes," Tamantha Wre said. "Other vid-views replay recent events you need to see for yourself." The *persai* moved to one of two chairs before the largest wall of vid-views. She offered the other to Antiquity, who sat down.

"Sadiya shared your discovery of Saph Fyre and the events that followed, Antiquity," the mistress of Pelail Eyrie continued. "Your great-grandmother had vision. Titanium is a powerful element for Erth. And that of the Imperium's stars, forming their ships, their weapons, their technology. Its possession keeps control. The Celestial in Luna Gold fulfilled an aspect of your great-grandmother's vision he deemed safe. He kept safe the knowledge of building mechs, put it to good use. The mechs beneath the House of Wisdom in Bayt al-Hikma are potent tools. In the right hands, they could free Erth from its repressive overlords; in the wrong hands, they could throw the planet into turmoil. Chaos could sunder the Erth as easily as the Imperium.

"The *persai* here hate mechs. We prefer . . . a more withdrawn and natural life. Technology can be a boon or a curse—it's all in the manner of how it is used. Rather than possess a mech, we fly upon the natural wings of the world. Dragons."

"Dragons will not win the day, not against the Imperium," Manson interrupted.

"You are correct, young Dreadth," Tamatha Wre said. "And mechs without their respective operating systems will not win the day either."

"It has to start with Saph Fyre. It possesses the only operating system that I know of besides the Imperium's lone mech on Erth, Star Sentinel. And there's no way we are getting near that mech, that's for sure," Antiquity said. "So. Where is Saph Fyre?"

"If I found her for you, what would you do?"

Antiquity looked to the bot. "Chekker is capable of a great deal, but even he has said he is far too limited to download a mech's sizable operating system. Too much data. What could you do, Chekker? If we had Saph Fyre."

"Saving Saph Fyre is only part of what needs to take place, Greychild," the bot said. "I am limited in what I can do. I need to be in close proximity to Saph Fyre as well as another mech. I can download from Saph Fyre even as I upload to the second mech. It would take time. But it should work, as long as a new mech's hardware is similar to Saph Fyre."

"Which brings us to your first concern," Tamantha Wre said. The *persai* brought shimmering light controls to life in front of her, twisting them this way and that. The vid-views in front of her changed, the first showing the city of Bayt al-Hikma.

Multiple warships hovered over the city, while smoke filled the skies.

"The Imperium has taken the city where the mechs are hidden," Elsana whispered.

Tamantha Wre nodded, looking grave.

"What of my brother?" Sadiya asked.

"A second worry." Tamantha Wre adjusted a screen, replaying old footage.

Royal Declarion Wit stood in front of the Rose Stronghold's throne, in the same hall where Sadiya and Rukh al-Za had fought. In front of him, the Lion pinned an *arabi* man's neck to the stone floor with his boot, a sword raised high, as Imperium guards kept their weapons trained on those watching in the hall. The sword came down, severing the man's head from his twitching shoulders. Blood streamed everywhere.

Antiquity recognized the dead man. Rose King Sayf al-Din.

Killed.

"The Imperium has taken over Bayt al-Hikma," Chekker said.

"And shared the feed with vid-views all over Erth," Tamantha Wre said.

"Sadiya, I'm not sure what to say right now," Antiquity said. "I'm sorry, I guess—"

"Do not be," the *arabi* said, eyes taking in the vid-view. "My brother brought this upon his head and the city of my birth. I just hope the rest of my family is safe. And few casualties have happened to those who live there."

"This does not bode well for us at all," Manson said, words gruff. "We have a city under new authority, with continually scanning warships. They either possess Saph Fyre already or will soon. And even if Saph Fyre hasn't been discovered and we took her back, we'd never get her close enough to the mechs beneath the House of Wisdom for Chekker to download and upload data."

"Complications—or a great boon—arise now," Tamantha said, changing the vid-view yet again to another area. "This is live."

It appeared to be a view from just outside of Bayt al-Hikma. Sunlight struck faded blue paint on a giant, and it took Antiquity's breath away.

Saph Fyre.

The mech flew slowly over the city, tethered at the shoulders to an Imperial warship. The mech appeared whole, showing no damage. The warship and its cargo moved out of the city toward the west.

"Why hasn't the Imperium ripped the mech apart by now?" she asked, puzzled by the Imperium's choice but so unbelievably happy to see the mech intact.

"And where is Saph Fyre being taken?" Elsana added.

Tamantha Wre pulled up a map of the continent. Projecting the warship's path had it flying to Solomon Fyre. She turned to look at the group. "Royal Declarion Wit ordered the death of Sayf al-Din and televised it all over Erth. It is a tactic, to quell any possible uprisings. *This* is what they do to those who rebel." She twisted the vid-view control again, showing Solomon Fyre. A giant mech stood upon the mountain rock that housed the eyries for Angelus and Dreadth. It was massive, much larger than Saph Fyre, and its white-plate exterior glowed in the sunlight.

"Star Sentinel, the mech of the governorship in Euroda," Manson snorted, shaking his head. "The only mech allowed by Imperium law to be on Erth. We can't fight that. It could destroy a city all by itself."

"Much has taken place since you fled Solomon Fyre, Antiquity Angelus," Tamantha Wre said, gesturing toward the vid-views. "The people of your city revolted after you destroyed that warship outside of Solomon Fyre. They tore down the Celestial consulate there, bringing the ire of the Imperium onto their heads."

"That's why the Imperium is hauling Saph Fyre to Solomon Fyre. Royal Declarion Wit wishes to make a statement," Antiquity said. "He said as much when we were in Luna Gold. That he would make the entire planet watch the destruction of Saph Fyre and make an example of all of us," Antiquity said, angry at the Celestial's depravity.

Sadiya pursed her lips. "Or he wishes to draw you out."

Antiquity had not thought of that.

"It will work," she decided.

Everyone in the room looked at her. Antiquity stared at the screen, thinking.

"You have to be protected at all costs," Chekker said.

"But why, Chekker?" Antiquity asked. "I have been giving a great deal of thought to this. Why here? Why now? The Angelus and Dreadth families. Why Luna Gold? Why Bayt al-Hikma? The Great Hall of Rostam beneath the House of Wisdom holds sixty mechs, each capable of great power. But sixty is not enough to account for the amounts of titanium that Vodard Ryce spoke about, that my great-grandmother wanted protected." She paused, thinking out loud now. "Vodard Ryce said there was enough titanium mined from the mountains of Luna Gold to keep the Imperium pleased for centuries. That's a lot. Where did it all go?"

"My great-grandmother had designs, but they were meant as a fail-safe if they lost the war against the Imperium," Antiquity breathed, putting it all together. "Vodard Ryce took her plans and made them his own. Out of loyalty. And friendship. He helped create the mechs beneath Bayt al-Hikma with the aid of Sadiya's father. But what about the rest of the titanium that he said he'd mined? Where would it be stored away?"

"In a different chamber beneath Bayt al-Hikma maybe?" Elsana said. "Or somewhere in Luna Gold? Something you never had the chance to see?"

"No, that doesn't feel right," Antiquity continued, searching for the answers but feeling hope rekindle. "Vodard Ryce would have wanted to keep it apart so no one city could possibly have all of the power in their hands."

"But still accessible to one of Laurellyn Angelus's heirs," Chekker added.

"Then there is more titanium somewhere else," Elsana said.

"Or more mechs created," Antiquity said.

"And placed elsewhere."

The room went quiet, everyone looking at the others.

"If that's true, we need to find them," Manson said, arms crossed. "The more we possess, the more power we have. I agree. Vodard Ryce would not have created only sixty. He would have prepared the world for war with the titanium reserves he had at his disposal."

"I am an old woman," Tamantha Wre said. She looked sad. "This is a dangerous thing you discuss. There are more lives at stake here than just those in this room."

"She is right. The people of Solomon Fyre are rising up," Elsana said.

"It could get them all killed," Manson observed.

"Or set them free," Sadiya countered. "Lull the viper, its fangs bite late. Royal Declarion Wit has fallen into a trap decades in the making."

"Well, where are the mechs?" Elsana asked.

"Remember what you asked in Tamantha Wre's washroom, El?" Antiquity said. The twin frowned, thinking. "You worried that you could never be a good fighter. Maybe it's not about fighting. Maybe it's about being smart. That's where true power lies."

Sadiya nodded. "It takes others a lifetime to learn that, Desert Rose."

"We must get home. Fast. Before Royal Declarion Wit and Saph Fyre arrive," Antiquity said, already formulating the needed plan. She looked at Tamantha Wre. "But first, Mistress of Pelail Eyrie, how well do your dragons fly in the desert?"

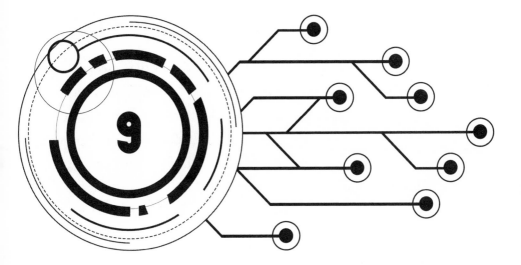

Antiquity gazed at the golden sunrise, one that could be her last.

It had not taken them long to cross the desert upon dragon wings. When Antiquity told Tamantha Wre and the others of her initial idea to reclaim Saph Fyre and retake Solomon Fyre from the Imperium, the old *persai* leader agreed they would need the dragons, that getting to the city ahead of Saph Fyre mattered above all else. For a price, to be named later through the wisdom of Sadiya. After mulling it over, Antiquity agreed. The mistress of Pelail Eyrie stayed behind— calling war a young person's pursuit—but she gave what she could to get Antiquity and her friends to the city. The dragons and riders would bear no affiliation upon their gear, nothing that could draw the ire of the Imperium upon Pelail Eyrie. Antiquity hoped it would be enough.

They had arrived cloaked by night's darkness, and after the dragons deposited them close to the city, the dragon riders flew to hide within the craggy canyons making up the plateau to the west of Solomon Fyre.

Now Antiquity sat cross-legged on a thrust of stone just beyond the city to the east, too distant to be seen, eyeing the gleaming plates of Star Sentinel.

The Imperium's behemoth mech still stood over the Angelus and Dreadth eyries, waiting. She wondered who piloted it. The governor himself? Royal Declarion Wit? His Lion? Or one of his other warriors?

Ultimately it did not matter. She would fight it before the day ended.

"When do we begin to worry?" Elsana asked, also sitting nearby.

"About Manson?" Antiquity asked, thinking. "He hasn't been gone long. It will take him and Kersus time to enter the city. We don't know what the Imperium is doing there, in the streets and in homes."

"But they also can't dally," Sadiya said. "Time is of the essence."

"No, they can't."

Elsana rubbed her forearm muscles. Her underdeveloped arm pained her now and then, especially in times of stress. "And you trust him to do this?"

"He knows the city better than me, at least that part of the city," Antiquity said.

"Let's hope he doesn't do something stupid," the twin said.

Antiquity nodded. She gazed into the desert. Saph Fyre and its warship were still not in view but they were coming. Soon enough. Antiquity and her friends had to put several wheels in motion at once before her mech arrived. She had no idea what the Imperium planned for her and Saph Fyre, but none of it could be good.

She had given a part of her plan to Manson, who was accompanied by the burly, bearded Kersus. The *persai* dragon rider had been chosen by Tamantha Wre for his leadership and dependability alongside the other dragon riders. Together, Kersus and Manson went into the heart of Solomon Fyre. To find the one person who held the key.

"With Star Sentinel already here and Imperium warships coming, we will be greatly outnumbered, not only in manpower but firepower," Antiquity mused, still considering different permutations for how the day could end.

"Kaihli would have known a way to bring that mech down," Elsana said.

"I wish she was here too."

"Sorry I won't be of much use."

"You will be, before the end of all this," Antiquity said, feeling a wry smile sneak upon her face.

Elsana frowned. "Why are you smiling like that?"

"Because I know something you do not," Antiquity said, standing to stretch her muscles again after their night flight.

"Tell me."

"And ruin the surprise? No," she said, serious again. She looked to the blue of the sky and took a long, deep breath. "I wish I could talk to my great-grandmother again," Antiquity thought out loud.

"You can, Grey-child," Chekker said.

Antiquity looked down upon the sapphire-embedded ring. The idea hadn't occurred to her. She had assumed her great-grandmother shared the totality of what she could, nothing left to learn. Perhaps she had been wrong. She took the ring off, letting the new day's sun be captured in azure. Chekker flew close, his hidden compartment opening. Antiquity placed the warm ring there.

The hole closed and she backed away from her longtime metal friend, hoping the bot was not mistaken. Light shot out of Chekker, forming an image upon the air.

"My great-granddaughter," the hologram of Laurellyn Angelus said, appearing exactly the same as the last time they spoke. "It pleases me to see you so. A woman is before me when last a girl stood."

"I discovered your secret," Antiquity said, back straight. The artificial intelligence before her was not wrong. She could feel how different she had become since she had last spoken with her ancestor. "The titanium. Mined by Vodard Ryce. And more. He built an army of mechs, spreading them throughout various caches on Erth to keep them safe from one person controlling all. I go to acquire one such cache."

"Vodard Ryce," Laurellyn Angelus said, eyes wistful. "He and his wife were very good friends. I knew I could trust him with the most important of secrets. With my very life. And the lives of those who would come after me."

"He saved my life."

"And sacrificed his, according to CHKR-11's data banks," the artificial intelligence said. "His dragonflies. His pets, his life. He always did have a penchant for the dramatic."

"He said he owed you."

"A life for a life."

Antiquity looked down. "He's not the only one. My friend Kaihli is also gone."

"I am sorry to hear that. Loss is a part of life," Laurellyn Angelus said. "The memories of the past must bolster your resolve now. What begins cannot be undone. My daughter and I have done what we can. The rest is on you."

Antiquity couldn't tell if her great-grandmother was trying to prepare her for more losses or if she only meant to instill a sense of magnitude for how events now occurred. Regardless, it wasn't necessary. Antiquity felt it all too clearly.

"I have one question for you. Am I doing the right thing?" she asked.

"The uncertainty you feel in your heart marks a good leader," the ghost of Laurellyn Angelus said, pleased. "Good leaders feel uncertainty, great leaders listen to it. I had doubts every day that rose with the sun. It kept me from being rash. It kept me focused on problems."

She paused, looking beyond her at the city. "Solomon Fyre, my favorite place in all of the world. The better question is this: Is fighting for that city the right thing?"

"I guess, but does it matter?" The strength she had just felt began to wane under her worry. "The Imperium. An *arabi* king. A *persai* queen. Even an Angelus. Someone will always lord over others. What makes one better over another?"

"Wisdom and counsel," Laurellyn Angelus said.

"Wisdom did not keep my friend alive."

"No. But if you honor your friend, you will learn and grow from the experience. To prevent others from her fate."

Antiquity looked at her feet. "I'm worried I could just make things worse for Solomon Fyre."

"I know this has not been easy for you, my sweet great-grand-daughter," Laurellyn Angelus said, eyes solemn. "You wear my ring, one similar to the one your grandmother also wore. You take us with you. Forever. If you slide the ring back onto your hand and you fight the Imperium that approaches, you do so as head of the Angelus family. And you will lead those of Erth who would see a brighter day tomorrow. Remember."

Before Antiquity could say more, the hologram of Laurellyn Angelus vanished.

The compartment in Chekker opened. Antiquity removed the warm ring.

And she slid it back onto her finger.

) ◗ ● ◖ (

Manson returned when the sun's full orb had risen above the horizon.

Antiquity and the others rose as the Dreadth and Kersus approached them manhandling a thin, tall man with long officious robes, hands bound behind him, and a rough burlap sack over his face. Antiquity stepped forward, pleased to see their first step in infiltrating Solomon Fyre had paid off. For now, at least. Manson pushed the man, who stumbled and almost fell. The Dreadth grinned. He was clearly enjoying this. A bully with a purpose could be a dangerous thing if not kept in line. Antiquity shook her head at him. To his credit, Manson looked away from her hard eyes and pulled the sack free of the man's head.

High Chamberlain Braun Pierce blinked at the sudden light. When his steely eyes finally fell on Antiquity, he gaped.

"It can't be," he said.

"It is though. Thank you for joining us."

"This is insanity!" the high chamberlain screamed, spine returned. "Treasonous! Take me back to my home at once!"

"Treasonous," Antiquity tasted the word. "As good a label as any, I suppose."

Braun Pierce turned to view Kersus and Manson. "And the Dreadth whelp. You no longer have a throne here, Manson. Your father is dead. Another rules in his place already. You should have grabbed Chat Higgum instead of me."

Before Antiquity could utter a word to stop him—not that she would have anyway, she realized—Manson gripped the bound man by his shoulders and threw him to the ground. Braun Pierce hit with great force on his shoulder and head. It didn't stop there. Manson stood over him and, foot against the high chamberlain's neck, ground the other's head into the bluff. The rock cut into cheek and chin, drawing blood.

Braun Pierce tried to twist free. "Call him off me, Angelus!"

"Now why would I do that?" Antiquity asked, but shook her head at Manson to stop.

He did, leaving the downed man sucking air.

"What do you want, Grey-shamed?" Pierce finally asked.

Antiquity wanted to let Manson go at the high chamberlain again for calling her that. With fists and all. Instead, she knelt before him, making sure he could see her. Blood ran in small rivulets where he had been cut but he was otherwise uninjured.

"I could have abducted Chat Higgum. But he would have been worthless to me. You hold the key. And what *I* want, *you* should want too."

"And that is?"

"To be free."

The high chamberlain snorted. He gazed at Star Sentinel. "See that!"

"I do," she said. "Star Sentinel is here. Other warships are on their way too."

"You think you can go up against Governor Ricariol Wit?" Braun Pierce's eyes were wild and incredulous. "The entire Imperium? With no more than a dragon, an *arabi* Will Master, a girl cripple, and an orphan boy?" He shook his head. "I've seen the vid-cam footage. Seen you no longer have Saph Fyre. Seen Bayt al-Hikma on fire, its Rose King killed by Royal Declarion Wit. You and Jackson Dreadth's son there should have turned that mech over to the Elders like we had planned! Things would be different!"

"Yes, the Elders would have become even more powerful. My family would still be in shame—if not by title then by poverty. And the Imperium would be none the wiser, safe, while the people you help govern still struggle under a yoke from the stars."

"You are going to kill us all!"

She hated saying it. "If that is what it takes."

"You've gone mad!"

Antiquity laughed. "I feel like I have! Kersus."

The bearded man crossed his thick arms—and nodded to his dragon.

The dark-brown giant beast stood on all fours, towering over all of them, but eyeing only the high chamberlain with its giant lantern eyes. Steam billowed from its jaws toward Braun Pierce. He shriveled into a ball, cowering. The dragon sniffed at the prostrate man, emitting a low rumble from deep within, as if the creature was deciding if the meal was worth the effort.

"What are you doing? Stop! Stop!" Braun Pierce cried, trying to crawl away until Manson put a boot in his back, preventing him from going any farther.

"It sounds like you are useless," Antiquity said. "And I have no need of useless tools."

The high chamberlain peered up—right into the maw of teeth.

"The Imperium will kill me if I help you!"

"Gaze upon the death in front of you," Sadiya said, dark eyes bright. The *arabi* stood off to the side, clearly enjoying the situation.

The high chamberlain did just that, going whiter than before. "Fine! What do you want? What do you want?!"

"A simple thing, really," Antiquity said. She looked to Kersus. The rider made several hand gestures to his mount. The dragon backed off. "We want admittance to the Hall of Elders. Now. You are the high chamberlain. You have the key to unlock the building and the responsibility of preparing the hall for admittance by the Elders. We have business there, and you will take us."

Braun Pierce's eyes narrowed. "Why would you want that? It's been shut down ever since the Imperium arrived after your attack. There is nothing there for you to use against Royal Declarion Wit, his Lion, or the lording governor of Erth." He paused before a snide look pinched his features. "It is folly. You should flee. Leave me. While you have the chance. More warships are on their way. Nothing will stop them."

"One ship comes. Do not lie," Sadiya pointed out. "The governor cannot direct more warships here because it would leave the garrisons in the other cities empty."

"Still, *arabi*, it will not matter," the high chamberlain said. "Star Sentinel will see you dead. Your friends dead. The revolt ended. I have no wish to be with you when that happens."

"You are right about one thing," Antiquity cut in. "I may have indirectly started the uprising here in Solomon Fyre, but I'm going to help the people as much as I can."

"Are you sure about the titanium? The mechs?" Manson asked.

"I'm not," she admitted. "Only one way to find out."

"If this doesn't go well, any Dreadths not put to death are going to be Grey and living in your home, Antiquity," Manson said with a small grin. The other's eyes held enough humor to soften the fear inside Antiquity. "How do you feel about that?"

"There could be worse company," she said, grinning back.

"Mechs? Titanium? Neither are in the Hall of Elders!" Braun Pierce said. "I would know. I have been high chamberlain for over a decade."

"I stand here at the edge of Solomon Fyre for multiple reasons," Antiquity said, becoming serious again. She thought of the Elders. Of Jackson Dreadth murdered by Royal Declarion Wit, of her enslaved city. Of Manson targeted as a traitor, unable to lead the council, with its Elders who would rather grovel at the feet of their slavers for political scraps. "This has never been about finding titanium. Or mechs, for that matter. This has been about waiting for the right time to challenge the power that chains us. We must break the chains."

"The Imperium has ripped our home apart," Manson said. "And after what my father did and his role in all of this, Royal Declarion Wit has probably invaded my home's eyrie and searched it as well. The mechs can't be there, Antiquity."

"Remember where our marriage would have begun, Manson?"

The Dreadth frowned—before his eyes lit in recognition. "Your great-grandmother and Vodard Ryce were sneaky dust devils."

"They were," Antiquity said. "Chekker, where is Saph Fyre now?"

Chekker spun and clicked. "Approaching. According to the Imperium's vid-cam feed, not far," the bot said. "Middle of the desert, still routed to Solomon Fyre. It will be here in two hours, perhaps a bit less."

"We must go then," she said.

"I do not want to be a part of this!" Braun Pierce whined, trying to wriggle free.

Manson hauled the high chamberlain to his feet.

"You are right to fear the Imperium," Antiquity said, walking up to stare in the other's eyes. Braun Pierce shrank from her. She then unbound his hands. "You should fear me more. I have nothing to lose now." She paused, nodding to Kersus. "Notify the dragon riders to be prepared for our return. We attack then. Manson, lead the way."

The Dreadth pushed Braun Pierce forward. The high chamberlain had no choice, giving them a dark look. Antiquity and Elsana followed with Chekker and Sadiya bringing up the rear. The desert sun warmed the day. They took twisted paths down, careful to not slip on pebbles that could send them falling to their deaths. Approaching from the north side of Solomon Fyre, they would have to gain the desert to the east first—there was no other way—but it was also the best way to escape notice by Star Sentinel and the Imperium's technology.

Antiquity drew in a dry breath when they reached the expansive sands. It had been almost two weeks since she had been here. She looked out over the world where she had found Saph Fyre, barely able to comprehend how much her life had changed.

They then entered the city from its lowest level, navigating the poverty-stricken outer districts of Solomon Fyre, every step bringing them closer to the center of the city. Early risers were already about.

Those who were stared at Antiquity and Manson. She realized that their faces had probably been on every vid-view for days and days. It made her push the others to walk faster.

It did not take long to enter the massive square of Solomon Fyre. More people were about but so too were Celestial guards, there to keep the peace but also hunt for those who had inspired the uprising. Manson walked next to the high chamberlain, a grip on the man's robes up by his neck. The grip said one thing.

If you try to warn anybody, you are the first to die.

They passed the water fountain where Antiquity and Vestige had once stood, its wet dragon glimmering in the sun. A deep pang filled her heart. The memory of talking to her grandmother, the wise words the woman said. Words that drew her home now. She focused on the situation, turning away from the memory, instead taking steps up toward the arched doorways that locked away the room she needed.

The building that housed the Hall of Elders.

"Not sure what you expect to find. There's nothing here. No titanium, certainly no mechs," Braun Pierce said, agitated. He produced a set of electromagnetic keys from his robe. "And there's no one else here to help you."

"All the better," Antiquity said.

Manson took the lead and Sadiya pushed Braun Pierce forward so he couldn't flee. Blue orbs of light flickered to life inside the vast structure, lighting their way. Footfalls echoed. A musty smell tinged the air, as if no one had disturbed the hall for days. They made their way through another set of rooms until they stood in an antechamber, a massive steel door before them. The same spot Antiquity had waited with her grandmother and Chekker before learning of her arranged marriage to Manson.

"Open it," she said.

Braun Pierce exhaled, annoyed. He did what he was told though.

More orbs came to life as they entered the Hall of Elders. The hexagonal room had not changed since her last visit, but the large vid-views upon the walls were lifeless, their light unable to chase darkness from the corners of the room. Antiquity strode forward, spinning the ring upon her finger. On this, all events hinged. She took several steps up to the dais that held the seats of the council. She ignored them. She only had eyes for the largest—the massive throne and the giant mech fist behind it.

"It is nearly the same as the House of Wisdom's hand," Sadiya said behind her.

"Let's hope it contains a similar secret."

"I see no other doorways," Manson said.

"That's because there are none, Dreadth," Braun Pierce smirked. "You have been lied to by this girl and her Grey-shamed family."

"My grandmother and I stood in this council chamber, looking to your father for answers, Manson. I hated her so much then, for even thinking to marry me to you. I fled, in anger and shame. She followed me, out to the fountain." Antiquity realized how it had changed her. "My grandmother was the wisest person I've known. Sad it took me so long to see it. But some of her last words stuck with me and here I am. She said, 'One day all too soon, you will stand before High Chamberlain Braun Pierce with Manson. It is the key to the future. Not only for you, but for Erth.' She then slid this ring upon my finger."

She stepped to the throne. She didn't touch it. Instead, she walked behind it to the massive fist. "Vodard Ryce gave us a clue through his words. That the truth was buried in Bayt al-Hikma. But he also said that a bot held a further secret. When Sadiya and I found the bot CyTak-5, I tried to figure out that secret. Took a while. Almost too late, I realized the bot's number held the key along with this huge mech fist."

The others watched as Antiquity removed the ring, the orb light catching the sapphires in the titanium. They winked at her. The ring held the power of her family within it. As Sadiya had done with her sword in the House of Wisdom, Antiquity pressed the ring first against the giant thumb and then each finger after that. She then touched it to the throne. And the wall behind the mech fist.

Nothing happened.

Antiquity lowered her hand, heart dropping in her chest.

"Told you," the high chamberlain snorted.

Before Antiquity could respond, the fingers opened like the closed petals of a flower suddenly in the sun, as if a giant below had woken and now flexed its gauntleted hand. Adrenaline flowed through Antiquity as she watched. The entire mech apparatus slowly sank into the floor, disappearing from view.

The others—even the high chamberlain—moved onto the dais to see.

Behind the throne, a maw of darkness lay revealed.

And stairs.

"The hand uncovers the way," Sadiya said behind them all. "The All-Father is with us."

"What say you now, High Chamberlain?" Elsana said.

Braun Pierce said nothing, gawking at the hole.

"Let us go. Chekker, light the way," Antiquity said. "Secrets await."

Manson pushed Braun Pierce forward, forcing him to go first. With the Dreadth at his back, the high chamberlain moved slowly, interested in what existed below. Antiquity went after, tamping down her excitement, knowing it could be an empty room. She didn't think so though. If dozens of mechs waited beneath the House of Wisdom, it stood to reason more were here, waiting to be discovered.

Chekker flew ahead of them, glowing to light the way, with Elsana and Sadiya bringing up the rear. Their footfalls echoed in the dark, and shivering at the cold, Antiquity could feel the weight of the stone about her and the enormousness of the room they entered. Just like below the House of Wisdom. She could not make out any other forms; Chekker would have to fly deeper and farther.

Before she could ask her friend to do that, another light flared to life in the far distance.

It approached and coalesced into a familiar style of bot.

"Welcome to the Great Hall of Fyre. I am CyTak-1. How may I be of assistance?"

The bot spun in the air, waiting.

"Can we get more light in here?" Elsana asked.

"Gladly," Antiquity said. "CyTak-1, more light please."

After scanning her like CyTak-5 had done below the House of Wisdom, the bot did as requested. It left them, floating higher and farther away, growing small. Then light exploded into existence, pushing back the darkness. Antiquity and the others had to shield their eyes, but they adjusted quickly, even as more lights blinked to life along the walls and floor. The sight left them all speechless.

Two rows of mechs, frozen in time, as far as they could see.

"Holy hells," Manson breathed finally. "You were right."

High Chamberlain Braun Pierce sat on the stairs, clearly awed by what he saw. "Beneath us. All this time."

"All this time," Antiquity echoed, trying to keep the excitement from her voice. "Look at the room's end: tunnels, used to get the mechs in here. I still cannot believe how Vodard Ryce managed it in secret." She paused, looking up at her bot friend. "Chekker, can CyTak-1 help in gaining the software we need from Saph Fyre?"

"He is a rudimentary bot," Chekker sniffed. "But he will suffice as a linking extension of me to one of the mechs."

"More than one maybe?"

"Yes, Grey-child, given time."

"Good," she said. "We will only have one shot at this."

"Shot at what?" Pierce Braun said, rising to his feet. "You have no pilots. No strategy. Nothing! The Imperium is going to kill all of us, no matter what's down here!"

"Not if we kill them first." Antiquity gave Sadiya a nod. "It is time."

"It is," the *arabi* said. She bowed briefly. "Time to see your fate accomplished."

In a moment of joy mingled with terror, Antiquity hugged Sadiya. The *arabi* did not respond at first but eventually let the close contact happen. Antiquity realized this could be the last time she saw Sadiya.

"Thank you," Antiquity said simply.

"We have more to do," the other said.

Antiquity nodded. She turned to Elsana and Manson. "Chekker will come with me. All things hinge on gaining Saph Fyre and not dying. We need that operating system, to infuse it into the mechs here. High Chamberlain, you may want to stay down here. It will be much safer than up there, trust me." Braun Pierce blanched at that but said nothing more. Antiquity turned to the room's guardian bot. "CyTak-1, I need you to work with CHKR-11. Can you do that?"

"You are the rightful heir of the Great Hall of Fyre. I am at your disposal."

Antiquity smiled but it didn't last long. She looked at her companions. They had seen her through the hardest days of her life. They had sustained and bolstered. They had watched her cry and given their strength. They had kept her safe. She sought to find the words to tell them this, to thank them, and to give back what they had given. But the words were not there, her heart stuck in her throat and cutting them off.

"Just go, Antiquity," Manson said, seeing her struggle. "Godspeed to you."

"And all of us," she managed.

She gave Elsana a hug. "Be ready. You will know when."

Before the twin could say anything, Antiquity turned to leave, unwilling to let the emotions she felt overwhelm her. She had to move. Fast. The second part of her plan completed—and Chekker with her to accomplish the third—Antiquity left her friends, taking the stairs two at a time back up to the sunlight.

And back to the fight for Solomon Fyre.

) ◗ ● ◖ (

When she regained the heights above Solomon Fyre, sweat ran freely.

The day had become hot despite it still being early morning. Kersus lounged in the shade of his great dragon, eating berries and drinking water. The dragon saw her first. His deep grunt alerted Kersus, who stood and, taking one look at her, offered his canteen. She drank greedily. Realizing it could be her last drink ever, she tipped the water back again, letting it refresh her. Antiquity needed to be clearheaded and prepared for what was to come. The simple act of drinking the water let her gather her thoughts. Giving the canteen back to Kersus, she looked out over the desert. Her playground. One that linked other parts of Erth she had once only dreamed about.

And out there, a warship carried Saph Fyre, to be used as a lesson of some sort to the people of Solomon Fyre, Erth, and perhaps the Imperium's universe.

She didn't let the thought linger long. She had a mech to save.

"Kersus, are your kin ready?"

"They are, Antiquity Angelus," he said. "They have flown into the mountains behind your eyrie home. Twenty strong. But a part of the might of Pelail Eyrie."

"How will they know to attack?"

Kersus patted his dragon, whose rumble sounded like a cat's purr. "Ever hear a full-throated male dragon roar before?"

"No."

"Let's just say you will want to cover your ears, lest you go deaf."

She grinned and nodded. She liked Kersus. Each one of her friends possessed a different strength from the rest. Kersus was solid like a mountain, immovable and stoic. The type of man who would die before failing.

She would need him to be that rock this day.

"Chekker, where is she?" Antiquity asked.

The bot spun and clicked. "Approaching. Your eyes should be able to see now."

Antiquity squinted against the rising sun. Chekker was right. In the distance, in a heat mirage that glistened with imagined water, a giant warship flew slowly toward Solomon Fyre. Beneath it, they could just make out the outline of Saph Fyre.

"It is almost time," Antiquity said.

"Mount Rorshak then, Antiquity Angelus."

She scrambled up the strange metal rungs after Kersus had done so, strapping herself in with leather and steel buckles. She looked back to the desert, heart pounding. The warship had slowed and descended toward the desert. Even from the great distance, Antiquity saw the Imperium lowering Saph Fyre to the sands still far removed from the city. The mech met the ground. The chains that secured and hauled the great mech from Bayt al-Hikma let loose, retracting into the warship. The vessel then left Saph Fyre, creeping toward the city. Its shadow fell briefly over Antiquity before it infiltrated the city proper and settled over its heart where Star Sentinel waited beneath it.

Antiquity wondered why the Imperium had left Saph Fyre out in the hot desert sands until she saw that the mech was trudging toward Solomon Fyre.

"How can that be?" Antiquity asked.

"The Imperium has somehow gotten control of Saph Fyre," Chekker answered.

Rage filled Antiquity. She hadn't expected this. "That shouldn't be possible."

"No, it shouldn't," the bot said. "Do we still proceed with the plan?"

"Why are they walking her into Solomon Fyre?"

"We cannot know their mind."

Antiquity thought about it. She gripped Kersus's shoulder. "This will be dangerous. Whoever commands my mech has full control of her arsenal too. It's not just her fists you have to be wary of."

"Life is dangerous, Angelus," the burly man said.

"Then let's be dangerous together," she said.

Kersus laughed, a big hearty sound. He kicked his heels into Rorshak. The dragon leapt into the air with powerful wing strokes and flew north, away from the city, to gain an altitude that would not be scanned by anyone. It grew cold the higher they flew. It did not bother Antiquity. Adrenaline sang through her veins, giving her heat and purpose. She would get Saph Fyre back. Become one with the mech again. And in so doing, be whole for the fight against Royal Declarion Wit.

Everything looked small from so high.

"Are you ready?" Kersus roared back at her.

Even from such heights, she could see Saph Fyre approaching the edge of the city where the desert met it. Antiquity gripped the leather belt strapping her to the dragon. Better now before innocent bystanders could be hurt or killed if the mech entered the city.

"Yes," she said, covering her ears.

When Kersus turned, he grinned. With both fists, he hit to either side of the dragon's lower neck, three times with urgency before covering his own ears. Rorshak understood the command. Gliding now upon the winds, the dragon drew in a deep breath that expanded its chest and let loose its roar, a sound that Antiquity would never forget. It vibrated through everything—her heart, her arms and legs, the very air about her, and even her mind. It seemed to fill the whole world. Antiquity didn't know how the dragon's kin could not hear the call.

When it finished, she uncovered her ears, looking toward the mountains that housed the Angelus and Dreadth eyries. The warship and Star Sentinel were still there.

A swarm of colorful wings and bodies rose behind the Imperium tech.

And fell on them like a swirling sandstorm.

The warship took action immediately. It began firing its laz-cannons in all directions, striking some dragons but missing most. Star Sentinel did not move, telling Antiquity that its pilot was not attached to its controls. They had caught the Imperium's mech by surprise. That would not last long though as she bet the pilot was scrambling for the cockpit even as the beasts tore at its titanium plate and joints. All in all, twenty dragons from Pelail Eyrie fought the warship and Star Sentinel, wreaking havoc.

The perfect diversion.

"We don't have much time!" Antiquity yelled. "Our window is now!"

"Hold on!" Kersus yelled.

Rorshak dove. Wind howled past her. The bottom of her guts curdled. She gritted her teeth, feeling as though at any moment she would detach and fall to her death. She didn't though. The city grew at an accelerated rate the closer they came to the desert. She blinked away tears, trying to keep her eyes open. Exhilaration mixed with dread—a potent combination.

When she began worrying they'd hit the ground if they didn't slow, Rorshak broke out his wings, a thunderclap of leather meeting air. They leveled off parallel to the ground, rushing toward the back of Saph Fyre as the mech still plodded toward the city.

Antiquity braced for impact as the dragon slammed into Saph Fyre.

The mech lurched forward, stumbling but keeping its feet. Rorshak gripped at the titanium plating, getting purchase. Saph Fyre's giant hands reached back, trying to dislodge whatever had struck it. The mech acted slow, as if asleep. It couldn't reach them, and the dragons attacking the warship and Star Sentinel kept the Imperium from knowing. For now.

"Where, Chekker?" Antiquity screamed.

"There! Where the lower back plates meet the side!"

Kersus directed Rorshak to the area, where structural damage was less likely. There was no way into the mech once it was in operation. Antiquity needed a hole. A fourth part of her plan. Heat gathered in the beast below her. And with a roar, flames erupted from the dragon's maw, blistering a small area of titanium. It took multiple blasts of dragon fire. Saph Fyre didn't stop shuffling toward the city. It was as though the mech pilot didn't care. Soon a hole appeared in the molten metal, dripping into the mech's hull and running in rivulets down its titanium skin.

"Go, Antiquity Angelus! And be safe!" Kersus thundered.

Wearing the burly man's heavy leather gloves, Antiquity undid the straps holding her in place and slid down Rorshak's scales.

To leap at the hole in the mech.

She almost missed it, only one hand finding a grip. She clung to it, flailing about, fear giving strength to her need. Throwing her other hand up, she pulled herself toward the cooling hole.

Antiquity dropped into Saph Fyre's interior, hitting hard. Chekker flew in after. Grimacing from the fall, Antiquity got her feet under her. She pulled a knife, given to her by Mistress Tamantha Wre before leaving Pelail Eyrie, and she climbed the ladder. The Imperium would have placed a trusted warrior in control of the only other mech on Erth besides Star Sentinel. She would have to be quick, and likely lethal. Chekker would help but some situations required more than an electric tase. She had her grandmother's words in her—be prepared. Always.

When she entered the cockpit, she paused, unsure what she saw.

Someone—some*thing*—floated in her mech harness.

Antiquity had no idea what it was. She knew it wasn't human. It repulsed her in a way that nothing had before. Wrong. Unnatural. The mech goggles and controls snaked over the creature as they would have with Antiquity, but it was only rudimentarily human-looking. Stubby arms. Short legs. A tiny torso. All four limbs and its body appeared as though made from cracked grey clay. The creature turned in her direction, sensing her somehow, a slow, inhuman way of moving. The mech goggles withdrew then. Its features were still hidden, but Antiquity could see pink skin like a baby's and stubbled hair on a warped head.

The opening into the cockpit closed, locking them in.

"Chekker," she said uncertainly.

Before the bot could respond, three vid-views in the pilot box came to life.

On all three, Royal Declarion Wit grinned at her, ruined face twisted.

"Catching flies with honey," the Celestial said, eyes filled with a cruel glint. "Or should I say, catching a fallen angel with a mech."

"What's going on?" Antiquity questioned, looking about her.

"I have done what my Lion could not do. Capture you," Royal Declarion Wit said. He floated in his own mech harness, but his wires and goggles were retracted so he could speak with her. He piloted Star Sentinel. It was the only place he could be. "You were clever, using the dragons as a diversion. I knew you'd come for your great-grandmother's mech. I knew you couldn't let it go. But I had no idea how resourceful you would be. Dragging a *persai* community into this fight. Ingenious. Although those flies don't quite like my mech's electrified plating. I haven't had to lift a finger. Yet."

Antiquity fought the fear rising up inside. She glanced at Chekker. The bot swirled in the air, seemingly not doing anything.

What could *he do?*

"You have brought me more to quell though," the Celestial said, thoughtful in the way that evil men could be. "I will discover which *persai* community is aiding you and end them too. It's the least I can do. The question is, should I keep you alive to watch?"

"Leave them be," Antiquity finally said. "This is between you and me."

"I wonder what you offered them." He paused. "No matter, really. Changes nothing."

"What is that thing in my harness?"

"A puppet. A pawn. The best kind, really," Royal Declarion Wit said, grinning all the more. Antiquity wanted to punch his face badly. "Would you like to give up now?"

"No."

"Tsk, tsk. Don't be so quick to answer. Think about this."

"No thinking needed. You killed my grandmother."

"Ahh, there is your one weakness."

Antiquity turned away from the vid-view and breathed a name to Chekker. A series of clicks and whirs whispered on the air from the bot. She turned back. "And what is my one weakness?" she asked, trying to buy some time.

"Love. You love. Therefore, your love can be used against you," the Celestial said, cleaning the goggles with a soft cloth—all of his tech newer than Saph Fyre's. "Pathetic. You are no leader. No great messiah. You have not the wit nor ability to be who you've been told you should be. You fell into my trap without a thought." He paused again, putting his goggles on. "But you are resilient. No doubt about that. And because you are, I cannot let you escape. Not again. My brother governor would have my head. Best way to keep you from breaking free is to restrain you."

A second set of cords, wires, and even goggles Antiquity didn't know existed shot out of the same compartment that housed the pilot's own. Shocked, she tried to fight them off, but it was too late. They gripped her like iron shackles. Saph Fyre began to draw her mind into it.

"And now you are mine," Antiquity heard Wit say.

The cockpit darkened about her as she was drawn into Saph Fyre, immediately realizing she was sharing the mech with another intelligence—one that seemed dull compared to her own but was just as strong and stubborn as she knew herself to be.

As Antiquity sank further into the machine, her horror grew as the creature's face looked up at her, blue eyes to blue eyes.

And the visage was her own.

) 🌒 ● 🌘 (

Antiquity could sense the golem that was her but not.

As she got drawn down into the darkness of Saph Fyre's core matrix, she understood what she was up against. Anger at what had been done bolstered her resolve, gave her strength. A violation, an abomination. The creature piloting the mech had been formed in a lab, grown at some accelerated rate. Knowing the Imperium killed Sayf al-Din and infiltrated Bayt al-Hikma, she should have expected the Celestial would take all material associated with Antiquity and her friends. That meant the artificial intelligence construct the Rose King had been working on—using the theft of Antiquity's memories along with her genetic information—had fallen into the hands of Royal Declarion Wit. The golem was made of her. And with a body composed of her genetics, it could operate Saph Fyre with the mech's locking mechanisms none the wiser.

She had hoped the Rose King hadn't gotten from her what he needed during his golem creation. Sadly, he had—and lost the golem to the Imperium after Royal Declarion Wit had him killed.

"Chekker! I need help now!" Antiquity screamed into the ether.

No response came. The bot might as well have been on the other side of Erth.

The golem had her. She could feel it. She couldn't see the creature, but she sensed it, deep in her mind, and it prevented her from swimming to the top of consciousness to be free. She fought to control Saph Fyre, but the mech did not respond. It was under the thrall of the golem as its primary pilot, and the golem was controlled by Royal Declarion Wit.

The chains didn't stop there though. The golem kept trying to push her further down in her own mind, into a place where madness resided.

She had to fight back.

It was like a dream she couldn't wake from.

She had to be smarter than the golem. Combatting the other entity would do nothing. It had the upper hand, in control of the system that kept her shackled in its depths. As long as it held the key, she could do nothing.

She realized she had to find a different way. The golem was once a part of her. It possessed enough of her mind and genetics to fool Saph Fyre.

With her memories, perhaps a weakness could be exposed.

It could be made vulnerable.

Antiquity gathered the most important memories, searching for the right one, a key to unlock her prison. She used her hurt, her pain, her hope. She opened herself up to her golem counterpart, trying to draw it into her mind. The golem kept her at bay—until they both crossed the memory of the day her parents died. Curiosity surfaced in the golem at the sorrowful recollection; the creature wanted to know more. Antiquity understood then. The golem saw her parents as her own. Using the connection, she shared her memories for the golem to know in their entirety. The golem sensed her efforts; it knew there were holes in its memory. Holes that needed filling. The golem became angry, buffeting her, trying to pull the memories by force. Antiquity offered to help the golem to know itself, how it came to be, and its purpose in life from here after.

Antiquity searched for one memory in particular. It came unbidden. A memory of her most horrible day, terrible because it would never change, never be different, never become more than the absolute pain residing in her heart forever.

Hoping it would be the key, Antiquity shared it with the golem. "Understand," she said to the dark creature, her twin, her jailer.

The darkness embraced the memory that hadn't been stolen.

It had been offered.

) ◗ ● ◖ (

The girl walks into the room, uncertain, scared, and alone.

The seven-year-old knows she isn't alone. Not really. She feels that way though. Her grandmother walks behind her, a presence lending the girl strength when she doesn't understand she needs it. The room is simple enough. It is sterile, white, and smells of strange chemicals. There is a vid-view on the wall, powered off. There are desert flowers in a vase, pale blue and yellow, ones her father picks for her mother all of the time. The sun shines in through the room's only window but there is no warmth to the light. The room is cold. And when she sees the bed with its medical bot technician, flashing support lights, and unmoving occupant, the girl realizes she wants to be anywhere but where she is.

She swallows her fear, and still moves forward. She approaches the bed, clutching a green teddy bear. She looks down at it. It is her oldest toy. She holds it like a shield. The girl then looks at the floor, hoping the world will fall away. It doesn't.

She can't bring herself to look up.

She knows who lies in the bed.

When she does look up, she regrets it. A woman lies there, hair matted red. Unmoving. Beaten. Swollen. Bloodied.

"Go to your mother's side, Desert Rose," her grandmother says.

The girl does. She can't see her mother in the person before her but she knows it is her. She remembers how her mother fought against the men who killed her father. She still sees the rock that slammed into her mother's head, how she went limp, how the man dragged her down behind a boulder. The day is one she will never forget.

Some part of her understands she would be dead too if not for her mother.

"Take her hand, sweet child," her grandmother says.

The girl looks at her grandmother. She is blind and old, but the girl has never seen her like this. Older than her age. Broken in ways the girl won't understand for many years. White eyes filled with tears that roll down weathered cheeks.

The girl turns back to the bed. She does as she is told, taking her mother's hand in her tiny one. The fingers are limp—fingers that used to brush her hair out of her eyes, fingers that fed her orange slices, fingers of hands of arms that hugged her close.

"Tell her that you love her."

The girl looks at her mother's ruined face. Tears come to her eyes then. The room swims with them. She takes a deep breath.

"I love you, Mama," the girl whispers.

Some part of the girl hopes her words will waken her mother. They do not. Her mother does not respond, does not stir.

She keeps breathing, the sound ragged in the room.

"I could have saved them," the girl says. She still holds her mother's hand and her teddy bear at the same time. "I should have stopped those men."

"They would have hurt you too," the grandmother says, putting her hands on the little girl's shoulders. "You did the right thing by running home, by telling me."

"How can you say that?"

The old woman kneels down, hugs the girl. "Because you are here. With me. And alive."

The girl doesn't know what to say. As she mulls it over, a bell chimes from the sensors in the bed. A series of warnings, blaring in the room. The medical bot technician floats to its patient's side, checking machines that flash red. The bot registers the warnings but does nothing. The bell continues as her mother takes a different breath, one heavier and longer than the rest. The next one comes shorter. The girl sees her mother fighting. The next breath is a gasp, hollow in her open mouth. The next one is a minute removed, barely a whisper of air.

The chiming bell becomes a flat drone of emergency.

"Do something!" the girl yells.

The bot moves to the medical unit and turns off the piercing sound. It tells the girl there is nothing that can be done.

The girl stares at her mother, unmoving, quiet.

She knows her mother is gone now too.

"My sweet daughter," her grandmother says, the words choked. She lifts the girl up, giving her a better view. The girl looks down on her mother—and can barely breathe. "You need to say goodbye to her, Antiquity. She would want that."

The girl is placed at the edge of the bed. Without realizing what she does, she leans down and kisses her mother's forehead.

It is still warm.

She realizes it's the last time she will see her. The tears increase, an ocean of sorrow rising up out of her depths. The girl can barely breathe. She turns away into the arms of her grandmother, who is waiting. The old woman is wiry strong and, lifting the girl clear of the bed, pulls her close. The girl buries her face in the other's neck. Grips her tight. And cries. It is one of the only times the two share a long embrace.

"You are all I have now, Desert Rose," her grandmother whispers, holding her granddaughter tightly too. The old woman is crying and her tears mingle with those on the girl's face, a shared moment that will forever be etched in the girl's mind.

The girl cries all the harder for it. She doesn't stop. "Why . . . did they . . . have to die?" She can barely say the words.

"I wish I knew."

The girl discovers a pinprick of anger in her heart. It helps stop the tears. "The men who killed my parents. They did so because we are Grey-shamed."

"Bad men do bad things all of the time," her grandmother says. "To Grey or not Grey."

"How do we stop being Grey though?"

"There is no answer to that," the old woman says, looking down on her unmoving daughter with milky white eyes that cannot see. "The Imperium

killed your great-grandmother, my mother. I was very young, like you are now. I still remember that day, like you will remember this day. People blamed my mother for what happened, the Splinter War and losing our world to the Imperium. We were Grey after that and have been ever since."

"The Imperium made us Grey then. It killed my parents."

Her grandmother moves a lock of the girl's hair out of her eyes.

"Indirectly, maybe."

The girl wipes her eyes free of tears. She looks down at her mother again before leaving the room, one last time, to forever remember what has been done to her. She says, "Maybe we can do something one day."

The grandmother hugs the girl. Both girls feel the hug—for there are two of them now, one girl remembering that day and one incorporating it as a new memory—and they hear the old woman's next words, like prophecy of a future they both will play a part in.

"One day you will."

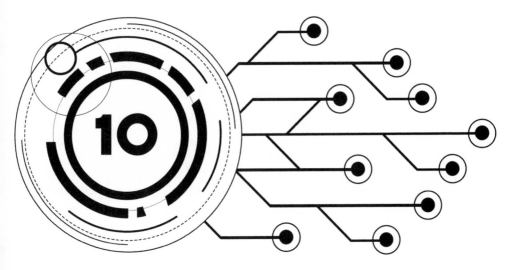

10

S uddenly freed, Saph Fyre became Antiquity's once more.

She felt the change immediately. The golem released its primary control over the mech. And her. The memory of her mother's death and how she had used it still heavy in her heart, Antiquity took control of Saph Fyre, one with the mech again, feeling its power thrum through her. It gave her strength when hers had been sapped. She returned to the world and ripped the goggles free, even as she powered everything down. The wires connecting her to the mech withdrew back to their compartment. Antiquity dropped to the floor, breathing hard from the emotional toll. She had gotten out. She was back. Royal Declarion Wit screamed at her and someone off camera from the vidviews but she ignored him—even as Saph Fyre powered them off too. She would deal with him in a second because he'd be coming for her.

Instead, Antiquity glanced over at the golem. It stared at her, its eyes shining with tiny tears. The golem saw Antiquity's mother as its own, the worst memory either of them shared.

"Kill me," it said, its malformed mouth barely able to articulate.

Antiquity picked up the *persai* knife that had clattered to the floor. It felt heavy in her hand. As if weighted with all of the most horrible decisions she had ever had to make—and this was the worst of them.

Chekker flew into her view, agitated with worry.

"Chekker, I gave you access to copy the system."

"Yes, yes, Grey-child," the bot said. "I recognized your command the moment it happened. The data is already streaming to CyTak-1. He is forwarding it onward to the first mech below the Hall of Elders. Are you okay?"

Antiquity nodded, pleased but still shaken. She walked over to the golem. She didn't know what to do. The creature before her withdrew its goggles with short arms and stubby fingers, the mech withdrawing its wires as well. The golem gently came to rest on the floor, a lump of Antiquity's genetics, clay, and stone.

"It is an aberration," Chekker said as if reading her mind. "Outlawed and not human."

"I know what I have to do."

Chekker said nothing more. Antiquity knelt before the golem.

"Kill. Me," it repeated, eyes imploring. "I am not real. You are."

Pain tore at Antiquity. She may have shared her mother's final moments, but she also had been given access to the golem's memories through their connection—its first breaths of life, the confusion, the fear instilled in it by Sayf al-Din and later by Royal Declarion Wit.

She knew the odd girl in front of her in a way no one could.

Antiquity lowered the knife.

"Why not kill me?" the golem implored. "I am not real."

"You are real enough," Antiquity said, decision made. "Besides, you are about the only family I have left. Now, can you move away from the main controls so I can access them? There is a war to fight."

The golem did not argue. It struggled across the floor, its arms stronger than they looked, pulling the girl's misshapen body across the floor.

"What are you doing, Grey-child?" Chekker asked. "It can't be left alive."

"I'm doing what needs to be done," Antiquity said, stepping into the space for the primary pilot. Saph Fyre sensed her immediately. Goggles and wires snaked over her once more, joining with her, giving her access to the mech and all of its power. Her mind became one with it, the two now so much more. She had not known how she would miss being connected to her great-grandmother's mech, but she embraced her future with her family's birthright.

Once within her metal skin, she felt Saph Fyre transmitting a massive amount of data to Chekker.

It would be heading toward her friends in the Great Hall of Fyre.

She flexed arms and legs and, with the mech's heightened sensors, gazed at the heights of the city where her eyrie existed.

There, dragons still fought the warship, but fewer circled the behemoth. And Star Sentinel's faceplate remained pointed in her direction even as the mech struck at its attackers. Antiquity felt Royal Declarion Wit staring at her.

But Star Sentinel did nothing.

"What is he waiting for?" Antiquity asked Chekker.

The bot spun in the air. "I do not know. The Royals have always been a scheming family. Be prepared for anything."

"We can't let those *persai* die," Antiquity said, getting Saph Fyre's legs under her to run through the streets. Careful not to kill innocent bystanders, she made her way toward the eyrie of her birth, to take on Star Sentinel. "They have risked everything. We have to return the favor. And keep the Imperium busy to give you and CyTak-1 time."

"There are other worries too. Look about you," Chekker pressed.

Saph Fyre did so. She saw what the bot meant immediately. The battle with the warship had set off chaos in the city. Parts of Solomon Fyre were aflame, some of the buildings smashed by falling dying dragons. The people of Solomon Fyre would be confused, frightened. Worse, if the battle continued, the entire city could succumb to the fight she would take to Royal Declarion Wit.

"I need my friends out here now, Chekker," she breathed.

She heard a couple of clicks in her com-link.

"Antiquity, are you there?" a familiar voice said in her ear, one she had hated her entire life but now loved hearing all the same.

"I am, Manson."

"CyTak-1 is connecting us," he said. "Are you okay?"

"Saph Fyre is mine once more," she shared, hoping Manson called with good news. "But the time the *persai* and their dragons have given us is almost at an end. I need you out here, now! CyTak should already have data streaming to him," she added, afraid of what the other would report. "Is he uploading it?"

"The bot says it will take time," Manson buzzed in her ear.

"Let's hope not too much time," she said. "The power I give you can move mountains. Be smart. We shall have our revenge but only if we do this together."

"For our families and friends."

"For Erth," she said. "Is Sadiya there?"

"I am," Sadiya said.

Antiquity wanted the *arabi* at her side. She hoped it would happen. Sadiya would be the most formidable warrior mech ever once she exited the Hall of Elders. "Keep safe there. And my friends. You know how to protect those who need it."

"By the time I have to, I will be wearing a very different kind of mettle."

Antiquity let the conversation go. She understood exactly what the *arabi* meant. And she had a fight to bring. Saph Fyre was now running through the streets, Antiquity yelling at Solomon Fyre's populace to take cover, to find safety. She entered the main square of the city—with its dragon fountain and the building that contained the Hall of Elders—and the closer she drew to her eyrie home, the more she saw. Dead dragons and their dead riders lay strewn throughout the streets. City residents were aiding those already injured by the conflict, pulling them to safety. It all sickened her. Antiquity had never seen war on this scale; the videos of the Splinter War focused only on the air battle. This was different. The streets were largely empty, giving Antiquity hope that casualties would be kept at a minimum.

But that would only happen if she stopped Royal Declarion Wit from destroying the city. She had to confront him, fight him. She tried to fire her flight capabilities, to gain the top of the bluff where Star Sentinel fought, but nothing happened. Cursing at her lack of ability even at this time of desperation, she gained the bottom cliff face and grabbed the bare rock that housed her eyrie to pull herself up to attack her enemies.

She was gripping the first boulders with her hands when a shadow leapt.

That's when the Lion slammed into her, hurtling Saph Fyre back to the streets.

) ◗ ● ◖ (

Titanium claws ripped into Saph Fyre, rending the mech's back.

Warning signals of the damage blaring in her mind, Antiquity acted on instinct. She rolled, the massive size of Saph Fyre forcing the Lion to let go or be crushed by the larger weight. The cat mech landed easily on all feet, its matte black titanium absorbing the day's light, massive jaws open and revealing rows of teeth. Antiquity saw no cockpit like that of Saph Fyre, but she knew the Lion was inside it. Watching her. Ready to attack when he saw an opening. The Lion's silver eyes followed her, titanium tail swishing back and forth, embedded with sharp spikes.

She brought Saph Fyre's fist up, launching a series of cram-missiles. The projectiles burned the air, coiling.

The Lion was fast, too quick for them. It danced aside, the firepower exploding into nearby buildings and the cliff beyond. Before Antiquity could shoot another set, the Lion leapt at her, taking advantage of the opening, slashing at her knees before bounding away again. Antiquity realized her danger. The Lion would continue to rip at Saph Fyre, a plate at a time, until there was nothing left.

She now knew why Royal Declarion Wit had not attacked her.

He had waited for his Lion.

"How does it feel, Antiquity Angelus?" Star Sentinel roared from above.

Antiquity didn't answer, anger fueling Saph Fyre as she and the Lion circled one another.

"All of Erth is watching. Your pet dragons are dead or have fled. The other cities of the planet will learn what happens to those who rebel against the Imperium and the governor's seat of Euroda. And you will be forgotten by all."

Rage twisted her insides but she tamped it down. Antiquity would not succumb to his bait, focusing on the fight at hand.

Instead, she kept her eyes on the Lion. It attacked again, a direct assault aimed at her head this time, launching so fast it would have destroyed the mech's cockpit and her inside it if it had struck. Saph Fyre was ready though; Antiquity felt more connected to the mech than ever before. She ducked aside, letting the Lion fly over her to slam into the rock face.

Too late, she realized it had all been a feint. The Lion gripped the cliff and pushed off with its powerful legs, straight back down to the ground.

When it hit, its tail lashed out, striking Saph Fyre behind her right knee. The force of it bent that leg's knee to the ground.

And Saph Fyre with it.

She tried to hit the Lion with her fist. It jumped aside only to vault back into Saph Fyre's chest. The Lion's inertia rammed Saph Fyre, until the mech toppled backward. She hit the ground hard, jarring even in her harness. The Lion tore at Saph Fyre's abdomen, titanium screeching as it rent. Warnings blared in her mind. Saph Fyre tried dislodging it, to grasp its leg and tear it apart. It was too strong, knocking her hands aside, going for her head.

It would reach her faceplate.

And kill her.

A dark shadow blotted out the sun over both of them then—as a mech fist not her own connected with her attacker. The Lion vanished in a heartbeat, flying sideways through the air to crash into a squat building that disintegrated beneath it.

"Looks like you needed some help," a familiar voice said in her ear.

"Manson Dreadth!"

She heard the man laugh at her exclamation. Antiquity couldn't believe it. The mech standing over her reached down, offering a shiny, unpainted hand, and Saph Fyre gratefully accepted it, Manson hauling her back upward. The Dreadth's mech was of a similar size and design to Saph Fyre. It possessed none of the battered plate and worn paint that Antiquity's mech had, instead looking as if it had just been assembled. It had never been painted, it held no house sigil. It glowed chrome beneath the sunlight, a powerful new ally for Antiquity and Solomon Fyre.

She couldn't stop grinning. The battle had evened up.

"Got a name for your mech?" Antiquity asked.

"I'm thinking Harbinger."

"I like it."

Before they could say more, a larger darkness fell over them. Both mechs turned. Star Sentinel had jumped from the eyries above to land between them and the Lion, the massive white mech larger than both, the Imperium's sigil glowing from its left chest plate. Much closer up, Antiquity could tell Star Sentinel possessed technology and design features greater than the mechs built decades earlier.

The Lion gathered itself from the rubble, showing barely any damage to its body. It moved to stand just behind and to the side of Star Sentinel.

"You are filled with all sorts of surprises, Angelus," Royal Declarion Wit boomed from his mech. "This is going to be better than I gave you credit for."

"Don't respond, Manson. We have to keep the others a secret as long as possible, and the Royal only wants to distract us," Antiquity said. "We end these two, then we go after the warship. This is going to take both of us."

"I want the Lion," Manson growled. "He killed my father."

Antiquity could hear the rage in his voice. He'd rather go after the Lion even if it threatened the sacrifices others had made. Before she could voice her concern, Star Sentinel crouched, a bunched coil of metal and Royal intention, preparing for an assault. Ports along its forearms opened, large laz-cannons emitting ribbons of fire at Saph Fyre and Harbinger. Antiquity leapt to the side; Manson rolled the other way.

That's when the Lion launched an attack—not at them, but the people of Solomon Fyre.

Before Antiquity could do anything, the Lion began killing any person remaining in the streets of Solomon Fyre.

Savaging men, women, and children of all races.

Batting them aside.

Crushing them beneath its claws and snapping them between its jaws. The screams reached Antiquity even within Saph Fyre.

"Can you keep Declarion Wit busy?" Manson asked. "I'm killing that Lion bastard."

"That's what they want! To separate us!" Antiquity yelled.

"That's what *I* want too," Manson said.

Antiquity took a deep breath, finding it difficult to say the words. "Don't do anything stupid."

"You know me."

Before she could change his mind, Manson went after the Lion, his running mech shaking the ground, leaving Saph Fyre to battle Star Sentinel.

"Careful," the golem warned at her feet. It had strapped itself into the side chair, to prevent being tossed about within the cockpit. "The Royal using you, gain his audience."

"Then let's give that audience something to cheer about."

She did not wait for the golem to reply. She prepared all weapon systems on board, hoping she had the firepower it would take to bring Star Sentinel down. She doubted she had it. Saph Fyre was a mech from an earlier age. She had different and lesser weapons, her size smaller than the much larger Euroda mech. Star Sentinel had been created by the finest minds in the Imperium, using the latest technologies available to them. But beating the Imperium with her great-grandmother's mech was not the point. Antiquity only needed to keep the Royal busy while not dying in the process.

The warship far overhead, now free of the dragon riders that had assaulted it, turned its weapons on Saph Fyre. Laz-blasts tore at her. She raised her hands up, running deeper into the city where the buildings were taller and offered cover.

And Saph Fyre took a hit from Star Sentinel that sent her sprawling.

In the cockpit, Antiquity felt it as if she had been punched. Star Sentinel had come at her from the opposite side where the warship attacked, a blind assault she hadn't seen coming. She landed hard, her momentum ripping up the streets. Before she could gather her wits, a missile exploded into her left thigh, scorching it, keeping her down. Star Sentinel fell on her, Royal Declarion Wit using his size advantage to keep her pinned. At least it kept the warship from firing on her.

The Imperium machine raised a massive fist and brought it down at her head. She rolled away—and kicked out, hitting Star Sentinel in its knee's side.

The Imperium mech shivered with the strike.

Antiquity rolled again.

"You are not going to hide from me or the Imperium, Grey," Royal Declarion Wit growled through his mech's speakers.

She ignored him. Instead, she tried to scramble to her feet, but Star Sentinel swiped at her leg, cutting the effort out from under her. The mech grabbed both of her feet, dragging Saph Fyre back to the dragon-fountain square where drone cameras shot wide angles of the battle.

As she was being dragged, Antiquity searched for Harbinger. She found Manson and it brought her hope. Somehow he had cornered the Lion within the broken confines of a building that had lost two of its walls and most of its roof and floors. The Lion stood upon rubble—face-to-face with the Dreadth's mech—looking about to pounce, shifting this way and that as if deciding where to attack. The next moment, the Lion changed its mind, turning to bound over the rubble and escape to fight in a different place.

Manson did not let that happen. He grabbed the tail despite its spikes and swung the Lion down through the air. The feline mech tried to rend Harbinger's hand like a captured desert possum but it lacked the time, and Manson drove the Lion into the broken rubble of the building. Stunned, the Lion scrambled to escape but Harbinger was faster. The shiny mech reached down, grabbed its foe by the neck and, with the strength of the entire mech behind him, brought the Lion down in a blur of speed and power to the square's stone courtyard.

The head of the Lion mech crumpled. Its silver eyes and skull shattered, jaw breaking and titanium shoulder, neck, and chest plates twisting beneath the blunt force of Harbinger.

Legs and tail thrashed for a few seconds before going still.

Manson didn't stop there. Harbinger brought both fists down, smashing the head.

"Your Lion is dead, Royal," Antiquity called.

"It does not matter. Star Sentinel is a match for you and your extra mech," Royal Declarion Wit said. He let go of Saph Fyre, flipping her to the stone. Antiquity hit hard again. She wondered how much damage her mech could take. "Who pilots that extra mech? Where did you find it?" He paused. "Dreadth. I bet it's that pup of a boy whose father died mewling like the traitorous bitch I always knew him to be."

Harbinger turned, fists clenched and already running at Star Sentinel.

"You will see my face before the end."

The Imperium mech let go of Saph Fyre and met Manson's machine, each trading punches. Manson didn't back down despite every delivered punch from Star Sentinel driving him back, pushing him down, forcing the much smaller mech to retreat. On her back, Antiquity fired ribbons of laz-fire into Star Sentinel's chest. The lines of red heat did barely any damage. The Royal ignored her and rammed his knee into the gut of Harbinger. It sent Manson sprawling, his mech lifted off his feet and thrown against one of the last buildings still standing in the main square of Solomon Fyre.

Star Sentinel turned to look down on her. She could sense Royal Declarion Wit inside, grinning at his power, his superiority oozing from the mech. Antiquity hated the truth. He did outmatch her and Manson. It was only a matter of time before he'd kill one of them.

And then kill the other just as quickly.

"I am here, Desert Rose," Sadiya said in her com-link.

"Me too!" Elsana added.

Desperation changed to excitement. Antiquity wanted to scream her elation to the heavens. Help had arrived. She had done what she had set out to do. Gotten the mechs belowground activated and piloted. The realization of her great-grandmother's dream was upon them. Solomon Fyre would be freed by a plan put in place decades before. Antiquity regained her feet, feeling renewed hope for the first time in days. She backed Saph Fyre away from Star Sentinel—not because she didn't want to fight Royal Declarion Wit but because she didn't have to fight alone now. Metal fist in the air, Antiquity roared Laurellyn Angelus's dream to the city.

She hoped the Imperium's vid-cams were catching all of it.

Because outside the Hall of Elders where the dragon fountain now slid aside, more of the buried past rose into the light.

) ◗ ● ◖ (

Star Sentinel stood transfixed as Sadiya and Elsana piloted toward him.

The two shiny mechs stepped clear of the now-revealed entrance to the catacomb beneath the Hall of Elders, their unpainted shiny titanium blinding in the early afternoon sunlight. Even though the mechs were the same, Antiquity could tell which of her friends piloted each one, one mech moving with a smooth grace that matched how the Will Master moved. They climbed over the remnants of smoking and wrecked buildings, entering the empty square to join Antiquity and Manson. Star Sentinel paused its assault, having gone silent, its pilot most likely assessing the change in the situation and formulating what to do against such a strong new show of force.

The mag-propulsion of the warship brought it around behind its master, cannons at the ready, covered in damage from the dragons and their fire—but still quite operational.

Star Sentinel had aid from the sky. Antiquity would have to change that.

"You wear that mech well, Elsana," she said to her longtime friend.

"I feel strong . . . for maybe the first time in my life," Elsana said, flexing her right hand. The twin's mind connected to the mech, overcoming her physical handicap.

"You've always been strong," Antiquity said. "If only Kaihli was here to see it."

"She'd be mad if she didn't have her own mech!"

"What did you do with High Chamberlain Braun Pierce?"

"I decided CyTak-1 could keep him jailed below," Sadiya said, stepping to Antiquity's side. "The All-Father does not release those who are still in His service." She paused, looking about. "I see this is not going as well as it could."

Joy at seeing her friend happy faded, and the destruction around them left Antiquity disheartened. The lives lost. The damage done. She had known the battle against the Imperium would involve sacrifice on some level. But witnessing it now in the city of her birth left her painfully aware of the consequences of her actions. She had few weapons left, her arsenal largely spent. But the friends who stood with her were weapons of a different sort, their bond to end the Imperium in Solomon Fyre and fix the lives of those who remained.

Star Sentinel brought his fists up, electricity arcing between them, a powerful feature that Antiquity's mechs did not possess.

"This ends now, Grey," Royal Declarion Wit said.

Using the thrusters in its feet, Star Sentinel blasted from the ruined city streets, flying right at Saph Fyre—while firing pulses of plasma at Harbinger to the left and Sadiya and Elsana to the right. Prepared for an attack, Antiquity backed up, opening more distance between them as she unleashed laz-cannons of her own, striking the Imperium's mech in the head.

The faceplate held strong but Star Sentinel turned aside, unable to see its foe. At the same time, the warship maneuvered directly overhead, releasing several high-speed single-pilot gunships, their distracting fire stinging like bees of titanium.

A continuous fount of fire and fury hit them from all fronts.

"Elsana, I need you to take care of these tiny ships," Antiquity ordered.

"On it!" the twin said, using her new weapons to shoot the ships from the air.

Antiquity turned to the *arabi*. "Sadiya, we have to take down the mech first. He's the main danger. He could destroy the city with his hands and nothing else. We can take care of the warship afterward. It's going to take all of us," Antiquity yelled to her friends. "All of us to fight back and end this—before more people are hurt and more of the city is destroyed."

"Then let's keep him busy," Sadiya said. Not wasting time, the Will Master moved smoothly, swiping the leg of Star Sentinel and bounding aside when the attack had been ineffectual. The two battled one another but Royal Declarion Wit never landed a blow, the *arabi* too fast. It gave Antiquity time to plan how they could combat such a foe. She wished Sadiya had some kind of mech sword to take the place of Oathmaster, one she could use to easily destroy the Royal. Instead, she had to strike and retreat, until Star Sentinel sent a rush of flame at the *arabi*, pushing her back.

Antiquity looked around, trying to come up with some idea. Elsana struck down another gunship. Then another. As if she had been born to the mech she now controlled.

"Or maybe we just need three of us," Manson said, sprinting at the freed Star Sentinel. "Attack once I've engaged him, both you and Sadiya. You'll know what to do."

"I said nothing stupid, Dreadth!" Antiquity said.

"And I told you that you know me!"

Harbinger tried its own flight capabilities, Manson managing to find control and jet into Star Sentinel. The two mechs met with a loud crash and, pounding at one another, separated for a brief instant as both returned to the ground. Manson did not let up. Harbinger swung. The punch landed solid. He did it again, against the other's chest plate. Star Sentinel staggered back. Manson finished with an uppercut into the Imperium mech's jaw. It looked like he had Royal Declarion Wit on the defense, Manson's rage fueling his mech's quick and powerful assault. But that ended fast. Star Sentinel caught the fist of Harbinger's next punch and pushed Manson down with his superior strength and height. Then he grabbed the mech's wrist with his other hand before twisting low to the side, bringing Harbinger's arm over Star Sentinel's thick-plated shoulder, and wrenched hard downward.

The screech of breaking metal punctuated the city—until arm tore from shoulder.

Harbinger dropped to its knees. Star Sentinel kicked the defeated mech to the ground and threw its arm upon the fallen titanium body.

Electricity sparked and spat from the missing arm.

"No, Manson!"

"Now, Antiquity!" he said in her ear.

Seeing Royal Declarion Wit distracted, Sadiya moved faster than any of them. Antiquity did the same from the other side. She understood what the *arabi* intended. Sadiya hit high while Antiquity chose to smash low, both mechs colliding into Star Sentinel at the same time.

At different heights. And from different directions.

The crash of titanium against titanium reverberated throughout Solomon Fyre like the hammer of one of the old gods striking an anvil. Antiquity felt like she'd just hit a wall at full speed. Saph Fyre blared titanium stress warning signals in her mind. She fought to keep focused, rolled to the ground, and looked up. Sadiya had vanished on the other side of Star Sentinel.

Or what remained of the Imperium mech. Legs torn asunder from the hips, the upper torso of Star Sentinel lay a hundred yards away, where Sadiya now regained her feet.

The Imperium's lone mech on Erth lay broken and ruined.

"He's going nowhere," Sadiya said.

"What now?" Manson asked, pushing himself up with his remaining arm. The pain in his voice was unmistakable. Connected to his mech, he had felt the loss of Harbinger's arm. "Kill him? Use him as a hostage?"

Antiquity hadn't considered this moment. She knew her own feelings but also had to take into account that of the Imperium. She had seen how cold and ruthless Royal Declarion Wit was, the things he had said about his brother and other Celestials. She doubted Royal Ricariol Wit, the older brother and great lord general of the Imperium's Erth, would barter for him or exchange him for the benefit of Solomon Fyre. Royal Declarion Wit knew that. But he could be useful in other ways.

"We will not kill him," she said. "We are not like them. And he has information that could be vital for us reclaiming Erth. He knows the world outside of this city better than we do. He will help us or live out the rest of his days groveling for his next meal."

"Antiquity, there is a sudden and growing heat signature within Star Sentinel," Chekker said. "There at its core."

Antiquity realized this was far from over. "What does that mean?"

"Royal Declarion Wit has triggered a self-destruct sequence within Star Sentinel's fuel cells. The readings I am gathering suggest those cells are quite large and dangerous."

"What is he doing?!" Antiquity asked.

Elsana clicked her tongue. "Look, the Celestial troops are pulling out of the city."

Antiquity saw it as well. Small soldier transports were lifting free of the ground all over Solomon Fyre, zooming from the city and back into the desert. The warship did the same. Whereas Elsana's voice carried excitement at the withdrawal of enemy troops within their city, a pit of dread grew in Antiquity's heart, a realization of what was actually happening.

"He's going to destroy the city," Antiquity breathed.

"He wouldn't," Elsana said.

"Royal Declarion Wit would do so if it meant having to face his brother in defeat," Antiquity said. She was at a loss for what to do. "He wants to win, even if that means his death." She activated Saph Fyre's voice. "Don't do this, Royal Declarion Wit!" she roared at the fallen Star Sentinel's faceplate.

No answer came. The mech's head settled to the street in defeat.

"A mega-explosion unlike anyone has seen since the Splinter War,"

Chekker said. "It accelerates. You do not have much time. It cannot be stopped."

"He will make Solomon Fyre a symbol," Manson said.

"Ash and rubble, for all the stars to witness," Antiquity said. She looked to the sky. She knelt down before the fallen Star Sentinel. "Step back," she ordered the others.

Her friends did as she asked. It made her sad as she suddenly understood the great truth of her family. She spent a lifetime studying her great-grandmother and the history of the Angelus leaders. Antiquity remembered hating those lessons; she never understood why they were important. Why would a Grey-shamed family ever need to lead again? To help people see the potential in not only themselves but those around them. To become a beacon of hope to those that had none. To lead and be followed, for the betterment of all.

Tears came to her eyes, hearing the words of her grandmother, finally understanding what the old blind woman had meant for all of those years.

Be the change of the moment.

Antiquity gripped Star Sentinel under its arms, lifting the giant mech free of the ground. It was much easier than she expected, the absence of its legs reducing weight.

"What are you doing, Antiquity?" Manson asked.

"What needs doing," she said. "Stand farther back from me."

The other mechs did so. Antiquity realized what needed to happen. She could never hope to drag Star Sentinel out into the wastes where the mech could explode. It would not only turn the desert to glass but it would spread its radioactive heart upon the winds. She would not do that to Erth's people. It would be as evil as the Imperium winning. There was only one direction she could go, a way she had not yet gone.

Looking upward, Antiquity delved inward. The key existed there, to a lock she had been unable to open ever since fleeing the Imperium. She knew the key now. It wasn't one made of every bit of pain she had experienced over her life. Or from the death of family and friends. Or the hardship faced as a Grey-shamed orphan girl tempered by experiences forged in a crucible on the journey from Solomon Fyre and back. All of that mattered but it wasn't what blocked her from flying Saph Fyre.

No, Antiquity realized what her great-grandmother and grandmother had always known, a lesson they had tried to instill in Antiquity but one that was never fully embraced. Until now. The lesson that working for the people—not herself, her family, or her friends, but everyone living in Solomon Fyre—was what mattered. What gave power. What pushed one to be more than they were. That to be Angelus was to be a servant beyond oneself.

Antiquity realized this in a maddening rush of insight—the responsibility she now carried upon her shoulders a part of her heart, mind, and soul. She took the key into the mech's depths, wielding it with conviction.

And for the first time, she truly became one with Saph Fyre.

The thrusters in Saph Fyre's feet erupted by her will, their power hers.

"Antiquity, do not do this," Elsana said, tears in her voice through the com-link.

"The city needs to see the might of the family Angelus," Antiquity said, already separated from the ground and in the air, still in control of Star Sentinel. "The world needs to see that even a Grey-shamed girl can beat the Imperium."

"All-Father speeds you on your way, Antiquity Angelus," Sadiya said, even her voice choked. "Your friends are with you."

Only Manson said nothing, merely watching.

The tears stinging her eyes starting to roll down her cheeks, she grimaced, trying to counter the weight she now carried with the weight she was familiar with. She kept Saph Fyre rocketing upward. Her friends grew small. Then the streets and buildings grew smaller. And after a few seconds, even Solomon Fyre became a shiny spot that slowly vanished and became one with the desert.

"You. Are. Strong," the golem stammered. Antiquity smiled, knowing the truth.

"We were made so by a strong woman."

The golem said nothing further, only gazing out the faceplate. Saph Fyre raced through a small bank of clouds, the world becoming misty white. Only the sound of her thrusters could be heard. Breaking free of the clouds, they shrank behind her, holes in the cover giving Antiquity a view of Erth's surface—a world of colors and textures and conflict and love and friendship. Humanity at its worst and best. Everything she knew was now gone. One of Star Sentinel's hands clamped over her arm. Royal Declarion Wit, having regained some control over his mech. Antiquity let him hold on to her arm. For now. It did not matter while Saph Fyre sent them skyward. She knew what was to come, was prepared for it.

He would win the battle but not the war. And he would die for it.

The azure of the sky thinned, losing its depth, until the blue faded and stars blinked into existence. Antiquity viewed Erth instead, marveling at its beauty from such a height—its wide deserts, its dark oceans, and even snow-capped mountain ranges. A world of dusty brown, rich blue, and white ridges. She took a deep breath, forcing Saph Fyre higher and higher, to get Star Sentinel beyond the winds of her world. She had protected it, done her job. Royal Declarion Wit would hurt no one again. It was up to her friends to take on the governor seat in Euroda with the new might they now possessed.

She gazed up again, at the heavens and beyond them, to the stars sitting within their velvet blackness. Everything she had learned from her grandmother and even great-grandmother served her well.

She was proud to bear the name Angelus and Grey at the same time.

"The end approaches," Chekker said.

"I love you, you crazy old bot."

"And I you."

Closing her eyes against the tears and what was to come, Antiquity released one hand on Star Sentinel. The Imperium mech did not fall. They were so high they were practically floating in space. She pried the Imperium's mech hand from her and let go with both, separating the mechs.

If she would die, it would not be chained to her enemy.

When the explosion tore the heavens asunder, it struck with such force Antiquity could feel it in her teeth, sending Saph Fyre hurtling back toward Erth. Warnings of her rate of speed blared in her mind. There was no way to slow down. Boosters would not help her now; her legs and their thrusters had disintegrated. The end approached. She grew faint, her descent's force threatening blackout. She knew there was nothing she could do, no ability the mech possessed that would prevent the inevitable. Saph Fyre would slam into Erth and be forever buried. Just like Antiquity found her.

But her steel would remain in those left behind.

Then darkness took her, the stars the last thing she saw.

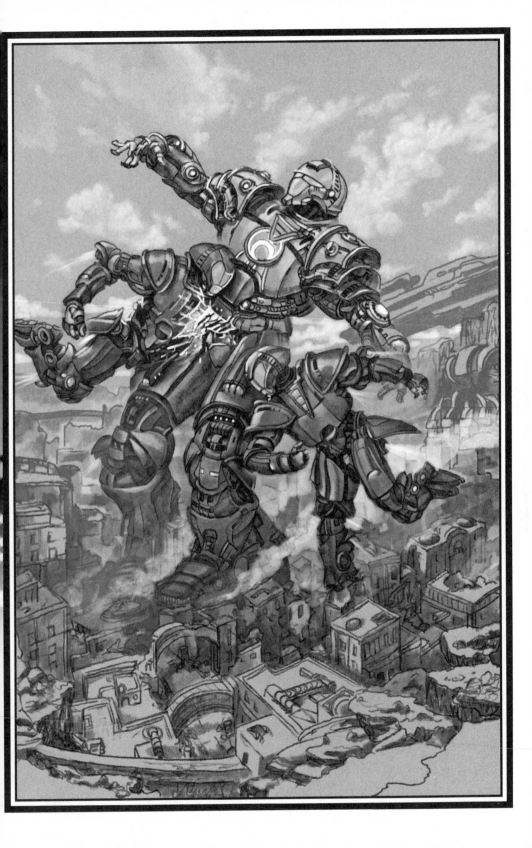

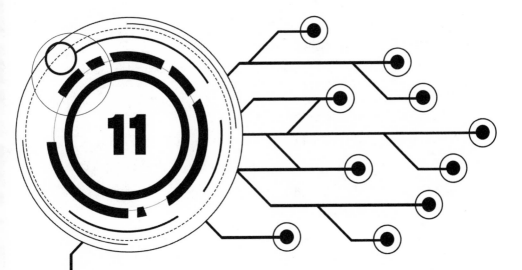

11

Antiquity stood upon the ruined stairs of the Hall of Elders building.

She marveled she was alive. Having fainted during her reentry to Erth, Antiquity had woken to a mech gripping Saph Fyre close, slowing her rate of fall. Puzzled by words in her com-link, she realized who they belonged to. Elsana, ridiculed all her life for her misshapen hand. Elsana, proud to live in her sister's shadow. Elsana, become like a god in titanium plate. The twin flew the remains of Saph Fyre back to Solomon Fyre, where the others worked Antiquity free. Now she looked about, recovered, glad to be alive.

The city still smoked, many buildings reduced to rubble, those citizens who survived now walking about the desolation or gathered below her in the square. They were innocent, those she fought to protect. She had not saved them all but she would make amends as only a leader could.

Sadiya stood to her right, Manson and Elsana to her left. The golem waited in the Hall of Elders, out of sight, shy, scared. Antiquity looked down at Saph Fyre—or rather, what remained.

It left her sad. Legs gone, chest rent apart from Star Sentinel's explosion.

But the mech would be rebuilt.

And it would continue to give hope to those who did not have it.

"Are you sure about this, Antiquity Angelus?" Chekker asked.

"Yes, my friend," Antiquity said, her resolve stronger than ever. "I am no longer the Grey-child you helped raise."

"You are not," the bot said. "You are a leader. You must lead. The blood in your veins is noble and carries power. Use that power wisely. You have a city to inspire, to care for, to grow. To protect. The Imperium will not sit idly by. They will try to kill you. And your friends."

"We need allies, yes. After we finish here, I will speak to the remaining Elders," she said, nodding. "I will consolidate whatever power remains in Solomon Fyre. Those who will not join me shall be stripped of authority. New voices are needed, new ideas made ready. The future is filled with promise but only if the leaders of the city are one. What Elders are with me will reach out to the other cities."

"A statement like the one you are about to give will bring the stars down on us," Sadiya said. Her hand resting lightly upon Oathmaster's pommel, the *arabi* stood proud and protective, no longer in her black robes but free of that past.

"That's what I want," Antiquity said. They both knew the next step. It would not be an easy one. While they had won the day and freed a city, the work done was only a grain of sand when compared to the desert they must conquer and free. They had lived in the desert a long time though.

They were used to the sand.

"We will need mechanics, technicians, and pilots most of all," Manson said from the side, his strong arms crossed. He had changed, their relationship had changed. He was no longer a bully. And if he was, he would be one tempered by her influence. "Not only for the mechs below but for those in the other cities."

"Brox survived. He will aid us in repairing the mechs as well as acquiring the right people as technicians," Antiquity said. "The pilots . . . well . . . who wouldn't want to be a pilot for Solomon Fyre?"

The others grinned. She smiled back. They were her new family now.

"Your grandmother would be proud," Chekker said.

Antiquity stood straight, shoulders back, chin up. "It is time, Chekker."

The bot twisted in the air, clicking this way and that. The two of them had come a long way in several weeks. Both were changed. For the better.

Blue light shimmered over Antiquity, recording her every word and movement.

And transmitting her to an entire world.

"People of Erth, I address you as a friend. I am Antiquity Angelus, once a Grey-child in shame," Antiquity said, voice steady, eyes earnest. "My grandmother Vestige Angelus used to say that the past should remain in the past until the present demanded that past for the future. I am here today, demanding the past be told. For our future is in the events of this present. And this present has seen power fall. And a new hope arise.

"The Imperium has kept Erth shackled for decades," she continued. "Draining our resources. Killing our people. To control the stars where their empire spreads. No more. My great-grandmother Laurellyn Angelus, the former leader of Erth and a woman betrayed during the Splinter War, led from her grave. Giving us a chance at that future. Through me. And through you." Antiquity pointed. Chekker changed his camera angle, to take in the three fully functional mechs that stood stoically in the square. "We will bring war to the Imperium. We shall take back what is ours. Besides these three, there are many more. And within their titanium hearts—titanium hidden from the Imperium—we shall rise again!"

The people who gathered below in the destroyed main square of Solomon Fyre shouted approval, their voices echoing for the entire world to hear. Not everyone did so, she noted. She knew why. Those with homes destroyed. Or worse, loved ones lost. She knew she'd have to work hard to win their trust.

Because before she could win the future, she had to care for the present.

"I am the pilot of Saph Fyre, Erth's oldest functioning mech," Antiquity said. "Our mech technology will spread over Erth again. To be free!"

The crowd cheered again, this time chanting her once forbidden surname.

"I have a simple question to ask of you, Erth!" Antiquity said, voice raised, eyes fiery. She had watched enough of her great-grandmother's speeches to know the power that such words had on those who needed to hear them. "One question! It is a simple one filled with all of the fire of a thousand suns!"

She looked into the depths of Chekker's camera—to those who watched.

"Will you fight and be free beside me?"

HERE ENDS *The Tempered Steel of Antiquity Grey.*
Book 2, *The Forever Foundry of Antiquity Grey,* continues
Antiquity's hardships of freeing Erth from the Imperium.

GLOSSARY

Abdur Hazim—scientist of artificial constructs for the Rose King

Airtafae al-Hisn—seat of ruling family in Bayt al-Hikma; translates to the Rose Stronghold

Airtafae Madrasa—university teaching how to master Will

Allamah—religious order of the *arabi*

All-Father—god of *arabi* faith

Angelus eyrie—home of House Angelus, built into plateau

Antiquity Angelus—"Grey-shamed"; granddaughter of Vestige Angelus; great-granddaughter of Laurellyn Angelus

arabi—kindred of *persai*

atlanti—rarely seen people of Erth

Azik—teen *arabi* boy

Bayt al-Hikma—*arabi* capital city

Baz al-Din—Sadiya's father; former Rose King

Beven el Ordett—merchant in Holstead

Braun Pierce—high chamberlain of the council

Brox Uphell—master mechanic; artificial construct hologram

cathari—rarely seen people of Erth

Celestials—former humans of Erth, returned from the stars

Chat Higgum—Elder whose family hates the Grey-shamed

Chekker—CHKR-11; spherical bot; friend to Antiquity Grey

Cinder—large cat; friend to Soren

Crock Bob—scavenger

CyTak-1—small spherical bot in Great Hall of Fyre

CyTak-5—small spherical bot in Great Hall of Rostam

Declarion Wit—Imperium Royal

Dragonell Mountains—mountain range to the east of the Splinter

Elders—men on ruling council in Solomon Fyre

el-hajida—wise *arabi*; creators of literature

Elsana El-Amin—Antiquity's friend; twin of Kaihli

Erth—planet

Euroda—Erth's new capital, under Imperium rule

glocks—underground animals

gold dirham—currency in Holstead

Great Cataclysm—the near destruction of Old Erth

Great Hall of Fyre—hidden underground chamber in Hall of Elders

Great Hall of Rostam—hidden underground chamber in House of Wisdom

Hall of Elders—in Solomon Fyre, where council meets

Harbinger—name of Manson's mech

High Dringlam Mountains—mountain range west of Solomon Fyre

Holstead—village within the Dragonell Mountains

House of Mourning Flowers—resting place of the dead in Pelail Eyrie

House of Wisdom—in Bayt al-Hikma; accumulation of the world's knowledge

Imperium—galactic ruling body spanning dozens of worlds

Jackson Dreadth—Manson's father; ruler of House Dreadth

Kaihli El-Amin—Antiquity's friend; twin of Elsana

Laurellyn Angelus—Antiquity's great-grandmother, Vestige's mother

Leesa—young *persai* woman; dragon rider

Lion, the—Celestial; hunter for Declarion Wit

Luna Gold—ruins of an ancient merchant metropolis

Madylia—Vodard's wife; Celestial

Manson Dreadth—son of Jackson; heir to House Dreadth

Marxa—Antiquity's mother

Mellex Dreadth—younger Dreadth kin

Mir Muhktar—Will Master; Sadiya's former teacher

Mohab al-Din—Sadiya's brother

Muthlaj Range—high eastern mountains where *arabi* settled

Old Era—long ago, when humanity ventured to the stars

Old Rizzo—scavenger

Pelail Eyrie—*persai* community in Dragonell Mountains

persai—kindred to *arabi*

Prather Anil—the oldest Hall of Elders councilman

Ricariol Wit—Imperium Royal; older brother of Declarion; lord general and governor of Erth

Rorshak—Kersus's dragon

Rose King of Bayt al-Hikma—ruler of *arabi* civilization

Rostam—ancient hero of the *arabi*, holy paladin

Royals—the Imperium Celestials in charge of Erth

Rukh al-Za—paladin; in service to the Rose King

Sadiya—Will Master; *arabi* princess

Saph Fyre—Laurellyn's mech; last mech of Solomon Fyre

Sayf al-Din—the Rose King; Sadiya's brother

scavengers—enhanced people of the desert

Sky Legions—army of the Imperium emperor

Smelly Nelly—scavenger

Solomon Fyre—once Erth's capital city

Soren—boy; friend to Cinder and Sadiya

Splinter War—Erth's mech battle against the Imperium

Star Sentinel—Imperium's lone mech on Erth

Syd Alyamin—Oathmaster; the name Sadiya gives her sword

Tamantha Wre—mistress of Pelail Eyrie

Tungstone—village within the Splinter

Vestige Grey—Angelus; Antiquity's grandmother; daughter of Laurellyn

Vodard Ryce—Celestial merchant

Will, the—a power manipulated by Will Masters

Woodlock Forest—forest in and between the Dragonell and Muthlaj Mountains

Word, the—text/philosophy of *arabi*, *cathari*, and *persai* religions

ACKNOWLEDGMENTS

Rachelle Longé McGhee
: Who helps produce a beautiful book every time out

Betsy Mitchell
: Who brought decades of SF&F editing experience to make this book the best it could be

John Joseph Adams, Terry Brooks, Robin Hobb, Mark Lawrence, Aidan Moher, and Janny Wurts
: Who lent their advice as well as encouragement

Todd Lockwood, Allen Morris, Marc Simonetti, Nate Taylor, and Kaitlund Zupanic
: Who brought colorful life to the book's black-and-white pages

Payton Lawson and Kendall Lawson
: Whose love of soccer inspired Antiquity and Chekker

Amanda Brooks and Kelle Ingham
: Who beta-read with red pens before everyone else

Kristin Speakman
: Who encourages me every day to not only be a better writer but also a better man

K:CKSTARTI∃R BACKE⌐S

Thank you doesn't even begin to express the appreciation I have for the following people (as well as those who did not wish to be named) who supported the Kickstarter campaign for this book and helped make it a success. I am sincerely grateful.

A

A G Carter • A Nony Mouse • A. Treamayne • Aaron Davenport • Aaron Dilday • Aaron Forderer • Aaron Guillot • Aaron Markworth • Abby Beasley • Adam Andre • Adam Holliday • Adam Klagues • Adam Yarbrough • adgroc • Adrian Cinca • Adrian Collins • Adrian Mørken • Adrianne • adumbratus • Aerronn Carr • Aidan Moher • Ailene Y. • Aj & Jenna Comfort • AJ LeFave • Alan D. • Alan Heinen • Alan Studzinski • Albene Dictine • Albert L. Hoyt III • Alex Beacham • Alex Fraser • Alex C. Hoffman • Alex Kostuk • Alex Lewis • Alex McKenzie • Alex Penchansky • Alex Strassburg • Alexander Dickinson • Alexander Johansen • Alexander Kalish • Alexander Nelson • Alexandra Babb-Johnson • Alexandre Tavares • Ali T. Kokmen • Alisa Peters • Allen Marsh • Allison Marie Caron • Amber de Haan • Amy Fearfield • Amy Grandelli • Amy Jarmuz Hoffman • Amy Schriever • Anaïs • Anders Walløe • Anders M. Ytterdahl • Anderson Yee • André Noel Joseph Gorley • Andrea Bicego • Andrew Cowell • Andrew Doherty • Andrew Fish • Andrew Godecke • Andrew Hildebrandt • Andrew Hogg • Andrew Lyons • Andrew Marmor • Andrew Mauney • Andrew Olsen • Andrew Ryan • Andrew Stoute • Andrew Williams • Andy Adams • Andy Barbieri • Andy Holcombe • Andy S. • Angel • Angela Walter • Angie Engelbert • Angie Ross • Ania Kwiecień • Ann Holland • Ann-Marie & Merle Dye • Anne Falbowski • Anthony M. Berardi • Anthony G. Rominske • Anthony Zielinski • April D. Moore • Aram Compeau • Arcturus Dobrica • Areeb Siddiqui • Ashley Strutt • Ashli Tingle • Atit Patel • Atthis Arts • Aurora Nicholson • Axiomwolf

323

B

B Lovrek • Bart Riepe • Bartimaeus • Baucom Family • Becky Beunton • Beks Opperman • Ben Hensey • Ben Jaeger • Ben Nichols • Ben Trehet • Benjamin A Brinkley • Benjamin Hayes • Benjamin Spademan • Benjamin Summers • Bernardo De Los Santos • Berta Batzig • Beth C. • Beth Hightower • Beth Tabler • Bethany Ritchey • Bhelliom Demian Rahl • Bill Cornette • Bill Moe • Bill Schneck • Bill Slaughter • Billy Clawson • Billy Lillard • Billy Taylor • Björn Henke • Blaise Ancona • Blake L. Duvall • Blake Unsell • BoA • Bobby McKnight • Bonnie J Ross • Bonnie Norton • Brad Kiewel • Brad Rohrer • Bradley MacDonald • Brandi Dimitroff • Brandi Plants • Brandon Babcock • Brandon Kanemori • Brayden Daniels • Brendan Morgan • Brenden Jackson • Brendon Grimm • Brennan Taylor • Brian Becker • Brian Carroll • Brian Cheek • Brian Crabtree • Brian Gressler • Brian Griffin • Brian Horen • Brian Horstmann • Brian Meadows • Brian Noonan • Brian O'Rourke • Brian J. Smith • Brian Scott Walters • Brian Whiting • Brittney Dirnbauer-Printy • Brooke Aquino-Ehlert • Bruce "Hoss" Collins • Bruce Fenton • Bruce Passey • Bruce Villas • Bryan Easton • Bryan Hill • Bryan M. Barnard • Bryan Marshall • Bryan Sears • Bryan The Wise & Powerful • Bryan Young • Bryon Chambers • The Bugge Family • Burgundy Featherkile • Burrhus Lang

C

C. L. Allen • C. Kierstead • C. Scott Kippen • C. Corbin Talley • C. D. Wright • Cade Marshall • Cailyn W • Caleb Barley • Caleb Hearth • Caledonia • Callum Kennedy-Clark • Calvin Park • Cameron Morris • Cameron Olsen • Cameron Rush • Capt. Nathan T. Schwarck • Carl Learned • Carl Plunkett • Carl VM • Carley Cowart • Carol Feeney • Carole Strohm • Carrick "Ben" Scott • Carson Sheffield • Cary Meriwether • Casey Johnson • Casey Mahoney • Catherine Book • Catherine Conklin • Catrina Ankarlo • Chad Nickalas • Chadrick • Chandra M. • Charlene Leubecker • Charles DeArmond • Charles Dewey • Charles Ryan • Charli Maxwell • Charlie Negyesi • Chawin Narkruksa • Cherloria & Simon • Cheryl Ruckel • Cheryl Rydbom • Chip P. • Chris Bone • Chris Bonn • Chris Brant • Chris Corke • Chris Fenton • Chris Gaboury • Chris Hansen • Chris Marsh • Chris Nicolls • Chris Seemann • Chris Stewart • Chris Ward • Christi 12ltrs • Christian Holt • Christian Pike • Christian Xavier • Christina Vandall • Christine Tate • Christopher Adolph • Christopher M Aldrich • Christopher Buser • Christopher A. Carlson • Christopher Horn • Christopher N. Hyde • Christopher Prew • Christopher Roland • Christopher Ward • Christy M. Schakel • Chuck Layton • Cindy Beehler • Cindy Melbye • Cliff Summers • Cliff Winnig • Clint Lewis • Clint Treadway • Colby Edrington • Cole P. Chapman • Cole Heap •

Colin Krueger • Collin M. Johnson • CompuChip • Corky LaVallee • Cory Padilla • Courtney Getty • Courtney Whitlock • Craig Dyson • Craig Gulbransen • Craig Massey • Craig T. Sanders • Crinaea Beck • Cristin Chall • Crystal • Cullen "Towelman" Gilchrist • Curt Iiams • Cynthia Lasley

D

D Chritchley • D. J. Goulding • D. M. Roberts • D.Max.D. • Daan Troost • Dagfinn Chr. Selvaag • Dale A. Russell • Damon & Jenna Bratcher • Damon M. Gelb • Damon Schofield • Dan Andrews • Dan Barnes • Dan Fritz • Dan Goodwin • Dan Grove • Dan K. Flowers • Dan K • Dan Martin • Dan McKee • Dan Norton • Daniel W. Ahrens • Daniel Anderson • Daniel Caridade • Daniel M. • Daniel J. Milligan • Daniel Nolansnyder • Daniel Priest • Danielle Pattee • Danleks • Dannel Stanley • Danny Soares • Danny The Dolphin Lundy • Darren Clarke • Darren Fry • Darryl Fortunato • Daryl Buckel • Dave & Joyce Bashford • Dave Baughman • David A. Bobbitt • David Bruns • David Lars Chamberlain • David Clarke • David D2 • David A. Dick • David Edmonds • David Galbis-Reig • David Johnson • David "Wyndhammer" Jones • David T Kirkpatrick • David Kitching • David McLoughlin • David, Caitlin & Eleanor Messina • David Moldawer • David Mulligan • David Parish • David Quist • David Renback • David Robinson • David Roc • David Rowe • David Salchow • David Tai • David N Taylor • Dawson Cowals • Dean Whirley • Deborah Yerkes • Denis Gagnon • Dennis Johnson • Derek Pritchard • Derek Roberts • Deric Paxson • Destineefarmgirl • Devyn Noto • Dipin Nayee • Dmitry Podpolny • Donald Dean McBride Jr. • Doni Savvides • Donny Lynskey • Dorothy Raniere • Doug Baer • Doug Cross • Doug Thomson • Douglas "Argowal" Reid • Douglas Cline • Douglas L Elmore • Dr. Charles Elbert Norton III • Dr. Rich Williams • Dr. Tanner Lee Nash • DresdenQ • Drew Henderson • Drew Hulburt • The Driscolls • Duncan Estes • Dustin Warford • Dusty Craine • Dylan Rose • Dyrk Ashton

E

E.D.E. Bell • ebarriusa • Ed Potter • Edward H • Edward Tolley • Edwin Roberson • Eileen Birdsong • Eldon Thompson • Eli O. Jakobsen • Elise Roberts • Elizabeth Davis of Dead Fish Books • Elizabeth F. Rovira • Ellen Feigl • Emily Omizo Whittenberg • Emily Reiff • Emmanouil Paris • Emmanuel E. Brown • Emmanuel MAHE • Eric Beach • Eric Lienhard • Eric J. Liles • Eric Munson • Eric Peters • Eric J Quartetti • Eric Severson • Eric Stamber • Eric Werner • Erica Martin Bradberry • Erik Stegman • Erin Nagy • ErinMH • Esapekka Eriksson • The Eskeli Family • Eskil Gjerde • Esko Lakso • Evan Kucera • Evan L • Evan Walter Scott Morgan • Evenstar Deane • Evonne

F

F Scott Valeri • Fazia Rizvi • Feldenthorne • Flynn Templeton • Francis Floyd Occena • Francis J. Wallace • Franck • Franti • Fred W Johnson • Fredrik Karén

G

G. Fisher • Gabriel Hernandez • Gabriele Ewerts • Galen W Miller • Gareth A Davis, Jr. • Garry Tickal • Gary Clark • Gary Maurer • Gary Olsen • Gary Phillips • Gary Rej • Gauthier Montejo • Gavin Martin • GeoffM • George Anadiotis • George J Evans II • George Tillman • Georgene Volintine • Gerald • Gerald P. McDaniel • Gerald "Jerry" Trapp • Gere • Gerry Dupuis • Giacomo Selloni • Ginger DeWitte • Giulia Ancona • Giulio Torlai • Giuseppe D'Aristotile • Glen Vogelaar • Gopakumar Sethuraman • Goran Zadravec • Graham Dauncey • Granofsky Family • Grant McCormack • Grayson Reed • Greg Bergerson • Greg Duch • Greg Hansford • Greg Yahle • Gregory Johnson • Gregory Tausch • Grimdark Dad

H

H. Quigg • Hailey • Hannah L. Hoehn • Hannah Maguire • Harro van der Klauw • Harvey Howell • Heath Shurtleff • Heather Harrington • Heather Shahan • Heather Smith • Heather V. • Helen & Nick Cowhan • Helen Smith • Henrik Sörensen • Henry Llantoys • Herb Neidner • Herm Wong • Herve Fraval • Holly Bowers • Hope Terrell • Howard R. Blakeslee • Hugo Essink • Hunter Domingue • Hyjinks

I

Iain Riley • Iake • Ian Bannon • Ian Greenfield • Ian Harvey • Ian Ségal • indylead • The Inghams • Ira Horo • Isaac "Will It Work" Dansicker • Island D. Richards

J

J Goode • J. James • J Lance Miller • J. Peretz • The J Randal MacKay Family (INRead.org) • J'aime Maynard • Jacob Magnusson • Jacob & Conor McCool • Jacqueline Skelton • Jafra451 • Jake Lawler • Jakob Barnard • Jakub Osiak • James W. Armstrong-Wood • James R. Aurandt • James Barron • James Calhoun • James S. King • James Kralik • James Matson • James "Yami" Mendez • James Pond • James Rao • James Robblee • James Schehr • James Strand • James Traino • James Wieman • James A. Young • Jamey Stegmaier • Jamie Mynott • Jamison Dobbs • Jan Buhagiar • Jan Clemens Gehrke • Janet L. Oblinger • Jannik Oyen • Jar Onaledge • Jared L. Lynn • Jarred Danner • Jasmine & Mathias Morgado • Jason • Jason Andrew Eubank • Jason Epstein • Jason T Green • Jason Laird • Jason & Cindi Martin • Jason Martinko •

Jason D Williams • Jason C. Wood • Jatt Mones • Javan & Emily Cook • Jay Brooks • Jay K • Jay Potts • Jayce Findley • Jazmin Quezada • Jean Bryan • Jeff Gardner • Jeff Granger • Jeff Hitchcock • Jeff Schock • Jeff Siegersma • Jeff & Deb Stauffer, in memory of Noah Stauffer • Jeff Thacker • Jeff Tiemann • Jeff & Laurie Whiting • Jeffrey de Lange • Jeffrey L Jones • Jelrik van der Meer • Jen Stroh • Jenna Galla • Jenna E. Miller • Jennifer • Jennifer Burns • Jennifer A. Johnson • Jennifer L. Pierce • Jennifer White • Jenny Busby • Jenny Sheldon • Jens Bejer Pedersen • Jeremiah Johnson • Jeremy Patelzick • Jeremy Rametes • Jerome P. Anello • Jerry L Albaugh Jr. • Jes Golka • Jess Turner • Jesse • Jesse Baartz • Jesse Snyder • Jesselyn Alvarrz • Jessica H Davis • Jessica L • Jessica Parks • Jessica Stark • Jeszika Le Vye • Jett Rink • Jim Bassett • Jim Gotaas • Jim Latimer • Jim Morris • Jim Saunders • JNM • Jo! • Jo Munro • Jo Ann Shores • Joan Digney • Joanna Rennix • Joanne OReilly • Joe Anders • Joe Brown (thunderw) • Joe Webster • Joe Zeigler • Joel Coleman • Joel Dupont • Joel Singer • Joey Hendrickson • John Adams • John M Allen • John Beis • John R. Bullock • John Exline • John Finch • John Franklin • John Hardey • John Hodgetts • John Idlor • John Markley • John Morrissey • John Morrow • John Osmond • John Reaper • John Riggs • John A. Spinetti • John B Spinks • John Winkelman • John Woosley • John Zerne • Johnny Fahan • Jon MF Adams • Jon Auerbach • Jon Hagen • Jon Moss • Jon Shelky • Jonah • Jonathan Hutchinson • Jonathan Jelsma • Jonathan Larson • Jonathan Piedmont • Jonathan Ryan • Jonathan Whittier • Jonny Nilsson • JonnyG • Jordan Charlton • Jordan Hibbits • Jordan Nelson • Jory Minyen • Jose Rojas • Jose Javier Soriano Sempere • Joseph Wells Aguiar • Joseph Goodrick • Joseph Livingston • Joseph Lopez • Josh Barratt • Josh Cleveland • Josh Creager • Josh King • Josh McWilliams • Joshua Barber • Joshua Beardslee • Joshua Bradley • Joshua A. Camp • Joshua Copper • Joshua C. Geiger • Joshua Hardy • Joshua Niday • Joshua Rebell • Joshua Robbins • Joshua Stingl • Joshua Tunstall • Josiah Jackson • Josie Noble • Josie Straka • Josue Pena • Journot • Joyce & Gary Phillips • Judy Bullock • Judy Hudgins • Jules Berglund • Juli • Julian Harris • Julie Higgins • Justin Barba • Justin Gallo • Justin Gross • Justin James • JW Merrow

K

K. Coleman • K Stoker • K. Webb Waites • K. Zwezdaryk • Kaitlund Zupanic • Kamash • Karen Blumst • Karen L. Cox • Karen M • Karina Noble • Karl Olsen • Kasper Grøftehauge • Kat Angeli • Katalin Ceskel • Kate Stuppy • Katherine Lee • Kathleen Q. • Katie Pawlik • Keenan Johnson • Keith Callaway • Kelly Flynn • Ken Denny • Ken Roberts • Kenneth E. Bragg • Kenneth J. Lindsey • Kenneth Skaldebø • Kenny Dickason • Kerry aka Trouble • Kevin • Kevin C •

Kevin "BigO" Daniels • Kevin Kennedy Dasakai • Kevin Harris & Ariana Barkley • Kevin & Nina Houston • Kevin "Nimbis" Kalenda • Kevin Kastelic • Kevin Grønberg Poulsen • Kevin G. Scott • Kevin Z • KHW • Kiel Siemen • Kim Alice • Kim Brodie • Kim Edströmer Lind • Kim May • Kimberly • Kimberly Adams • Kramer Walz • Kris Alexander • Kris Wirick • Kristian Handberg • Kristie M. • Kristopher Horatio Mason • Kristopher Jerome • Kryla Gonzales • Krystal Drommel • Krzysztof Klimonda • KurtD0g • Kyla Patton • Kyle Baker • Kyle Niemeyer • Kyle Smith • Kyle Spencer • Kyra Freestar

L

L. E. Custodio • L. Wills • Labtroll • Lairian Paige • Lajos Kovács • Lark Cunningham • Larry Gilman • Larson Steffek • Laura • Laura Allen • Laura Miller • Laura Winfree • Lauren G • Lauri Ciani • Laurie Lachapelle • Lawrence Lynn • Leah Slater • Lee Drummond • Leila Ghaznavi • Leokii • Leslie Davis • Lester D. Crawford • Liam Simmons • Linda Lenard • Lisa Herrick • Lisa Kruse • Liz • Liz Jacka • LLyon • Logan Applebaum • Logan Roe • Lora Waring • Lorelei Owen • Loren Aman • Loren Bagby & Kelly Williams • Lorrie • Louis-Andre Pelletier • Louise Lowenspets • lrnwardncr • Lucas Martin • Lucas Nicholes • Luis Quiñones • Luke DeProst • Lynn Kempner • Lynne Everett

M

M. Ahmar Siddiqui • Mackenzie Moody • Maggie Stoner • Malissa Little • Mamma Shroud • Mandy & Brad A. • Marc Harpster • Marc Rasp • Marcel de Jong • Marco & Tina • Marco Nahrgang • Marek Fukas • Margaret St. John • Margie "Max" Novak • Maria Aponte • Maria Shugars • Maria Teresa Chamorro • Marian Goldeen • Marilena Ghita • Marilyn Donahue • Mario Poier • Mark Flemmich • Mark Hindess • Mark Holt • Mark Matthews • Mark A. Moore • Mark Nellemann • Mark Rollison • Mark Vach • Mark Zaricor • Markus Morrice • Marnilo C • Marten Keashly • Martin Eichman • Martin Jackson • Marty Lloyd • Marty Wichter • Marvin Langenberg • Mary Alice Kropp • Mary Anne Howard • Mary B Allen • Mary Charrett • Mat Meillier • Mathias Rotestam • Matt • Matt Armstrong • Matt (Doc) Bowman • Matt Bunker • Matt G • Matt Klawiter • Matt Koballa • Matt Moerdyk • Matt "Screng" Paluch • Matt Smith • Matthea W. Ross • Matthew "Bubba Moose" Adams • Matthew Bean • Matthew Bess • Matthew Brantley • Matthew J Clark • Matthew Fairfax • Matthew E. Hart • Matthew Aaron Heiser • Matthew Kopchick • Matthew LaRose • Matthew Pemble • Matthew Siadak • Maura B. • Maurice Gir • MC Abajian • The McClelland Family • Mecca Lynette • Megan Lindholm • Meida M. Lockhart • Melanie Bannister • Melissa Goodwin-Dikkers •

Melissa Harkness • Melissa Lahmann • Melissa Shumake • Michael • Michael Brooker • Michael Carrig • Michael C Cluff • Michael J. Conway • Michael DeLong • Michael Dukes • Michael Emerson • Michael Alan Klippert • Michael Leaich • Michael Mattson • Michael L Mcintosh • Michael J. Millman • Michael B. Mitchell • Michael Murphy • Michael Proch • Michael Spredemann – 2 Old Guys Games • Michael J. Sullivan • Michael Sweitzer • Michael Ude • Michael L. Van Scyoc • Michael Yigdall • Michał Kabza • Michelle Beninati • Michelle Findlay-Olynyk • Michigan Don Forster • Midhun Mathew • Mikael Mortensen • Mike • Mike Benjamin • Mike Kitchell • Mike Klein • Mike Lannon • Mike Olson • Mike Parsons • Mike Pitts • Mikhail Ransquin • Mitchell Tyler • Mo Moser • Molly Thomson • morgan • Morgan Fuery • Morgan Herriott • Morgan Stoneman • Mortimer C Spongenuts III • Mosby Oliphant • Mrinal Singh Balaji • mud • Myron Fox

N

N. Scott Pearson • Nabeel Moloo • Nadia Kay • Nancy & David Boulton • Nastyfox • Natalie • Natasha Mench • Nate Cutler • Nate, Sarah, Kate & Owen McBride • Nate Taylor • Nathan Beins • Nathan K. Foote • Nathan Jameson • Nathan Mills • Nathan Turner • Nathaniel "Aexoyir" Berliner • Nathaniel Blanchard • Neal McAuley • Ned Hearn • Neen Tettenborn • Neil • Neil Musser • Neil Ratna • Neil Shapiro • Nic Baltas • Nichelle Fromm • Nicholaus Chatelain • Nick Cat • Nick Chapin • Nick Newman • Nick Toepper • Nick W • The Nickels • Nicolas Lobotsky • Nicole Nishimura • Niki & Toby Turner • Niki Mclamb • Niklas Henningsson • Nina • Nina Semjonous • Nina Silver Ch. • Noah M. Bruemmer • Noah Torrez • Nora K. Vinghøg • Norm • Norman P. Gerry

O

Øyvind Nordli

P

P. A. Geisler • P. Karns • P. Roberts • Pam Wicker • Pamela Wissenbach • Pancho Espejo • Pat Spanfelner • Patrick Boyle • Patrick J Cerra • Patrick Dugan • Patrick L Hayde • Patrick Heffernan • Patrick High • Patrick King • Patrick Perrault • Patrick Swenson • Paul Charlebois • Paul Downey • Paul Edmunds • Paul Genesse • Paul Lynch • Paul Mikkelsen • Paul Niedernhofer • Paul Perez • Paul Quinn • Paul Shepherd • Paul Stansel • Paula Fernández • Paula Meengs • Per Axel Stanley Willis • Peter Engebos • Peter Gnodde • Peter Helmes • Peter Kah • Peter Edmund Mullins • Phil Hucles • Phil Miller • Phillip H • Phillip Steele • Phillip Wood • Pierce Erickson • Pieter Willems • PJDEMPC • pjk • Preston Creed • Professor Stephen Candy

Q

Quentin Foster

R

R Grundy • R J Powell • Rachel Beittenmiller • Rachel Vrchoticky • Raine Hasskew • Ramon Castillo • Ramon M Balut • Randal Bozza • Randee • Randy Arnold • Randy Chrust • Rasol Y Mitmug Jr • Raven Oak • Rebecca Davidson • Rebecca Larson • Reed Bens • Remi • Remon Waasdorp • Renee Beauford Weekley • Renee G • Renee Relin • Rex Tanner • Rhonda Moore • Rhonda M. Silva • Riccardo Franchi • Rich Reading • Rich Velez • Richard L. Fellie • Richard Forsyth • Richard Greenbaum • Richard Hawks • Richard Hiebl • Richard Erik Larsen • Richard Lebrun • Richard Parker • Richard Plemons • Richard Resnick • Richard Robinson • Richard Unz • Richie Parnell • Richzrd, Dark Lord of All • Rick Brown • Ricky Lyn Mohl Sr. • Riki Martin • Rissa Lyn Floyd • RJ Jones II • Rob Alley • Rob Bakker • Rob Campbell • Rob Kutob • Rob Muszalski • Robert James Bruce • Robert de Villa • Robert N. Emerson • Robert Glodowski • Robert Karalash • Robert Kusiak • Robert McGeary • Robert McPeak • Robert Napton • Robert Parks • Robert A Pritchard • Robert Quimbey • Robert L. Vaughn • Robert Za • Robert Zumbrun • Robin Allen • Robin Douglas • Robin Hill • Robin Snyder • Robyn DeRocchis • Rod Cressey • Rodabaugh • Roe Jivers • Rogan Wright • Roger Christie • Roger Sandri & Lorraine Jonsson • Rogue Rich • Roland Xander Jones • Ron Bachman • Ron Gerrans • Ron Lasner • Ronald L. Weston • Rose D. • Rosie Vincent • RtG Gary • Rumen Ganev • Russell Dunk • Russell Lindsay • Russell Ventimeglia • Ryan Willes Brady • Ryan Carty • Ryan Colbeth • Ryan Elledge • Ryan Filkins • Ryan Garms • Ryan & Caroline Gaterell • Ryan Groh • Ryan Leduc • Ryan Reasor • Ryan Smrekar • Ryan Weaver

S

S Bernescut • S Busby • Sage • Sally • Sam Gearing • Sam Hart • Samantha Carlin • Samantha E Goodwin • Samantha Landström • Samantha Whitney • Samuel Trevor Beesley • Sandhya Harris • Sandra K. Lee • Sanzaki Kojika • Sarah Corbeil • Sarah G. • Sarah Palmer • Sarah Phillips • Sarah E Webb • Sci Fi Cadre • Scot Mealy • Scott Dell'Osso • Scott Handren • Scott Hinshaw • Scott Pare • Scott R • Scott A. Sizemore • Scott Twelves • Sean Bulloch • Sean Burns • Sean Lynch • Sean Manear • Sean Myer • Sean Stockton • The Searle Family • Sebastiaan Henau • Sebastian Kleinschmidt • Sebastian Z. • Serena Beneze "Zyraphyre" • Serge Broom • Seth Alister-Jones • Seth Lee Straughan AKA TrashMan • Shahazadei • Shane Ede • Shane Stein • Shannon Tusler •

Sharon Eastridge • Sharon Ogan • Sharon Su Plasser • Shawn T Huffman • Shawna JT Dees • Shayne/Lori Sampson • Shelley Blake • Shelli Carter • Sheri Gurney • Sherry Hare • Sherwin K Meeker • Si2Au • Simon Dick • Singed Minge • Snowman • Sokota Ireland • Sola Balisane • Sorkin Lidor • Spencer C. Woolley • SporadicReviews.com • "Squiggle" • Stacy Lee Sundgren • Stef Anderson • Stefan J. Torres • Steffan Arndt • Steffen Nyeland • Stephanie Maxwell • Stephanie White • Stephen Barr • Stephen Bateman • Stephen Crawford • Stephen Hall • Stephen Hikida • Stephen Ivelja • StephenB • Stephenie Morales • Steve Cobb • Steve "El Queso Grande" Drew • Steve Lindquist • Steve Nadel • Steve ofn • Steve Phelps • Steve Pickering • Steve Pulley • Steve Smith – Alaxis Press • Steve Soltz • Steve Zielinski • Steven Cox • Steven Flewallen • Steven Hall • Steven Makai • Steven Nesdore • Steven Nicoll • Steven Peiper • Steven Ribaudo • Steven Thornton • Steven Varnier • Stuart Gillespie • Sue DeNies • summervillain • Susan Araiza • Susan F • Susan, Tom & Anthony Ferrara • Susan Sampso • Susan J. Voss • Susan Wilson • Suzanne Gouin-Boudreau • Svemir Brkic • Sven Felske • Sydney Cohen • Sylvia L. Foil • Sylvia van der Vlies

T

Talei Lawson • Tamara Shiver Young • Tammi Spencer • Tank Thomson • Tari Parr • Team Boxley • Ted Stevens • Terri A Rae • Terry Brown • Terry Davis • Terry Foster • Tharathip Opaskornkul • Thomas R Bonaparte • Thomas Cocchiaro • Thomas Houseman • Thomas Jones • Thor Gervasi • three west • Throm • Tim Bennett • Tim Brugman • Tim J Doel • Tim Gross • Tim Hempstead • Tim Jordan • Tim Knox • Tim MacCannell • Timothy Lee • Tod McCoy • Todd J McCaffrey • Tom Branham • Tom McDermott • Tom Snyder • Tom Stephens • Tom Thurman • Tomas Bowers • Tony Hamlin • Tony Pedley • Tony Salva • Torian Ironfist • Tracy Erickson • Tracy Fettig • Tracy Frost • Tracy R. • Tracy Schneider-Morstad • The Trainer Family • Travis Hayden • Travis J. Richins • Travis Stockton • Travis M. Triggs • Tristan Ragan • Troy D. Erickson • Troy Osgood • Tuffin • Ty Larson • Ty Staheli • Tyke Beard • Tyler • Tyler Alexander • Tyler Ebby • Tyler Griesinger • Tyler Nixon • Tyler Trent • Tyler Willis

U

Urs Hiller

V

Valery Trubnikov • Vicky Wahlqvist • Victor Morgan • Vince Dutra • Vince T Vo • Vincent Mak • Virany M. Kreng

W

Wade Leibeck • Walt Lange • Wayne • Wayne Fullmer • Wayne Naylor • Wednesday • Whit • Wilfredo Quiles Jr • Will Hodgkinson • William Murdoch • William O'Connell • William Smart • William A. Tomlinson • Wolfsbane • Wraithmarked Creative

Y

Yankton Robins • Yazmin Ferman • Yegor • Ylva von Löhneysen • Yogesh Yagnik • Yvonne Cook

Z

Zach Sallese • Zack May • Zephaniah Mauro

SHAWN SPEAKMAN is the award-winning editor of *Unbound* and three *Unfettered* anthologies, and the author of *Song of the Fell Hammer* and *The Dark Thorn*, an urban fantasy novel Terry Brooks called "a fine tale by a talented writer." An avid fan of SF&F, he owns The Signed Page and Grim Oak Press, where he is surrounded by books. He currently lives in Seattle, Washington, with his wife and two sons.